D1008040

Paige Turner Mysteries by Amanda Matetsky

MURDERERS PREFER BLONDES
MURDER IS A GIRL'S BEST FRIEND
HOW TO MARRY A MURDERER
MURDER ON A HOT TIN ROOF

continued . . .

Praise for
MURDERERS PREFER BLONDES

"A beautifully realized evocation of time and place; 1950s New York City comes alive for those of us who were there and even those who weren't. Amanda Matetsky has created a very funny and interesting female protagonist, Paige Turner, and put her in the repressed and male-dominated year of 1954, which works like a charm. This is more than a murder mystery; this is great writing by a fresh talent."

—Nelson DeMille, author of *Night Fall*

"Prepare to be utterly charmed by the irrepressible Paige Turner, and take an enchanting trip back in time to New York City, circa 1954 . . . A thoroughly fun read."
—Dorothy Cannell, author of *The Importance of Being Ernestine*

"Amanda Matetsky has created a wonderfully sassy character in the unfortunately named Paige Turner. In her 1950s world where gals are peachy and cigarettes dangle from the lips of every private dick, a busty platinum blonde finds herself at the wrong end of a rope and Paige is on the case of a swell whodunit, sweetheart. Delightfully nostalgic and gripping. Irresistible."

—Sarah Strohmeyer, author of *Bubbles All the Way*

"A great idea well-executed—funny, fast, and suspenseful." —Max Allan Collins, author of *Road to Perdition*

Murder on a Hot Tin Roof

Amanda Matetsky

BERKLEY PRIME CRIME, NEW YORK

THE BERKLEY PUBLISHING GROUP
Published by the Penguin Group
Penguin Group (USA) Inc.
375 Hudson Street, New York, New York 10014, USA
Penguin Group (Canada), 90 Eglinton Avenue East, Suite 700, Toronto, Ontario M4P 2Y3, Canada
(a division of Pearson Penguin Canada Inc.)
Penguin Books Ltd., 80 Strand, London WC2R 0RL, England
Penguin Group Ireland, 25 St. Stephen's Green, Dublin 2, Ireland (a division of Penguin Books Ltd.)
Penguin Group (Australia), 250 Camberwell Road, Camberwell, Victoria 3124, Australia
(a division of Pearson Australia Group Pty. Ltd.)
Penguin Books India Pvt. Ltd., 11 Community Centre, Panchsheel Park, New Delhi—110 017, India
Penguin Group (NZ), Cnr. Airborne and Rosedale Roads, Albany, Auckland 1310, New Zealand
(a division of Pearson New Zealand Ltd.)
Penguin Books (South Africa) (Pty.) Ltd., 24 Sturdee Avenue, Rosebank, Johannesburg 2196,
South Africa

Penguin Books Ltd., Registered Offices: 80 Strand, London WC2R 0RL, England

This is a work of fiction. Names, characters, places, and incidents either are the product of the author's imagination or are used fictitiously, and any resemblance to actual persons, living or dead, business establishments, events, or locales is entirely coincidental. The publisher does not have any control over and does not assume any responsibility for author or third-party websites or their content.

MURDER ON A HOT TIN ROOF

A Berkley Prime Crime Book / published by arrangement with the author

PRINTING HISTORY
Berkley Prime Crime mass-market edition / November 2006

Copyright © 2006 by Amanda Matetsky.
Cover art by Kim Johnson.
Cover design by Rita Frangie.
Interior text design by Kristin del Rosario.

ISBN: 0-425-21293-9

BERKLEY® PRIME CRIME
Berkley Prime Crime Books are published by The Berkley Publishing Group,
a division of Penguin Group (USA) Inc.,
375 Hudson Street, New York, New York 10014.
The name BERKLEY PRIME CRIME and the BERKLEY PRIME CRIME design are trademarks belonging to Penguin Group (USA) Inc.

PRINTED IN THE UNITED STATES OF AMERICA

10 9 8 7 6 5 4 3 2 1

For Harry, Sylvia, Matthew, Molly, Rae, Joel, Ira,
Liza, Tim, Tara, Kate, Mary Lou, and Dick—
my favorite cast of characters

Acknowledgments

I am, as always, most grateful to family and friends—especially Harry Matetsky*, Molly Murrah, Liza, Tim, Tara and Kate Clancy, Ira Matetsky, Matthew Greitzer, Rae and Joel Frank, Sylvia Cohen, Mary Lou and Dick Clancy, Susan Frank, Ann Waldron, Nelson DeMille, Dianne Francis, Dorothy Newmark, Craig Hughes, Art Scott, Betsy Thornton, Santa and Tom De Haven, Nikki and Bert Miller, Herta Puleo, Esther Schoenhorn, Marte Cameron, Mirella Rongo, Al Faust, Cameron Joy, Sandra Thompson and Chris Sherman, Donna and Michael Steinhorn, Stephanie and Burt Klein, Mark Voger, Gayle Rawlings and Debbie Marshall, Judy Capriglione, Martha Cevasco, Judy Dini, Betty Fitzsimmons, Nancy Francese, Jane Gudapati, Carleen Kierce, April Margolin, Margaret Ray, Doris Schweitzer, Carol Smith, Roberta Waugh and her heavenly helpmate, Joseph.

My good friends at Literacy Nassau are a source of much-needed encouragement, as are my fellow mystery writers and readers at Sisters in Crime-Central Jersey. And my co-agents, Annelise Robey and Meg Ruley of the Jane Rotrosen Agency, and my editor at Penguin Group (USA), Martha Bushko, are the most inspiring and indulgent supporters any writer could ask for. A million thanks to them and every one of my readers.

*Cheers to my husband, Harry, for writing the odd, incomprehensible poems of Jimmy Birmingham. What can I say? The beat goes on.

Acknowledgments

Prologue

DANGER IS A POWERFUL DRUG. IT MAKES your heart throb, your head buzz, your limbs quiver, and your skin crawl. It sends adrenaline shooting through your veins like a bolt of electricity. It can make you weak as a kitten, or stronger than Charles Atlas. It can fill you with terror, or cause you to feel so brave and defiant you'd gladly challenge Senator Joe McCarthy (and all the rest of his hateful red-baiting House Un-American Activities Committee vigilantes) to a duel.

You have to be very careful, though. Danger is such a devious, potent, and seductive stimulant that once you develop a taste for it, you can easily become addicted.

As I seem to be.

I'm Paige Turner (more about the preposterous name later), and I'm the only female on the six-person staff of a sensational (okay, *trashy*) true-crime magazine called *Daring Detective*. Normally, my job wouldn't be especially dangerous—except for the fact that, as an abnormally assertive woman, I'm always in danger of getting fired—but since I'm also the only female writer in the whole darn detective magazine industry, and since I'm always trying to prove myself to be as tough and capable as any man . . . well, let's just say I have a tendency to put myself in a teensy bit too much peril.

Like the time I was writing about the rape and murder of an unwed mother/call girl and nearly got raped and murdered myself. Then, last Christmas, when I was working on the story of a young Macy's salesgirl who was killed over an oatmeal box full of diamonds, I got shot! And just a few months after that—after my leg and shoulder wounds had healed and I was running all over Manhattan investigating the so-called suicide of a famous TV star—I was almost thrown to my death over a mezzanine railing.

Get the picture? Danger clings to me like a possessive lover. Or maybe, as I noted before, it's the other way around. But whatever the case (i.e., whoever's doing the clinging), one thing is inescapably true: Danger and I have a *very* intimate relationship.

This drives my boyfriend, NYPD homicide detective Dan Street, right out of his cautious, crime-busting mind. Every time I begin working on another unsolved murder story, he pops his cork altogether. He starts stomping around like a storm trooper, smoking one Lucky Strike after another, getting all red in his glowering yet gorgeous face, and flatly forbidding me to get further involved. If Dan had *his* way, I'd quit my job, take up embroidery instead of writing, and never again set foot outside the confines of my tiny, roach-infested Greenwich Village apartment.

It's nice that Dan worries about me so much, I guess. I surely wouldn't like it if he didn't *care*. But as a twenty-nine-year-old Korean War widow who has to make her own way in the world . . . and who prides herself on her own pluck and ingenuity . . . and who has longed to be a crime and mystery writer since she was an innately curious (okay, insanely nosy) girl of fourteen—well, I'm forced to admit that I sometimes find Dan's concern for my safety a bit bothersome (all right, annoying as hell). And, as much as I admire and respect Dan's noble and steadfast authority—in both his personal and professional life—there are times when, if I want to get on with my own life, I simply have to ignore it. And go on about my business. (And, though it pains and shames me to admit it, tell Dan a few lies to cover my tracks.)

I never had this problem with my late husband, Bob Turner. Not because Bob was more supportive and understanding than Dan, but because Bob and I weren't together long enough for any such power struggle to arise. We had been married only one brief, blissful month when he was called overseas to help General Douglas MacArthur fight the enemy in North Korea. I saw my brave, beloved husband off at Grand Central Station, hugging and kissing him as if my life depended on it, and begging the Fates to bring him back home to me soon.

Well, the filthy, fickle Fates must have been really ticked off at me about something, because I never saw him again.

Bob was killed in action three years and seven months ago, on the first day of December, 1951. And I've been on my own ever since. Except for some breathtakingly bittersweet memories, a small government-issued insurance policy, a few khaki-colored U.S. Army T-shirts, and—natch!—the hindmost half of my embarrassingly comical name, Bob didn't leave me anything when he died. So, I've had to support myself. Totally. Which isn't easy when you're a woman living alone (and striving to do a man's job) in the dog-eat-dog world of Manhattan. Which is why I've become the hardest-working (not to mention most danger-prone!) crime writer ever to nab a piece of the *Daring Detective* payroll pie.

Though most of my *DD* duties consist of making coffee and attending to all secretarial and clerical chores (the boring, servile stuff my chauvinistic boss, Brandon Pomeroy, calls "women's work"), I have, on occasion—as mentioned above—probed into an unsolved homicide, identified the murderer, and then written an in-depth, first-person story so shocking, scandalous, and exclusive that our editor-in-chief, Harvey Crockett (the ex-newspaperman who's in charge of the whole *DD* operation) has overruled Brandon Pomeroy's objections and published my work in the magazine. And a couple of my *DD* stories have even been expanded (by me, of course) and somewhat fictionalized (for legal reasons) and then published as mystery novels in twenty-five-cent paperback form.

If I were a man, I'd be making darn good money by now. I'd be living the life of Riley (or at least Mickey Spillane) in a snazzy bachelor pad uptown, wining and dining a slew of glamour girls at the Stork and the Copacabana. But nothing like that happens to you when you're a woman. When you're a single working gal like me, you get paid a fraction of what your male coworkers earn. You live in a dingy little duplex over a fish store on Bleecker Street, and you dine alone on Campbell's soup and crackers at your secondhand yellow Formica kitchen table. You also risk your neck (as well as your hotly developing romance with the city's most handsome homicide detective) to fight your way up the sexist professional ladder.

My best friend and next door neighbor, Abby Moscowitz, is really proud of me for having the courage (she calls it the *chutzpah*) to stick to my girlhood goals. She says a woman has to have "balls" if she wants to make it in America's biggest and hardest city. And, you can take it from me, Abby knows what she's talking about. She's a fabulous freelance magazine illustrator (the best I've ever seen!), yet the only way she managed to get any work in the field was by barging into publishing offices and threatening to camp out in the waiting room—cooking beans on a hot plate and washing her stockings out in the ladies' lavatory—until somebody looked at her portfolio.

And by using a male signature on all her work.

And by flaunting her female curves in front of the male art directors who dole out the assignments. (Abby's breasts, you should know, are as fully developed as her hypothetical balls.)

But as bold and brash as Abby is, she never gets herself into even half as much trouble as I do. You'll see what I mean if you read the shocking and terrifying true story I'm about to start writing (i.e., expanding into a dime store mystery novel) for you right now. You'll see how Abby somehow rises—almost floats—above the most atrocious and hazardous of situations, while I flap around in the dirt like a beheaded chicken, blindly scratching my way toward disaster and flipping feathers all over the place.

The story starts out innocently enough (don't they all?), but soon degenerates into a steamy tale of forbidden love, uncontrollable passion, unthinkable desperation, and—you guessed it!—murder. And that's where you'll find me—right in the murderous middle of things as usual—working my twitchy little tail off to get to the truth, and endangering my own twitchy little life while I'm at it.

But here, my dear reader and friend, is the 64,000-dollar

question: Am I courting danger, or is danger stalking me? Is danger my greatest affliction—or my deadliest addiction?

I honestly don't have a clue. Read the story, then you tell me.

Chapter 1

IT WAS A HOT TIME IN THE OLD TOWN that night. Seven o'clock on a Friday evening—July 1, 1955, to be exact—and even though the sun had slipped below the skyscraper skyline, the mercury was still stuck at a blistering 98.3 degrees. The steamy, jam-packed subway ride home from work had left me weak, wobbly, and drenched in perspiration (mine or somebody else's?—it was hard to tell), and as I staggered down Bleecker Street toward my apartment, the hot sidewalk under my swelling feet was scorching the soles of my stilettos.

I needed a drink, and I needed it now. If Abby wasn't at home—standing at her kitchen counter and mixing me up a tall, icy-cold Tom Collins—I'd have to kill myself.

No call for concern. The minute I opened the door to our building and began climbing the narrow chute of stairs to the small landing between Abby's apartment and mine, I heard the ultra cool sounds of John Coltrane pulsing through her open door. Then Abby poked her head and one hand—the hand that was holding my cherry-topped Tom Collins—out into the hall.

"You're late to the gate, Kate!" she piped, speaking in rhyme as she often liked to do, and giving me a new name in the process. She flipped her thick, black, waist-length braid of hair off her shoulder and stepped all the way out onto the landing. "Half the ice in your drink has already melted! This gunk is sunk."

I tried to think up a clever reply, but couldn't. My brain had melted, too. "That's okay," I said, wiping my sweaty forehead on my sweaty forearm and trudging the rest of the way up the steps. "I'm so thirsty I'll drink anything—as long as it's wet." To prove my words, I grabbed the glass from Abby's hand, threw my head back, and poured a good third of the diluted cocktail down my dehydrated throat.

I considered pouring the rest of the drink down inside the front of my lavender linen dress, but quickly ditched that idea. It would cool me off for a few glorious seconds, I knew, but then later—as the sugary concoction warmed to the rising temperature of my skin—I'd feel steamier and stickier than ever. And my new dress would be ruined. So, instead of giving myself a Tom Collins dunk, I guzzled the rest of the watered-down gunk. (Okay, you caught me. I don't often speak in rhyme, but I have, on occasion—I'm thoroughly embarrassed to admit—been known to write that way.)

"Way to go, Flo!" Abby said, her stunning Ava Gardner face lighting up in a satisfied smile. Aside from drawing and painting, listening to jazz, and pursuing her bohemian interest in the taboo practice of free love, the preparing and sharing of exotic alcoholic beverages was Abby's all-time favorite pastime. "Come on in," she said, beaming. "I'll make you another one."

A welcome breeze was blowing in Abby's apartment. Actually, three welcome breezes. One came from the electric fan sitting on the floor at the rear of the kitchen area, right in front of the wide-open back door (which led out to the rusty fire escape landing, which led down to the small, weed- and, no doubt, rat-packed courtyard behind our building). A revolving draft blew from the fan perched on the kitchen counter, and another came wafting from the tall, whirring contraption set near the easel in Abby's living room-cum-art studio.

I plopped myself down at the kitchen table, in the spot I thought most likely to benefit from all three breezes, and lit up an L&M filter tip. "Oh, God!" I exclaimed. "Please kill me right now! I can't endure this unbearable heat for even one more second." (I am, as you will eventually discover, somewhat prone to hyperbole.)

"Yeah, it's pretty awful," Abby said, sighing. She poured a healthy dose of gin into my fresh drink, gave it a vigorous stir, then, nestling the glass in a cocktail napkin, carried it from the kitchen counter to my place at the table. "I was working on a new illustration all day," she said, nodding toward her easel, "a cover for *Husky Male* magazine, and it was so crazy hot in here I thought I was going to faint." She sat down at the table, lit up a Pall Mall, and took a deep swig of her own drink. "It got so bad I had to take off all my clothes and work in the nude."

Uh oh. I knew what that meant. It meant the crazy heat wave had probably been of her own making—that Abby had likely worked with a handsome young *Husky Male* model that afternoon, and that she'd spent more time seducing (or, as she would say, *shtupping*) him than painting him.

"I take it you weren't alone," I said, letting more than a shred of sarcasm seep into my tone. (I disapprove of Abby's promiscuous ways, you should know, while she thinks I'm a total prude.) "Anybody I know?" I asked. "Or did the model agency send you a brand-new toy?"

"Oh, shut up, Paige! You're such a prig!"

"I am not. I'm a healthy, passionate, open-minded woman who just happens to believe that the beautiful and intimate act of procreation should be enjoyed with one's husband, not every Tom, Dick, and Murray in Manhattan."

"Yeah, well, that's all fine and good if you're *married*," Abby snorted. She gave me an impish smirk, hoisted one eyebrow to the hilt, then blew a perfect smoke ring in my direction. "And need I remind you, Little Miss Morality, that neither one of us is?"

Her smoke ring hit the crossbreeze and disappeared.

"I'm not the one who needs reminding," I said with a sniff. "I'm painfully aware of my single-woman status. You, on the other hand, seem to think you're married to all mankind."

Abby laughed out loud. "No, I'm a *lover* of all mankind, you dig? I'm not ready for marriage yet. Who knows if I'll ever be?" Taking another big gulp of her drink, she eyed me over the rim of her glass. "And I think any woman who waits till she's hitched to indulge in the pleasures of sex is a dope. Present company included."

"Oh, yeah?" I said, putting my mental dukes up for round two of our favorite fight. "Well, I think any woman who gets pregnant out of wedlock is an even bigger dope!"

Abby rolled her eyes. "Do you see anybody here who's pregnant?" she huffed.

"Not *yet*," I needled.

"And you never will!" she said, flipping her long braid from one shoulder to the other. "I'm no dope, you dig? I've got a diaphragm, and I know how to use it."

(I had a diaphragm, too, I should tell you—courtesy of the Margaret Sanger Clinic on 16th Street. I'd had myself fitted for the contraceptive device right after Dan and I started dating, when I came to realize how thoroughly attracted to him I was. I hadn't used the contraption yet—nor did I intend to anytime in the near future—but my desire for Dan was so intense, I couldn't be sure of my self-control. And like any good Girl Scout, I believed in being prepared.)

"The diaphragm isn't infallible, you know," I said, turning serious and giving Ab the evil eye. I hated to be such a nag and a killjoy, but I felt it was my solemn duty. Abby was the best friend I'd ever had in my life. I loved her like a sister. And if she ever had to suffer the brutal social ostracism of unwed motherhood, or the wrenching torture of giving up her baby for adoption, or—worse—the pain and horror of a squalid backstreet abortion, I didn't think either one of us would be able stand it.

Abby tossed her head and let out a loud guffaw. "Chastity ain't the answer, either, babe!" she insisted. "It may keep you from getting pregnant, but it still makes your life miserable!"

"How would you know?" I teased. "You've never tried it."

We were both laughing now—which was the way most of our sex-focused sparring matches ended: in a draw, with a couple of chuckles and no hard feelings.

"Speaking of chastity," Abby said, "will the sex-starved Detective Street be dropping by to see you tonight?"

"Not a chance," I said, heaving a pregnant sigh. (No pun intended. I swear!) "He left town early this morning and drove up to Maine with his daughter. They're spending the holiday weekend with his parents. And since Monday is the big day—July Fourth, I mean—they won't be back till Tuesday."

"Did he invite you to go with them?"

"No."

"Why not?"

"Because Dan planned the trip just for his daughter—he wants Katy to get to know her grandparents better. If I had gone with them, it would have changed everything. The focus would have been on me instead of Katy. Dan has told his daughter about me, but I haven't met her yet. And I don't think Dan wants me to—not until he's absolutely sure our relationship's going to last." I snuffed out my cigarette and poured some more gin down my throat, dabbing at my steamy cheeks with the soggy cocktail napkin.

Abby shrugged her shoulders. "Sounds like Danny the dick is as uptight as you are."

"He's not uptight, he's up*right!*" I cried, springing like a Doberman to Dan's defense. "He's strong and sensible and protective and considerate! He went through hell with his unfaithful ex-wife, and their divorce was pretty awful, and he doesn't want Katy—or himself—to be subjected to anything like that ever again. Katy's fifteen now—that's a very emotional age, you know!" I was getting pretty emotional myself.

"Cool down, kiddo," Abby said, lifting her heavy braid off her neck, letting the breeze circulate underneath. "Don't say another word. I get the picture already! You're a prude, and Dan likes it that way. He'd rather trust you than *shtup* you. And you—you're even worse! You'd rather suffer than be satisfied! You're both just a couple of straitlaced *shlumps* who've forgotten how to enjoy life." She let her braid fall down her back and gave me a goofy grin. "You're perfect for each other."

I laughed. In a way, she was right. Dan and I *were* a couple of straitlaced characters, doing our best to live by—and even help enforce—society's rules. But Abby was dead wrong about one thing: we had not—repeat, *not*—forgotten how to enjoy life. (Though I hadn't yet taken Dan into my bed and we hadn't yet gone all the way, we'd been having a darn good time taking side trips on the couch.)

"Has he told you that he loves you yet?" Abby wanted to know.

"Well, no," I sadly admitted.

"Have you told him?"

"No!" I sputtered. "I'm the woman! I can't say it to him till he says it to me."

Abby rolled her eyes. She thought my feminine inhibitions were absurd. "Look, I'd like nothing better than to sit around talking about sex all night," she said, suddenly plunking her empty glass down on the table and adjusting the plunging neckline of her black halter-top dress. "It is, after all, my favorite subject. But I'm afraid I have to cut this conversation short right now." She squashed her cigarette out in the ashtray, scraped her chair away from the table, and stood up. "There's no more time for chitchat. We have to get ready to go."

"Huh? What did you say?"

"I said we have to get ready to go."

"Go? Where?"

"To the theater, my dear," she said, pronouncing her words in a snooty British accent and playfully sticking her nose in the air. She turned and began circling her apartment, closing and locking the kitchen door, turning off the hi-fi and all the fans. The dense humidity settled on me like a wet wool blanket. I could barely breathe.

"Drink up!" Abby urged. "We have to hurry. The curtain goes up at eight."

"What the hell are you talking about?" I snarled. I wasn't in the mood for any jokes or surprises. It was too darn hot.

Abby shot me a mischievous smile. "You've heard of the *theater*, haven't you, my dear?" she asked, still speaking in a pompous tone. "Because that's where you and I are going tonight. To a smash-hit play on Broadway. And the show starts at eight." She looked at her watch. "*Oy vey!*" she cried, suddenly dropping her British airs and reverting to her Yiddish roots. "It's almost seven thirty already! We've got to leave right this minute or we'll miss the opening curtain. C'mon, Paige, get up! Let's go!"

Now I don't know about you, but I really *hate* being yanked around like a poodle on a leash.

"I'm not going anywhere!" I growled, crossing my arms over my chest and staying firmly glued to my chair. "I just got home from work! I'm exhausted. I'm hungry. My feet hurt. I'm perishing from the heat!"

"The theater will be air-conditioned," Abby said.

"Right," I replied. Then I hopped up, grabbed my purse, and pranced like a poodle to the door.

WE WERE LUCKY. THE VERY MINUTE WE descended into the Sheridan Square subway station and stepped out onto the platform, the uptown local arrived and whisked us away. "Hey, bobba ree bop!," Abby crowed, lurching against me as the train whipped around a sudden curve in the tracks. "If we can catch an express at fourteenth street, we'll make it just in time."

"In time for what?" I snapped. "You still haven't told me what play we're going to see. I hope it's not *The Pajama Game*—but, knowing you, it probably is." (I didn't name this particular play just so I could make a snippy reference to Abby's love of bedroom sports. No lie. I really didn't want to see the popular musical. I'd read the reviews and thought it sounded silly.)

Abby gave me a dirty look. "No, it's not the goddamn *PJ Game*!" she said, shouting to be heard above the clamor of the train. "It's a serious drama, not a comedy. It was written by Tennessee Williams—that sensitive Southern cat who wrote *A Streetcar Named Desire*—and it's directed by Elia Kazan, whose latest movie, *East of Eden*, is—to use a moldy but apt expression—the cat's pajamas. This play is cool, you dig? Everybody says it's gonna win the Pulitzer."

I was shocked right out of my seamed (and uncomfortably damp) silk stockings. "You mean *Cat on a Hot Tin Roof*?" I asked. "We're going to see *Cat on a Hot Tin Roof*? That's the hottest ticket in town! Kilgallen and Winchell can't stop talking about it. They say the show's booked up until next year. How the hell did you ever get seats? Did you sleep with the producer or something?"

"Very funny," Abby said with a sneer. "And you can get that snotty look off your face right now, because no, I did *not* sleep with the producer."

"Then who *did* you sleep with?" I bellowed, just as the train pulled to a stop at 14th Street. My question went unanswered as we hopped off the local and changed to an express.

"Knock it off, Paige," Abby yelled into my ear after the

train had resumed its noisy hurtle through the tunnel, "I'm getting tired of your nasty insinuations about my sex life. They're repetitious and boring."

She had me there. I was even beginning to bore myself. "Okay, okay!" I cried. "No more catty remarks. I promise! But, please, just tell me this: how in the name of all that's holy did you ever get tickets to *Cat on a Hot Tin Roof*?"

"I don't have them yet," she admitted. "I have to pick them up at the theater. Somebody was supposed to leave them at the box office for me."

"Oh, no!" I groaned, feeling a big wave of doubt crash over me. "Who was supposed to do that? How do you know the tickets will be there? And what'll we do if they're not? Jesus, Abby! We could be making this miserable trip for nothing!" In an effort to curb my rising temper (and rising temper*ature*), I gazed up at the Catalina swimsuit ad plastered above the seats across the aisle, imagining that I was the pretty redhead in the green-and-white strapless one-piece, bouncing in the surf instead of the subway.

"Hang loose, Paige!" Abby sputtered. "Don't sweat it. The tickets will be there. Take my word for it. Gray is a very good friend of mine. He won't let me down."

"Gray?"

"Yeah, Gray Gordon. He's the understudy for Ben Gazzara, the actor who plays the male lead in the show. Gray called me up a few hours ago and said that Mr. Gazzara had collapsed from heat stroke this afternoon, and that he— Gray—was going to have to take over for him—Gazzara— and play the lead role in the performance tonight! Isn't that fabulous? My good friend Gray is making his debut in the peachiest play on Broadway, and he wants me to be there. I'm so proud I could *plotz!*"

The train zipped into the 34th Street station and then out again, with barely a blink of awareness from me. My brain was focused on more pressing matters.

"Gray who?" I asked again. "What did you say his last name was?"

"It's Gordon!" Abby shrieked, patience strained to the limit.

"Gray Gordon," I repeated, still doubtful about the phony-sounding name and the whole iffy situation. "Never heard of him."

"Of course you never heard of him! He's an *understudy*, for cripe's sake! Tonight will be his first time appearing on the legitimate stage! How the hell could you have heard of him?" She was getting mad now.

"I meant I never heard *you* mention him before," I said, barreling on in my naturally inquisitive (okay, normally intrusive) style. "Just how good a friend is he?" I pestered. "How long have you known him? Does he do anything besides act? Where does he live? Does he have any family? Why haven't I ever met him?"

What I really wanted to know was if *he* was the one she had slept with, but I didn't dare ask.

Abby moaned and threw her hands in the air. "God, Paige, you're worse than my mother!" she wailed. "What the hell does any of that stuff matter? All that matters is that my friend Gray is playing the lead in a hit show tonight, and he left two free tickets for me at the box office. Eighth row center. Thanks to Gray, you and I get to sit in a posh, air-conditioned theater all evening—lolling in the lap of luxury and digging the coolest drama on Broadway—instead of panting like dogs in the stifling heat of our apartments and taking cold showers just to stay conscious."

Abby glared at me and her cheeks turned crimson. "You should be kissing Gray's *tuchus* in Macy's window," she fumed, "instead of asking me all these stupid damn questions about him!"

I was about to utter something wise and witty about the importance of being vigilant and well-informed, when our train screeched into Times Square station, cutting off my train of thought. Then, before I knew what was happening, Abby vaulted out of her seat, stomped across the aisle, slipped through the opening doors, and stormed off toward the station exit.

"Hey, wait for me!" I called, running like a fool to catch up with her.

Big mistake. If I'd had any idea of the danger she was leading me into, I'd have run like a thief the other way.

Chapter 2

ABBY WAS SO MAD SHE DIDN'T TALK TO me during the entire three-block trek uptown. She didn't even say anything when I asked if I could make a quick stop at Nedick's for a hot dog. She just shook her head (rather violently, I thought) and kept on walking (okay, *charging*) past the strip joints, rifle ranges, novelty shops, penny arcades, and peep shows strung, like gaudy charms on a bracelet, along the blinking neon borders of Broadway.

When we got to 45th Street, Abby made an abrupt right turn and led me halfway up the block to the Morosco Theatre. I was happy to see the words *Cat on a Hot Tin Roof* displayed on the theater's marquee. At least *that* part of Abby's story was true. And the large posters hung near the theater's entrance made it clear that Ben Gazzara was, indeed, the male star of the show. Now there were just two questions left to answer: Would Mr. Gazzara's understudy be playing the lead tonight, and would two free tickets actually be waiting for us at the box office?

I followed Abby into the crowded lobby, expecting the worst (as I usually do) but praying to be wrong. All I wanted in the whole wide world at that moment was to sit down in a cushioned seat, pry off my painful high-heels, and surrender my feverish body to a comforting blast of refrigerated air. (I had given up all hope of a hot dog.)

Without a word, Abby turned her back to me and began pushing her way toward the box office, quickly disappearing in the crowd. Exerting an uncharacteristic effort to be confident and optimistic, I decided to wait for her near the main door to the theater, in the ticket-holders line. (I hadn't read Dr. Norman Vincent Peale's number-one bestseller, *The Power of Positive Thinking*, for nothing!)

I didn't have to wait long. Abby reappeared within minutes, waving two tickets in the air and wearing a very smug smile on her self-satisfied kisser. "See?!" she crowed. "I told you they'd be here. My friend Gray is a man of his word. And I trust him a hell of a lot more than you trust me! So, what do you have to say about that, Miss Snotnose?"

"That's great!" I exclaimed, hoping those two little words, coupled with the joyful-yet-apologetic look on my face, would convey my sincere repentance and gratitude.

Abby, you should know (if you don't already), is a more forgiving and accepting person than I am. "This is so groovy!" she said, dropping all signs of anger and impatience and replacing her smug smile with a happy one. "I can't wait to see Gray perform here tonight. He's going to be great. I know he will!"

"What makes you so sure?" I asked, trying, but failing, to suppress my still-burning curiosity. "Have you seen Mr. Gordon perform anywhere before?"

"You bet I have," she said, "but it wasn't on the stage!" She grinned and gave me a big fat bawdy wink that answered my unspoken question. "Now, come on!" she chirped, linking her arm through mine and tugging me toward the ticket taker. "Let's go inside."

HAVE YOU EVER HAD THE SUDDEN DREAM-like sensation that you died and went to heaven? Then you know how I felt the instant I stepped into the hushed, cool, velvet-soft sanctuary of the elegant Morosco Theatre. It was as if I had left the real world altogether and walked into a cushy cloud.

Abby and I made our way to our seats (eighth row center,

just like she said), and sat down in a flurry of excitement and petticoats. (Abby was wearing at least three of the starched and swishy things. I had on just one.) I looked over the playbill and scanned the cast list, spotting three names I recognized: Ben Gazzara in the role of Brick; Barbara Bel Geddes in the female lead of Margaret, a.k.a. Maggie the Cat; and Burl Ives in the role of Big Daddy. I read down the list of the understudy's names and, sure enough, Gray Gordon was there.

"Can you see all right?" Abby asked me. Her tone was sarcastic, not serious. She knew we had great seats, and she was prodding me to admit it.

"Perfectly," I said, delighted to give her the satisfaction. I didn't mention that the wide-brimmed hat on the head of the woman sitting in front of me was blocking part of my vision. I'd complained enough for one night. "Everything is ideal, Abby. Especially the air-conditioning. Thanks so much for bringing me. I'm sorry I was such a—"

My apology was interrupted by an abrupt squeal of static on the loudspeaker, then a brief, static-free announcement: "Good evening, ladies and gentlemen," a deep male voice intoned, "and welcome to the Morosco Theatre. Due to a sudden but, thankfully, not serious illness, Ben Gazzara is unable to appear in tonight's performance of *Cat on a Hot Tin Roof*. His leading role—the role of Brick Pollitt—will be played by his understudy, Gray Gordon. We trust you will enjoy Mr. Gordon's fresh and exciting interpretation, and we thank you for your support of the dramatic arts."

A slight murmur of disappointment swept through the audience, but there was no further reaction. No outburst or uprising. Nobody jumped out of their seats and stormed into the lobby for a refund. The only person who seemed deeply affected by the announcement was Abby, who was squeezing my hand so hard I thought my fingers would fall off.

"This is so atomic," she whispered, "I think I'm going to explode! Gray must be going out of his mind right now."

I sincerely hoped not. I felt cool and comfortable for the first time all day. I wanted to sit in that red-velvet-covered seat forever. I wanted to kick off my shoes, wiggle my toes, and lose myself in the trials and turmoil of somebody else's drama. Longing for the curtain to rise, and for Gray and the rest of the cast to put on a good show, I closed my eyes and said a silent prayer of encouragement for thespians the world over—but primarily for the one who had *shtupped* my soon-to-explode best friend.

"Ladies and gentlemen," the loudspeaker voice continued, "the Morosco Theatre is proud to present the most talked-about new play of the season, Tennessee Williams's *Cat on a Hot Tin Roof*."

A hush fell over the audience and the theater went dark. Abby gasped and squeezed my hand even tighter. Then the footlights clicked on and the heavy red-and-gold-trimmed curtain began its smooth, otherworldly ascent. I sat back in my chair, slipped off my shoes, and exhaled a grateful sigh. It was showtime.

I WISH I COULD RELATE THE WHOLE play to you—describe every detail of the lush, dramatically lit stage set and repeat every word of the emotion-charged dialogue—but I can't. It would take way too long. And I'd be infringing on every copyright law in the book.

So, in the interest of brevity and legality, just let me say that the play was excellent, the acting was terrific, and Gray Gordon was probably the most gorgeous, glowing, well-built man I'd ever seen in my life. With his golden-brown hair, clear blue eyes, and tall, lean, muscular physique, he looked like a Greek god (or a Hollywood cowboy hero, take your pick). And his stage presence was dynamic. His voice was strong yet mellifluent, and his fake Southern accent (the play was set in Tennessee, but Abby said Gray was born and raised in Brooklyn) was thoroughly convincing.

Actually, his whole performance was convincing. Assured and utterly believable. The way I saw it, Gray Gordon had been born to play the role of Brick Pollitt—an alcoholic ex-football player who may be more in love with his dead teammate, Skipper, than he is with his beautiful, sensual, and very much alive wife, Maggie.

When the curtain came down on the final scene, there were a few breathless moments of silence, followed by a thunderous standing ovation. Everybody in the audience (myself and Abby included) jumped to their feet and shouted "bravo" at the top of their lungs. We applauded and shouted until the cur-

tain was raised again and the cast returned to the stage to take
their bows. Lots of bows. And most were taken by Gray, who
was showered with so much applause and so many bravos I
thought he would break in two from the bending.

"This is so fab!" Abby whooped, grinning and clapping
like there was no tomorrow. "I think I'm going to die. Gray's
such a good actor! He's on his way to the top!"

"That could be true," I said. "All the columnists will be
singing his praises in the papers tomorrow. I wonder if Brooks
Atkinson is here. He's the most influential theater critic in the
city. If he caught tonight's performance, Gray's career will be
made in the shade."

"Critics schmitics!" Abby scoffed. "Gray doesn't need any
help from those clowns. Just look around at the people in the
audience. They're enraptured. They're madly in love with
him. *They're* going to make him a star."

She was right. Every face I looked at was euphoric. The
entire audience was caught up in some kind of weird religious
ecstasy. Billy Graham couldn't hold a candle to our boy Gray.

"Let's go backstage," Abby said, after Gray had taken his
final curtain call. "I want to thank him for the tickets and give
him my up-close and personal congratulations." (I knew what
that meant: she wanted to give him a tongue kiss so deep it
would shock his socks off.)

"Will they let us in?" I asked.

"We won't know till we try," she said, "so let's go find
out!" She turned and began inching her way toward the aisle,
sticking so close to the line of people slowly exiting our row
that she seemed to be attached.

I stuffed my feet back into my shoes and followed along
behind her, hoping that we *would* be admitted backstage. I
was curious to meet Abby's gorgeous and gifted loverboy, of
course, but I was even more curious to see how long we'd be allowed to remain in the blissful comfort of the air-conditioned
theater.

Abby stopped at the end of our row, waited for the aisle to
clear, then sauntered over to the side door closest to the stage.
"I'll bet this leads to the dressing rooms," she said, pulling the
door wide and sashaying through it as if she owned the place.
I scurried through right behind her, surprised that no usher or
doorman sprang from the shadows to turn us away.

The narrow, dimly lit corridor on the other side of the door led to a short flight of steps, which led up to a wider, slightly brighter hallway. And when I climbed the steps and saw that this hallway was full of laughing, chattering, well-dressed people—each holding a cigarette in one hand and a glass of champagne in the other—I knew we had come to the right place.

Wriggling her way through the crowd, Abby headed straight for the star dressing room, which actually had a gold star painted on the door. I scooted after her as quickly as I could. Was that where the champagne was being served? Maybe they were handing out canapés, too! I was so hungry I'd have swallowed a fistful of live tadpoles, no questions asked.

But there was no such delicacy in sight. No more champagne, either. Just five empty bottles piled in the trash can near the door. *Jeezypeezy!* I complained to myself. *These show-biz vultures work fast!*

There were so many people crammed in the tiny star dressing room I knew we'd never work our way inside. The entire cast was in there, including all five of the child actors (or, as Maggie the Cat had called them, "no-neck monsters") who had provided the play with some very unruly and annoying moments. Several columnists, reporters, and photographers were in there, too, shouting out toasts and questions and popping flashbulbs to beat the band.

"Gray! Gray!" Abby yelled, standing on her tiptoes and waving her arms furiously in the air. "It's Abby! I'm over here! Can you see me? Thanks for the tix, babe. You were great! Better than Humphrey Bogart or Cary Grant. Way better than Marlon Brando!"

If Gray actually saw Abby waving out in the hall, or managed to hear any of her enthusiastic accolades, it was impossible to tell. He was completely surrounded by fellow cast members and other well-wishers, who were all kissing him and slapping him on the back and sticking to him like glue. (When the vultures sense you're taking off for the top, they all want to hitch a ride. At least that's what I've been told. I can't speak from firsthand experience since I'm still squirming around on the bottom.)

"Oh, it's no use!" Abby said, finally lowering her waving

arms and coming down off her tiptoes. "He can't hear me. Those no-neck monsters are making too much noise. And I'll never get into that dressing room. It's packed tighter than an old maid's hope chest."

"There's no more champagne, either," I whined. "And nothing to eat."

"Come on then," Abby said. "Let's make like a tree and leave. I've got some more gin at home and we can grab a pie at John's." (She meant John's Pizzeria, which was on Bleecker, right across the street from us.)

"Sounds good to me," I said. "But what about Gray? I thought you wanted to give him your 'up-close and personal congratulations.' " My tone was just the teensiest bit sarcastic. I swear.

"I'll do it tomorrow," she said. "I'll hop over to his apartment in the morning, before he has to leave for the theater. And you'll come with me, you dig? He lives real close to us, just a couple of blocks away on Christopher Street."

I didn't say anything. It was sweet of Abby to invite me, but I had no intention of tagging along to watch her give Gray a gooey french kiss (or whatever else she had in mind). Tomorrow was Saturday! I didn't have to go to work. I didn't have to hop around all day serving coffee to my demanding male bosses and coworkers. I wouldn't have to work like a slave to compose all the captions, proofread all the galleys, file all the invoices and photos, rewrite and retype all the head staff writer's boring and ungrammatical stories, and fend off the oily art director's offensive advances and annoying jokes about my name.

No, tomorrow was the first day of a long, luxurious holiday weekend. It belonged to me, and I was going to do what *I* wanted to do. I planned to sleep until noon, take a cool shower, put on a sleeveless blouse and my cool new capris, pop into Chock Full o'Nuts for an iced coffee and a datenut-and-cream-cheese sandwich, then spend the rest of the afternoon in an air-cooled library or museum.

Ha! I might as well have planned to go swimming with Frank Sinatra. Destiny had a very different agenda in store for me, and there would be nothing cool about it.

Chapter 3

I WAS AWAKENED AT NINE INSTEAD OF noon. Somebody was ringing my buzzer and throwing something—or, rather, a lot of little somethings—against the screen of my open bedroom window. I opened my eyes and stared up at the ceiling, wondering who I was, where I was, and why my entire, near-naked body was slick with sweat.

"Paige Turner!" a familiar voice shouted from the street below, giving me a pretty good clue to my identity. "Are you dead or alive? If you don't come to the window this minute, I'm going to freak out and call the cops!" Another round of hard little somethings blasted into my window-screen insert, knocking it loose from its unstable moorings and sending it crashing to the floor.

I groaned and rose to a sitting position, swinging my sweaty legs over the side of the bed. *Bed*, I said to myself. *I must be in my bedroom . . . Hot*, I slowly comprehended. *It's hotter than a furnace in here.* I dropped my feet to the floor and tried to stand up. "Yikes!" I shrieked, as my feet came down on several round little somethings and rolled right out from under me.

I fell flat on my rear like a sack of potatoes.

And that's when I saw all the radishes on the floor.

Huh?! Radishes?! What the holy hell is—

I was crawling over to the window to see what was going on when another batch of little red missiles came hurtling through the screenless opening, pelting me in the face and chest.

"Hey, Paige!" Abby hollered. "You'd better get up right now! Angelo doesn't have any more radishes. I'm gonna have to switch to turnips!" (Angelo, I should tell you, is the owner and sole proprietor of the fruit and vegetable store under Abby's apartment.)

I hurriedly pulled myself to my knees and leaned over the sill, sticking my head all the way out the window. "Are you out of your mind?" I screeched, gaping down to the sidewalk where Abby was standing. (My bedroom is on the top floor of our tiny duplex, directly above my living room and two floors above Luigi's street-level fish market.) "What the hell are you doing down there? Why are you ringing my buzzer and throwing groceries into my bedroom? I have a door, you know! Can't you just *knock* on it like a normal person?"

"I *tried* that, you dodo. I practically knocked a hole in the damn thing! But I couldn't wake you up. No matter how loud I pounded and shouted. And your phone must be off the hook or something. All I could get was a goddamn busy signal. I didn't know what was going on! I thought you had a stroke and died!"

At that particular moment, I sort of wished I had. I was so hot and sweaty and achy and groggy that being conscious was a pain in the ass. Literally. (My radish-induced flop to the floor had bruised my bottom bigtime.)

"So, what do you want?" I said, heaving a thunderous sigh. "Make it snappy. I'm going back to bed."

"Oh, no you don't! I want to talk to you! And I can't keep yelling to you from down here. I'm disturbing the peace!" She was right. A slew of nosy neighbors and morning shoppers had begun to gather on the sidewalk around her. "I'm coming upstairs," she said. "Come down to your door and let me in." Before I could protest, she disappeared inside the building.

Cursing under my breath and kicking radishes out of my way, I staggered out into the hall, grabbed my robe off the hook on the bathroom door, and hurried down the steps to the main floor of my apartment (i.e., the single narrow room that housed the kitchen, dining, and living areas combined). Abby was already at my front door, banging on it with her fist (or maybe her head).

I pulled on my robe and yanked the door open. "This better be good," I snarled, giving her a really dirty look.

If Abby noticed my indignation, she didn't let on. She just breezed into my kitchen, plopped herself down at my yellow Formica table, lit up one of my L&M filter tips, and asked if I had any coffee.

"Yes, but it isn't *made*," I said, growing angrier by the second. "I don't usually perk a pot of coffee while I'm *sleeping*."

"Then, you'd better perk some now," she said, exhaling a stream of smoke in my direction. "You look like you need it."

Aaaargh!

"I do *not* need it!" I growled, stomping my bare foot on the linoleum. "The minute you finish telling me whatever it is you have to tell me, I'm going back to bed. And then I'm going back to sleep. So, I don't want any damn coffee since it will just keep me awake."

A look of pure desolation fell over Abby's beautiful face. "You mean you're not going to Gray's apartment with me?"

"No. It's too hot and I'm too tired. I took the phone off the hook for a reason, you know. I really need to get some sleep. Now I'm going back to bed."

"But you said you would go with me!"

"No, I didn't. *You* said I would go with you."

"Don't you want to meet Gray? I thought you wanted to tell him what a good actor he is."

"He doesn't need me to tell him that. After last night, the whole world will be telling him."

"Yes, but—"

"No buts!" I snapped. "I'm going back to bed and that's that!"

Abby looked so sad I thought she might start crying. "Uh . . . well, okay . . . if that's the way you want it," she said, staring down at my kitchen floor as if it were the boulevard of broken dreams. She took a deep drag on her cigarette. "It's just that I really need some company today."

"Two's company, three's a crowd," I said. "Gray will provide more than enough togetherness. I'd just be in the way."

"Oh, no you wouldn't! Gray has to go to the theater, don't forget, and there's a matinee today. He won't have any time for me. He'll only be home for a short while this morning, and that's why we have to go so early."

Uh oh. She was using the we word again.

"Why this sudden need for company?" I asked her. "What's wrong? Is something troubling you?"

"No . . . yes . . . well, sort of . . ."

"Then tell me what it is already! The sooner you get it off your chest, the sooner I can go back to bed."

She smashed her ciggie in the ashtray and gave me a pleading look. " I guess I'm just lonely," she said. "I'm so restless and depressed, I didn't get any sleep at all last night. I've been feeling pretty low since Jimmy moved out."

She was talking about Jimmy Birmingham, her most recent live-in lover, an absurdly handsome beatnik poet who wrote absurdly silly poems. Jimmy was very popular in the Village bars and coffee houses where he gave frequent readings of his work, but I'd never been able to pinpoint the reason for his success. I supposed it had something to do with his youth (Jimmy was just twenty-two years old), or his outrageous good looks (Tony Curtis, with a little Gregory Peck thrown in), or the adorableness of his little dog, Otto—the miniature dachshund who was always at his side. I was pretty sure it didn't have anything to do with his poetry. Or his dopey personality.

"You mean you actually *miss* having Jimmy around?" I asked, in disbelief. "You said you were bored with him—sick and tired of being his muse. You claimed you'd rather eat nails than have to listen to one more of his pompous recitations. You practically begged him to move back to his own apartment! Are you telling me you've had a total change of heart?"

Abby's lips curled upward in a shameless smile. "Not total, just partial."

She didn't have to tell me which part had changed. "So, you miss having him at your beck and call in bed," I said, trying not to sound too judgmental. "That's easy to fix. Just give him a buzz and tell him to come back."

"And subject myself to more boring poetry readings? You must be crazy!"

She hit a nerve with that one.

"You're *driving* me crazy!" I cried, grabbing two fistfuls of my shoulder-length brown hair and pulling it out by the roots.

(Well, sort of, anyway. A few strands got caught in my finger-nails and came loose from my scalp.) "I've had enough of this ridiculous conversation. I'm going back to bed. Lock the door on your way out." I turned and headed for the stairs.

"No, Paige!" Abby cried. "Please don't leave me! I wasn't kidding before. I feel really, really lonely today, you dig? I don't know why, but I do. And since Dan is away for the weekend, you must be lonely, too. Can't we spend the day to-gether? You could come with me to see Gray, then we could have lunch at Louis', and then we could catch a movie at the Waverly. They've got air-conditioning."

I'd never known Abby to be so blue. Her shoulders were sagging, her chin was drooping, and every breath she heaved was a hefty, heartbreaking sigh.

"Could we go to Chock Full instead of Louis' for lunch?" I asked.

Her face flashed bright as a sun lamp. "Any place you say, babe!"

"Okay," I said, heaving a hefty sigh of my own. "You make us some coffee. I'll go get dressed."

IT WAS A SHORT BUT SIZZLING WALK TO Gray's apartment. Just ten thirty in the morning and already the temperature had climbed to 97.4 degrees. (At least that's what Angelo's outdoor thermometer had shown.) Abby and I were wearing our coolest, lightest street clothes—cotton capris, midriff halter tops, thin-strapped platform sandals—but we were wilting in the humid heat. My naturally wavy hair had curled into something resembling an eagle's nest.

"You should have called first," I said, as we were slogging across Seventh Avenue. "Maybe Gray is still sleeping. Maybe he doesn't want any visitors. Jeez, he's probably not even home!" Just call me a cockeyed optimist.

Abby grunted impatiently. "Knock it off, Paige. If he doesn't want to see us, or if he's not there, we can hop over to Washington Square Park and groove to the sights and sounds around the fountain. Jimmy might be there."

Oh, great. Just what I want to do. Stand out in the blister-ing sun and pretend to be digging some fey young composer's new folk song, or—worse—Jimmy Birmingham's latest in-comprehensible opus.

(The circular rim of the Washington Square Park fountain is, in case you didn't know, Greenwich Village's theater-in-the-round. Actually, some would call it the theater of the ab-surd. All the Village idiots—I mean, *artists!*—gather there to perform their music, poetry, monologues, or whatever, to a roaming, free-wheeling audience.)

Hoping that Gray would be at home and receptive to our unannounced appearance (thereby sparing me from the Wash-ington Square fountain festivities), I quickened my pace across Seventh and followed Abby's lead down Christopher Street. The sooner we could give Gray our congratulations, get to Chock Full, and then to the air-conditioned movie the-ater, the better.

Gray lived in a neat four-story brownstone. There were eight apartments in the building, and according to the num-bers on the mailboxes in the entryway, Gray resided in 2B. Abby rang the appropriate buzzer, but there was no answer. She rang again. Still no reply.

"I *knew* he wouldn't be home," I said, with a loud har-rumph. "How the devil did I ever let you talk me into this wild goose—"

Before I could finish my sentence, Abby moved her finger over to the buzzer for 2A and pressed it repeatedly.

"Go away!" a tinny male voice came over the intercom. "I'm not home. Unless you're Rock Hudson, that is. Or Mont-gomery Clift. If you're Rock or Monty, you can come on up. But be quick about it. I haven't got all day!" Then, without an-other word (or any answer from us), he buzzed us in.

Abby gave me a puzzled but triumphant look, then promptly charged up the stairs to the second floor. I scooted up right behind her. "Gray's probably in the shower," she said, heading straight to the door marked 2B. "That's why he didn't hear us ringing. I bet he'll hear me knocking, though!"

As she raised her balled fist in the air and prepared to begin banging, the door to 2A was pulled wide open. And out stepped one of the oddest-looking men I'd ever seen in my life. He was short, pudgy, uncommonly potbellied, and his thick blond hair was slicked back from his face with gobs of goopy pomade. His pug nose was dotted with freckles and his bulging blue eyes were as big as . . . well, radishes were the first things that came to mind. And you wouldn't believe what he was wearing! It was a short, yellow silk kimono with black embroidery and a tasseled sash! On his feet were a pair of black satin slippers. I guessed him to be about forty.

"Omigod!" he squealed when he saw us. "Who are you? What do you think you're doing?" He suddenly ducked back into his apartment and shielded himself behind the door. Just his head was sticking out. I could tell from the growing pinkness on his pudgy cheeks that he was embarrassed to have been seen in his unusual . . . um . . . outfit. "I thought you were somebody else!" he said, speaking a bit louder than was necessary. "What happened? Did you ring my bell by mistake?"

Nice of him to provide us with a credible explanation.

"Gee, I guess I did!" Abby said, hitting him with her most charming smile. "I'm so sorry we bothered you, sir. I must have gotten the buzzers mixed up. I meant to ring 2B, Gray Gordon's apartment."

"Oh," he said, blue eyes popping wide as golf balls. He blotted his damp cheeks on the billowy sleeve of his kimono, then quickly pulled his head inside and slammed his door. I could hear him clicking the locks. The show was over.

"What a kook!" I whispered to Abby. "Did you see what he had on?"

"Yeah," she whispered back. "He's a fashion idol—a real gone geisha. I'll have to find out where he shops." Then she turned back around to Gray's door and pounded on it with all her might.

To our great, jaw-dropping surprise, the door flew open and crashed against a nearby wall.

"Oh, my Lord!" I cried. "You broke it!" I was on the verge of wigging out again. "We could be arrested for this, you know!" Breaking and entering? This was more like *bashing* and entering, except we hadn't entered yet.

Abby gave me a weary look. "Don't be stupid, Paige. I didn't break a thing. The door wasn't locked, it wasn't even all the way closed." She stepped into the dim, narrow hallway and started walking toward the sunlit room ahead. "I wonder where Gray is. He must have heard the noise . . . Hey, Gray!

Gray! Are you here, babe? It's me, Abby. I came to tell you what a great big gorgeous star you are!"

There was no answer to her call. There was no sound at all. I held my breath and strained my ears, but no noises came from inside the apartment. No clattering dishes, whistling tea kettles, or irksome radio commercials. No singing in the shower. Not a creature was stirring, not even a mouse.

Except for Abby, who had breezed all the way down the hall and was now entering Gray's living room with such ease and abandonment you'd have thought it was her own. She turned the corner to her left and disappeared from my view. "Where are you hiding, Sweetpants?" she warbled. "Come out, come out, wherever you are!"

Still no response.

Feeling certain that Gray wasn't at home, and that I wouldn't be disturbing him in any way, I finally ventured into the apartment and began slinking through the shadows toward the sunny room at the end of the corridor. I was about halfway there when Abby started screaming.

Chapter 4

I HURTLED TO THE END OF THE EN-
trance hall and rocketed into the living room. What was
happening? Where was Abby? Was she hurt? Had somebody
attacked her? Was she unconscious? She wasn't screaming
anymore.

She *was* crying, however, and although I couldn't see her
anywhere in the large bright room, I had only to follow the
sounds of her sobbing to figure out where she was. I found her
down on her knees behind the couch, hugging her arms tightly
across her breast like a distraught mental patient strapped in a
straitjacket. She was kneeling in an enormous pool of blood.

At first I thought it was her own blood, but—praise be to
every deity who ever rented space in Heaven!—it wasn't. It
was the blood of Gray Gordon, whose dead and naked body
was lying just four feet away—splayed out like a poor sacri-
ficed lamb—in the middle of the wide passage between the
back of the couch and a wall of windows. His throat had been
slit and there were numerous stab wounds in his chest. There
were many other deep slashes in his limbs, belly, and groin,
but I won't say anything about that. Believe me, you
don't want to know.

I didn't want to look at the butchered mess of bone and
flesh before me, but my inquisitive nature overpowered my

revulsion. What monster had done this hideous thing? When had the murder taken place? How long had Gray been lying here like this? Judging from the thick coagulation of his blood, and the dry opaqueness of his gaping eyes, and the sickeningly rancid stench that permeated every breath I took, it had been a few hours at least.

Fighting back my own tears, and a violent urge to throw up, I dropped down to my knees next to Abby and threw my arms around her. Still sobbing and gasping for air, she turned and wrapped her arms around me. Then we held on to each other for dear life, rocking to and fro in a steady, continuous rhythm, like two orthodox Jews in prayer.

After a few anguished and mournful minutes of kneeling, hugging, rocking, and praying, I grabbed hold of the back of the couch and pulled myself to my feet. Then I helped Abby stand up. Our knees, shins, and shoes were covered with blood. Abby's hands were coated, too, until she wiped them— over and over and over again—on the cotton contours of her powder blue capris. Struck dumb by the carnage, she didn't utter a word.

"I think you'd better sit down," I said, putting my arm around her shoulders and gently guiding her around the couch. Then I steered her across the floor to a chair on the opposite side of the room, where the body would be out of her sight. "Will you be okay here for a couple of seconds?" I asked, helping her lower herself into the dark green club chair. "I need to go next door and call the police. I don't want to put my fingerprints on Gray's phone. You stay right here, okay? Don't move. Don't get up and walk around. And don't touch anything."

She stared straight ahead and mumbled something I couldn't understand. But then she nodded in my direction, so I figured she wasn't in a total daze.

"Just sit tight," I reiterated, using the calmest and firmest voice I could conjure up. "I'll be right back."

Careening out into the hall, I lurched over to the door marked 2A and started knocking as hard as I could. "Help! Help!" I bellowed. "There's been a murder! Please open up! This is urgent! I need to use your phone!"

Gray's strange-looking neighbor opened his door right away, looking not quite so strange as before. Instead of a yellow silk kimono, he was wearing a crisp white shirt and a pair of tan trousers. He even had on a tie.

"Murder?" he spluttered, eyes bugged to the limit. "Did you say *murder*?" He yanked his door wide and motioned me inside, eyes protruding even further at the sight of my gory shins. "Omigod!" he shrieked. "Is that *blood*? What happened? Are you hurt? Who's dead? Where is the killer? Is he still in the building?" The man was scared out of his wits. As soon as I walked through his door, he slammed it and locked it again.

"Don't worry," I said, hurrying to calm the poor fellow's fears. "The murderer's gone."

But the minute those words flew out of my mouth, I realized how wrong they could be. I didn't know if the killer was still there or not! What an idiot I was! I hadn't searched the rest of Gray's apartment! Thinking that Gray had been dead for hours, I had jumped to the conclusion that his slaughterer had fled the premises. But what if I was mistaken? What if the fiend was still in there—hiding in the bedroom closet or behind the shower curtain—waiting to plunge his bloody knife into another hapless victim?

Oh, my god! I shouldn't have left Abby in there by herself!

"Open up!" I cried out to Gray's neighbor, jumping back over to his double-locked front door, so frantic to get out of there he probably thought I'd lost my senses. "I've got to go back across the hall! Please let me out right now! And then call the police immediately. Tell them there's been a murder and they've got to come at once."

"Who, me? I can't call the police! I don't like them and they don't like me. And I don't have their number!"

"Then get it from the operator!" I screeched, unlocking and opening his door myself. Then I sucked up all my courage (and a big supply of stench-free air) and scrambled back to the murder zone.

ABBY WAS NOWHERE IN SIGHT. THE club chair I'd left her sitting in was empty, and the partially concealed passage behind the couch—the area where Gray's body was lying—was devoid of any other bodies, alive or dead.

There were lots of bloody footprints, though, stamped all over the floor around Gray's corpse, and tracked across the thick beige carpet in the living room. A slew of ruddy smudges were concentrated around the legs of the club chair, and several rust-colored streaks stretched from the chair to the small hallway leading to the rear of the apartment.

Oh, no! What happened while I was gone?! Did the killer grab Abby and drag her into the bedroom to slit her throat?

"Abby!" I screamed at the top of my lungs, following the rusty streaks across the carpet and part of the way down the hall. "Where are you?!" I was so panicked I was practically howling.

"Keep your shirt on, Sherlock," Abby yelled back. "I'm in the bathroom!"

I felt a giant whoosh of relief, which comforted me for a moment or two, but quickly turned into a blinding surge of anger. "What the hell are you doing in there?" I roared, wrenching open what I thought was the bathroom door. "I told you not to move or touch anything!"

Oops. Linen closet. I was screaming at a stack of beige bath towels.

The toilet flushed, then Abby exited the bathroom one door down. "When you gotta go, you gotta go," she said, "and I wanted to wash the blood off my hands." When she saw me standing nose-to-nose with the towels, she gave me an exaggeratedly puzzled look. "What are you doing now, Miss Marple? Interrogating the terry cloth?"

She was putting up a good front—doing her best to act as brave and brazen as usual—but I could tell from her colorless complexion, and the way her lips were quivering, that she was all torn up inside.

Sidestepping Abby's sad attempt at humor, I gave her a deceptive but perfectly reasonable explanation for my discourse with the bath linens. "After I went next door to call the police," I said, using my most professional tone, "I realized the killer could still be here, hiding in Gray's apartment. I thought I'd better come back and check the place out, inspect all the rooms and closets, make sure you weren't in any danger."

"That was very sweet of you," she said, with just a hint of a whimper, "but as you can see, I'm quite safe. The bastard who killed Gray is long gone. There's no sign of him any-where. No murder weapon, either."

"You looked?"

"In every room."

"What about the closets?"

"They're clean."

"Well, then, the *doorknobs* aren't so clean," I said, worry-ing about the evidence again. "They've got your bloody fin-gerprints all over them now. I thought I told you not to touch anything."

"I didn't!" she protested. "I opened the doors with a dish-towel over my hand. Which is more than I can say for *you*, Little Miss Perfect." She shot a glance at my bare hands, then aimed her gaze at the open linen closet. "Whose prints do you think are decorating *that* doorknob?"

She had me there. I'd left my share of fingerprints at the crime scene. And my bloody footprints were probably all over the place, too. The homicide dicks were not going to be happy.

"Okay, so we both goofed up," I admitted. "But we can't do anything about that now. All we can do is make sure we don't corrupt any more evidence. We've got to vacate this apartment immediately. We have to go next door and wait for the police to come."

"Oh? . . . well . . . if you think so . . ." Abby reluctantly agreed. Some color had returned to her cheeks, but her lips were still trembling. "It breaks my heart to leave Gray here all alone," she said, dark thoughts gathering like storm clouds in her grief-stricken eyes, ". . . but I guess he won't mind."

Chapter 5

TWO HOURS LATER, ABBY AND I WERE still sitting on the purple couch in apartment 2A—the poshly decorated domain of Gray's pudgy blond neighbor, Willard Sinclair—answering Detective Sergeant Nick Flannagan's relentless and repetitious questions.

"So, let me get this straight," Flannagan said for the umpteenth time, "you both got covered with the victim's blood because you were *kneeling* in it?" His thin, youthful, clean-shaven face was wrinkled in disgust and disbelief (as it had been every time he'd made the same inquiry). "And then you hopped up and tracked it all over the place without realizing it?"

"Yes, that's right, Detective Flannagan," I wearily repeated, "except for the hopping part. I'm sure we didn't *hop* anywhere." I was so ashamed of my heedless behavior at the crime scene that I couldn't raise my voice above a murmur. "We were both in shock, you see, and in a kind of stupor. We didn't know what we were doing."

"Yeah, that's what you stated before," he said, glowering at me as if I were his prime suspect. "You also claimed you didn't notice whether or not there were any bloody footprints on the carpet *before* you discovered the body. But, you know what, Mrs. Turner? Much as I want to believe you, I just can't bring myself to accept that explanation. It seems farfetched to me. It seems very unlikely that—"

"Things aren't always as they seem," Abby interrupted, brown eyes flashing with fury. Detective Flannagan was getting under her skin. Way under her skin. "Paige has given you the facts, ma'am, just the facts," she seethed, quoting the corny, overused line from the *Dragnet* television series—and casting aspersions on Flannagan's masculinity in the same breath. And with a totally straight face.

Luckily, Flannagan didn't catch on.

Under different circumstances, I'd have laughed my head off. (Abby really slays me sometimes.) In my current state, however—slick with sweat, sticky with blood, sweltering on the hot seat in a weird-looking stranger's insufferably warm apartment, trying to defend my thoughtless actions at the scene of a brutal murder—well, I couldn't muster up a snicker, much less a laugh.

I was about to apologize, once again, for the way Abby and I had messed up the evidence at Gray's apartment—thereby causing a whole lot of confusion and extra work for the medical examiner and crime scene investigators—when one of the uniformed cops who'd been stationed out in the hall marched into Willard Sinclair's living room and told Detective Flannagan that he was needed next door.

"All right!" Flannagan said, grinning like a kid at an amusement park, obviously raring to return to the recreation at the murder scene. He took off his suit jacket, loosened his tie, and rolled up the sleeves of his white cotton shirt. "That'll be all for today, ladies. You're free to go. We know where you live and we have your phone numbers. But you're under strict instructions not to leave town, understand? And I want to see you both in my office tomorrow morning at ten."

"What?!" I sputtered, sounding like Donald Duck on the brink of a breakdown. "Tomorrow is Sunday—the day of rest. Don't you want to spend it with your family? This is the Fourth of July weekend, for Pete's sake! We're all entitled to a little time off."

Flannagan looked at me and grinned again. "When you're on the homicide squad, and there's been a murder, there's no such thing as time off." He was having the time of his life. I swear he was. You could tell from the way his small hazel eyes were sparkling. "That goes for the people who discovered the body, too."

"But we've told you everything we know," Abby said, keeping her anger under admirable control.

"We'll see about that tomorrow," he replied. "Ten o'clock sharp." Hooking his suit jacket on one finger and slinging it over his shoulder, Flannagan turned and headed for the door. Then, just as he was about to step out into the hall, he swung back around and glared at Willard Sinclair, our potbellied host—the queer little man who'd been sitting in shock on a chair in the corner, saying nothing and chewing his nails to the quick.

"As for *you*, Mr. Sinclair," Flannagan said, puckering his boyish features in obvious but uncalled-for aversion, "stay right where you are. That's an order. Don't set foot outside this apartment. I'll be back to question you later."

AS SOON AS FLANNAGAN WAS GONE, Abby let out a humongous groan. "That man is a raving *putz*!" she croaked, jumping up off the couch and pacing around the living room. "I wanted to knock his snotty block off! He was treating us like we were the ones who killed Gray. He should be spanked. No, he should be fired!"

I agreed with her, but I didn't say anything. I didn't have the energy.

Willard Sinclair, on the other hand, had energy to burn. He sprang out of his chair like a jack-in-the-box, shot across the room in a flash, and then quickly, but ever so quietly, pushed his front door all the way closed. "Oh, mercy me!" he cried, darting back to the middle of the living room and joining Abby in her anxious pacing. He was wringing his hands as well. "What am I going to do now?" he said, speaking with a faint Southern accent I hadn't noticed before. "That awful little worm is coming back to give me the third degree. I know the way he works! He'll grill me till I'm limp as a wet noodle, and then he'll do it all over again, just for fun—like the last time."

I snapped to attention and sat up straighter on the couch. "The last time? You mean Flannagan has questioned you before? About another murder?" My wheels were spinning like crazy. Could it be that Gray's peculiar, kimono-wearing next door neighbor was a deranged serial killer?

Sinclair stopped his frantic pacing and combed his fingers through his gummy hair. "Yes . . . Flannagan has interrogated me before," he admitted, staring down at his pink-flowered living room rug, avoiding eye-contact like the plague. "But it didn't have anything to do with murder."

"Then, what *did* it have to do with?" I probed, suddenly driven to launch an interrogation of my own.

"Oh, nothing . . ." He kept on staring, bug-eyed, at the field of flowers beneath his feet. "Really. It was nothing at all."

"The cops don't usually give somebody the third degree over *nothing*," I pressed, hoping to provoke a revealing reaction.

"What dream world have you been living in?" he cried, shifting his gaze from the floor to my face, then rolling his protruding eyes up toward the ceiling. "They do it all the time, honey. You just don't hear about it so much. It's their dirty little secret, and they usually manage to keep it out of the papers."

"He's right, Paige," Abby said, sitting down and lighting a cigarette. "Not all Manhattan detectives are as swell as your man Dan. Especially the ones who work down here in the Village. A lot of them don't dig the free thinkers and artistic types who live in this area. They think a groovy, far-out cat with a beard is nothing but a mangy dog."

"That's a fact!" Sinclair crowed, nodding at Abby in grateful agreement. "And they drag us off to the pound every chance they get."

"Oh? Do you consider yourself a groovy, far-out cat?" I asked him. "You sure don't have a beard."

"No, but I have other . . . um . . . eccentricities." He was staring down at the floor again. "And the police *do* treat me like a dog. I've been hauled off to the pound more than once."

Look, I wasn't a total dope. I had already figured out that Mr. Willard Sinclair was a homosexual. If the yellow silk kimono and pink-flowered rug hadn't convinced me, then the ruffled throw pillows on the purple couch—not to mention the fringed shades on all the living room lamps—surely would have done the trick. (See what an observant sleuth I am?)

And I wasn't totally in the dark about the way the police

treated homosexuals, either. I had written a story on the subject for *Daring Detective*, so I knew that popular homosexual
hangouts, and even private parties, were frequently raided,
and that these raids generally resulted in numerous arrests. I
also knew that many of the detainees had suffered brutal beat-
ings while in police custody.

Homosexuality was illegal, and some of the city's more
"manly" law officers considered it the world's most heinous
crime. And they felt it was their solemn duty (though others
might call it their pleasure) to prosecute (or rather, *persecute*)
the criminals. I was not, I should tell you, in accordance with
either the law or the so-called public servants who delighted
in carrying it out. As a matter of fact, I found the whole situation abhorrent.

So, in an effort to spare Mr. Sinclair any further discomfort
or embarrassment about his forbidden sexual preferences, I
quickly dropped my line of questioning about his previous
dealings with the police, and switched my focus to the subject
that interested me the most: his relationship with Gray
Gordon.

"Tell me, Mr. Sinclair," I began, "how well did you know
your next door neighbor?"

"Call me Willy," he said. "My friends all call me Willy."

I didn't know that I was—or was ever going to be—his
friend, but I was glad to be offered the use of his first name.
It would make it so much easier for me to pry into his personal
life. "Willy it is!" I chirped, giving him an earnest smile.
(Okay, so it wasn't a really *earnest* earnest smile, but it was
the best I could do considering the fact that I'd only just met
the man a couple of hours ago and was now trying to figure
out if he was a throat-slashing, chest-stabbing, gut-ripping
killer.)

"So tell me, Willy," I cooed, "were you and Gray good
friends? Had you known each other long?"

"Not very," he said, standing slumped in the middle of the
room, shoulders sagging toward the floor. "Gray moved into
the building two years ago, but we never became close
friends. He was so busy going to acting school, freelancing as
a model, and bussing tables at Stewart's Cafeteria, that he
didn't have time for me. Then after he became an understudy,
I hardly saw him at all. I longed for a deeper, more intimate

bond, but I knew it would never happen. He was a young, strapping, gorgeous Greek god, and I was a flabby old frog. And there isn't a kiss in the world that could turn me into a prince."

Willy flopped down in a chair across the room and covered his face with his hands. He looked so wretched and pathetic, I felt drawn to comfort him in some way. Pat him on the back. Massage his sloping shoulders. Uplift his sunken ego with heaps of flattery. But such gestures were out of the question, of course. Willy's unrequited passion for Gray might have been the motive for the murder! How could I, in good conscience, try to bolster the self-image of a possible slasher? (And besides—as much as it discomfits me to disclose it—he really *did* look like a frog.)

"*Oy vey*!" Abby cried out, jumping up from the couch again. "It's hot as fire in here! If I don't get some air, I'm gonna die! I need some lunch, too. C'mon, Paige, let's go. Flannagan said it was okay for us to leave."

I was hot, but I wasn't hungry. The bloody scene next door had murdered my appetite. And there were still tons of questions I wanted to ask Willy. "Gosh, I don't know, Ab," I said, piercing her with a pointed stare. "I think I'd like to stay for a while and—"

"Yeah, what's your hurry?" Willy broke in, wringing his hands again. He stood up and walked over to Abby, a pleading look in his protruding eyes. "I'll fix you a nice lunch," he said. "I made a lovely batch of chicken salad this morning. And a pitcher of iced tea. With fresh mint." He clearly didn't want us to leave.

"Thanks, but no thanks," Abby said, ignoring both Willy's and my respective appeals. "No offense, pal, but we've got to blast off before Flannagan comes back. Otherwise we'll get stuck here for the rest of the day."

Abby's warning hit home. Suddenly I was in a hurry to blast off, too. I felt uneasy about leaving Willy to face the intolerant—possibly abusive—authorities alone, but I couldn't afford to get caught up in Flannagan's afternoon inquisition. I simply couldn't spare the time. I had my own investigation to conduct.

Chapter 6

ABBY AND I WALKED HOME IN TOTAL silence and as fast as we possibly could. The blood on our knees, shins, and shoes had dried, but the crusty streaks were still very much in evidence—both to the people on the street and to our own horrified senses. We couldn't wait to shower and change our clothes.

"Come over as soon as you're finished," Abby said, as we each opened the door to our own apartment and stepped inside. "We'll go get something to eat."

"Okay," I said, quickly shutting my door and locking it, hoping to keep the demons at bay. It was a wasted effort. The demons crawled in under the door, followed me upstairs to the bathroom, and sat on the edge of the bathtub while I tore off my gory, sweaty clothes and dropped them in a pile on the floor. Then the nasty little devils got into the shower with me and haunted me with horrible visions as I scrubbed Gray's blood off my legs and watched it swirl in a bright red whirlpool down the drain.

Poor Gray, poor Gray, poor Gray, I repeated to myself like a mantra. *Poor, poor Gray. Last night he was on top of the world; today he's gone from the world altogether.* Is there any more fickle fate, I wondered, than to be dealt the lowest blow at the moment of your highest glory?

After I finished my shower and dried myself off, I put on another pair of capris, a different halter top, and my white ballerina flats. Then I gathered up the clothes on the bathroom floor and carried them downstairs, thinking I'd throw them in the garbage. I never wanted to see them—much less wear them—again.

But as I was about to toss the clothes in the trash, I changed my mind and stuffed them into a brown paper shopping bag instead. Then I set the bag on the floor of my coat closet and kicked it deep into the darkest corner. Maybe some of the blood on my sandals and capris had been shed by the killer instead of Gray. (There had, after all, been a whole lot of slashing going on!) Maybe Flannagan would want to run tests on the bloodstains. If two different blood types were discovered—either at the scene or on Abby's or my clothes—then the police would have at least one true, indisputable clue to the killer's identity. I decided I would take the bag of bloody clothes to Flannagan tomorrow.

Feeling much more alert and responsible than I'd felt all morning, I closed the closet door, grabbed my white leather clutch bag off the kitchen table, and hurried next door to Abby's.

"Let's go!" she said, lunging out onto the tiny landing between our apartments before I'd even had a chance to knock. "I'm so hungry I could eat a moose. Do they serve moose at Chock Full?"

"Sure," I said, chuckling. "They make a great mooseburger. But you won't be having one today since that's not where we're going."

"Oh, really?" she said, leading the way down the stairs to the street, long black ponytail swaying with every step. "Then where *are* we going? To Twenty-One? El Morocco? The Copa?" She was trying to act gay and chipper, but I could tell from the catch in her voice she was still feeling as sad and shaky as I was.

"None of the above," I said, as we exited the building and came together on the sidewalk. "We're going to Stewart's Cafeteria, on Christopher near Seventh. We passed it twice today. Looked like a nice place to eat." I turned and began walking down Bleecker toward Seventh Avenue.

Abby caught up with me and followed alongside, face

screwed up in a crabby frown. "Why the hell do you want to go there?!" she squawked. "The food is lousy. Mostly steam-table stuff. And you have to stand in line and get it yourself."

"How do you know? Have you been there before?"

"Sure. Lots of times."

"But if the food's so bad, why did you go so often?"

"I didn't go there to eat, silly. I was just looking for models."

"What?!" Now I was the one who was squawking. (Just when you think you know everything there is to know about her, Abby pulls another squirming rabbit out of her hat.) "Looking for *models*?!" I cried, tossing my hands up in wild confusion. "What the devil are you talking about?"

"Enough with the dramatics, Paige. It's not as crazy as it sounds." We came to a stop at Seventh Avenue and stood waiting for the light to change. "I'll explain everything when we get there," she said. "It's too hot to talk while we're walking. And the cafeteria's right across the street."

As rabidly curious as I was, I didn't try to argue with her. When Abby set her mind to something, it was carved in stone. And besides—it really was too hot to walk and talk at the same time.

THE LIGHT CHANGED AND WE CROSSED over Seventh to Christopher. Stewart's was right around the corner and the double entry doors were propped wide open. My heart sank at the sight. The gaping portal could mean only one thing: no air-conditioning. And if Abby was right about the steam tables, it was probably hotter inside the restaurant than out.

Yep. The indoor temperature was at least five degrees higher. And the air was so moist and heavy you could barely breathe—which turned out to be a good thing since the sickening smell of fried fish was overpowering. The ceiling fans were going full speed, but their only effect was to move the hot, greasy air from one spot to another. As a result, the place was practically empty. Except for a skinny middle-aged man sitting at a table near the windows, and the hairy, husky man behind the food counter, and two sweaty young busboys in wilted white uniforms, Abby and I were the only ones there.

Abby headed straight for the food service area and grabbed a brown plastic tray from the stack at the end of the counter. Then she began to move down the food line, asking the husky server for a slab of this, and two scoops of that, and a heap of that stuff over there. You'd have thought she was a starving longshoreman, the way she was piling it on. When she finished making her selections, the mound of grub on her plate was as high as the Matterhorn.

The sights and smells at the food counter—particularly the slimy display of boiled beef and the repulsive odor rising from a pan of steamed trout—were making me nauseous. I took a small roll, a puny portion of the fruit salad Jell-O mold, and a glass of iced tea.

"Okay, out with it," I said, as soon as we were seated at a front table near the row of large windows and the open doors. "Whatever gave you the yo-yo idea to come here looking for models? Are they running an agency in the kitchen?"

"No, silly," Abby said, digging into her meatloaf and mashed. "Ith juth tha a lop of goop loofing ghys ang hout ear and—"

"Stop! I can't understand a word you're saying. Can't you swallow before you speak?!" My patience was wearing a little thin.

Abby gulped and gave me a goofy grin. "Sorry, babe, but my mooseloaf is calling." She took another bite and gobbled it down. Then she looked up and said, "What I was trying to tell you was that a lot of really good-looking guys hang out here at Stewart's, and some of them are only too happy to do a little modeling for me. Sometimes they'll even do it for free. And that's a whole lot less than the twenty-five bucks an hour the agency charges. And that's why I come here looking for models. Get what I mean, Jean?" She shoveled a fresh load of mashed potatoes into her mouth.

"No! I don't get it at all. What's so special about this crummy place? Why do good-looking guys like to hang out *here*?"

Abby swallowed her spuds and widened her eyes in surprise. "You mean you don't know?"

"Know what?" I urged.

"About Stewart's," she said.

"What about Stewart's?" I begged.

"I can't believe you don't know," she said. "I thought *everybody* knew about Stewart's."

"Well, *I* don't!" I shrieked. My patience wasn't wearing thin anymore. It was officially worn-out.

"Shhhh! Keep your voice down. You're making a scene."

"You're *making* me make a scene! And if you don't tell me everything you know about this place right now, I'm going to jump on the table and hoot like a monkey!"

"Do monkeys hoot? I always thought of them as screechers, not—"

"Abby!!"

"Okay, okay!" she finally relented, leaning forward and lowering her voice to a whisper. "Here's the dirt, Bert: Stewart's Cafeteria is known in these parts as Queer Central Station. You dig my meaning? It's where all the fairies meet and greet. See the fellow sitting at that table over there, staring out the window? He's probably a queer looking for company. And see the sidewalk right outside this row of windows? They call it the chicken run. That's where all the chickens strut up and down and back and forth, flouncing their feathers and flexing their muscles, angling for potential . . . um . . . boyfriends. Or, in some cases, modeling jobs."

"Chickens?"

"Yeah," Abby said, smiling. "You never heard that term before? It's what the older homosexuals call the younger, more attractive ones. The chickens are the handsomest, most well-built, most sexy guys of all. A lot of them live in the Village and a whole flock of them live right here on Christopher Street. They're always prancing by these windows on their way to and from one place or another.

"On normal days," she went on, "there's a constant parade out there. And all these chairs and tables here, right inside the windows? They're like the bleachers. On normal days they're packed with enthusiastic . . . uh . . . spectators."

"What do you mean by *normal* days?"

"I mean days when it isn't over a hundred goddamn degrees in the shade. And when it's *not* the Fourth of July weekend. The bleachers and the runway are deserted today because every homo who has two nickels to rub together is out on Fire Island. And all the others are tucked away at home, sitting naked in front of the fan and soaking their feet in ice water."

Or being grilled about a murder by a hotheaded homicide detective, I brooded, thinking of Willy.

Abby started chowing down again. "So, what's your excuse?" she asked between mouthfuls. "Why did *you* want to come here? You certainly aren't in the market for a homosexual lover. Or a male model. And don't give me that crap about how it looked like a nice place to eat, either. Because it doesn't. And it isn't. The food stinks to high heaven," she said, forking a huge pile of gray string beans into her mouth.

I nibbled on my roll and took a sip of iced tea. "It was something Willy said," I told her. "He mentioned that Gray had been bussing tables here. I thought I'd check the place out and see if that was true."

"It was true all right. *I* could have told you that. Jeez, Paige, why didn't you just ask me? I would have given you the dope, and then we wouldn't have had to come here to eat!" She took another bite of meatloaf and chomped it eagerly.

"So you knew that Gray worked here?"

"Of course I did. This is where I met him. I was about to start working on a new illustration, and I needed a new model, so I came here to check out the chicken run. But then I saw Gray clearing the tables, and I really dug the way he looked, so I skipped the whole sidewalk show and asked him to pose for me. I had just landed a cover assignment from *Real Men* magazine."

"So what did he say? Did he accept?"

"In a flash."

"When did this happen?"

"Oh, a couple of years ago. Right after Gray moved from Brooklyn to the Village. Both of his parents were killed in a car accident, so he packed up his meager belongings and moved to the city to start a new life—to pursue the acting career his parents had never approved of. He was working as a busboy just to pay the rent while he took acting lessons and went on auditions. When I offered him ten dollars to pose for me, he pounced on it like a hungry tomcat."

"Ten dollars an hour? Wasn't that a little high for somebody with no modeling experience?"

"Well, yeah, but Gray was so gorgeous he was worth it." Her eyes lit up and her lips curled into a sinful smile. "He was worth it in other ways, too."

Oh, brother, I groaned to myself. *Doesn't her libido ever take a nap?*

"Other ways?" I said, widening my eyes in imitation innocence. "What other ways do you mean?" Though I knew all-too-well what Abby was hinting at, I wanted to make her say it. That way, she couldn't get mad and accuse me of making snide remarks about her sex life.

"Oh, shut up, Paige!" she snapped. "You know exactly what I mean. And your cute little Shirley Temple act is getting on my nerves."

Curses, foiled again.

"I slept with Gray once or twice," she went on, "and that's all there was to it. He was a good lay and a great model. We didn't stay lovers for long, but we did remain friends. He kept on modeling for me, too."

"So, Gray wasn't a homosexual?"

"No way, Doris Day!"

"But he worked here at Stewart's," I said, wondering about the coincidence. "And he lived on Christopher Street, too."

"So what? Not every man who works and lives here is gay. Just some of them are. And you can take it from me, babe, Gray *didn't* belong to the club."

"Then why was your affair with him so brief?" I asked. "Did you dump him for somebody else?" (This wasn't an impertinent question, I swear. It was fair and perfectly reasonable. Abby was so beautiful and voluptuous and smart, no man ever willingly broke up with her. Whenever there was dumping to be done, *she* had to be the one to do it.)

"Nobody dumped anybody," Abby insisted. "Gray simply decided to commit himself to just one of his flames and stop *shtupping* all the others. I was one of the others."

"How many of those were there?"

"How the hell should I know? I didn't ask him for an itemized list!" She was getting touchy again. She ripped her roll apart, swiped a piece of it through the leftover gravy in her otherwise empty plate, then poked the gloppy morsel in her mouth.

I took one taste of my canned fruit and Jell-O mold, then shoved the warm, half-melted mess aside. "Do you know who Gray's chosen mate was?" I asked. "The one he finally committed himself to, I mean?"

"No," she said, eyeing the gooey remains of my gelatin salad. "I never met her, and he never told me her real name. I only saw Gray when he was posing for me, you dig, and he didn't talk about his girlfriend much at all. And the few times that he did bring her up, he just called her Cupcake." Abby stretched her arm out over the table and picked up the plate of oozing Jell-O. "Are you finished with this?" she asked.

"Unconditionally," I said. "Have a party."

While Abby was polishing off whatever edibles were left on the table, I sat back in my chair and smoked a cigarette, silently watching the ghost-white fumes vanish in the gyrating air. I probably looked quite serene and relaxed, but my mind was spinning faster than the ceiling fans above. I smelled something fishy, and I knew it wasn't just the food.

Chapter 7

"WANT TO GO TO THE MOVIES?" ABBY asked as we stood up from the table and headed for the cafeteria exit. "*Dial M for Murder* is still playing at the Waverly. I wouldn't mind seeing that again."

I wouldn't have objected to seeing the clever Hitchcock mystery again, either, but at the moment my thoughts were focused on a different murder. "Two killings in one day?" I said. "That's two too many for me."

"I guess you're right," Abby said, growing sadder by the second. "I just thought it would take our minds off—"

"Hold on a minute," I broke in, coming to an abrupt standstill three feet inside door. "I want to talk to the busboys before we leave." I looked around and saw them standing together near the entrance to the kitchen. "Wait here for me, okay?"

"No! Why should I? What do you want to talk to them about, anyway? If they have anything interesting to say, I want to hear it, too. I'm coming with you!"

"Please don't, Abby. Please stay here. I just want to ask them a couple of questions about Gray, and I think I'll get more answers if I talk to them alone. The two of us together might be too overwhelming."

To my great surprise, she reconsidered and agreed. "Oh, all

right!" she huffed, flipping her ponytail off her shoulder and letting it swing down her back. "But you'd better make it quick, Dick. I haven't got all day." She made a big production out of looking at her watch and tapping her foot. (In case you haven't noticed, Abby has the patience of a gnat.)

I hurried over to where the two busboys were standing and gave them both a cursory once-over. One was young, tall, thin, and had shoe-polish black hair. The other was young, tall, thin, and had peroxide blond hair. Standing shoulder-to-shoulder in their identical white uniforms, they looked like a matched pair of salt and pepper shakers.

"Hello, boys!" I said, baring my teeth in a huge Dinah Shore smile. "Enjoying the heat wave?"

"Not much, ma'am," the blond one said, in a sincere, aw-shucks kind of way. "Guess we better get used to it, though. Radio says it's gonna last another week."

"I may not live that long," I said.

Blondie smiled; Blackie scowled.

Okay, that was enough small talk. "Hey, do either of you guys know Gray Gordon?" I blurted. "He's a busboy here, too. I was hoping to see him here today, but I guess this isn't his shift. Do you know if he'll be working tonight?"

"No he won't, ma'am," Blondie said. "Not tonight or any other day or night."

The hair on the back of my neck bristled. Did Blondie know that Gray was dead? "Gee, why not?" I asked, flapping my lashes in imitation innocence. "Is he on vacation or something? Gosh, I hope he's not sick!"

Blondie smiled again and shook his head. "No, ma'am. He's not sick. He just quit this job and took a better one. He's in a play on Broadway now."

"What?!" I exclaimed, agape, agog, and aghast. "I don't believe it! I knew he wanted to be an actor, but I never dreamed . . . Broadway, you say? Wow! When did this happen?"

"About four months ago," Blondie answered. "Sometime in March. Gray was supposed to work the lunch shift with me one day, but he marched in and quit instead. Right on the spot. Said he got a job as an understudy in a play on Broadway, and if the play was a hit, he wasn't ever coming back. I haven't laid eyes on him since."

"I guess the play was a hit," I mused.

"Sure was," Blondie said. "*Cat on a Hot Tin Roof.* You must've heard of it. Everybody's talking about it . . . or at least whispering about it."

"Whispering?" I coaxed. "Why are they whispering?"

Blondie gave me another smile, but this one was kind of crooked. "I haven't seen the play myself, but a lot of the customers here have, and they're all excited and hopped-up about it. They say it has something to do with a man being in love with another man, and—"

"Shut your trap!" Blackie cut in, jabbing Blondie in the ribs with his elbow. "You shouldn't be telling her what Stewart's customers do and say. It's against the rules. And it's none of her business."

Blondie stared at Blackie for a couple of seconds, then turned his eyes back to me. "He's not very polite, ma'am, but he's right. I've got a big mouth sometimes. But you don't need *me* to tell you about Gray Gordon or the play he's in. You can read all about it in today's *Times*. They say the star of the show got sick last night, and Gray had to step in and play the lead, and he was so good he's now the toast of the town. They put his picture in the paper and everything."

"Really?" I said. "Thanks for the tip. I'll pick up a paper as soon as I leave. But before I go, may I ask if either one of you knows where Gray lives? I'm an old friend of his from Brooklyn, and I haven't seen him in quite some time, and I sure would love to pay him a surprise visit and congratulate him on his success." I wasn't fishing for an address, you realize (the location of Gray's apartment was permanently—and painfully—fixed in my brain). I was just trying to find out if either Blondie or Blackie was privy to that information.

"Yeah, I know where he lives," Blondie replied. "His pad is right down the—"

Blackie jabbed him in the ribs again.

There was no point in continuing my little charade. Blackie was determined to keep Blondie from revealing any significant information, and Abby was so restless she was having an all-out nervous breakdown (a detail I discovered when I glanced over in her direction and saw that her face was turning blue). I took a deep breath, thanked the busboys for their time, and made a beeline for the door.

• • •

ABBY STARTED COMPLAINING THE VERY
second we hit the sidewalk. "You sure took your own sweet
time!" she croaked. "How could you keep me standing there
like that? I almost fainted dead away from the heat."

"I'm sure you never fainted in your life," I replied. "You
aren't the swooning type."

She gave me a dirty look. "There's always the first time,
you know!"

"Yeah, but this wasn't it." I wasn't in the mood for Abby's
fiery histrionics; I had more burning issues on my mind.

"So, what do you want to do now?" she asked, abandoning
her temper fit as soon as she realized it wasn't having the de-
sired effect. "I know! Let's walk over to Washington Square
Park. It'll be a lot cooler there. We can sit in the shade under
the trees, eat ice cream, and dig the folksingers at the fountain."

Folksingers, my foot. What she really wanted to do was
look for Jimmy Birmingham. I knew from Abby's and my talk
earlier that morning that she was missing Jimmy (or rather,
missing sex with Jimmy) like crazy, and I also knew there was
a very good chance he'd be at the park that afternoon, reciting
one or two of his preposterously silly poems at the fountain.
So, it didn't take me more than a split second to deduce why
Abby wanted to go there . . . and why I didn't.

"You can go to the park if you want to," I said, "but I've
got other plans."

"Huh? What plans?"

"I'm going to *Times* Square, not Washington Square."

"What the hell for? Don't tell me you're still craving a
Nedick's hot dog."

I snorted and shook my head. "No, I'm going back to the
Morosco Theatre. I want to see if I can talk to some of Gray's
fellow cast members and friends."

"Are you out of your mind?" she cried, looking as if she
might fly into another fury. "That's the craziest idea I ever
heard in my life! The lead actor must've recovered from his
heatstroke by now, so he and the rest of the cast are kind of
busy *on stage* at the moment, you dig? The matinee performance is in full swing! And they'll never let you inside without a ticket. And just look at what you're wearing! You're

dressed for a goddamn hayride, not a Broadway show!"
(That's Abby for you. Always concerned about the clothes.
She's a regular Coco Chanel—or Edith Head, take your pick.)

"Oh, for Pete's sake!" I sputtered, about to fly into a fury
of my own. "I'm not going to sit in the theater and watch the
damn show! I'm going to look for a back door and try to sneak
backstage. I don't have to be all dolled up for that."

Abby gave me the kind of look Dan would've given me if
he'd gotten wind of what I was up to. "*Now* I get the picture,"
she said, one eyebrow arched to the limit, dark eyes boring
into mine. "You're angling for another big fat news flash—another sensational exclusive inside story. You think you're
gonna ace-out the whole Homicide force and find Gray's
killer all by yourself. *Oy vey iz mir!* You're cruisin' for another
bruisin', Paige, and if I know you, you're gonna get it. You
won't stop snooping until you're dead yourself."

"Thanks, Ab. Your encouragement and support mean a lot
to me."

"Well, what am I supposed to do?" she screeched. "Knit
you a sweater? Send you off to battle with a fresh-baked batch
of cookies in your duffle bag? Pray night and day for your im-
mortal soul, and then—when the unimaginable but inevitable
finale occurs—praise God that you didn't die in vain?" Gasping for air, Abby wiped the perspiration off her forehead with
her hand and then wiped her hand on her hip. "Sorry, Laurie,"
she said, voice cracking with emotion, "but that's not the way
this cookie crumbles."

I grabbed her by the arm and pulled her into the shade
under the awning of the candy store next door to Stewart's.
"Jeez, Ab, you'd better calm down or you'll catch a case of
heatstroke yourself. You're getting all worked up over nothing."

"Nothing?!" she shrieked, stamping her foot on the cement. "A good friend of mine was just murdered! You call that
nothing? And now my best friend in the whole world is about
to run off half-cocked looking for the killer, putting herself in
so much danger she'll probably get slashed to ribbons, too. If
that's *nothing,* then I hope to high heaven I never find out
what *something* is!"

"I'm sorry, Ab. You're upset about what happened to Gray
and I understand that. You wouldn't be normal if you weren't

wigged out about it. But there's no reason on earth for you to be so wigged out about *me*. I won't be putting myself in any danger today at all. I swear! I just want to sniff around a little bit, get the lay of the land. And it's important that I do this right away, before the news about the murder gets out. It's a cinch that Flannagan hasn't notified the show's cast and crew yet, so they won't be suspicious or try to hide anything from me. They don't even know that Gray is dead."

"The murderer knows," she said.

"Yes, but he doesn't know that *I* know. And who says he'll be there anyway? The killer may have nothing whatsoever to do with the theater. Maybe he's a member of Gray's family, or one of his old friends or enemies from Brooklyn—in which case I won't be running into him today. And besides, the chances that I'll actually be able to get inside the theater and talk to anybody who was closely connected with Gray are practically nil. See? What I said before is true, Ab. You really are getting worked up over nothing."

"But I worry about you, you know!" she whined. (Which prompts me to point out something else I've learned about Abby during our tight three-year friendship: As bold and brazen a sexpot as she most assuredly is, she is also, at heart, a ranting, raving—i.e., loving—Jewish mother. But please don't tell her I said so!)

"Gosh and golly, Polly—what's gotten into you?" I said, chuckling and nudging her with my elbow, trying to cheer her up and make light of the situation. "You used to egg me on and call me a sissy. You said if I had any *chutzpah*, I'd live up to my absurd name and go after the big, sensational stories. You told me if I was going to write for a magazine called *Daring Detective*, I should have the balls to become one myself. Remember?"

"Yeah, well, that was before," she muttered.

"Before what?"

"Before you were nearly raped and strangled on the stairs at your office . . . before you were almost thrown to your death over a mezzanine railing . . . before I saw you shot and bleeding on your kitchen floor."

"Oh," I said, staring down at the sidewalk, unable to dispute those disturbing particulars.

A heavyset woman in a flowered sundress came out of the

candy shop, peeling the wrapper off a large Hershey Bar. She had a copy of *Confidential* magazine tucked under arm. Abby and I moved aside to let her pass by, then waited for her to walk a few yards down the block before continuing our conversation.

"Look, Ab, I know some awful things have happened in the past," I said, "but that doesn't mean something awful's going to happen today. If anything, today will be the safest time of all to snoop around. That's why I'm so anxious to get going. Maybe I can pick up a few clues to deliver to Flannagan tomorrow—something that will help him in his investigation, and also help me get over my embarrassing and incompetent behavior at the crime scene this morning. Most importantly, I want to do whatever I can to make sure the sick monster who killed Gray is caught as soon as possible."

"Okay, you convinced me," she said, changing her attitude in a snap. "What are we waiting for? Let's go!"

Chapter 8

I REALLY DIDN'T WANT ABBY TAGGING along. I was afraid she would complicate my undercover (and hopefully inconspicuous) investigation with her passionate and unpredictable antics. But I didn't bother to protest. I knew it wouldn't do any good. I could see that invincible, uncompromising, stubborn-as-a-mule look in her eye. She was coming with me, and that was all there was to it.

"Hold your horses, Ab," I said, with a plaintive sigh. "I want to get a couple of newspapers before we go." I turned and stepped toward the open door to the candy store. "You want anything?"

"That's a definite yes, Bess!" she whooped, following close on my heels as I entered the tiny shop. "I want a Tootsie Roll. A great big one!"

Abby headed straight for the candy counter while I checked out the news rack. I picked up the last copy of the *New York Times*, and also a copy of the *Journal American*, thinking Dorothy Kilgallen had probably written something about Gray in her daily column, "The Voice of Broadway." I would have grabbed the *New York Daily News* as well—just to take a look at Ed Sullivan's "The Toast of the Town" column—but there weren't any left.

Abby and I reconnected at the cash register and paid for

our items. Her giant-sized Tootsie Roll was half-eaten already. I folded the newspapers, cradled them in the crook of my elbow, and led the way out of the store. Abby joined me on the sidewalk, then we strolled in total silence around the corner and up the block toward the Sheridan Square subway stop. It was too hot to walk fast, and Abby was too busy chewing to chat.

It was a bit cooler underground and the train came almost immediately. We got on, sat down, and I handed Abby the *Journal American*, telling her to search for write-ups about Gray. I opened the *Times* and looked for the article Blondie had mentioned.

I found it in the middle of the second section, near the theater listings and movie ads. There, under the headline A STAR IS BORN, was a short article by Brooks Atkinson, and a small photo of Gray. It was an extreme close-up, and the rapturous, ecstatic smile on Gray's face led me to believe that the picture had been taken just the night before, in the star dressing room, while the very much alive, but unsuspecting, understudy was reveling in the triumph of his stellar Broadway debut.

The article accompanying the photo was brief and to the point. An unknown actor by the name of Gray Gordon had played the lead in last night's performance of *Cat on a Hot Tin Roof*, and his portrayal had been so brilliant he would not remain unknown for long. Mr. Gordon was—according to the famous *Times* theater critic, and as the title of his article proclaimed—the brightest new star in the Broadway firmament.

Although the Atkinson piece was full of praise, it was sadly short on information. Aside from the fact that Gray had come from the Carnarsie section of Brooklyn, and that he was currently studying his craft under the "admirable tutelage" of Lee Strasberg at the "renowned" Actors Studio in Manhattan, there were no useful (for me) revelations. I dropped the paper to my lap and heaved another mournful sigh, wishing with all my heart that Gray were alive to read this fabulous review, but sickened by the knowledge that tomorrow's *Times* could very easily (and very truthfully) run the headline A STAR IS DEAD.

"Look," Abby said, shoving the *Journal American* under my nose. "Kilgallen gave Gray a rave. She says he's handsomer than Marlon Brando and James Dean put together. A lot more talented, too. She says if Gray doesn't become an even bigger star than Brando or Dean, she'll eat the chic new sunbonnet she bought for her upcoming Mediterranean cruise."

I hope Dorothy enjoys her lunch, I thought, keeping my bitterly sarcastic reaction to myself. Abby seemed to be in an equable mood, and I didn't want to upset it. "Brooks Atkinson gave Gray a good review, too," I told her. "You want to read it?"

"Absolutely not!" she said emphatically, emphasis on the *not*. "My heart's broken enough as it is. Life's so freaking unfair! I can't stand reading these bubbling accolades. They would have made Gray so happy—but they make me want to kill somebody."

So much for equable.

I refolded the newspapers with the articles about Gray on top, then set them down on the seat beside me, hoping other passengers would pick them up and read about Gray's success. If more people read the reviews, I reasoned (i.e., intentionally deluded myself), it would be like keeping Gray and his budding career alive just a little while longer.

"We should have changed our *focockta* clothes, you know!" Abby griped, still worrying about the wardrobe. "It isn't proper for us to go uptown like this. We should have put on dresses. Or at least skirts."

"Since when do you care about being *proper*? I never even heard you use that word before. And besides, this is the hottest Fourth of July weekend in history. The way I see it, all clothing rules have been suspended until Tuesday."

"Have it your own way," she said, with a disparaging sniff. "But when everybody stares at us like we're creatures from another planet, don't say I didn't warn you."

When we emerged from the subway at Times Square and began walking up Broadway toward the theater, I saw that Abby was right. All of the women were wearing summer dresses, seamed stockings, and heels. Some even had on hats and white gloves. I'd have bet my last dollar they had on girdles, too. (From the stiff and snooty way they were glaring at Abby and me, you could tell they weren't too comfortable.)

"See?" Abby said, smirking. "You should have listened to me. If we ever get inside the theater and get to talk to anybody in the show, they're gonna wonder why the hell we're dressed like this. Nobody wears capris and halter tops on Broadway! They'll probably think we're streetwalkers from 42nd Street, or lowly extras from the *Bus Stop* cast."

Bingo.

"Hey, that's a great idea!" I yelped. "I've been wondering what kind of cover we could use—what we could say to make our sudden appearance backstage, plus our nosy fixation on Gray, seem logical and reasonable. And this is it, Ab! It's like somebody wrote the script just for us. It's so perfect I'm beginning to believe it myself."

"Have you flipped your wig, babe?" Abby gaped at me as if I'd just turned into a unicorn. "You think we should pretend to be streetwalkers? Ha! That's a total crack-up! I could probably carry it off, but you—you look more like a peach-picker than a prostitute."

"No, you've got the wrong idea!" I took her by the arm and pulled her off to the right of the crowded sidewalk, under the overhang of a souvenir shop entryway where we could talk. The Morosco Theatre was just two blocks up and I wanted to get our stories straight before we got there.

"We're going to be *Bus Stop* extras!" I crowed, flushed with excitement. "It's the best of all possible disguises. Thank God you thought of it! *Bus Stop* is playing at the Music Box Theatre, you know, and that's right across the street from the Morosco. Did you ever hear anything so ideal in your life? We can say we're in intermission or between scenes or something, and that we just hopped across the street to see our good friend Gray and congratulate him on his fabulous performance last night."

Abby frowned, then arched one of her eyebrows to a peak. "I don't know, Paige. Sounds pretty sticky to me. How do we know the people in the *Cat* cast don't know all the people in the *Bus* cast? And what if they've seen each other's shows? Then the *Cat* people would know that the outfits we're wearing aren't real *Bus* costumes."

"So what? The styles are pretty similar, so if anybody wonders about the costumes, we can say we just got new ones. And if anybody questions our place in the cast, we can say we just got hired to replace a couple of extras who just got fired."

"But if we're supposed to be Gray's good friends, how can

we go around asking a bunch of questions about him? Won't that seem just a dinky bit suspicious?"

"Okay, okay!" I said, hooking my arm through Abby's, tugging her back out to the sidewalk, and urging her onward toward 45th Street. "You've got a point," I admitted, "but it's really easy to fix. We don't have to be Gray's good friends. We can be more like fans, or recent acquaintances from his acting class. That way our curiosity will seem totally natural." I quickened our pace, but kept on talking. "Don't you see what a slick strategy this is? It's so tight it's right. I'm telling you, Ab, this plan is foolproof!"

"That depends on who the fool is," she said, still skeptical. "And in this case, it could be you."

WHEN WE ARRIVED, STILL ARM-IN-ARM, at 45th Street, I tried to pilot Abby around the corner toward the Morosco. But she suddenly started straining in the opposite direction. "Come across the street for a second," she insisted, charging like a bull for the Loew's State movie theater and dragging me along with her.

"Stop!" I hollered. "What do you think you're doing? I told you before—I'm not going to the movies!"

"Don't be a goose, Paige. This isn't about that!" she said, steadily pulling me toward the brightly lit marquee. *The Seven Year Itch* was playing. Even if I hadn't been able to read the title on the signboard, I would have known what movie it was from the enormous banner hanging above. The four-story-high image of Marilyn Monroe—standing legs apart on the subway grate while a blast of air blows her skirt up past her panties—was a pretty good clue.

Abby drew me into the shade under the movie marquee and then backed me up against the exterior wall of the theater, next to a large glass-enclosed poster display case. Inside the case was another big image of Marilyn. She was wearing a low-cut dress and leaning over in such a way as to expose yet another amazing aspect of her celebrated anatomy.

"Stand still," Abby ordered, opening her purse and taking out a tube of lipstick. "If you're going to pass for a *Bus Stop* extra, you have to wear a hell of a lot more makeup than you've got on. You need some greasepaint, baby!" She mashed her fingers against my face and began smearing a thick coat of red lipstick on my stretched-out lips.

"Ith thith reewy nethethary?" I whined—well, tried to, anyway. (I'm not a big fan of heavy cosmetics. And I didn't like the way people were gawking at us.)

"Of course it's necessary," Abby insisted. "Now, shut up! Stop moving your lips." She finished applying the lipstick and then started to work on my eyes, slathering the lids with bright blue shadow and blackening the lashes with gobs of mascara. After that came the eyebrow pencil and the face powder and the rouge. And when she was through with me, she added a few finishing touches to her own makeup.

"There!" she said, dropping the last weapon in her arsenal of cosmetics back into her purse and snapping the clasp closed. "All done. Now that wasn't so bad, was it?"

"Ugh," I said, checking my reflection in the glass of the poster display case. "I look like a clown."

"Better to *look* like a clown than to *be* one," Abby huffed. "Trust me. If you tried to masquerade as a showgirl with that schoolgirl face of yours, they'd kick you in the seat of the pants and then shoot you out of a cannon."

Chapter 9

NOT ONLY WERE OUR CLOTHES, MAKEUP, and cover story perfect, but our timing couldn't have been better. As we rounded the corner and headed across the street for the Morosco, the doors to the theater flew open and the audience began pouring out onto the sidewalk. The matinee was over! We wouldn't have to search for a back entrance to sneak into, or beg some doubtful stage door custodian to let us inside. All we had to do was push our way through the exiting crowd, slip past the ushers into the slowly emptying theater, and then make our way to the side door we had used the night before—the door that led to the stairs leading up to the dressing rooms.

"We have to stick very close together," I whispered to Abby as we huddled in the dark, deserted passage just inside the door. "And you'd better let me do all the talking. That way, we won't tell any conflicting stories or ask any incongruous questions." *Or attract too much attention*, I said to myself—but not to Abby. (I didn't want to offend my wildly attractive, attention-grabbing friend . . . or give her any wild ideas.)

"Okay, chief!" Abby said, surprising me with her quick and easy compliance. Was she really deferring to me or just humoring me? There was only one way to find out.

"Okay," I said. "Let's go upstairs."

The scene in the hall outside the dressing rooms was more subdued than it had been the night before. There was a light flurry of activity, but nothing at all like the hullabaloo inspired by Gray's knockout debut. Some of the children from the play were chasing each other down the hallway, and a few well-dressed people were milling around in the vicinity, smoking and chatting, probably waiting for their friends or family in the cast to change their clothes and join them for an early supper before the next show. But that was the extent of it. There were no gossip columnists and photographers. No shouts and cheers and popping flashbulbs. No champagne, either.

I studied the arena before me (i.e., cased the joint), trying to decide which target to hit first. I knew I didn't want to talk to any of the show's main stars. Their status and success would, I figured, make them the candidates least likely to know much about the personal life of a mere understudy. I believed I'd have better luck talking to the more "humble" members of the cast and crew—other understudies, or stagehands, or technical assistants—people who, until last night, were on a parallel professional level with Gray and, therefore, more inclined to know him well.

As Abby and I ambled down the hall, peering through every open door, looking for promising people to question, I saw that several people were looking back at us. They obviously noticed our odd clothes and garish makeup, but seemed to take our appearance for granted. Nobody asked who we were or challenged our right to be there. I felt stronger and safer—and more like a *Bus Stop* extra—with every step.

Bypassing all the star dressing rooms, even the communal ones, I led Abby down toward the end of the corridor, to a dim, quiet area that seemed to be abandoned. "I'm looking for the other understudies," I explained to her, speaking in a very low voice even though we were alone in that part of the hall.

"Why?!" she squawked, totally unmindful of her own noise level. "I want to meet the stars! I caught a glimpse of Ben Gazzara when we passed his dressing room just now, and he wasn't wearing a shirt. Oooh, baby, talk about hot! We *have* to go back and interrogate him. Right this minute, you dig? Before he puts his shirt on." She turned and bolted in the opposite direction.

"Whoa!" I cried, lunging after her, grabbing hold of her ponytail and reining her back in.

"Ow!" she cried. "What the hell are you doing?"

"You promised to stick close to me, remember?" I snapped. "And we're not going anywhere near Gazzara's dressing room! There's no reason to question him; we have to focus on what's important. And in case you've forgotten what *that* is," I said, forcing the words out between clenched teeth, "let me refresh your memory. We're here to look for a god-damn murderer, *not* to gawk at an actor's bare chest. *You dig*?" (I pronounced those last two words with enough acidic sarcasm to strip the enamel off my firmly clamped molars.)

Abby pouted and stuck out her chin. "Well, that's not *all* I wanted to see!" she said, stamping her foot on the bare wood floor. "I was thinking about the murderer, too, you know! So I wanted to see what Gazzara is really like. That could be really important! I mean, is he the jealous type? Does he go crazy when his superiority is threatened? Could Gray's fantastic performance last night have made him jealous and crazy enough to kill?" She crossed her arms over her chest and glared at me with a smirk that said, *So there!*

I rolled my eyes at the ceiling. Only Abby would try to turn a burning sexual impulse into a righteous quest for the truth. "That's utter nonsense," I said, "and you know it. Gazzara did not kill Gray. He was in the hospital last night, getting pumped full of fluids and massaged with shaved ice, over-coming his heatstroke and getting in shape for today's perfor-mance. Get real, Abby! Pull yourself together and stop acting like a—"

I was about to say "slut" when the door to my right shot open and a striking young blonde sprang out into the hall. She was about five foot six in her bare feet (I mean that literally, since she didn't have on any stockings or shoes), and her plat-inum locks and shapely curves were comparable to those of Marilyn Monroe, whose bombshell image she was obviously trying to ape. Besides her bra and panties (which I assumed were comfortably settled in their proper places), she was wearing nothing but an ivory satin slip.

"Hey, pipe down, willya?" she croaked, giving Abby and me the evil eye. "I'm trying to get some sleep in here!"

"Sorry," I hurriedly replied, before Abby could get a word

in. "We didn't mean to wake you. We were just looking for a friend from our acting class. Gray Gordon. He's an understudy in this show. Do you know him?" I watched her face for a revealing reaction.

Her sleepy scowl turned into a creepy smile. "Sure, I know him," she said. "Gray and I are just like this." She held up two closely joined fingers. "We're Lunt and Fontaine. Romeo and Juliet. Ozzie and Harriet. Get the idea?"

She was either claiming to be Gray's girlfriend, or telling us that she was his closest castmate—i.e., the play's female lead understudy. Either way, I wanted to know more.

"You must be the stand-in for Maggie the Cat," I ventured, figuring her scantily clad presence backstage made that answer the right one. (I'm so clever sometimes, it kills me.)

"Well, whaddaya know," she said, sneering, looking me over from head to toe. "It has a brain."

Uh oh. I had no idea why the young actress was being so rude to me, but I knew I had to pacify her immediately. Otherwise, Abby would leap to my defense and start telling her off—or, gasp, beating her up!—and that would bring a sure end to the interview. And I couldn't afford to let that to happen. I had to get on the boorish blonde's good side. Fast.

"So you're Rhonda Blake!" I blurted, grinning from ear to ear (and giving myself a silent cheer for remembering her name from the Playbill). "Gray has told us so much about you! He says you're such a wonderful actress you're going to be famous someday." I batted my lashes, shuffled my feet, and let out a fawning gasp of delight. "I'm so thrilled to meet you! May I please have your autograph?"

Mission accomplished.

"Why, of course you can!" she said, brown eyes beaming with vanity and pride. Her mood had turned on a dime. "Got anything to write with?"

I opened my purse and shuffled through the contents, deliberately ignoring the pad and pencil I carry with me always. "Oh, no!" I wailed, doing a swell imitation of Anna Karenina right before she throws herself in front of a train. "I must have left my pen at home!"

"Oh, that's okay, sweetie," Rhonda cooed. "We have one in the lounge. Some paper, too." She turned and wiggled her

happy, ivory satin-sheathed hips back through the door she'd
just exited, motioning for us to follow.

THE "LOUNGE," AS RHONDA HAD CALLED
it, was nothing but a windowless room furnished with one
dressing table, a few chairs, and three folding cots. One of
the cots was open and sloppily covered with a white sheet;
the other two were closed and rolled against one wall. There
were several floor lamps in the room, but only one was
turned on, giving off a dim yellow light that made everything
look murky. Clothes, underwear, towels, magazines, full
ashtrays, and dirty coffee cups were scattered all over the
place. The room was cool, praise the Lord (or, rather, the
saint who invented air-conditioning), yet the smell of sweat
was strong.

Rhonda walked over to the dressing table and started
rummaging through the stuff that littered its surface.
"Cripes! There was a pen here just this morning," she said,
sweeping makeup sponges, eyebrow pencils, combs,
brushes, lipsticks, and dirty Q-Tips from one place to another. "Where the hell did it disappear to? I used it to write
down a slew of phone messages for Gray, and I . . . Oh, here
it is!" she squeaked, "hiding behind the cold cream!"

She snatched up the pen, then bent over and grabbed a
tablet of paper off the floor. "What's your name, honey?"
she asked, walking toward the middle of the room where I
was standing, flipping over several pages of scribbles
(*Gray's phone messages?* I wondered) to get to a clean
sheet. "You want this made out to you, right?"

"Uh . . . yes . . . that would be nice, please." I was so focused on watching the action unfold I almost forgot what I
was supposed to be there for. "You can make it out to
Phoebe Starr," I said, dredging up an old alias I'd used several times before. (My ridiculous real name was hardly well-
known, but it was entirely too memorable to mention. And I
was in no mood to be laughed at.) "That's Starr," I repeated,
"with two r's."

"Got it," Rhonda said, sticking the tip of her tongue between (and quite a bit beyond) her lips as she wrote. Then
she signed her name with a flourish, ripped the whole sheet

off the pad, and handed it to me. "And what about you, sister?" she said to Abby. "You want one, too?"

I froze. What would Abby do now? Would she be a good girl and accept Rhonda's offer of an autograph, or would her true personality break loose and blow our carefully planned cover to smithereens?

"Yes, please," Abby said, fluttering her lashes and panting like an overheated sheepdog. "I'd simply *love* to have your signature. Just your name will do. It would make my pitiful, lonely, and hopeless life complete."

I cringed. Would Rhonda pick up on the contempt in Abby's voice? Would Abby's belligerent, legs-apart, arms-folded posture lead Rhonda to realize that we were both just blowing air up her skirt?

Nope. Looking as satisfied as a cat with a saucer of cream, Rhonda blithely signed her name to the paper, tore the sheet off the tablet, and handed it over it to Abby. "It's all yours, sis," she said, tossing the pen and the pad down on the mattress of the open cot. "Better keep it in a safe place. It'll be worth big money someday."

"Oh, I know right where I'm going to put it," Abby said, curling her lips in a nasty smile. She didn't actually say the words "trash can," but you could tell that was what she was thinking.

"Thank you so much, Rhonda!" I jumped in, hoping she wouldn't notice Abby's scornful expression. (She didn't. Instead of looking at Abby, she was looking at herself in the mirror.) "We really do appreciate this! And we can't wait to tell Gray we met you. Is he here now? Can you tell us where to find him? We want to congratulate him on his fab performance last night."

"Yeah, you and everybody else, honey," she grumbled, sitting down at the dressing table and looking at me in the mirror's reflection. "The phone at the end of the hall's been ringing off the hook all day. And I had to go out and answer it, and take down all of Gray's messages, because he never bothered to show up! If you don't believe me, take a look in the men's lounge next door. He's not there! He didn't even call in. Can you believe that? One stupid night on stage and he's acting like a freaking superstar!" Rhonda snatched up a hairbrush and started yanking it through her platinum fluff.

"You know what else?" she rattled on. "He didn't come in for Thursday's show, either. And that was *before* his goddamn dazzling debut. I had to take down a bunch of messages for him that night, too. What am I, his freaking secretary?"

"Well, it's very nice of you to do that for Gray," I said, just to keep the ball rolling. "I'm sure he's very grateful."

"Ha!" she scoffed. "That's a laugh and a half. He was so busy taking bows last night, he never even looked at the messages to see who called. That's how grateful he is!" She angrily tossed the hairbrush back down on the cluttered table. "And I'll tell you something else. If our director, Mr. Kazan, ever finds out Gray wasn't here Thursday or for the matinee today, he'll fire him on the spot. An understudy has to be in the house for every single performance, no matter what!"

Even if he's dead? I muttered to myself.

"Gray better show up for tonight's show," Rhonda went on, "or I'm going to report him myself. He can't disappear whenever he feels like it. It's not fair!" She spun around on her stool and then suddenly, out of the blue, took a long, cold, appraising look at both Abby and me. "Hey, what are you two pretending to be? What's with the makeup and the sporty little outfits? Is your acting class working on a scene from *Picnic*?"

"Good guess," I replied, "but actually we're crowd scene extras in *Bus Stop*. It's playing right across the street. We dashed over here the minute the matinee ended, hoping to catch Gray before he left the theater. That's why we're still in costume—we didn't have time to change."

"What a crock!" Rhonda said. "You're really asking for it, you know!"

"For what?" I asked, getting nervous.

"For trouble, sister. And I mean *big* trouble."

"Why? What are you talking about?" I was on the verge of panic now. Had Rhonda heard me and Abby arguing—and discussing the murder—out in the hall before? Did she know that everything we'd said and done since then had been a big fat act? Had she guessed our real reason for being there, and then put on a big fat act of her own?

"Don't play the ingenue with me, honey!" Rhonda exclaimed. "You know darn well that all cast members of all Broadway shows are forbidden to wear their costumes in the street. That's totally against the rules! And don't say you didn't have time to change, either. That's a complete crock. You're supposed to *make* the time, no matter what. So, you know what I say? I say you and your sour-faced sidekick over there have broken one of the most basic laws of Broadway—and you ought to be fired for it!"

Whew. Is that all? For a lowly understudy, Rhonda sure took her job (and everybody else's!) seriously. I was staring at the floor, trying to think up a good excuse for Abby's and my bad Broadway behavior, when a very soft, muted tinkling sound seeped into the lounge and captured my attention.

"Hey, what's that?" I asked. "Do you hear a bell or something?"

"Cripes! It's the goddamn phone again!" Rhonda snapped. "They keep it muffled in case it rings while the show is on."

"Do you have to answer it?" I asked, hoping she would.

"Yeah, yeah, yeah," she said, wearily rising to her bare feet and padding toward the door to the hall. "You and Tonto have to leave now, anyway," she added, shooting us a snotty glance over her shoulder. "I'm going back to sleep, and if you know what's good for you, you'll run back across the street and take off your goddamn costumes."

"Oh, we will!" I assured her, as she sashayed out the door and disappeared down the hall to the right. "And thanks for the autographs!" I called out, even though I knew she wasn't listening. (I can be—and often am—polite to the puking point. Abby swears I'm related to Emily Post.)

Abby erupted as soon as Rhonda was gone. "What a bitch!" she spluttered, looking as if the top of her head would blow off. (Considering the pressure that had surely been building up in her stubborn, short-tempered skull, such an event wouldn't have surprised me in the least.) "I never met such a sniveling, pretentious, big-mouthed broad in my life! She's a tattletale and a tramp. And I bet she's a murderer, too. She probably killed Gray for taking too long for lunch!"

"Shhhhh!" I cautioned, holding a silencing finger up to

my lips and tiptoeing over to the cot where Rhonda had tossed the pad and the pen. Glad she hadn't taken the message pad with her to the phone, I promptly snatched up the tablet full of scribbles, hid it under my purse, and scrambled for the door. Abby scrambled right along with me and—fleeing down the hall to the left like Bonnie and Clyde (or, more precisely, Lucy and Ethel)—we made a clean getaway.

Chapter 10

MOST OF THE SCRIBBLED NOTES IN THE pad really *were* phone messages for Gray—a fact Abby and I determined as soon as we were seated on the subway headed home. Somebody named Bradley had called to say "Bravo!," a fellow named Lloyd had phoned to say goodbye since he knew Gray would never talk to a "nobody" like him again, and somebody calling herself Aunt Doobie had left her room number at the Mayflower Hotel.

There were other messages as well—some of them congratulatory, most with first names only, just one with a phone number. No days or dates were noted, and there seemed to be no order to the listings, so—unless a message was congratulatory—I couldn't determine if the call had been made last Thursday night or this afternoon. As far as I could tell, Cupcake hadn't called on either day. I flipped the pad closed and tucked it under my purse, saving my careful clue-hunting inspection for later, when I could concentrate.

"Are you going to give the notebook to Flannagan in the morning?" Abby asked.

"I don't know yet," I said. "Depends on how well he behaves. If he's a good dog, I'll give him the bone."

"Ha!" she yelped. "Then you might as well bury it in the back yard. That man will always behave like a bastard."

I laughed. "You're probably right. He might even arrest me for stealing, or tampering with evidence. I'd better leave the pad at home."

We got off the train at West 4th Street and climbed the steps to the street. The steamy heat engulfed me and I suddenly felt very weak. I hadn't eaten much all day and—though I still wasn't the least bit hungry—I knew I needed fuel.

"Want to grab a bite at the White Horse, Ab?" I asked, naming the popular tavern on Hudson Street that was famous for its cheap beer, lousy hamburgers, and literary clientele. They didn't have air-conditioning, I knew, but very few places in the Village did.

"No way, Doris Day!" she said, shaking her head so violently her ponytail was twitching from one side of her back to the other, like a real horse's tail swishing off flies. "I'm still full from lunch, babe. I'm just gonna mosey on over to the park, get a purple snow cone, see if Jimmy is there. Wanna come?"

"No, thanks. I'm too hot. And my head is too crazy for poetry or folk music. I think I'll just go home, have a sandwich, catch some TV, and wait for Dan to call."

The minute Dan's name flitted out of my mouth, my heart started doing the hula. And my clammy forehead broke out in another sweat. I wanted to talk to Dan. The only thing in the whole wide world I wanted to do at that moment was talk to Dan.

I pulled Abby to a stop on the sidewalk and sputtered, "He'll call me tonight, don't you think? He probably tried to last night, but I was at the theater all evening, and after that my phone was off the hook. And he couldn't get hold of me today since I haven't been home. So he must be going nuts by now, wondering where I am and what I've been doing. Right? He's going to call me tonight for sure, don't you think?" (To say that I was eager to hear from my daring detective would be like calling the cruel heat wave cozy.)

"Be cool, fool," Abby said, smiling. "If there's one thing I know in this *focockta* mixed-up world, it's that a man likes a challenge. So it's great that you're playing hard-to-get. The harder you are to reach, the harder he'll try to get there. You dig my meaning?"

I understood what Abby was saying, but I couldn't accept her prognosis. She had never played hard-to-get in her whole darn hard-and-fast life, so what the heck did she know about it? And besides, I wasn't playing games with Dan! I had gone to the theater at Abby's insistence, and I had taken my phone off the hook to avoid a call from her, not him. And I had been out all day discovering a dead body and investigating a murder, for God's sake, not toying with my boyfriend's peace of mind. (Although now that I think of it, I guess that's exactly what I *was* doing. I mean, if Dan had known what I'd actually been up to, his peace of mind would have been pretty much shot.)

"Take it from me, Paige," Abby added. "When you chase after a man, you're just keeping him from catching you."

"And that's why you're going to the park to look for Jimmy?" I teased. "To make yourself uncatchable?"

"Oh, shut up!" she said, giggling, nudging me with her elbow. Then she gave me a little bye-bye wave and quipped, "Catch you later, alligator. Tell Dan I said hi!" Before I could reply, she made an abrupt left turn and galloped across Sixth Avenue, her ponytail flapping wildly down her back.

I BOUGHT A LOAF OF ITALIAN BREAD AT Zito's bakery, a few slices of salami and cheese at Faicco's deli, and a green pepper at Angelo's fruit and vegetable store before I went home. (That's one advantage of living on Bleecker between Sixth and Seventh—anything you could possibly want to eat is right downstairs.) It was hot as hell in my apartment, but after I opened the back door and turned on the electric fan in the living room, it was almost sufferable.

Switching on the radio and searching the dial for some cool music, I finally settled on Sarah Vaughn. She was singing "Whatever Lola Wants," and—since Lola always got whatever she wanted—I wondered how hard it would be to change my first name. *Lola Turner*, I thought. *Has a nice ring to it. A tad too close to Lana's label, but at least it's not a stupid pun!*

I took a bottle of Orange Crush out of the ice box, rolled its cold surface across my forehead, then pried off the metal cap using the handle of my kitchen drawer as an opener. Setting the soda pop down on the table, I removed the salami and cheese from the bag and slapped the slices on a plate. Then I grabbed a sharp knife from the kitchen drawer and—doing my best not to think of it as a murder weapon—used it to slash off a few pieces of bread and green pepper.

Dinner was served.

By the time I finished eating, the Four Aces were singing "Love Is a Many Splendored Thing," and I was bawling like a baby.

(Well, I'd had a pretty hard day, you know! And I hadn't spoken to Dan in over thirty-six hours. And I was so hot and tired and depressed I wanted to die. And poor Gray Gordon *was* dead, lying gashed to ribbons in the city morgue, and I had to go to the police station in the morning to explain to a hotheaded homicide dick why Abby and I had tracked blood and fingerprints all over the crime scene, making a godawful mess of the evidence. . . . And to make matters worse, even if Dan did call me tonight, I couldn't tell him what was happening because it would not only ruin the rest of his weekend with his daughter, but he'd get so mad at me for getting involved in another dangerous murder case, that . . . oh, why am I pestering you with all these whiney details? I'm sure you get the picture.)

I was still blubbering at the kitchen table, feeling sorry for myself and listening to the Penguins sing "Earth Angel," when the phone rang. I sprang out of my chair, leapt into the living room, and—wiping my eyes and nose on the paper napkin clutched in my hand—yanked the receiver up to my ear.

"Hellooooh," I said, trying to purr like Kim Novak, but surely creaking like Jerry Lewis with a head cold.

"Hi, babe," Dan said. "What's the matter? You sound awful. Do you have a cold?" (See, I told you!)

"No, I'm just a little stuffed up," I said. "I think it's from the heat and humidity."

"Or maybe you've just been crying because you miss me so much," he teased. (If I haven't said it before, then let me say it now: Dan is a *really* good detective.)

"I haven't been crying," I lied, "but I *do* miss you. Like crazy, if you want to know the truth."

"I miss you, too, baby," he said, and the way his deep, delicious voice rolled around in my ear made my whole body vibrate. "I called you several times yesterday and today, and all I got was a busy signal or no answer. Has your phone been out of order?"

And thus another perfect cover story landed in my lap.

"It sure has!" I said, hating having to lie to Dan (again), but feeling certain it was for the best. "It's so hot a bunch of cables melted, or some gaskets blew up, or something drastic like that. Workers from the telephone company have been hanging around this block for two days now, trying to fix the problem. It looks as though they've succeeded now, since you were able to get a connection, but who knows how long the service will last? A couple of phone company trucks are still parked outside." (I figured I'd better lay the groundwork for future communication failures. Dan would be out of town for two more days, and god only knew where I was going be!)

"How's your trip going so far?" I asked, hurrying to change the subject. "Are you and Katy having a good time?"

"Katy's having the time of her life." Dan's voice was crackling with enthusiasm and good humor. "My folks have taken her clamming and fishing and to the whale museum. Turns out she's fascinated with marine life."

"And what about you? Didn't you go on these outings, too?"

"Oh, I tagged along, but I'm not very seaworthy. I'm a city boy, don't you know. I like to hook worms, but only the human variety."

I smiled. Dan was a man after my own heart (my body and soul, too, I hoped). "What's on your agenda for tomorrow?" I asked. "Are you celebrating in any special way?"

"We're going to the beach in the morning and to Captain Billy's Mermaid Cove for lunch. Then we're taking a glass-bottom boat ride in the afternoon. After dinner, it's back to the beach to watch the fireworks. I'll probably duck for cover every time a Roman candle explodes."

I laughed. It was hard to imagine Dan sitting in shorts on the sand. Would I even recognize him without his trench coat, fedora, and shoulder holster?

"What are you doing tomorrow?" he asked. "Got any hot

holiday plans? I bet Abby's taking you to some wild bohemian bash where reefers instead of firecrackers will be the cause of all the smoke."

He was trying to sound cool and cocky, but I detected a distinct note of discomfort in Dan's voice. He was feeling insecure about me. I was certain of it. (As a woman who's spent her whole life flailing in a giant vat of insecurity, I know what I'm talking about!) I was glad that Dan was concerned about me (it sure beat indifference), but I didn't have the slightest desire to make him squirm. He'd be doing enough of *that*, I knew, when he found out what was really going on.

"I don't have any plans at all," I assured him. "All I'll be doing is trying to stay cool. I'll probably make a pitcher of lemonade and take it up to the roof after it gets dark. Maybe I'll be able to see the fireworks from there."

"Lemonade?" he said, chuckling softly.

"With a hint of vodka," I conceded. "And a box of animal crackers instead of firecrackers."

Dan chuckled again, but then turned serious. "I miss you so much, Paige," he said. "I wish you were here with us. I think you and Katy would really hit it off."

Now he thinks of it?! Now that he and his daughter are a million miles away baking clams on the coast of Maine while I'm baking alive in Manhattan, knee-deep in blood and murder?! Dan's timing, I felt, could have been a bit better.

Still, now was a whole lot better than never. I stifled my exasperation and focused on the heartfelt emotion I'd heard simmering in Dan's voice when he said he missed me. "I wish I were there with you and Katy, too," I said, simmering with emotions of my own. "And I know Katy and I will get along very well whenever we finally do meet. We have a lot in common already," I added. "We are, for instance, both nuts about you."

Dan let out a satisfied snort. "That's just what I needed to hear, babe. Now I can go clean the smelly fish heads off the deck of Dad's boat with a song in my heart."

I giggled. "Which song will it be?"

"'The Ballad of Davy Crockett,' I think. Old Dave must've dispensed with a lot of fish heads in his day."

"Have fun," I said, grinning like a lovestruck fool. "Will you call me tomorrow?"

"It's a date," he promised. "First thing in the morning."

"I hope my phone's still working."

"If it's not, I'll fly home and fix it myself."

Chapter 11

THERE ARE—IN ALL OUR LIVES— certain times to feel good, other times to feel bad, and many more times to feel in-between. This was, for me, one of the hopelessly stuck-in-between times. I felt great about Dan's declared longing for me, but I felt awful about the way I was deceiving him. Six of one, half a dozen of the other. Would I ever break loose from this gut-twisting tug of war? Would I ever be free to give Dan my wholehearted devotion and unrestricted allegiance?

Maybe someday, but not tonight. Tonight I had to study the smudged and wrinkled pages of a scribbled-up message pad, and search for clues to a brutal killer's identity.

I filled a jellyglass with Chianti and took it into the living room, setting it down on the table near the couch (or, rather, the homemade daybed contraption I try to pass off as a couch). Then I scooted into the kitchen, grabbed my L&M filter tips and the message pad, hurried back to the couch (or whatever you want to call it), and seated myself directly in front of the fan (which made it hard for me to light my cigarette—but where there's a will there's a way). A puff of smoke, a sip of wine, a chorus of "Only You" by the Platters, and I was ready to tuck into the task at hand.

Three glasses of wine, umpteen cigarettes, and who knows

how many hit tunes later, I was all tuckered out. I had read all thirteen of Gray's messages nine or ten times over, studying each word as if it were a hieroglyph and I were an Egyptian scholar (which wasn't so far from reality since Rhonda's handwriting was almost indecipherable). I had hoped to pick up at least one truly significant clue—something that would send me shooting, like an arrow, straight toward the homicidal bull's eye—but that hope never materialized. Aside from Aunt Doobie's hotel room number, I learned only a couple of things that I thought might be helpful.

I now knew, for example, that Gray had had a lot of friends, and that four of them were named Randy. (Okay, okay! So it was probably more likely that all four messages had been left by the same Randy, but I couldn't be certain of that now, could I?) I knew from the preponderance of masculine names that most of Gray's friends were male. Aside from Aunt Doobie, the only female name on the list was Binky—"Binky from acting class," to be more precise.

Binky's message was the only one with a phone number, and I decided to dial it that very night, before the morning papers with the news of Gray's death hit the stands. I drained the dregs from my third wine glass, lit up another cigarette, and placed the call.

One ring, then two, then a brusque "Hello." It was a man's voice, and it didn't sound happy.

"Oh, hello," I said, trying to sound calm and cool as a cucumber (which was impossible since I was hotter than a roasted chicken, and as calm as Daffy Duck on the opening day of hunting season). "May I speak to Binky please?"

There was a long pause, and then the brusque voice growled, "Who is this?"

"Uh . . . mm . . . you don't know me," I stammered, madly searching for the right thing to say. " My name is Phoebe Starr and I'm a friend of Gray Gordon's and I'd like to talk to Binky if I—"

"You're a friend of Gray's?" The man's tone had turned from curt to curious.

"Yes, that's right. We're neighbors in the Village."

"So, what do you want to talk to Binky for?"

I was reluctant to answer the question. Who was this impertinent man? And why was he screening Binky's calls? Was he her father, brother, husband, boyfriend, or lawyer?

"Well . . . uh . . . see, I'm an actress," I began, taking my own sweet time, speaking as slowly as I could without seeming retarded (I didn't want to reveal too many personal facts—okay, fables—until I knew who was on the other end of the line) " . . . and I've been looking for a new drama coach. So, when I ran into Gray on the street the other day," I continued, still stalling, "I started asking him a bunch of questions about his acting workshop. I wanted to know how much it cost, and if you had to audition, and if he thought I'd be able to get in. But Gray didn't have time to talk to me since he was in a big hurry to get to the theater . . . so he gave me Binky's number and said I should talk to her about it."

The man burst out laughing. "*Her?*" he croaked, between guffaws. "Are you sure Gray said 'her'?"

Boo-boo alert. Right name, wrong gender.

"He didn't actually use the word 'her,'" I hurried to explain. "I just assumed . . ."

"Then, you assumed wrong, sweetheart. Do I sound like a girl?"

"*You're* Binky?"

"The one and only."

"Please pardon my mistake, Mr. . . . uh . . . um . . . er . . ." I stumbled, hoping he would fill in the blank of his last name.

"Kapinski," he said. "Barnabas Kapinski. But you can call me Binky. Everybody does."

"Okay, Binky," I said. "If it's all right with you, it's all right with me."

He laughed again. "It's not a very manly name, I know, but then, neither is Barnabas."

I giggled, just to keep the good will flowing. "You're in Gray's drama workshop, right? You're studying at the Actors Studio? With Lee Strasberg?"

"Guilty as charged."

"Ooooh, that's so wonderful!" I gushed. "You must be a really good actor! I know Mr. Strasberg only accepts the best. And some of his students are famous stars already! I mean, James Dean and Marilyn Monroe are studying at the Studio now, aren't they?"

"Yeah, but you don't see them around much. They're kind of busy making movies."

"And what about you?" I probed. "Are you starring in any movies or shows?"

He laughed again. "Not unless you count my starring role at the Latin Quarter every night. I'm the best bartender they have."

I let out another giggle and tried to think of a way to get him to talk about Gray. "Well, that's a better job than Gray had," I stressed. "He was just a busboy before he landed the *Hot Tin Roof* understudy job. And now he's a star! At least that's what Brooks Atkinson says. Did you read his review of Gray's stand-in performance in the *Times* today?"

"Of course. Atkinson is the best drama critic in the city. I read every word the man writes."

"So, what do you think about what he said? Is Gray as good an actor as he claims?"

"Yeah, yeah, Gray's okay, I guess," Binky replied. "He seems pretty skillful when he's doing scenes at the Studio. I didn't see him on stage last night, though, so I don't know about *that* . . . But what the hell does it matter what *I* think, anyway? Brooks Atkinson said he's good, and that's all that friggin' counts. Gray's a lucky guy. He'll be getting more offers than he can handle. He's on a friggin' free ride to the top."

I couldn't see Binky's face, but judging from his grudging tone of voice and vulgar choice of words, I'd have wagered it was green with envy.

"I bet you'll be next," I said, hoping to soothe his jealous soul and turn his attentions to more important matters (i.e., the things that mattered to *me*). "Everybody who gets accepted at the Actors Studio eventually hits the big time, right?" I asked. "That's why I want to study there so much. Do you think I have a chance? Is it as hard to get in as everybody says?"

"Yeah, it's pretty tough," he said, warming to the role of the wise advisor. "First of all there has to be an opening in the Studio. Mr. Strasberg likes to keep the headcount under control, and sometimes he won't accept a new student unless he's lost an old one. And then—if a space does open up and you want to apply—you've got to do at least two auditions, have excellent recommendations, and be super serious about pursuing an acting career. You've got to have some experience, too.

Professional experience, I mean. Not just high school or college stuff."

"Gee, that *is* tough," I said, with an exaggerated sigh. "Still, I *am* really serious about being an actress, and I *do* have some professional experience. I've done some summer stock and a slew of radio commercials. Does that qualify?"

"It might be enough," Binky said, "but all the experience in the world won't do you any good unless you perform really well at the auditions. That's what Mr. Strasberg cares about the most—whether or not you have an exciting stage presence, and whether or not you can act."

"Oh, I can act, all right!" I said, with unshakable self-confidence. (Am I a good actress, or what?) I wanted to convince Binky of my talent and drive so that he would accept me as a striving colleague, and show me around the Studio, and introduce me to his and Gray's fellow drama students (be they friend or, more importantly, *foe*).

But Binky wasn't very receptive to my performance. He paused for a moment, then muttered, "You sound pretty damn sure of yourself, little girl."

Uh-oh. His tone had turned gruff again—especially when he pronounced the words "little girl." Had I overstepped my feminine bounds? Had I threatened Binky's masculinity with my forceful (albeit fake) self-esteem?

"Oh, that's just an act," I hastened to admit, working to recover lost ground and get back on Binky's good side. "I kid you not. I'm nothing but a nervous Nellie inside. I'm so full of self-doubt, I'm bursting at the seams." (This part was a snap for me to play since it was completely in character.)

Binky let out another laugh, and I breathed a sigh of relief. The "proper" male/female order had been restored.

"That's another reason I wanted to talk to you, Binky," I went on, simpering, making my voice sound as girlish and fluttery as possible. "Gray said you might be willing to meet with me, help me get all the right application forms, and take me into the Studio to show me around. If I could just meet some of the other members of the program, watch a workshop in progress, and see what the audition area is like, I think it would help me get over my nervousness. Don't you agree? Do you think you could help me, kind sir?"

If Binky had been able to see me, I'd have been gazing at

him like a puppy and batting my lashes to beat the band (the way Abby had taught me to do). As it was, though, I was free to cross my eyes and stick out my tongue (just to relieve the pressure, you understand).

"Yeah, maybe," Binky said. "I guess I could take you to the Studio someday. But not right now. It's closed for the Fourth. Won't be open till Tuesday."

"Oh, Tuesday will be fine!" I exclaimed, jumping to seal the bargain before he could change his mind or delay the day. "I can't tell you how much I appreciate this, Binky! And Gray will be delighted to hear how helpful you're being. I'll call you on Monday so we can set up a time and a place to meet."

"Er . . . well . . . okay," he mumbled, sounding unnerved and somewhat dumbfounded.

And with any luck, I thought—bidding him a fast farewell and hanging up the phone in a flash—he would stay that way.

I WAS AS TIRED AS A MARATHON TAP dancer, but it was too early—and too hot—to go to bed. I considered going uptown to the hopefully air-conditioned Mayflower to pay Aunt Doobie a surprise visit, but simply didn't have the energy. Thinking I'd call her room at the hotel instead, I got the address and phone number of the Mayflower from the phone book and wrote the info down on the message pad. But then, just as I picked up the receiver and began to dial, I was besieged with second thoughts. Who *was* this woman, anyway? Maybe she was Gray's aunt, and maybe she wasn't. She could be Eisenhower's aunt, for all I knew! So, what the devil was I going to say to her? How could I get her to talk about Gray? What kind of story was I going to make up this time?

Aaaargh!

Finally realizing that I was too addled and exhausted to deal with Aunt Doobie at the moment, I dropped the receiver back in the cradle, deciding I'd try to get in touch with her tomorrow.

Shuffling into the kitchen in a daze, I washed Abby's gloppy makeup off my face at the sink, gave my arms, neck, and shoulders a cold sponge bath, cranked open a new tray of ice, and loaded a tall glass with cubes. Then I held the glass under the faucet and filled it to the brim with tap water. By the time I staggered back into the living room, turned off the radio, and turned on the TV, half the water had been drunk (by me, I guess, but I don't remember doing it).

Sitting back down in front of the fan, I sucked on an ice cube and tried to focus my attention on the final monologue of *The George Gobel Show*. I was hoping the casual comedian's folksy, down-home humor would soothe my frazzled nerves and take my mind off the murder. Ha! I might as well have hoped for a snow storm. The memory of Gray's slashed and bloody body was as intense and unrelenting as the temperature.

Even *Your Hit Parade*, the next show to come on the screen, offered no relief. The sunny lyrics of the most popular songs—not to mention the beaming faces of the cheerful singers—only made me feel worse. (Mourners like the rain, you know. It makes them feel that the cosmos is crying, too.) And then later in the show, when Gisele MacKenzie came out and sang "It's a Sin to Tell a Lie," I got *really* depressed. If the words to that song were true, I was going to burn in hell for all eternity—not just for the duration of the heat wave.

When Snooky Lanson came on the screen and started singing a heavy rendition of Tennessee Ernie Ford's smash hit, "Sixteen Tons," I couldn't take it anymore. I had too much weight on my shoulders already. Standing up from the couch and turning off my rented Sylvania, I unplugged my electric fan and lugged it into the kitchen. Then I retrieved my glass from the living room, refilled it with ice and water, closed and locked the back door, turned off all the downstairs lights, and trudged—glass grasped in one hand, fan gripped in the other—up the stairs to my oven of a bedroom.

The night would be unbearable, I knew.

What I didn't know was: The worst nights were yet to come.

Chapter 12

I HAD BREAKFAST NEXT DOOR THE FOL-
lowing morning. (My bountiful neighbor is as quick to serve
up a bagel as she is to shake up a cocktail.) Jimmy was sleeping upstairs, but Abby was fully awake and "properly"
dressed for our command appearance at the police station. In
her prim white Ship 'n Shore blouse, navy blue pencil skirt,
and navy-and-white spectator pumps, she looked almost innocent.

The key word here is *almost*, because one peek at the satisfied smile on her sensual Ava Gardner face and you knew
she had to be guilty of something. And it wasn't hard to
fathom what that something was.

"I guess you had a good time with Jimmy last night," I
said, trying to keep the judgmental (okay, jealous) tone out of
my voice. "You look like the cat that ate the canary."

"That's one way to put it," she said, grinning like an idiot,
pouring us each a glass of iced coffee. "And how did your
evening go? Did Dan call?"

Now it was my turn to smile. "Yep." I stirred some cream
and sugar into my glass and took a sip. "He called me last
night and this morning, too. He said he misses me a lot."

"Did he tell you he loves you?"

"No, but he sounded like he does. He said he really wishes

I were there with him. He thinks Katy and I would be getting along great."

"Yeah? Well, too bad he didn't think of that before," Abby said, with a derisive snort. "The temperature's fifteen degrees lower in Maine, you dig? You could be having a really cool time right now. Ocean breezes, moonlight swims, half-naked bodies on the beach."

"Yeah," I said, sighing. "There must be plenty of *those* lying around . . . and I bet none of them are dead."

I wished I hadn't said that. Now Gray Gordon's eviscerated corpse was lying on the table between us, calling a halt to our cheerful banter, wrenching our thoughts from romance to murder.

"Did you go over Gray's phone messages last night?" Abby asked.

"Yes, of course I did. Several times."

"Find any clues?"

"A few," I said, "but nothing really solid. I wish Rhonda had dated the messages, or at least put them down in the order she received them. Then I might have learned something important. But the list is just a mish-mash. It's as messy and disorganized as Rhonda's dressing table at the theater."

"Do the dates really matter that much?"

"Of course they do!" I said, surprised by Abby's naiveté. "If I had the dates, I'd know which calls came in before Gray was killed, and which ones came in after."

"But what difference does that make?"

I rolled my eyes at her inane question. "Jeez, Abby! Just think about it for a second. If somebody telephoned Gray the day *after* he was murdered, then it's a pretty safe bet that person *wasn't* the murderer, wouldn't you say? Why would anybody call him up if they knew that he was dead?"

"To plant a false clue," she said. "To make himself look innocent."

"Oh," I said, embarrassed by my own shortsightedness. Abby had a good point. Why hadn't *I* thought of it?

"So what *did* you find out?" Abby asked, not rubbing it in. Either she was letting me off the hook, or she hadn't noticed my impatient tone. (Considering the fact that Abby really loves to one-up me, I figured it was the latter.) "Solid or liquid," she said, "every clue is worth something."

Taking her words under advisement, I told Abby about the various names and numbers I'd gleaned from Rhonda's list, reporting on every aspect of my study. Then I sat back in my chair, lit up one of Abby's Pall Malls, and related all the details of my phone conversation with Binky.

"Ve-ry interesting," Abby said, when I'd finished my summary. "Binky-Winky sounds kind of stinky. Maybe he murdered Gray himself. "

"Could be," I said, remembering how Binky's tone and vocabulary had turned angry when we were discussing Gray's rave review. "I'll have a better idea after I meet him on Tuesday."

"I'll go with you!" she said, getting excited. "I'm a really good judge of character, you know. And I'd love to take a stroll around the Actors Studio, get an up-close and personal look at James Dean. I think he's in town now. And he's my fave new screen boy. He's so hot it hurts!"

I didn't say a word. I had no intention of taking Abby with me, but I didn't tell her that. I knew she'd have a complete fit. Then she'd dig in her heels and torment me until I surrendered and let her come—a consequence I simply could not allow to happen. Abby's presence at my meeting with Binky would rattle my concentration, play havoc with my cover, and lead Binky to question my "true" motives for contacting him (i.e., wreck the whole darn operation!). Better to keep my mouth shut, keep the peace, and wait until Tuesday to crush Abby's hopes of meeting her fave new screen boy.

I glanced at the clock on Abby's kitchen wall. It was nine thirty-five. "Holy moley, would you look at the time?!" I cried. "I've got to run home and change my clothes. If Flannagan saw me in this outfit" (a pair of short shorts and one of Bob's old army T-shirts), "he'd arrest me for sure."

"Then you'd better scurry, Murray," Abby said. "From what I've heard, It ain't too cool in the cooler."

THE SIXTH PRECINCT STATION WAS JUST a few blocks away on West 10th Street. Abby and I walked there as fast as we could—which wasn't very fast since the heat, humidity, and our dangerously high heels slowed us down to a stroll. I bought a newspaper on the way over, but didn't take the time to look for any articles about the murder. We were late enough as it was. Entering the busy station through the streetlevel double glass doors, we headed straight for the main desk to our right, stilettos clicking across the scuffed brown linoleum.

A tall, well-built young man with an exceptionally long, narrow face was standing like a sentry behind the counterlike partition. He was wearing the standard summer uniform (same as the winter but with short sleeves)—no jacket or hat. A badge was pinned to his shirt, and a gun was holstered on his hip. As Abby and I approached the desk, he snatched a white handkerchief out of his pocket and quickly mopped the sweat off his handsome, shoebox-shaped mug. "Hello, ladies," he said, stuffing the handkerchief back in his pocket. "How can I help you?"

"We're here to see Detective Flannagan," I said. "We had a ten o'clock appointment but, as you can see, we're a few minutes late."

"Then I'll have to take you into custody," he teased.

"I can think of worse punishment," Abby said, batting her lashes so hard and fast I felt a breeze.

Oh, brother! She was flirting with him. She was flaunting her so-called charms all over the place. You'd have thought our horrific reason for being at the station (or, at the very least, her randy reunion with Jimmy last night) would have stifled her seductive ways—but noooo. There she stood, one hand propped suggestively on her jutting hip, making eyes at a horse-faced policeman as if she were a filly in heat and he were the last stallion on earth.

Luckily, I found my voice before they galloped off to the nearest stable together.

"Detective Flannagan is expecting us, sir," I said, with a loud sniff of annoyance. "And we don't want to be any later than we already are. Can you let him know we're here, or direct us to his office, please?" I was doing a swell immitation of Susan Hayward in a righteous huff, but I felt like Milton Berle in a prom dress (i.e., more likely to attract ridicule than respect).

"Oh, uh . . . sure," the young officer said, reluctantly turning his attention from Abby to me. "I'll just give them a call upstairs. They'll send somebody down to get you."

"Can't you show us the way yourself?" Abby said, batting her damn lashes again. "That would give us a little more time together."

His rectangular face turned as pink as a primrose. "Oh, no, ma'am," he said. "I couldn't do that. I'm not allowed to leave my post. But hang on for a second, I'll get you another guide right away."

While he was dialing and then talking on the intercom, I gave Abby my sternest look. "Cut it out!" I whispered. "We're here to help the cops find a killer, for God's sake! Your search for a new lover can wait!"

"That's not fair!" she hissed. "I'm looking for a new model, not a lover!"

"Same difference," I said.

"IT'S SEVENTEEN MINUTES AFTER TEN," Flannagan said, looking at his watch, shooting me a nasty scowl, then standing up behind his desk. His jacket was draped on the back of his chair, his sleeves were rolled up to his elbows, his collar was unbuttoned, and his tie was loose and lopsided. "It's about time you showed up," he growled. "I was beginning to think I'd have to send somebody to your place to get you."

"Please forgive us, Detective Flannagan," I said. "We got off to a bit of a late start this morning."

"Yeah, well, your 'bit of a late start' has thrown my whole damn schedule off track," he griped, looking at his watch again. "I have to be somewhere else at eleven, so we don't have much time."

"Oh, what a shame!" Abby cried, putting on a big sarcastic show of contrition. "I could just kill myself for taking so long to eat that extra bagel."

Her jeering tone was making me squirm. Would Flannagan realize that she was mocking him? Would he get mad and give us an even harder time than originally planned? I tried to think of something soothing to say—something that would calm the choppy sea between the surly detective and my irascible best friend—but finally decided it would be safer to just leave things alone.

"Let's get started," Flannagan said, showing no more anger

(or awareness) than usual. He gestured toward the two old wooden chairs positioned in front of his old wooden desk and muttered, "Sit down."

We did as we were told. (I don't know about Abby, but I was glad to get off my feet.)

Flannagan sat back down behind his desk and began shuffling some papers around. While he was getting organized, I took the opportunity to look around his office—or, rather, the large bullpen in which his work area was situated.

Flannagan's desk was one of seven in the drab, greenish-gray room, one side of which was lined with windows so dirty they barely let in any light. The desks all faced the door and were aligned along the outside wall like cars in a parking lot. A row of tall, beat-up file cabinets stood against the wall opposite the windows, narrowing the aisle running down the center of the office to a width of about four feet. (A rhino might have made it through, but never an elephant.) Except for Flannagan and the rhino-size man sitting at the first desk in the front, there were no other homicide detectives in sight (unless you want to count *me*, which you probably don't).

Flannagan slapped the papers down on his desk and lit up a Camel. His boyish, clean-shaven face was scrunched up in an ugly frown. "Okay, first things first," he said. "Give me the names of your doctors."

"What?!" we cried, in unison.

"The names of your doctors," he repeated.

"Why?!" we harmonized.

"Because I told you to," he said, sticking out his jaw and crossing his arms over his chest. He not only looked like a little boy, but he was acting like one, too. He was the bully of the playground—the one who would push you off the seesaw and steal your lunch money.

"But may I ask *why* you want our doctors' names?" I said, jumping to take the lead in the conversation before Abby could cause a scene. (One glance at her rigid posture and clenched fists, and I knew she was about to blow her stack.) "It seems such an odd request, if you don't mind me saying so, sir. I'm sure I'm a complete dunce, but I can't help wondering what our doctors have to do with the murder of Gray Gordon."

Sometimes it pays to be polite. My courteous and feminine

(okay, totally self-deprecating) demeanor had a pacifying effect on Flannagan's mood. His ugly frown faded, then he uncrossed his arms and removed them from his chest. Retrieving his lit cigarette from the ashtray and taking a long, slow drag, he cocked his head in my direction and tweaked his lips into something resembling a smile.

"I really don't have to explain myself or my methods to you, Mrs. Turner," he said, "but since you asked so nicely . . ." He paused for another puff on his cigarette. "I want your doctors' names so I can contact them to verify your blood types."

Oh, so that's it! I said to myself. *They did find more than one blood type at the crime scene. Guess they won't be needing my bag of bloodstained clothes after all . . .* which was a good thing, I realized, since I'd forgotten to bring the bloody stuff with me!

"After seeing the excessive carnage at the scene," Flannagan went on, proudly launching an account of his own outstanding powers of detection, "I had a hunch the victim put up a big fight before he died. Which meant the murderer could have been wounded, too. We took blood samples from several different places in the apartment—including the bathroom, where we think the killer took a shower and changed into clean clothes before he fled—and then we rushed the samples to the lab for overnight testing.

"Sure enough," he continued, "the tests turned up two distinct blood groups: type A and type O. Mr. Gordon, we've learned, was type O, so we believe the killer was type A. Therefore, if you two ladies can each swear that you're not type A, and if your doctors will verify your statements, then we can let you both off the hook."

That's when Abby's stack finally blew. "*Off* the hook?!!!" she sputtered, turning red in the face. "We never should have been *on* the hook in the first place! Your suspicions are so absurd they're stupid. Can't you flatfoots tell the difference between a couple of horrified dames in distress and a savage, cold-blooded killer?"

Flannagan's baby-soft face turned even redder than Abby's. "The way I see it, sweetheart," he said, glaring at her through squinted eyes, "you are as cold-blooded as they come."

Now they were *both* acting like children.

And I had to be the babysitter.

"I think I'm type O," I said, leaping to steer the rocky situation to shore, "but I don't know for sure. And I don't have a regular doctor you can talk to, either. I was a patient at Saint Vincent's Hospital a few months back, though, so maybe you could check with them. I had to have a transfusion, so they must have noted my blood type in their records." I left out the part about *why* I'd needed the transfusion. Revealing that I'd been shot would have just made Flannagan more suspicious of me.

Flannagan gave me a nod, mashed his cigarette in the ashtray, and made a few marks on his memo pad. Then he raised his eyes and aimed them at Abby. "And what about you, Miss Moskowitz?" he said, pronouncing her name as if each syllable tasted worse than the first. "Do you want to cooperate with the investigation or continue to be a prime suspect in the murder of Gray Gordon?"

She didn't say anything (for once). She just tapped her foot on the floor and rolled her eyes at the ceiling.

Flannagan looked at his watch and vaulted to his feet. "Okay, that's enough!" he blustered, buttoning his collar and straightening his tie. "I've had it up to here with your crap. I'm leaving for another appointment, so you have to decide *now*. Off the hook, or on, sweetheart? It's your call."

"I'm AB," Abby said, smirking, enjoying herself to the hilt. "Rh-positive. If you don't believe me, you can ask my uncle, Dr. Seymour Katz. He's really hip to hemoglobin."

Chapter 13

AS WE WERE HEADING ACROSS THE lobby toward the police station exit, Abby pulled me to a stop in the middle of the floor. "Hold on a second, Paige," she said. "I want to talk to that cute officer at the front desk again. I just got a cover assignment from *True Police* magazine, so I really do need a new model, you dig? And he would be perfect for the job. I want to see if I can get him to pose for me in uniform."

"Oh, sure," I said. "And after that, you can see how long it takes you to get him *out* of uniform."

I thought my snippy remark would make her angry, but it didn't. She gave me a cunning wink and replied, "Just one of the perks of my occupation."

"Yeah, well, you don't need me to help you plan your perking. Go ahead, Ab. Talk to Officer Longface as long as you want. I'm going home."

"Okay," she chirped, obviously glad to be getting rid of me. "See you later, gator."

I was glad to get rid of her, too. Trying to conduct a serious murder investigation with Abby in tow was like standing under a palm tree during a thunderstorm, waiting for the coconuts to break off and fall on your head.

It was calmer and quieter outside than in. The streets and

sidewalks were practically deserted. It was late Sunday morning on a holiday weekend, and much too hot to be out on the move. I turned right at the corner and began the two-block trek to Seventh Avenue, wondering if I could make it that far without a camel and a canteen.

I did. And when I found myself at the corner of Seventh and Christopher—at the wide-open entrance to Stewart's Cafeteria—I staggered inside to get a glass of iced tea. And to read my morning paper. And to see if Blackie and Blondie were there. And to check out the clientele and the chicken run for suspicious-looking characters.

Blackie was there, but Blondie wasn't. I wished it were the other way around. (Blondie had been the talkative one, if you recall, and Blackie's lips had been sealed tighter than a pharaoh's tomb.) I nodded to the ebony-haired busboy (there certainly wasn't any point in questioning him again!), bought an enormous glass of iced tea at the counter, and then carried it toward the bleachers—the chairs and tables near the row of windows that looked out on the now-vacant sidewalk where, according to Abby, the chickens usually liked to strut.

There were three customers sitting in that area of the cafeteria. All of them were male. Two were together at the table nearest the door, chowing down on bacon and eggs (sunny-side-up, if you must know). The third man was sitting sideways at the very last table in the back, nibbling on a piece of toast and staring out the window in a trance. I couldn't see his face full-on, but one peep at his pudgy, pug-nosed profile, and his thick, slicked-back blond hair, and I knew who he was.

"Well, if it isn't Mr. Sinclair!" I said, approaching Willy's table with a big smile on my face. (And it wasn't a fake smile, either. For some reason I didn't fully understand, I was genuinely glad to see the strange, funny-looking fellow.) "Remember me?" I asked. "I met you yesterday at the . . . uh . . . at the . . ." I didn't know how to finish that sentence. At the bloodbath? At the slashing? At the scene of your neighbor's hideous murder? Nothing seemed acceptable. I finally gave up and asked, "May I join you?"

Willy had turned his head toward me, but he was still in a trance. His enormous blue eyes were looking straight through me, and his mind was someplace else entirely. He took a tiny bite of his toast and chewed it vigorously, but he seemed totally unaware of his actions. Setting my tea down on his table, and my newspaper and purse down on an extra chair, I took the seat directly across from him and leaned my face so close to his I could have counted all his freckles.

"Hello, Willy?" I said, peering smack into his distant eyes. "Are you okay?"

The nearness of my voice (not to mention my nose) must have jarred his sleeping senses, because he came to in a start and focused on the first thing that came into his sight—my looming kisser.

"Eeeeeek!" he shrieked, looking shocked and horrified— as if he'd just seen a ghost. (I guess my makeup had worn off.) "What are you doing? Get away from me! Shoo!"

"Sorry, Willy," I said, backing off in a flash. "I didn't mean to frighten you. I was just trying to get your attention."

"You sure succeeded!" he cried, voice still shrill and trembling. "Mercy me! I almost fainted dead away." His Southern accent was more noticeable now than it had been yesterday.

"You were lost in another world," I explained, "and you didn't respond when I spoke to you. I got a little nervous."

"Yes, but *I'm* the nervous one now!" he squealed, throwing his hands up in the air. His piece of toast flew out of his fingers and thwacked against the wall behind him.

"I can see that," I said, smiling.

Willy leaned over, picked the toast up from the floor, and daintily dropped it on his empty plate. "Well, I've got a lot on my mind, you know! The police think *I* killed Gray! You should have seen how they treated me yesterday. They gave me a really hard time after you left."

"I'm sorry to hear that," I said, checking his face and arms for scratches and bruises. He was clean as a whistle. "They didn't hit you, did they?"

"No, this time they just pummeled me with questions and accusations. For hours and hours and hours. I was so scared and exhausted when they left, I curled up in a ball on the carpet and cried myself into a coma." He gave me a shamefaced smile, then dabbed the perspiration off his upper lip with his napkin. "And I stayed there all night long, honey. I didn't get up off the floor until six thirty this morning, when Flannagan phoned and started pounding me with questions again."

"What kind of questions?"

"Humpf! You name it, you asked it. First yesterday, and then again this morning. How long had I known Gray? Did we spend much time together? Am I a homo? Was Gray a homo? Had we been screwing each other? Was I jealous of his other boyfriends? Did we hang out at the same bars? Did we eat at the same restaurants? Was I obsessed with him? Was he getting sick of me? Who were his friends? Who were his enemies? What did I want from him? Did I want him dead? Did I kill him for revenge or just for fun? Did I enjoy gashing his throat, and stabbing him in the gut, and watching his blood spill out on the floor?"

I hated to admit it, but these were the same questions I wanted to ask Willy—except I would have phrased them in a gentler way, and omitted the last three altogether. (Which compels me to make yet another admission: As much as I've always prided myself on not jumping to hasty conclusions, I had already made up my mind that this whimsical little pot-bellied man was no murderer.)

"Sounds pretty rough, Willy," I said, reaching across the table to touch his stubby, freckled hand. I felt very sorry for him—both for the way he'd been treated by the police and for the way he would always be treated by society. "But you can't really blame Flannagan for asking so many questions," I added. "It's his job, after all. He's the one who has to track down the killer."

"Yes, but he's convinced *I'm* the killer, so how much tracking do you think he's going to do? I'll tell you how much! None! He's just going to hammer me with relentless gibes and interrogations until I cave in and confess to a crime I didn't—and never, ever, ever *would*—commit." He paused for a few seconds while he gnawed one pinkie nail to the nub. "You want to know what he was grilling me about at six thirty this morning, honey? My blood type, of all things! Can you believe it?! What does that have to do with anything? He even demanded the name of my doctor so he could get positive proof."

"What did you tell him?" I asked. "Do you even know what your blood type is?"

"I sure do, honey," he proudly pronounced. "I donated to the big Red Cross blood drive last month, and they gave me the best grade of all—an A."

• • •

I SAT AND TALKED TO WILLY FOR AN-
other half-hour or so, trying to steady his frazzled nerves and
dig up some new leads at the the same time. I failed at both
endeavors. Willy remained as jumpy as a jackrabbit, and I was
left as clueless as a Keystone Cop. Aside from his incriminat-
ing blood type (which, in the interest of preserving Willy's
shaky sanity, I chose not to explain the importance of just
then), he didn't give me any new information at all. (I'm talking zilch. Zero. Or, as Abby would say, *bupkes*.)

I asked Willy if he'd ever met any of Gray's friends or rel-
atives—specifically his girlfriend, Cupcake, or his Actors Studio cohort, Binky, or a persistent fellow named Randy, or
somebody calling herself Aunt Doobie—but Willy swore he'd
never even heard those names, let alone met the people they
belonged to. He also insisted that—in spite of his own enormous crush on "the gorgeous golden-skinned god next
door"—he had no firsthand (or any *other*-hand) knowledge of
Gray's true sexual proclivities.

After all was said and done, I concluded from our brief
but intimate interview that Willy hadn't known Gray very
well at all.

Hoping the newspaper would offer a new clue or two, I
opened the copy of the *Daily Mirror* I'd bought that morning,
and scanned the pages for news of Gray's murder. The story
appeared on page seven, under the headline BROADWAY ACTOR
SLAIN, and I read it quickly. The article was, like its headline,
short and to the point, revealing nothing that I didn't already
know. The two women who discovered the body were mentioned but not, thank God, by name. I passed the paper over to
Willy and he read the story, too, much more slowly than I had,
chewing on his nails the whole time. We didn't have much to
say after that.

Willy and I left the cafeteria together, but parted company
outside, on the abandoned chicken-run sidewalk, after ex-
changing phone numbers and promising to keep each other
posted on any new developments in the case. Willy went
home to "wash out a few underthings" and to make himself a
"monster mint julep," while I scooted over to Sheridan Square
to catch a subway train uptown.

It was time to pay a call on Aunt Doobie.

• • •

THE MAYFLOWER HOTEL WAS ON CEN-
tral Park West at 61st Street. I walked the block and a half
from the Columbus Circle subway stop to the entrance of the
hotel with my nerves tied up in knots. Was Aunt Doobie still
a registered guest? Would she be in her room? How could I
get her to talk about Gray? If she was really his aunt, she
would probably be mourning his death. Should I give her my
real name and tell her why I came? What would I do if she had
already checked out? How would I ever find her again?

I ventured into the rather drab and narrow lobby, hurried
past the news and candy counter, then made a beeline for the
elevators on the right. Both cars were open and attended by
uniformed operators. I stepped into the first one and asked to
be taken to the ninth floor—where, I assumed, room 96 would
be located.

"Sí, señorita," said the skinny young Puerto Rican operator. He pulled the elevator door closed and then yanked and
latched the metal gate across the door. Slowly cranking the
brass control lever to the right, he turned and gave me a sly
wink as the elevator began its jerky ascent. Then, turning back
around to face the door, he mumbled something that sounded
like "cute chicky" under his breath, and released a series of
soft, nearly inaudible clucking sounds.

Oh, for heaven's sake! The cocky little fellow was coming
on to me! Had flirting with strangers become a national epi-
demic, or had he just caught the bug from Abby?

The elevator boy lurched his lever farther to the right,
sending us into a much swifter ascent, and then, when we
reached the ninth floor, he brought the car to a stop so suddenly my stomach did a somersault and sank like lead to my
toes. He was showing off, I realized. He had been driving fast
just to impress me. And when he gave me another wink and
opened the gate and the door to let me out, I saw that he'd
overshot the landing by a good eight inches. I had to step
down to exit the elevator. (I've met some smooth operators in
my day, but this character wasn't one of them.)

Still feeling a bit woozy from the stomach-turning touch-
down, I stumbled along the dimly lit, red-carpeted hallway to
my right, looking for the door marked 96. I found it quickly,
but didn't knock right away. I just stood there like a dope, tak-

ing a few deep breaths and staring at the room number as if it were an indecipherable algebra equation. Finally, after several more moments of nervous hesitation, I raised my hand and rapped my knuckles on the door.

No answer.

I knocked again.

Still no answer. I put my ear to the jamb and listened for noises inside the room, but all I could hear was the thumping of my own heart. I tapped on the door again and again, but there was no response at all. Finally accepting the evidence that nobody, not even Aunt Doobie, was there, I groaned and turned back toward the elevators. But right before I walked away, just for fun (okay, spite), I gave the door one last knock. A really loud one this time.

To my enormous, eye-popping surprise, the door flew open and an exceptionally good-looking man with a towel wrapped around his head off at me. "Shut up, already!" he roared. "Stop that goddamn knocking and get lost! I'm trying to get some sleep in here!" His brown eyes were blazing and his bare chest was heaving. With his dark wavy hair falling down over his forehead and his lips pulled back in a toothy snarl, he looked like a cross between Dean Martin and a rabid Great Dane.

"Oh, I'm so sorry, sir!" I exclaimed. "I didn't mean to disturb you. I must've made a mistake. I thought this was my Aunt Doobie's room."

Was it my imagination, or did his eyes grow fiercer when I mentioned my dear auntie's name? Did he know who Aunt Doobie was? Was he related to her in some way? Was he, perchance, Uncle Doobie?

"You're nuts," he growled. "Do I look like somebody's aunt?"

I had to admit that he didn't. There was nothing at all auntlike about his broad shoulders and brawny biceps.

"You'd better go down to the desk and get the *right* room number," he said, pulling his shoulders straighter, and his towel tighter around his hips. "There's no Aunt Doobie here."

"But this is room ninety-six, isn't it?" I asked, doing my best to look and act like an anxious niece. "That's what it says on the door. And that's where I was told to come. My cousin

Gray said Aunt Doobie was expecting me." (If the first bell doesn't ring loud enough, try a gong.)

"Gray?" he muttered.

"Yes, *Gray*," I stressed, studying his face for a reaction. "Gray Gordon."

If the name meant anything to him, he showed no sign. "Look, I don't care who told you to come here," he said, glowering, "but whoever it was made a mistake. This is *my* room, not your aunt's. And I booked it so I could get some *sleep*. So will you please get the hell out of here and go bother somebody else? I'm going back to bed."

To emphasize the import of his words, he stepped back from the door and then closed it, like a book, in my face.

Chapter 14

THE ELEVATOR RIDE GOING DOWN wasn't as eventful as the one going up. The other Puerto Rican operator was older, less excitable, and more attentive to the landing than the takeoff. He piloted our car to a sure, steady descent and parked it perfectly at the bottom. I gave him a grateful smile, then swooshed into the hotel lobby, heading straight for the main desk.

The gaunt, middle-aged man behind the counter gave me a look of total boredom and exhaustion. "May I help you?" he asked, clearly hoping my answer would be no.

"Oh, yes, please!" I begged, adopting, once again (and much to the desk clerk's dismay), the role of a frantic neice. "I'm very, very upset! I was supposed to meet my aunt here today, in her room on the ninth floor, but now there's somebody else in ninety-six! I don't know what happened! Did she move to another room, or did she check out altogether? I don't know where to go or what to do!"

The man sighed and shrugged his thin shoulders. "Room ninety-six, you say? Let me check on that for you. What's your aunt's name?"

"Aunt Doobie," I said, madly searching for an appropriate surname to tack on the end. "Isn't that funny?" I stalled. "I'm so used to using her nickname, I can't think of her real name . . . Oh, now I remember!" I cried. "It's Gordon!" (At least that seemed a likely choice.) "Mrs. Dorothea Gordon."

"I'll take a look," he said, heaving another weary sigh, opening the guest ledger and slowly sliding his finger down the page. "Gordon . . . Gordon . . . Gordon . . . uh, no, miss . . . nobody by the name of Gordon is registered in the hotel at this time. Is it possible your aunt made a reservation under a different name?"

"Gee, I don't know," I said, fluttering my lashes and giving him an urgent, pleading look. "All I know is she was supposed to be in room ninety-six. And I'm supposed to be meeting her there right now!" I was working myself up to ask for the name of the room's current occupant, but it turned out I didn't have to.

"Well, there must be some mistake," the droopy desk clerk said, "because a Mr. Jonathan Smith checked into that room on Friday and reserved it for the rest of the holiday weekend." He paused and gave me a pleading look. "Are you sure your aunt isn't registered in room ninety-six of another hotel? Perhaps the Plaza? It's just across the park, you know." He inched his hand toward the phone. "If you'd like, I could call the Plaza and ask them—"

"No, thanks!" I hurriedly replied. "I'll just pop over there and see for myself." I gave the tired but dutiful fellow an appreciative smile, then made a run for the hotel exit. I saw no reason to stick around.

Except for the air-conditioning, I soon realized (i.e., the very second I stepped outside to the street). The thick, steamy afternoon heat was so overwhelming I wanted to duck back into the Mayflower and reserve a nice cool room for myself. I would have done it, too, if I could have been sure to get a room on the ninth floor, or—to phrase it in a simpler, more direct way—if I'd had enough money.

But all I had left in my purse was a half dollar. One measly fifty-cent piece. It was enough to get me home on the subway, but it wouldn't buy me a hamburger at the White Horse, or a pizza at John's, or even a chicken salad sandwich at Chock Full—which was a rotten shame because I was hungry.

Maybe Abby will be home, I thought as I trudged back to the Columbus Circle subway stop. *Maybe she has some bagels left over from breakfast*. It was either that or the leftover bread, salami, cheese, and green pepper I had in my own Frigidaire. I focused my hopes on a bagel—not because it was my dining preference, but because it would come with some lively conversation and an ice-cold gin and tonic on the side.

"AUNT DOOBIE IS A MAN?!" ABBY croaked. She was obviously excited by the news.

"I didn't say that!" I cried. "What I said was, there was a man in Aunt Doobie's room. There's a big difference, you know. You're always jumping to conclusions!" I took a quick drag on my cigarette and exhaled with a swoosh. "The guy could be Aunt Doobie's son, or her lover, or her husband, for all we know. Or, he could be a man named Jonathan Smith who just happened to check into room ninety-six right after Aunt Doobie left."

"Doobie who?" Jimmy asked. The brilliant and beautiful bearded poet had been sitting at Abby's kitchen table with us for over an hour, listening to every detail I recounted about my afternoon crime-busting adventures, and he still didn't have a clue.

"Never mind, Daddy-O," Abby said, curling her fingers through his sleek dark Vandyke and blowing her words directly into his ear. "Mama will tell you all about it later, when we're alone. Here, have another piece of pizza." She held the last slice of our cheese and tomato pie up to his mouth and fed him like a baby—or a dog, depending on your point of view.

Speaking of dogs, Jimmy's best friend and constant canine companion—the miniature dachshund named Otto—was at the table, too (or under it, I guess you would say). He was curled up in a soft brown wad and sleeping soundly in his master's lap. I was dying for Otto to wake up and and come sit on my lap instead, as he'd often done in the past. That way I wouldn't feel so lonely, or so much like a third wheel.

"John Smith!" I barked, trying to get Abby's attention again (and wake Otto up). "Did you ever hear a more obvious alias? Couldn't the lazy creep have made up a better pseudonym than that? He may be handsome but he sure as hell isn't creative!"

"He's handsome?" Abby asked, perking up like a flower in a shower. "You didn't tell me that!"

"Some things are better left unsaid." I took another sip of my drink (gin and tonic, just like I'd wanted), and another drag on my cigarette. "Besides," I added, "what do the man's physical attractions have to do with anything? Apart from your ongoing quest for new models, that is."

"Maybe nothing," Abby said, gazing off into the mysterious distance like a daft fortuneteller, "or maybe everything." She emphasized the last word in her sentence with a deep, spooky undertone. You could almost hear the thunder rolling in the background.

I put out my cigarette and lit another. "Get real, Abby! With you, it's always the looks that count. With me, it's the name. And I'd bet my whole bankroll this guy's real name is *not* John Smith. It could be Hamlet or Heathcliff or Alfred Hitchcock—but it's not John Smith. Maybe it's Randy. The burning question is, why did he register at the Mayflower under an alias?"

"Oh, don't be such a cube, Paige!" Abby scoffed. "There are thousands of reasons why people use phony names when they're checking into hotels. Do I have to list them for you?"

"Please spare me," I said, realizing the futility of pursuing the issue. Maybe John Smith was Aunt Doobie, and maybe he wasn't. Maybe he knew Gray Gordon, and maybe he didn't. He could be a vicious, cold-blooded killer, or just an out-of-town businessman trying to sleep off an all-night bender in his private, air-conditioned hotel room. Since there was no way on earth either Abby or I could know the truth at this point, why continue this silly guessing game?

"What about Willy?" I asked, flipping the page to a different puzzle. "You don't think he could be the killer, do you? I'm convinced he's not. He's too high-strung and squeamish. The only reason he'd ever use a knife would be to chop celery or carve a radish rose."

"Who's jumping to conclusions now?" Abby said, arching one of her eyebrows to a peak and spreading her lips in a contemptuous smirk. "Willy was obviously in love with Gray, and Gray wouldn't have anything to do with him. Unrequited love, you dig? That's the likeliest murder motive known to man. And Willy has the same blood type as the murderer! How can you ignore the only bit of real evidence that has come up in the case so far?"

"I don't know," I said, feeling foolish, realizing that Abby was right. "It's just that I *like* Willy," I mumbled in self-defense. "And I feel a strong urge to protect him."

"Oh, yeah?" Jimmy said, speaking in the same deep, sexy baritone that had made him a celebrated reader of his own dopey poems. "Maybe you got it backwards, babe. Maybe what Willy needs is an *erection*, not *protection*." Jimmy shot up straighter in his chair and started snickering like an idiot, so proud of his feeble rhyme he was about to pop.

Abby giggled and started twirling her fingers through his beard again.

Startled by the sudden noise and movement, Otto jumped off Jimmy's lap and skittered over to me. He huddled around my ankles and gazed up at me—with the softest, sweetest, sleepiest brown eyes you ever saw in your life. I picked the little pooch up and settled him in my own lap, stroking his head and velvety back until he feel asleep again.

Sometimes, I mused, happily petting the warm little weiner-shaped pup, *there actually is such a thing as justice in the world.*

LATER IN THE EVENING—AFTER WE'D discussed the inscrutable murder case to death, and worn the grooves off Abby's new Miles Davis record, and consumed at least five gin and tonics and a hundred cigarettes each—Abby stood up from the table and announced that it was time for us to go.

Oh, no, not again. "Go where?!" I sputtered. Remembering the last time she'd dragged me off to points unknown, I sat rooted to my chair, firmly deciding that I wasn't going anywhere but home.

"To the Vanguard, of course," she said. "Jimmy's going to recite his new poem there tonight. It's a masterpiece! It's a far-out Independence Day epic, and he's going to read it at the stroke of midnight. Isn't that cool?"

"It's totally cool," I said, "and I appreciate the invitation. But I can't possibly go out tonight. In the first place, I'm not dressed for it." (My yellow piqué sundress and red patent stilettos belonged at an afternoon tea party, not a midnight soiree at the local jazz joint.) "And in the second place, Dan's supposed to call me later—right after twelve, when the rates change."

"But you already spoke to him this morning!" Abby yelped.

"So what? Is there some law that says I can't speak to him twice?"

"How can he afford two long-distance calls in one day? It'll cost him an arm and a leg."

"Dan's not a pauper, you know. And maybe he'd rather lose limbs than lose contact with me." I shot her a stubborn smile.

Abby flipped her long braid from one shoulder to the other and leaned over the back of her chair like a gargoyle. "Oh, come on, Paige!" she said, whimpering (just like Otto does when he has to pee). "Jimmy and I both really want you to be there. It's important. You dig what I'm saying?"

I dug what she was saying all right. She was dreading the poetry reading every bit as much as I was, and she expected me to come with her—whether I wanted to or not.

I groaned to myself and gave her a nasty, I'm-going-to-make-you-pay-for-this look.

She grinned and gave me a look that said, *Stop whining, sister. I just treated you to a feast of pizza and gin. The least you can do is keep me company in my hour of need.*

"Oh, all right!" I snapped, picking Otto up off my lap and setting him down on the floor. "You win! But if Dan has a fit wondering where I am, it'll be on your head. He worries about me a lot, you know."

"I worry about you, too," Abby said, with a snort. "Now hurry up. Go change your clothes."

Chapter 15

IN SPITE OF THE HEAT AND THE HOLI-
day, the Vanguard was packed. All the tables were full, and
black-clad bohemians were standing three-deep at the bar,
drinking beer, smoking weed, and snapping their fingers to
the live sounds surging from the piano, bass, guitar, and
drums ensemble on stage. In my black capris, sleeveless black
shell, black ballerina flats, and heavy black eye makeup, I
blended in perfectly with the hip, cool (and, if you ask me,
corny) crowd.

"Hey, Birmingham!" one of the bartenders called out to
Jimmy, as we stood near the entrance looking around for
seats. "Come park your pets over here!" I hoped he was referring to Abby and Otto—not me.

Jimmy led us to the single empty stool at the end of the bar
and sat down on it himself. Cradling Otto in the crook of his
left arm, he rested his other elbow on the counter and ordered
a Pabst Blue Ribbon. "You girls want anything?" he asked, finally remembering that Abby and I were there.

"I'll have a beer, too," I quickly replied, before he could re-
scind the offer. "Whatever's on tap. In a frosted mug."

"And another G and T for me, sweetcakes," Abby said,
slithering up as close to Jimmy's side as she could. If she was
annoyed that he'd taken the seat instead of offering it to her,

she didn't let it show. (As I may have mentioned before, Abby's a tad more forgiving than I am.)

It was hard to talk above the music and the noisy crowd, so as soon as I got my hands on my beer, I slipped away from the bar scene. Then I wandered into the depths of the club and leaned against the back wall for a while, watching the Negro jazz quartet perform their musical miracles. And when I tired of doing that, I began a thorough, table-to-table survey of the audience. (I can't help it, you know. I'm just naturally nosy. Even when I'm not looking for a murderer.)

That's when I saw her.

She was sitting at a table right next to the stage, so close to the spotlights that her face and figure were fully illuminated. Her eyes were closed and her fluffy, platinum-blonde head was thrown back against the shoulder of a large, completely bald man in a suit and a tie. The skirt of her white *Seven Year Itch*-style halter-top dress was hiked high above her knees, and her legs were crossed. (Well, sort of, anyway. One of those slim, shapely appendages—the top one, of course—was also draped across the lap of the huge, hairless man she had either cuddled up to or collapsed upon.)

You could have knocked me over with a feather—or any other flimsy utensil. It was Rhonda Blake (Gray's *Hot Tin Roof* understudy partner, in case you need reminding), and she looked drunker than any skunk I'd ever seen.

I gasped with delight and started searching for a way to get to her table. What an incredible stroke of luck! I'd been wondering how I was going to get to chat with (okay, interrogate) Rhonda again, and now here she was—laid out like a blooming buffet at a wedding banquet—just waiting for me to help myself to her secrets. Praying that Rhonda wasn't too intoxicated to carry on a conversation, I handed my beer to the thirsty-looking young man standing next to me and began winding my way through the crowded tables toward the stage.

I didn't get very far, though. All of a sudden the jazz quartet stopped playing, the audience burst out in applause, and the emcee for the evening bounded onto the stage and took over the microphone. "Are these cats crazy, or what?" he exclaimed. "Let's have another hand for the Fountainbleu Four!"

Some of the people near me jumped to their feet and began

clapping like there was no tomorrow. I ducked my head to my chest and tried to bulldoze a path to Rhonda's table. I was about halfway there when the emcee motioned for everybody to quiet down and take their seats again. Too polite (and self-conscious) to remain standing like a monument in the middle of the room, I sank to my haunches and tried to waddle my way forward.

It was no use. The tables were too close together, and the thick jumble of jostling legs, knees, and feet at my face-level made further waddling impossible. I was about to stand up and retreat to the rear when the emcee returned his mouth to the mike and announced, "Now it's time for another treat, guys and dolls. Are you ready to have your socks rocked and your inhibitions defrocked? Are you ready for a hot transfusion? Then let's hear it for the cat with the dog! Here comes Jimmy Birmingham and his sidekick, Otto, to give us the midnight truth—the groovy, far-out gospel of today and tomorrow!"

Aaaargh. I was stuck like a pig in a poke. I had no choice but to sit down on the floor and enjoy (okay, endure) the show.

Carrying Otto in the crook of one arm, Jimmy walked onto the stage in a thunderstorm of applause. He pulled a tall stool up close to the mike, planted one buttock on the seat, and arranged his oh-so-young-and-sexy body in an oh-so-casual half-sitting, half-standing pose. Then he stretched Otto out on the shelf of his thigh (the one that was propped up on the stool) and gave him a long, slow stroke from the tip of his pointy nose to the end of his stringbean-size tail. Otto snorted and put his head down on Jimmy's knee. Was it my imagination, or was the little dachshund as unimpressed with Jimmy's act as I was?

To signal that he was about to recite his poem, Jimmy cleared his throat into the microphone. Then, when the applause had completely died down, he unleashed his pompous, theatrical baritone and began:

> Pounding, resounding
> Moonlight noises,
> Slams me in
> And out of my mind.
> A high and low life

Cerebral celebration,
A garden of madness.
Maggot salad
Spiced with lice,
Bottles of holiday frenzy,
All sucked up
Into tomorrow's rushing,
Failing day
Of push and pull.
Put my snail in your pail.
A love thrill
Keeps me slowly
Burning away,
Smoldering like a fire in
The rain.

The people sitting around and above me were transfixed. They sat in silence for a couple of seconds, letting the full impact of Jimmy's, um, verses sink into their sodden brains. Then, all at once, they rose from their chairs and broke out in a wild shouting, clapping, cheering, whistling, finger-snapping ovation.

"He's so deep!" one woman cried out. "He's real gone."

"And his words are true, man," a bearded fellow bellowed. "Like, really true."

Yeah, true twaddle! I said to myself, laughing out loud and jumping up off the floor. Then, as Jimmy tucked Otto under his arm and proudly strode off the stage, I began pushing and shoving my way toward Rhonda's table again.

I could have saved myself the trouble. When I finally got there, she was gone. Real gone.

"RHONDA BLAKE WAS HERE?" ABBY said. "Are you sure it was her?"

"Yeah, I'm sure," I said. "She was sitting so close to the stage she was lit up by the spotlights. I got a good look at her."

"Maybe she's in the bathroom?"

"Nope. I checked."

"Did you see when she got up and left?"

"No. I was sitting on the floor. I couldn't see anything but the people right around me and what was happening up on the stage. Actually, I'm surprised you didn't see her leave, Ab. With her platinum blonde hair and bright white dress, she really stood out in this dark-as-doom crowd. And she must've passed right by you on her way out."

"I was concentrating on Jimmy's performance," she said, with a sniff. "All I could see was the poetic vision of my genius loverboy's face." She turned to Jimmy, who was now sitting on the barstool next to hers, and gave him a juicy nibble on his neck. "You were great, babe. Really great."

"Thanks, doll," he said, swiveling away from the bar and stepping down off the stool. "Be back in a few. Takin' Otto for a stroll."

I hopped onto Jimmy's vacated seat, ordered another beer, and lit up a cigarette. My head was spinning with questions about Rhonda. What had brought her to the Vanguard tonight? Did she come here often? Did she live in the Village? Did she know that Gray's apartment was just a few blocks away? Who was that man she was with? Had she been as inebriated as she seemed? Had she heard the news about Gray's murder and gotten drunk to escape the pain? Or maybe she was trying to wipe out the memory of the hideous crime that she herself had committed! Why did she disappear so suddenly? Had she seen me trying to get to her table?

"I know what you're thinking," Abby said, "but please don't say a word about it." She gave me a threatening look and took a deep swig of her gin and tonic.

"Huh? What?" I sputtered, wondering what the hell she was talking about.

"Jimmy's poem," she said. "I know you didn't like it."

I spat forth a great gush of smoke. "Oh, I wouldn't say that," I teased, coughing, abandoning the unanswerable questions about Rhonda and returning to the issues at hand. "The 'maggot salad' part was pretty darn entertaining."

Abby giggled. "Yeah, that was a scream, wasn't it? If only he had *meant* it to be funny. I could really dig it then!"

We looked at each other for a couple of goofy seconds and then cracked up laughing. And once we started, we couldn't stop. We cackled and crowed and shrieked and guffawed, letting all the tension of the last two days spew out of our souls onto the beer-splashed, ash-strewn bar. We were out of control. We were insane. Everybody at the bar was staring at us, wanting to be let in on the joke. It was pure heaven.

When our howling laughter had finally dwindled to intermittent chuckles and I was able to catch my breath, I asked, "How do you do it, Ab? How do you keep putting Jimmy's childish ego ahead of your own true feelings and opinions? Doesn't it make you nuts?"

She gave me a knowing smile. "Honest communication would be nice," she purred, "but nothing beats a good snail in the pail."

AS SOON AS JIMMY AND OTTO RE-turned, I chugged the rest of my beer, snuffed out my cigarette, and hopped down off the barstool. I wanted to go home. If I hurried, I thought, maybe I could get back to my place before Dan called. I bid a quick goodnight to my friends, gave Otto a pat on the head, and headed for the door.

Halfway there, though, I thought of something I wanted to do before I left (or rather, something I knew a good reporter or detective would want to do). So I spun around on my heels, darted over to the middle of the bar, and questioned each of the two bartenders in turn:

Had either one of them noticed the blonde in the white dress?

"Sure did," said one.

"What man wouldn't?" said the other.

Did they know who she was?

"Nah," said one.

"No idea," said the other.

How much did she have to drink?

"Enough," said one.

"Too much," said the other.

Did they know who the man she was with was?

No, two times.

Was either the blonde or the bald man a regular Vanguard customer?

"Not since I been working here," said one.

"Never saw 'em before tonight," said the other.

Was there anything at all they could tell me about the couple?

"One thing," said one. "The man is loaded."

"What do you mean?" I asked. "He's drunk?"

"No, he's rich."

"What makes you say that?"

"Three things," he said. "One, he's got a girlfriend who looks like Marilyn Monroe; two, I saw through the window that they drove away from here in a long black limousine; and three, the dude offered me a C-note to tell him who *you* were."

"What?!" I was thunderstruck. My heart started beating like a wild pair of bongos and every inch of my skin broke out in goose bumps. "Why the hell was he asking about *me*?" I said (okay, screeched).

"Don't know, doll. But he must've wanted the scoop on you pretty bad to be flashin' a hundred-dollar bill in my face."

My heart stopped racing and came to a dead standstill. "What did you tell him?" I asked.

"Not much," he said, with a shrug. "Told him I've seen you around the Village a few times, and that you come to the Vanguard once in a while, when Jimmy 'the Bard' Birmingham is doing his thing, but that's all I said. Nothing else. Couldn't tell him your name since I don't know what it is."

Whew! As hard as I'd worked to make a name for myself as a true crime reporter and mystery writer, this was one time I was glad my success had been minimal.

"Did he give you the money anyway?" I asked.

"Yep," the young bartender replied, pulling the bill out of his shirt pocket and showing it to me. "Easiest hundred I ever made. I'm gonna split it with Jerry, though," he said, nodding toward his fellow barkeep, who was busy at the far end of the counter. "Jerry didn't speak to the man, but he took care of all the drink orders while I talked to him, so he earned his half. And we always split all the tips anyway."

Figuring I'd learned all he could tell me about Rhonda and the bald man, I thanked my informant for his time and trouble, and offered my hand for a shake. "I'd give you a C-note, too," I said, "but I don't have one on me."

"That's okay, babe," he said, with a flirtatious wink. "Just give me your name and phone number and we'll call it even."

"Down, boy," I said, smiling and shaking my head. "That information's not for sale."

Chapter 16

ON MY WAY OUT, I WANTED TO STOP and get Abby and Jimmy and Otto to come home with me—or at least fill them in on the freaky stuff I'd just learned from the bartender—but I couldn't get anywhere near them. They were surrounded by hordes of fawning poetry fans, avid dog lovers, and rapt admirers of beautiful women. They were having a really good time. I didn't have the heart to bring them down to my level of anguish and anxiety. Besides, I was in a hurry.

Still hoping against hope that I would get home in time for Dan's call, I barreled out the door and hit the street running. I'm not kidding. I was really *running* (ballet flats are a frantic girl's best friend). The dense heat slowed me down a bit after just half a block, but I kept right on going, throwing one foot in front of the other, huffing and puffing till I thought my lungs would collapse, hurling myself onward like a racehorse—or a total nut case, take your pick.

Okay, I admit it. It wasn't just the desire to talk to Dan that was spurring me on. It was also fear. (I'm such a sissy sometimes!) I was scared to death that the bald man's long black limousine had been lurking in the darkness, waiting for me to leave the Vanguard and head for home. I was afraid that the sinister people in that sinister car were following me now—

looking for a good opportunity to shanghai me (or watching to find out where I lived so they could shanghai me in the near future).

I kept twisting my head around, checking all the nearly empty lanes of southbound Seventh Avenue traffic, peering up and down the intersecting side streets, looking for the long black limo as I ran. But I didn't see the car anywhere. And no suspicious headlight beams were creeping along behind me.

Finally, when I reached Sheridan Square, I allowed myself to decelerate. It was either that, or pass out. My lungs were strained to the bursting point, and so much sweat was streaming down my forehead and into my eyes I could barely see. By this point I felt pretty sure the limo wasn't tailing me, but to be on the safe side, I made a sharp left turn onto Washington Place—which was a one-way street going west, which meant no motor vehicle could follow in the direction I was going (east) without breaking the law. (Am I tricky, or what?)

The sudden detour would add an extra block to my trip home, but I didn't care. It was worth it for the peace of mind. Groaning, wheezing, and gasping for air, I slowed my pace to a stagger and pushed myself onward to Sixth Avenue (another one-way street leading *away* from my destination). Then, one block down Sixth, I branched off onto Cornelia (another one-way street, etc., etc.) and headed—at last!—for Bleecker.

When I neared the end of the block, however, I freaked out again. What if the limo had secretly snaked its way into my neighborhood and was now slithering around the area, waiting for me to reappear? What if Rhonda Blake and her big bad rich bald boyfriend were now searching the Village streets with binoculars, hoping to see me enter my building, and thereby ascertain my address?

(Okay! Okay! So I was probably overdoing it a bit—dreaming up more than my share of scary scenarios—but when you've been stalked, molested, strangled, and shot as I have in the past, you tend to get a little wary around the edges.)

So instead of hurrying to the end of the street, turning the corner on Bleecker, and going straight to the front door of my building as I normally would do, I pulled to a stop on Cornelia, next to the locked and gated passage to the tiny courtyard behind my apartment. Unlocking the tall metal gate with the key I always carry with me for emergencies, I pulled the gate open, slipped inside, and then closed and locked it again.

Stealing like a cat burglar down the narrow cement path to the inner recesses of the courtyard, I could feel my heart banging against my ribs and my hot breath surging through my lungs. I was even more frightened now than before. (You would be, too, if you suddenly found yourself in a pitch-black enclosure crawling with worms and spiders and God knows how many different species of rodents.)

I scurried down the overgrown walkway as fast as I could and hastily climbed the rusty metal stairway leading to the rusty metal landing outside my back door. Then I unlocked that door, pushed it wide open, and lunged headfirst into my kitchen. I was so glad to be home I fell to my knees and kissed the black-and-white-checked linoleum floor. (Okay, so I didn't really kiss the floor, but I was so crazed I considered it.)

After closing and relocking the back door, I tossed my purse on the kitchen counter, gulped down a couple of handfuls of water at the sink, splashed some water on my overheated face, and then stumbled into the dark living room and over to the front window. I didn't turn on any lights. I didn't want to let anybody know that I was home. And I wanted to be able to peek out the window without anybody being able to peek in.

Standing to one side of the window, I stuck my nose through the gap between the blinds and the glass and peered out at the sidewalks and the street below. There were several cars parked at the curb, but not a single black limo in sight. And there was no moving traffic on the street at all. No people on the stoops or sidewalks, either—which kind of surprised me at first (Bleecker is usually a very busy byway), until I remembered the time (almost 2 A.M.), and the heat, and the holiday.

In spite of the inactivity, I stayed next to the window and stared down at the street for a few more minutes, keeping my eyes peeled for a black you-know-what. But when no such vehicle appeared, I started feeling kind of silly (really stupid, if you want to know the truth).

For God's sake, Paige! I scolded myself. *What on earth's the matter with you? Why do you always imagine the worst and make such a big fat deal out of everything? You just tore*

*through dark city streets and cut through a courtyard full of
rats for nothing! Nobody was following you! Do you hear
what I'm saying, you imbecile? Nobody was following you!
And nobody is out there spying on you now!*

Which was my second big fat misconception for the night.

And if I had let down my guard and turned away from the
window at that moment, I never would have realized my mistake. I never would have known that a tall thin dark-haired
man wearing dark pants and a dark T-shirt was lurking in the
doorway of the laundromat across the street, keeping watch
on my apartment.

But, as bad luck would have it, I didn't turn away from the
window. I was still standing there, staring out at the street in
a dopey dither, when the slim dark figure emerged from the
unlit laundromat doorway and—keeping his eyes trained on
my building—slunk out to the curb. I saw him crouch down
behind a baby blue Studebaker for a second while he tied his
shoe. I saw him sidle over to the lamppost and hold his watch
up to the light to check the time. And then, right before he
left—when he tilted his head back and gazed up at the windows of my apartment one last time—I saw his face.

Bathed in light from the streetlamp, his menacing mug was
clearly visible. And I stared at it in shock. It was the face of
the tightlipped Stewart's Cafeteria busboy—the one I called
Blackie.

I NEVER WENT UPSTAIRS TO BED THAT
night. I just threw myself down on the daybed in the living
room and then sat there like a stump, smoking cigarettes in the
dark and praying for the phone to ring.

It never did, of course. I figured Dan had tried to call me
shortly after midnight as promised, and then, when I didn't
answer, had simply gone to bed. I hoped he hadn't flipped out
and started worrying about me too much (although considering the dreadful day and night I'd had, such a reaction would
have been warranted). I hoped he was sleeping soundly and
having the sweetest, most soothing dreams imaginable.

At some point during my nocotine-and-nerve-wracked
night, I fell asleep, too. But I had nightmares instead of

dreams. (I won't disturb you with the details of those feverish visions. Believe me, you don't want to know.)

When I began to regain consciousness in the morning—still dressed in my black capris and black knit shell, eyelids glued shut with mascara, face mashed into the mattress of the daybed—I felt like a dead monkey. (Sorry, but that's the best way I can think to describe it.) My sweaty hair was matted, like a damp carpet, to my head, and my outspread arms and legs were as leaden as pipes (the plumbing kind, not the musical or smoking variety).

So when the doorbell rang—jolting me like a jack-in-the-box out of my horizontal stupor to a sudden sitting position—I almost fainted dead away. No exaggeration. My head was so dizzy I couldn't see straight. And when I tried to stand up, I almost fainted yet again. Every object in my living room (the TV set, chair, lamp, radio, bookshelf, electric fan, telephone table, potted plant) was swimming in circles before my eyes.

Groaning, I flopped back down on the couch and cupped my spinning head in my hands. *I just won't answer the door*, I decided. *I don't have to. Nobody can make me.*

The bell rang again, but I ignored it. I was *not* in the mood to see anybody. And I was definitely in no condition to be *seen*. I was curious to know who was out there, of course (curiosity is my constant companion), but I didn't have the energy, or the equilibrium (or, I'm ashamed to admit, the *chutzpah*), to go peek through the window and find out. If it was Blackie or the bald man, I reasoned (okay, rationalized), I might have a heart attack and die. And that wouldn't do me any good.

The doorbell rang again . . . and again . . . and again. *Aaaargh!* Whoever was out there wasn't giving up. I stuck my fingers in my ears, trying to block out the persistent piercing sounds, but it wasn't any use. The bell just kept on ringing and ringing till it drove me clear out of my mind. I threw my hands in the air, leapt to my feet, sprang over to the door, and—without a single precautionary peek through the front window—buzzed the unknown caller in.

Yikes! I shrieked to myself, as soon as I realized what I'd done. *Why did I do that? How could I be so stupid?* And when I put my ear to the door and heard the slow, heavy, Frankenstein footsteps ascending the stairs to my apartment, I almost wet my pants. *God help me! I'm a goner! A strong man could bust down this door in an instant!*

Madly searching for a way to protect myself, I scrambled into the kitchen and—using every ounce of strength in every cell of my 5-foot 7-inch, 119-pound body—pulled the refrigerator away from the wall. (That's right. The refrigerator! Shows you what a blast of adrenaline can do.) Then—thinking I'd make like Superman again and shove my Frigidaire across the room and park it in front of the door—I yanked the plug out of the wall, anchored my shoulder, hands, and forearms against the back of the appliance, and pushed with all my might.

The damn thing budged about an inch, but that was all. My adrenaline was all used up. (But you saw that coming, didn't you? Hell, anybody with half a brain would have seen that coming! I, on the other hand, was utterly bewildered by my profound power failure—which will no doubt confirm your suspicions about the state *my* half a brain was in.)

I was standing in the kitchen like a dolt, struggling to catch my breath and wondering what to do next, when the mysterious intruder started wrenching my doorknob in a frenzy and pounding hard, really hard, on the door.

I didn't answer this time. (I usually try not to make the same mistake twice in one morning.) Overcome with exhaustion and dismay, I collapsed against the refrigerator and slid down to a squat on the floor. I didn't know what else to do. The fat lady was singing at the top of her lungs. The end was near. I might as well give up and "go gentle into that good night." (Dylan Thomas, in case you're wondering, with just a couple of words left out.)

The pounding on my door grew even louder. "Open up, Paige!" a gruff male voice shouted. "I know you're in there."

First I melted in joyous relief, then I stiffened in stark apprehension.

It was Dan, and he didn't sound friendly.

Chapter 17

HAVE YOU EVER HAD TO FACE THE MAN you love with gobs of mascara smeared all over your cheeks, a hairstyle that resembles a bathmat, a damp, wrinkled, all-black costume fit for a witch (or a crow), and a great big suitcase full of secrets? Then you know how I felt as I scraped myself up off the floor, steadied myself against the refrigerator for a second or two, and then wobbled over to open the door. (*Aghast*, *appalled*, and *ashamed* are the first words that come to mind, starting with the A's.)

I flipped the latch, released the deadbolt, slipped off the chain, and slowly cracked the door open. "Hi," I said, gazing down at my feet as if they were the eighth wonder of the world. "What are you doing here? I thought you weren't coming back until tomorrow."

Dan pushed the door wide and lunged inside. His anger was so intense I could taste it. "Don't give me that crap," he said. "You know why I'm here."

"No I don't!" I cried, telling the god's honest truth (for once). I raised my eyes and met his irate glare head-on. "What's the matter?" I begged. "What are you so upset about? Has something bad happened? Oh, my god! Where's Katy?"

"She's still in Maine with my folks," he said, quickly relieving my mind on that score, but letting my other questions dangle.

"So what's going on?" I spluttered. "Are you okay? Why are you so mad? Please tell me what's wrong!!!" I was teetering on the edge of another emotional breakdown.

Dan grabbed me by the shoulders, pulled me close, and peered deep into my eyes for a moment, obviously trying to judge the credibility of my frantic and concerned response. (I couldn't blame him for that. Dan was a trained and efficient homicide dick; it was his duty to be suspicious. And, then, there was always the little matter of my less-than-stellar track record in the honesty department . . .)

Finally satisfied that I wasn't putting on an act, Dan squeezed my shoulders, gave them a shake and growled, "Okay, so maybe you *don't* know why I'm here." Then, in a very sarcastic tone, he added, "But since you're such a cunning, clever, and *daring* little detective, I'm sure you can figure it out."

His voice was still angry, and his fingers were still digging into the flesh of my upper arms, but as he stood there staring at me, the expression on his gorgeous, stubbled, well-tanned face underwent a conspicuous change. Instead of fierce and furious, he now looked kind of quizzical and . . . well, amused.

"What is it?" I snapped, unnerved by his sudden shift in mood. "What are you smiling about?"

"Your face is all black," he said, "and your hair's kind of frizzy. Have you joined a minstrel troupe?"

"Very funny," I said, resisting the urge to run and hide in the coat closet. I was embarrassed about my appearance, but really glad it had given Dan a chuckle. (Call me a boob, but I'd rather be laughed at than yelled at.)

"Hey, what's your refrigerator doing in the middle of the room?" Dan let go of my shoulders and walked over to the wayward appliance, brow wrinkled in a Mr. Fixit frown. "Is it broken? How long has it been unplugged?"

"Oh, er, just for a little while," I stammered, feeling even more embarrassed than before. "And, no, it's not broken. I've been thinking of redecorating the kitchen, and I wanted to see what it would look like on a different wall." (Well, what was

I *supposed* to say? That I was trying to shove it in front of the door so a deranged slasher couldn't burst in and kill me?)

Dan shot me a sneer of disbelief, stuck the plug back in the socket, and—with barely an oof or a grunt—wriggled the Frigidaire back into place. Then he took a tray of ice out of the freezer, cranked the cubes loose, and stacked a bunch of them in a glass. "Okay, out with it, Paige," he said, filling the glass with water and carrying it over to the kitchen table. "No more lies and deception." He yanked a chair away from the table and sat down. "I want a full confession and I want it *now*."

My head started spinning again. How was I going to deal with this one? Dan had obviously learned something about me since I'd last spoken to him—something that upset him so much he'd cut his vacation a day short, left his daughter with his parents in Maine, and driven all night to get to my apartment. But what exactly had he learned, and how had he learned it? How could I make (okay, make up) a good confession when I had no idea what I had to confess to?

(I know what you're thinking. You're thinking I should have made a clean breast of everything right there and then— told Dan all about Gray's murder and my subsequent involvement in it. And, looking back, I can see the wisdom of that view. But hindsight is better than foresight—well, *my* foresight, anyway—and at this particular point in time all I could think about was how I was going to get to the heart of the murder without losing Dan's heart in the process.)

"Lies?! Deception?! Confession?!" I squawked, putting on a big show of righteous indignation (which is hard to do when you look like a cross between Al Jolson and the Creature from the Black Lagoon). "I don't know what you're talking about! What crime am I being accused of now?" (The best defense is a good offense, they say—or is it the other way around?)

"Quit stalling, Paige." Dan pulled a pack of Luckies out of his shirt pocket and fired one up. "It took me nine straight hours to drive here from Portland. I'm too tired to play games. Just tell me the goddamn truth."

"Can I wash my face first?" I stalled, walking over to the kitchen sink and turning on the water. "Then I'll tell you anything you want to know. Promise."

He released a loud groan of exhaustion. "Yeah, okay. And make a pot of coffee while you're at it. I'm really beat." Setting his burning cigarette in the ashtray, he leaned back in his chair and stretched his long, strong legs out in front of him. Then he crossed one burly arm over the other and closed his bloodshot eyes.

I scrubbed my face clean and filled the coffeepot with water. Then, spooning Chase & Sanborn into the filtered metal basket, I snuck a long, hard look at Dan while his lids were shut. Maybe his unguarded facial expression and body language would clue me in to the secret workings of his mind . . .

Nope. I couldn't see that far inside. All I could see was the outside: . . . the sexy jut of his hips . . . the unusually casual and sporty way he was dressed (khaki shorts, blue and white seersucker shirt opened halfway down the chest) . . . the way his disheveled dark brown hair was flopping down over his forehead.

Mmmmm. My temperature soared a good ten degrees. I had to open the back door and let in some air. I was so over-heated (okay, turned-on), I came this close to throwing myself at Dan's feet (okay, on his lap) and begging for mercy.

But I put the coffeepot on the stove instead. And turned the burner on. And then—combing my fingers through my hair, straightening my clothes, and doing my best imitation of Jane Russell, or Lauren Bacall, or Lana Turner, or any other screen goddess you can name (besides Debbie Reynolds, I mean)— I sidled over to the table and sat down in the chair closest to Dan's.

"Are you hungry, honey?" I simpered. "I've got some bread and cheese. Or I could run down to the bakery and get you a Danish." (I don't always act so slavish and sub-servient—except at work, that is—but I felt the circumstances called for it now.)

Dan arched an eyebrow, opened one eye and aimed it, as if through a gunsight, at me. "No!" he grumbled, piercing me to the core with his Cyclops stare. "I don't want any food. And I don't want you to feed me any more of your flap, either." He sat up straight, rubbed his tired face in his hands, and then glared at me again (with both eyes this time). "All I want is the truth," he said, taking one last drag on his nearly burnt-out Lucky and angrily crushing it in the ashtray. "Is that too god-

damn much to ask? I want you to tell me where you were—
and what you were doing—all day yesterday and last night."

Oh, so that's it! I whooped to myself. *Maybe Dan really
was just crazy worried about me! Maybe the fact that he
couldn't reach me on the phone sent him into such an insecure
and jealous spin that he jumped in his car and drove here in
a possessive rage. Maybe he's just as nuts about me as I am
about him!*

*And maybe he doesn't know anything about the murder
after all . . .*

"I was with Abby all day and night," I told him. "We had
breakfast at her apartment yesterday morning (true), and we
messed around the Village for a while (true—if you can call
our mission to the Sixth Precinct police station 'messing
around,' which, in the meddlesome sense of the phrase, it kind
of was), and then, in the afternoon, we went to the Waverly to
see *Dial M For Murder* (total lie, except for the title of the
movie and the name of the theater where it was, in truth, playing). We had pizza for dinner at Abby's apartment (true), and
after that we went to watch her boyfriend Jimmy perform his
inspiring Independence Day poem at the Vanguard (also true,
except for the 'inspiring' part)."

A lot more Trues than Falses, wouldn't you say?

I took a deep breath, proudly stuck out my chin and asked,
"Anything else you want to know?" I almost added the word
"buster," but thought better of it.

"Yeah," he said, not missing a beat. "Why did you tell me
your phone was out of order when it wasn't?"

Uh oh! How did he find out about that?

There was no point in contradicting him. (Unlike *some*
people I know, Dan's a confirmed straight shooter. He
wouldn't make such a bold, accusatory inquiry unless he
knew it was legit.) I was stuck. I had to come clean (sort of).

"You probably won't understand," I mumbled, "but I let
you believe my phone was out of order because I knew I was
going to be out of the apartment a lot—missing most, if not
all, of your calls—and I didn't want you to worry about me."
I was aware of how lame that would sound to him, but it was
the only excuse I could think of on such short notice. And besides, every single word of it was true. (It was all the words I
left out that would have caused a problem.)

"You bet I don't understand!" Dan said, dropping his fist down hard on the tabletop. "Whatever made you think that a goddamn lie was going to keep me from worrying?"

"I didn't really lie to you!" I protested. "You jumped to the conclusion that my phone was out of order yourself, and I just let you believe it."

"But why? Why didn't you simply tell me that you weren't going to be home? Then I wouldn't have had to keep calling and calling and wondering if you were okay. I wouldn't have been worried at all."

"That's what you say now, but when we spoke on Saturday night, I had the impression that you were vexed about not being able to get in touch with me, and more than a little concerned about how I was going to be spending the rest of the holiday." (I didn't actually use the word "jealous." Why threaten his pride and arouse his masculine ego? I had enough hard feelings to deal with already!)

I must have hit a nerve, because for a second Dan looked as though he would accept my explanation. He softened his eyes, relaxed his scowl, and took a deep swig of ice water, clearly giving more thought to the matter. But then his scowl came back, and his eyes narrowed into slits, and he twisted his luscious mouth in a knowing (i.e., nasty) smirk.

"Nice try, Paige," he said, "but your cover-up won't work. You've been lying through your teeth all along. You told me two phone company trucks were sitting outside your apartment. You made references to melted cables and blown-out gaskets. You said phone company workers had been hanging around your block for two days. If those weren't lies, then what do you call them? Misinterpretations?" There was enough sarcasm in his voice to sink a ship.

"I . . . uh . . . well, I was just trying to—"

"Stop it!" he shouted, pounding his fist on the table again. "I don't have the energy to listen to any more of your crap. You must think I'm a total moron, the way you keep telling me one cock-and-bull story after another. But I've got news for you, Paige. I'm *not* a moron. I'm a trained, experienced, and well-connected NYPD detective. It took me all of two minutes to contact the phone company and find out that no repair work was being done in your area—and that your own phone was in perfect working order."

"Yes, but I—"

"So now it's official," he barreled on, ignoring my attempts to explain. He looked tireder and sadder than I'd ever seen him look before. "You're a liar and a fake. And nothing you can say or do will change those facts—or the way I feel."

"Oh, no, Dan! Please don't say that! Please let me tell you—"

"No, that's enough." He scraped his chair away from the table, rose to his feet, stuffed his pack of cigarettes in his pocket, and turned toward the door. "If you have any more song and dance acts you'd like to perform, I'd thank you to wait until I'm gone."

"You're leaving?" I whimpered, in shock.

"As fast as I can," he said, walking over to the door and pulling it open.

"No! Wait! Please don't go! Just give me one more chance. I swear I'll tell you the truth about everything!"

"It's too late, Paige," he said, withering my soul with his weary goodbye glance. "I don't care anymore."

Chapter 18

DAN HAD WALKED OUT ON ME BEFORE.
Several times. And always for the same reason: My willingness to lie to him while I was working on a dangerous murder story. I'd spent untold hours wracking my brain and
crying my heart out, trying to find a solution to this pressing
problem, but it was no use. There *was* no solution. Dan was
never going to accept my dogged pursuit of the facts at the
expense of my own safety, so I was always going to have to
dodge the truth to keep him happy (unless I quit my job and
gave up my lifelong career goals—which I definitely did not
want to do).

But no matter how many battles and breakups we'd suffered as a result of this predicament, something had always
drawn Dan and me back together in the past. Our mutual
physical attraction had proved unshakable, and our more emotional attachments—i.e., our sincere affection and grudging
respect for each other—had compelled us to stay connected.
And even though Dan hated, hated, *hated* to be lied to (you
can blame his lying, unfaithful ex-wife for that near-phobic
obsession), I had always had the feeling that—way down deep
in his secret heart—he understood my basic motives and
would eventually forgive me.

But I didn't feel that way this time.

This time was different.

Two seconds after Dan stormed out, I ran to the window and snapped open the shade, praying with all my might that when Dan reached the street he would look up and wave at me the way he usually did (when he wasn't mad at me, I mean). But that didn't happen, of course. The instant Dan stepped through the door of my building to the sidewalk, he made a sharp right turn and walked briskly away toward Jones Street, where he often parked his car. His eyes were glued to the cement.

And mine were gushing with tears.

Oh, Lord! What's happening? I sobbed to myself. *Is this the way it's going to end? Has Dan left me for good this time? Will I ever see him again?*

I was bereft. I felt more desolate and alone than I'd ever felt in my life (except for the hideous blur of time following my notification of Bob's death in Korea). I curled myself up in a ball on the couch, hugged my knees in close to my chest, and, wailing like an inconsolable baby, replayed the last few moments of Dan's dramatic exit scene over and over in my mind.

He had seemed far more sad than angry, I recalled, hugging my knees tighter and wailing even louder. Rather than looking as if he wanted to kill me, he had looked as though he'd just lost his best friend. That was not a good sign. And what had he said when I begged him to stay and hear my confession? "It's too late," he'd insisted. "I don't care anymore."

Dear God. Don't let it be true. Please don't let Dan stop caring about me . . .

Bam! Bam! Bam! Someone was banging on my door.

My heart did a somersault in my chest. Was it Dan? Had he come back?

"Let me in, Paige!" Abby shouted. "What's that horrible howling noise? It sounds like you're skinning a cat in there!"

"Go away!" I hollered, mewling and puling and gasping for air. "I want to be alone."

"No go, Garbo! You'd better open the door right now, or I'll break it down. Either way, I'm coming in!"

Knowing Abby was fully capable of demolishing my door (it wouldn't surprise me if she kept an axe in her broom closet), I pried myself up off the couch, staggered across the floor, and—wiping my tears on my sweaty forearm—opened it myself.

"*Oy vey!*" Abby yelped when she saw me. "You look awful! Are you sick or something?" She breezed into my apartment and gave me a head-to-toe onceover. "Yuck! There's a glob of snot the size of New Jersey hanging out of your nose!"

Great. A broken heart and a giant booger. Now my life's complete.

"That's the least of my problems," I said, slogging over to the kitchen counter and blowing my nose on a paper napkin. As I was throwing the napkin in the trash under the sink, the coffee pot caught my attention. Steam was shooting out of the spout and the loosened lid was rattling and snapping like a pair of novelty store dentures. How long had the pot been perking? I had no idea.

I turned off the stove and squinted through my swollen eyelids at Abby. "Want some coffee?"

"Sure," she said, looking fresh, clean and ravishing as usual. Her shiny black hair was loose and streaming down her back like a waterfall. Her white peasant blouse and bright red capris looked as if they'd just been washed and ironed. There wasn't a drop of perspiration on her perfectly made-up face—or anywhere else on her person, for that matter.

(Just par for the course, you should know. Abby usually looks like a Walt Disney princess, while I often resemble a scarecrow . . . or a dead monkey).

While I was pouring the coffee, Abby popped into the living room and turned the fan to face the kitchen table. Then she walked over to the table, positioned a chair in the center of the airflow, and sat down.

"So what's the matter now?" she asked. "Tell me all your troubles, Bubbles."

I carried our coffee over to the table and sat down across from Abby. "I don't even know where to begin," I said, choking back a rising tide of tears. "So much has happened since I last spoke to you."

"You mean since you left the Vanguard last night?"

"Since five minutes before I left."

"But that was just eight hours ago." She spooned some

sugar into her cup. "How much could have happened since then?"

"Plenty," I grumbled, disgusted with myself and revolted by my entire lifestyle. I was reluctant to tell Abby about what had happened with Dan (I didn't want to start crying again), so I lit up an L&M and began recounting the details of my most recent misfortunes from the beginning.

"Before I left you last night," I told her, speaking in a voice so dead it was dirgeful, "I went over to talk to the bartenders. I wanted to find out if they knew anything about Rhonda Blake or the man she was with. So I asked them both a few questions and—"

"*Feh!*" Abby erupted, spraying coffee out of her mouth and all over the tabletop. "This stuff is foul! It's as thick as house paint and it tastes like dirt!"

"Oh . . . I guess I cooked it too long."

"Uh, yeah! I'd say you did. When did you put it on the stove? Last summer?"

"Ha ha," I said, not laughing, just pronouncing the words.

"It's like acid," she needled. "I wonder if it damaged the spoon." She picked said utensil up off the table, held it up close to her nose, and—doing a swell imitation of Jerry Lewis at his crazy, cross-eyed best—examined it from every angle.

I knew what Abby was doing. She was trying to make me smile. She was trying to tease me out of my mournful mental state and nudge me back to the land of the living. But it wasn't working. I didn't *want* to be alive.

I took a drag on my cigarette and exhaled slowly. "Ha ha," I said again, as mirthlessly as before.

"Oh, come on, Paige!" Abby said, slapping the spoon down on the table and throwing her hands in the air. Her patience was fading fast. "Snap out of it! Whatever it is, it can't be *that* bad."

"Oh, yeah?" I retorted, summoning enough energy to plant myself firmly on the defensive. "First listen to everything that's happened to me since I last saw you, and *then* you can decide how bad it is."

•   •   •

A JILLION CIGARETTES AND FOUR CUPS of coffee later (yes, we both drank the filthy stuff anyway), I concluded the tale of my latest pitfalls and perils.

"That's really *bad*!" Abby admitted, referring to the whole disturbing picture, but mostly to my disturbing conflict with Dan. (As you no doubt know by now, Abby believes man trouble is the worst kind of trouble any woman can have.) "Why the hell didn't you just tell Dan the truth?" she ranted. "Then he wouldn't have broken up with you! Then he could help us look for the murderer, and protect you from Baldy and Blackie at the same time."

"But it never would have worked out that way," I sadly replied. "Don't you see? Instead of helping us look for the killer, Dan would've ordered us to drop our investigation altogether. He would have insisted that we leave the whole case—and poor Willy Sinclair's entire future—in Detective Flannagan's homophobic hands. And I could not, in good conscience, allow that to happen. I would never, ever forgive myself if Willy went to jail—or got the death sentence!—for a murder I know he didn't commit."

"What makes you so sure he's innocent?" Abby inquired. "His blood type is guilty as sin."

"Right. And that may be all Flannagan needs to convict him. But lots of people have type A blood, you know. And they're probably all more homicidal than Willy. Willy wouldn't hurt a fly—or even a flea. He's a nervous little mama's boy. I'll bet the closest he ever came to cutting a man was during his girlish youth, when he was cutting out paper dolls. Take my word for it, Ab. Willy's frilly and he's silly—but he's not a murderer."

"You may be right," Abby conceded. "I wouldn't peg him as a killer, either. But we've been over all of this before, you dig, and *you're* the one always warning me not to jump to conclusions. You always say there has to be solid proof. And right now the only proof we have is the blood type."

"Which proves nothing."

"Maybe, baby. But what if you're wrong? What if you're screwing up your relationship with Dan and putting yourself in danger to save Willy when you should be trying to bust him instead? Gray's murder was obviously a crime of passion. And Willy strikes me as both passionate and *meshuga*. You might have to call your next mystery novel 'The Killer in the Yellow Silk Kimono.'"

I smiled (finally). "That's not a bad title," I said, "but I doubt I'll ever be using it. I think 'A Killer Named Cupcake' is the better choice."

"Oh, really?" Abby said, arching one eyebrow to the roof. "Have you been holding out on me, Paige? Have you found out who the mysterious Cupcake is?"

"No, but she's still a prime suspect. Most murderers turn out to be really close to their victims, and if she was Gray's steady girlfriend as you say, then she was the closest. Her real name will come out eventually."

"I'll bet it's Rhonda Blake," Abby said, with a sniff. "That dame even *looks* like a cupcake—all soft and buttery and slathered with poisonous vanilla frosting."

"Yes, but remember how annoyed with Gray she was— how she threatened to turn him in to the director if he didn't show up for the next show? A real girlfriend wouldn't feel that way. Instead of reporting him, she'd try to protect him."

"Or slash him to ribbons," Abby said, refusing to grant Rhonda any concessions. She lit another cigarette, exhaled a thick stream of smoke, and watched it disappear in the churning gust of air from the fan. "So who else is on the table, Mabel? Do you consider Aunt Doobie a prime suspect?"

"Of course. And after last night, Baldy and Blackie have been promoted to the list. I'm still wondering about the guy named Randy, the one who left four messages for Gray, and I don't know about Binky yet. When I spoke to him on the phone, he sounded very jealous and contemptuous of Gray's sudden success. But would he have been carrying on that way if he had already eliminated the source of his envy and contempt? I can't judge until I see him in person."

"Gee, I forgot about Binky!" Abby exclaimed, perking up considerably. "When are we hooking up with him? Tomorrow, right? And then we're going to the Actors Studio!" She fastened her bright gaze on my face. "I can't wait! I'm dying to meet James Dean, and give him my up-close and personal good wishes."

I rolled my eyes at the ceiling. How was I going to get out of this one?

"I don't have any idea what's going to happen tomorrow,

Ab," I demurred, looking for a way to let her down easy. "I haven't spoken to Binky yet. And I have to go back to work in the morning. After a holiday I'm always up to my eyebrows in extra paperwork. If I know Pomeroy," I said, referring to my immediate boss at *Daring Detective*, "he'll keep me chained to my desk until Christmas. He'll make me pay through the nose for having the day off today . . .

"Oh, by the way," I added, "happy July Fourth."

"Same to ya," she chirped, smiling widely, distracted (for the time being, at least) from the subject of Binky. "What're you going to do today, Paige? Jimmy and I have a really cool sked. We're going to Child's for lunch, and then to the Gramercy to see *East of Eden*. It stars James Dean, you know! Then we're going to John's for spaghetti and meatballs, and to the park later to listen to music, dance like fools around the fountain, and light up some sparklers and firecrackers. Come with us! It'll be fun."

"No. I don't feel like doing anything."

"You're just going to sit alone in your hot apartment and mope?"

"Yep."

"That's really dumb. Come out and play with us. It'll take your mind off Dan."

"No it won't. Nothing can."

"But it'll help you pass the time!" Abby said, growing impatient again. "You can't just stay here and wallow in your misery like a pig in the mud."

"I can if I want to," I said, pouting—sounding, even to myself, like a cranky and stubborn four-year-old. "I don't care what anybody says, I'm going to wallow in the mud for as long as my piggy little heart desires!"

I really meant it, too. I was going to stay home all day and night, have a few more crying jags, drink some more putrid coffee, smoke a thousand cigarettes, listen to Billie Holiday sing the blues, and pray with all my might for Dan to call. I was going to eat stale bread and cheese for dinner, and commemorate our country's independence with a glass (or whole bottle) of cheap Chianti. There would be no dancing or fireworks for me. I intended to lock my doors and stay inside where it was safe.

Too bad I didn't stick to the plan.

Chapter 19

AFTER ABBY LEFT I WENT UPSTAIRS AND took a shower (there's only so much mud-wallowing a girl can stand). I put on a pair of shorts and a clean blouse, then went back downstairs to sit in front of the fan—or, more importantly, right next to the phone. I wasn't the least bit hopeful that Dan would call, but I wanted to answer on the double if he did.

So, two seconds later when the phone rang, jerking me to attention and launching my spirits toward the sun, I pounced on the receiver in a flash. "Hello?" I croaked, too excited to even try to sound sexy. "Is that you, Dan? Thank God you called! I'm so sorry I—"

"Who's Dan?" the caller asked. From the high-pitched voice and slight Southern accent, I knew right away it was Willy.

"He's my boyfriend," I said, hoping against hope that that statement was still true.

"So where *is* your man Dan? Why isn't he there?" Willy asked. "Isn't he spending the holiday with you?"

"Uh, no, he—"

"Good!" Willy exclaimed. "Then can I come over and spend the afternoon at your place?"

I was so taken aback, I didn't know what to say. "Gee,

well, maybe . . . I mean, I guess you could . . . But why would you want to—"

"I've got to get out of my apartment!" he screeched. "Flannagan's driving me out of my mind! He keeps calling and calling and calling—every blessed minute of the day and night—asking me one appalling question after another, and making horrible accusations. He says I have the same blood type as the killer. He says he knows I killed Gray and it won't be long before he can prove it. He's trying to torture me into confessing. I know he is!"

"Take it easy, Willy," I said, speaking as calmly and reassuringly as I could. The poor fellow sounded even worse than I felt. "Don't fly into a panic. That's what Flannagan *wants* you to do. Have you tried taking your phone off the hook?"

"Mercy, no!" he squealed. "That would make it even worse. Then he might show up and torture me in person! I've got to get out of here now! Can I come over to your apartment for a while? Please, please, pretty pretty please? He'd never think of looking for me there."

"Um . . . uh . . . okay," I said, spirits sinking as low as they could go. I didn't want any company. I wanted to wallow in my own troubles, not Willy's. "Do you know where I live?"

"Yes, I heard you give your address to the police. It's two-sixty-five Bleecker, right? Just a few blocks from me."

"Right. I'm one floor up, over the fish store."

"Kiss, kiss, kiss," he said. "I'll be there in a jiffy."

Click.

(Okay, you can stop shaking your head that way! I get the message already! You're thinking I was certifiably crazy to let Willy come to my apartment when I had no sure way of knowing whether he was the murderer or not. And you're one-hundred-percent right, of course. It was a really stupid move. Dan and Abby would be tearing their hair out if they knew what I'd just done. And there's nothing I can say in my own defense, either—except that I truly believed in Willy's innocence, and I trusted him completely, and I was bound by my own sense of justice and compassion to help him in any way I could. If that makes me a brainless twit, so be it.)

•   •   •

MY BUZZER RANG TWENTY MINUTES later. I darted over to the living room window and peeked through the shade to make sure it was Willy. (At least I was being *somewhat* cautious. I even shot a glance across the street to see if Blackie was lurking in the laundromat doorway. He wasn't. There was no black limousine parked at the curb, either.) After taking a second look at Willy's slicked-back bleach-blond hairdo and the plump contours of his colorful shoulders (he was wearing a pink and orange Hawaiian shirt!), I went over to the door and buzzed him in.

Willy climbed the steps to my apartment with difficulty; his legs were short and his arms were full of packages. He carried a foil-wrapped bunch of long-stemmed roses in one hand. "Greetings!" he said, when he reached the top landing. His pale lips were stretched in an ear-to-ear grin. "I come bearing gifts!"

"I can see that," I said, pulling the door wide and motioning him inside. "But what's the occasion? My birthday was over a month ago."

"It's the Fourth of July, silly," he said, setting the packages down on the kitchen table and handing the roses to me. "Better put these in water quick. It's so hot they're already starting to wilt."

I stepped over to the kitchen counter, filled my empty flour cannister with water, and plunked the flowers in. "What else have you got there?" I asked, carrying the roses across the room and setting them down on the table. I hoped he'd brought something edible. *Anything* edible. (I was so hungry I'd have eaten a hamster, providing it was properly cooked).

"Just wait till you see!" he warbled, his enormous blue eyes glistening with glee. "I'll open this one first." Tearing the brown paper wrapping off one of the parcels, he proudly produced a bottle of champage. "Voilà! Isn't this fabulous? I believe every holiday should be celebrated with sparkling French wine, don't you? Quick! Put it in the refrigerator before it gets warm."

I happily did as I was told. (Nothing like a bottle of champagne to turn a blue mood bubbly.) When I returned to the table, Willy was unwrapping a box of Russell Stover chocolates.

"Here!" he said, opening the box and holding it out toward me. "Have one. You look like you need it."

"Thanks," I said, popping a chocolate-covered caramel in my mouth and chewing it like gum. "Mmmm. Thith ith good." (It's hard to enunciate when your teeth are stuck together.) When I swallowed that, I took a nougat. My mood was sweetening by the second.

"I've brought other goodies, too," Willy chirped, taking lots of small jars and tins out of a large paper bag and arranging them on the table. "We've got beluga caviar, Vienna sausages, deviled ham, smoked oysters and clams, sardines and anchovies, lichee nuts, pickled beets, Greek olives, and capers!" The way his pudgy, freckled hands were gesturing toward the lavish display of delicacies, you'd have thought he was presenting jewels at Tiffany's. "And here's a beautiful baguette!" he added, pulling a long, thin loaf of French bread from another brown paper bag and setting it down on the table with a flourish.

All I could say was, "Mmmm." My mouth was watering too much to speak. I had never tasted any of those unusual things before in my life (except for sardines), but I couldn't wait to get started.

"Shall we have our feast now, or wait till later?" Willy asked.

"Now, please," I said. I was probably whimpering like a hungry puppy.

Willy took a step back, folded his arms over the top of his pink-and-orange-swathed potbelly, and studied the table scene as if it were a movie set. "Do you have a pretty tablecloth, honey? No offense, but this yellow formica is atrocious! I won't be able to eat a thing until it's hidden from my sight."

Oh, brother! I was annoyed by Willy's criticism. I'd always thought my yellow tabletop was cheerful. "I've got one," I reluctantly admitted, "but I never use it. It's on the top shelf of my closet upstairs. It's hand-embroidered white linen and it belonged to my grandmother."

"Perfect!" Willy whooped, clapping his hands in delight. "While you're getting the tablecloth, I'll open the wine. Where do you keep your champagne glasses?"

Ha! Did Willy think I was a relative of the Rockefellers?

"I don't have any," I said. "All I have are four tall water glasses and three small jellyglasses."

He wrinkled his freckled nose and shrieked, "Eeeeeeeek! What a disaster! If only I'd known, I would have brought some from home. You can't drink champagne from a jellyglass! It's a travesty!"

"Would you rather drink it from a shoe?" I snapped. I was getting a little tired of Willy's high-pitched histrionics. "I've got an old pair of pumps upstairs."

Startled by my peckish tone, Willy gasped and gave me a hurt look. Then he stared down at the floor in shame. "I'm sorry, Paige," he mumbled. "I can be a little overbearing sometimes. I didn't mean to upset you. I was just trying to forget about Gray, and Flannagan, and all the ghastliness of the last few days. I was just trying to make everything elegant and festive."

I felt like a heel. "No, I'm the one who's sorry, Willy! Please forgive me for being so short-tempered. I was in a really bad way before you came, and now, thanks to you, I'm about to enjoy some fabulous food, fine wine, and good company. You *have* made everything festive, Willy. And as soon as I bring down my grandmother's tablecloth, it's going to be elegant, too!"

Willy raised his eyes from the floor and gave me a shaky smile. "You really mean it, Paige?"

"Of course I mean it. And to prove it, I'm going to run upstairs and get the tablecloth right now. It's party time! So hurry up, pal. Pop the cork and pour the champagne, willya?"

"You bet I will!" he squealed, bounding over to the refrigerator to get the bottle. "Where do you keep your jellyglasses?"

AN HOUR AND A HALF LATER WE WERE still sitting at the kitchen table, telling each other our life stories, nibbling chocolates and sipping champagne. My grandmother's tablecloth was littered with bits of caviar, a few stray capers and olive pits, and enough bread crumbs to feed all the pigeons in the park (I'm talking Central!). Our plates and most of the tins and jars were empty; our stomachs were full.

Except for the lichee nuts, which I found to be pretty yucky, I had relished every peculiar morsel.

"That was really good, Willy. Weird but wonderful. Where did you get all this stuff anyway? Every store in the city is closed."

"I had it all at home. Even the roses. I'm always prepared for emergencies."

"That's good to know," I said, smiling. "Next time I have a smoked oyster crisis I'll give you a call."

He giggled, took another sip of his wine, then turned serious. "Thanks for letting me come over today, Paige. You saved my life. One more afternoon of Flannagan's relentless questions and accusations, and I'd have jumped right out the window." His bulbous blue eyes were on the verge of tears.

"I'm glad you came, Willy," I said, really meaning it (and hurrying to stop the saline flow). "You saved my life, too. But now do you think you could stand it if I asked you a few more questions? About you and Gray and the murder, I mean. I'm working on a story, and I'm hoping I can figure out who the real killer is before Flannagan hangs the rap on you. And there's so damn much I need to know!"

"Fire away!" Willy said, poking a chocolate-covered cherry in his mouth. "I'm really grateful for your support. *You* can ask me anything."

"Okay, here goes." I sat up straighter in my chair, determined to find out everything Willy might know, even if my intrusive inquiries embarrassed him. I took a deep breath and began: "First things first. Are you a homosexual?"

"Of course I am, honey!" he squeaked. "I thought you knew that already!"

"I sort of did, but since we've never spoken the actual *word* . . ."

Willy gave me an indulgent smile. "Sticks and stones may break my bones, and words will also hurt me. So let's get them all out in the open right now. I'm not just a homosexual; I'm a fairy and a queer and a faggot, too. I'm a flit, a fruit, a queen, a pansy, and an auntie. I'm a sodomite and a pervert and a deviant. And according to some people—Detective Flannagan included—I'm also a sex fiend and a psychopath. There! Are those enough words for you? Did I leave anything out?"

"Gay," I said. "You didn't mention that you were gay."

Willy cracked up laughing, as I'd hoped he would. (Laughing feels better than crying, wouldn't you say?) He laughed so hard his pale face turned as pink as the hibiscus blooms on his Hawaiian shirt.

I waited until he'd expelled his last snicker, then continued the discomforting inquest. "'Auntie?'" I probed. "I never heard that word used in this context before. Is it a very common term?"

"It's not as popular as 'fairy' or 'queer,' but it gets tossed around a bit. Even by the fags themselves."

"You mean they call each other 'auntie'?"

"Not exactly. What they do is use the word in a nickname. If I had a good friend named Salvatore, for example, I might call him Auntie Sal or Aunt Sally. It's a term of endearment. But only when it's used by one homosexual talking to another. When a straight man uses the word, it's totally derogatory."

"I see," I said, wheels turning. "So it wouldn't be strange for a gay man to call another gay man Aunt Doobie."

"Not at all. It would just signify that they had a close relationship."

"A sexual relationship?"

"Most likely."

"As I mentioned to you yesterday, Gray had somebody in his life called Aunt Doobie. Would that mean that Gray was gay?"

Willy slicked his fingers through his heavily pomaded hair. "That's a tough one to answer, Paige, but offhand, I'd say yes. Gray never *told* me that he was queer, but I always sensed that he was. It takes one to know one, you know!"

"But yesterday you told me you *didn't* know!"

"And I don't know for sure. I just have a feeling. Gray never gave me or anybody I know a tumble, so I can't swear that he was gay. And you can't go by the whole 'auntie' thing, either. It's possible Gray had a real aunt called Aunt Doobie."

Back to square one.

I paused to collect my thoughts, then proceeded. "Okay, here's another question I've already asked you, but now feel pressed to ask again: Are you quite sure you never heard the name Aunt Doobie before?"

"I'm positive. That's not the kind of name you forget."

"Aaaargh!" I growled, rolling my eyes at the ceiling in despair. "Aunt Doobie could be the murderer, for God's sake, but I may never be able to find out who he or she is!"

"Maybe I can help," Willy said. "I'm going to a private party at the Keller Hotel tonight. It's for gays only. Should I bounce the name around and see if anybody's heard of it?"

"Absolutely not!" I insisted. "You could be putting yourself in grave danger that way. And with Flannagan hot on your tail, you're in more than enough trouble already." I lifted my jellyglass to my lips and drained the rest of my champagne. "You said the party is for gays only. Does that mean no women are allowed?"

"Mercy, no!" Willy said, tossing his head and flipping one pinkie—extended hand in the air. "There'll probably be quite a few women there. But they'll all be lesbians."

"Then you'd better give me lesbian lessons," I said, "because I'm going to the party with you."

Chapter 20

HAVE YOU EVER HAD THE FEELING THAT you've lost touch with your real self altogether—that you're floating around in the stratosphere without any skin? Then you know how I felt that night, as I dressed myself in long pants and a white shirt—just as Willy had told me to do—and prepared to make my fraudulent debut as a lesbian. I was uncomfortable, not to mention too warm, in the stiff masculine attire, and I couldn't wait for the painful charade to be over.

I went downstairs, put some money in my pants pockets (Willy had forbidden me to carry a purse), then stuck a pack of cigarettes in the breast pocket of my white cotton shirt. I looked at the clock on my living room table. I was too early. It was 8:00 P.M. and I wasn't supposed to meet Willy until 9:00. I had plenty of time to call Binky.

Taking the pad with Gray's phone messages out of the table drawer, I sat down on the couch, lit up an L&M, and dialed Binky's number. He answered on the second ring.

"Hello. Who is it? Speak up! I'm in a hurry."

"Hi, Binky," I said. "It's Pa—I mean Phoebe Starr. I spoke to you the day before yesterday, remember? I'm the actress who wants to enroll in the Actors Studio. You said you'd take me there tomorrow and show me around, so I'm calling to confirm that appointment."

There was a short silence, then Binky said, "You're Gray Gordon's friend, right?"

"Yes."

"Then what the hell do you think you're doing? Are you nuts? Why are you calling me *now*? Maybe you haven't heard, but Gray's dead! He doesn't friggin' exist anymore!" Binky sounded like an overactive volcano—boiling and ready to blow.

"Yes, I know," I said. "It's so horrible, I still can't believe it. It's a sickening, hideous tragedy. Gray was such a wonderful person. Who would do such a terrible thing to him?"

"Don't ask me," he said, lowering his voice to a more mournful tone. "But you want to know something, sweetheart? I think what *you're* trying to do is pretty terrible, too."

"What do you mean?" I asked, starting to squirm. What did he think I was trying to do? And why was it so terrible? "I really don't know what you're talking about."

Binky let out a derisive snort. "I'll tell you what I'm talking about! I'm talking about the way you're swooping in like a vulture, trying to pick the meat off Gray's bones and fill the sudden vacancy at the Studio. Gray's only been dead for three friggin' days, little girl. He's probably not even cold yet. And here you are, already trying to take his place in Strasberg's class."

"I am not!" I cried, defending myself vociferously. "How could you say such an awful thing? I called you tonight because I *told* you I would the last time we spoke. And that was *before* I knew that Gray was dead. Don't you remember? We spoke on Saturday and the news of Gray's murder didn't appear in the papers until Sunday!"

"Saturday, Sunday—what's the difference? You're still just trying to get into the Studio."

"Yes, I would like to join, but so would every other actress under the sun. We *all* want to study under Lee Strasberg, you know. I've wanted to work with him for as long as I can remember. So I am not—repeat *not*—trying to take advantage of Gray's tragic misfortune. I'm just continuing my pursuit of a lifelong dream. And Gray wanted to help me achieve that dream, if you recall. That's why he told me to call you."

"Oh, all right!" Binky said, letting out a loud groan of exasperation. "I'll take you to the damn Studio sometime. But I can't talk about it now. I'm late for work."

"So when *can* you talk about it?" I urged, desperate to pin him down. "Can I call you later, when you get off work?"

"Are you nuts? I won't get home till five in the morning. On big holidays like this, the Latin Quarter bar stays open all night. You can call me tomorrow if you want to—but not before noon."

"Okay, thanks," I said. "I'll talk to you tomorrow."

Binky's only goodbye was a beastly grunt, plus the sound of the receiver crashing into the cradle.

EVEN IN THE DARK OF NIGHT, I FELT extremely self-conscious when I left my building and stepped out onto the sidewalk. What if somebody I knew saw me looking like this? No makeup, no high heels, no purse, no wavy, shoulder-length hairdo (I had pulled my hair back in a rubber band, the way Willy told me to do). Thank God Abby and Jimmy weren't there to witness my defeminization. Abby would have a heart attack and die; Jimmy would just die laughing. Otto would probably bark his head off for a few seconds and then cover his little brown eyes with his paws.

I was glad all the neighborhood stores were closed. If Angelo or Luigi got a load of my lesbian get-up they'd probably run down the street to St. Joseph's to light candles and pray for the salvation of my soul. And I hated to think how Dan would react—so I tried not to. One good thing could come from my disguise, though, I realized. If Baldy or Blackie happened to be hiding in the shadows in ambush, they might not know who I was!—a lucky ramification which could save me from a shanghaiing (or any other dastardly deed either one of them might have in mind).

Keeping my head down and walking as fast as I could in the stifling heat, I crossed Seventh Avenue, made my way over to Christopher, and—shielding my face whenever I passed a streetlamp—made a beeline for the four-story brownstone where Willy lived. I stepped into the well-lit vestibule and, feeling a very strong sense of déjà vu, rang the buzzer for 2A.

As I stood there waiting for Willy to answer, I couldn't

help noticing that both the mailbox and the buzzer for 2B still bore the name GRAY GORDON. The sight of Gray's carefully hand-printed capitals broke my heart. He had probably been very happy when he'd lettered those labels, I mused—excited about beginning a new life in his new apartment and looking forward to a fabulous future.

"Is that you, Paige?" Willy sputtered into the intercom.

"Yes, it is," I said, although considering the way I looked and felt, I wasn't at all sure.

"Okay, hang on! I'm coming right down."

Eager to escape the sad specter of Gray's name, I left the vestibule, crossed to the edge of the cement stoop, and sat down on the top step. Two young men were strolling up the street holding hands, but when they spied me sitting on the stoop ahead, they quickly loosened their fingers and dropped their hands to their sides. Then, when they drew closer and saw in the light from the vestibule that I wasn't a homophobe prowling for prey, but rather a woman in mannish clothing (i.e., one of them, in a flip-flop kind of way), they relaxed, gave me a smile and a nod, and took hold of each other's hand again.

The wardrobe was working.

Willy came out a few seconds later and, after he'd checked out my lesbian garb and given it a passing grade, we started walking west on Christopher, in the opposite direction of the strolling hand-holders.

I was feeling nervous about the whole expedition. "Where did you say this party is being held?" I anxiously inquired. "At a hotel?"

"That's right," Willy said. "The old Keller Hotel. It's over by the river, on West Street. It was built in 1898, and it used to be a thriving hotel for seamen. Now it's just a fleabag dump. We have parties in the hotel bar because it's one of the few places that will serve homosexuals. And because it's so far off the beaten track we don't attract too much attention."

"Does Flannagan know about this place?"

"He sure does, honey. The bar gets raided about once a month. All the Keller Hotel regulars are regulars at the Sixth Precinct police station, too."

Oh, no. Just what I need—to get arrested at a gay bar dressed like a lesbian. Dan would lose every last one of his marbles over that! "You mean the party might be raided tonight?" I croaked. I was getting more nervous by the second.

"It could happen," Willy said, "but I don't think it will. This is the Fourth of July, don't forget. The cops will be too busy with other crimes and disturbances of the peace to pay any mind to us."

Pow! Pow! Bang! Boom!

As if on cue, a bunch of firecrackers went off in the near vicinity. Willy jumped like a jackrabbit and squealed like a girl. (So did I, if the truth be told.) "Eeeeeek!" he wailed, grabbing hold of my arm and twisting it so hard he almost dislocated my elbow. "What's that? A machine gun?"

"I don't think so," I said, groaning and giggling at the same time. "Sounds more like firecrackers to me."

"Oh, yeah," he muttered, looking embarrassed. "I forgot about the fireworks." He let go of my arm and quickened his pace toward Hudson Street. I hurried to catch up with him. After we crossed Hudson and neared the intersection of Greenwich Street, there was another loud explosion. "Yeeee-oww!" Willy shrieked. "That was a bad one! I bet somebody threw a cherry bomb in a trash can. Oh, how I hate all this dreadful noise! It scares the stuffing out of me!"

"Well, you'd better get used to it," I said, breathing heavily from our brisk clip. "The pyromaniacs are just getting started. And the closer we get to the river, the worse it's going to get."

My apprehension was mounting with every step. There were very few streetlamps in this part of town, and many of those were broken. And after we crossed Washington and continued down Christopher toward the Hudson River, I realized how rundown and deserted the neighborhood was. Battered trucks, boarded-up warehouses, and dilapidated maritime buildings lined the ill-paved streets, and there were no stores or restaurants in sight.

But at least Willy and I weren't walking the streets alone; quite a few other people were out treading in the same direction, rapidly making their way toward the waterfront to shoot off their skyrockets and torpedoes. The riverside fireworks were just getting underway, I observed, as the bright comet of a Roman candle whooshed into the black sky above, then exploded and released its vast shower of red and gold stars.

By the time we reached West Street, the sky was alive with fireballs and pinwheels. And our ears were ringing from the blasting bombs, cannons, crackers, and whiz-bangs. People near the river, on the other side of the elevated West Side Highway, were cheering and screaming and dashing in all directions—blazing sparklers thrust high in their hands—and the hot, humid nighttime air was filled with acrid smoke. The Villagers were staging their own little war.

Willy had stopped squealing every time a bomb went off, but he was still scared stuffingless. He grabbed my arm again and pulled me to the left, hastily leading me down West Street, and then around the corner on Barrow, to the entrance of the Keller Hotel.

The sight of the square, six-story, red stone structure gave me the shivers. The narrow windows were filthy, the canvas awning over the door was faded and tattered, and the low cement stoop was crumbling away. The dimly lit red-lettered sign sticking out from the corner of the building offered one sad, solitary word: HOTEL.

Even with the door propped wide open, the entryway was far more forbidding than inviting. And the groups of jittery young men hulking around near the door, smoking cigarettes and speaking in strained whispers, did nothing to ease my anxiety. I wanted to turn on my heels and run home like the wind.

Which would have been the smart thing to do, of course. But, as you well know by now, I'm more accomplished at doing the stupid thing. And tonight was no exception (not by a long shot!). Stupidly ignoring my fearful misgivings, I took a deep breath, straightened my spine, and—affecting what I hoped was a manly John Wayne swagger—followed Willy inside.

Chapter 21

THE SMALL BARROOM WAS SO CROWDED, hot, and smoky you could barely move or breathe. The barstools were all taken and the booths were tightly packed. There was no room but standing room—and very little of that. Leading with his prodigious potbelly, Willy forged his way into the center of the crush, then began wriggling toward the bar. I stayed as close on his heels as I could, trying not to brush against any burning cigarettes or step on any toes.

"What do you want to drink?" Willy shouted to me over his shoulder. His chubby round face was red from exertion.

"A bottle of Ballantine!" I shouted back. (I really wanted a champagne cocktail, but since Ballantine sponsored the Yankees, I figured that would be the more masculine choice.)

"Stay right where you are," Willy hollered. "I'll be back in a minute." He turned and kept pushing toward the bar.

I stood still in the middle of the room and glanced around at the faces close (very close!) to me. They were all male. Various shapes, sizes, and ages, but the vast majority were young and attractive (in a smooth, big-eyed, feminine sort of way). *Abby should conduct a search for new models here*, I said to myself. *This place is crawling with chickens.* Some of the guys had their arms around each other, clinging quietly together like sweet, just-married couples; others were more boistrous and communal—laughing, chatting, posturing, gesturing, trying to make an impression. I wondered how short, pudgy, middle-aged Willy would fare in this callow, good-looking crowd.

"Here you go!" Willy said, appearing out of the throng and handing me my beer. "It's a madhouse in here. I thought I'd never make it back alive!"

"Well, I'm glad you did," I shouted. "I was starting to feel lonely and out of place. I thought you said there'd be some other women here."

"There are," he said, standing on his tiptoes and yelling directly into my ear. "Two are sitting at the bar. And I bet a few more are sitting in the booths against the wall. Chivalry is not dead! The girls still get the seats!"

"Oh, yeah? Then if we went over and stood near the booths, do you think somebody would get up and let me sit down?" (I didn't really care about getting a seat. I was just hoping it would be quieter in a booth—that maybe I'd get to talk to some people without shouting, and actually be able to hear their replies. It was time to do a little name-dropping and pop a few questions.)

"Probably," Willy said. "C'mon, let's go see."

It took us a while to get across the floor. Even more revelers had pushed their way into the party, packing the room so tightly I felt surrounded by sardines instead of chickens. Some of the men were dancing—if you could call it that. Feet rooted in place, they stood locked together like lovers, heads on each other's shoulders, swaying to the music from the jukebox. The Maguire Sisters were singing "Sincerely," but you could barely hear their harmony above the clamor of the crowd.

"Hey, Farley!" Willy cried out, spotting somebody he knew and waving frantically. He was so thrilled to find a friend his metaphorical tail was wagging. "Look, Paige, I want to go talk to Farley for a while, okay?" he hollered. "You stay here. See if you can get a seat in a booth."

"Okay," I said, not eager to be left alone, but wanting Willy to have a good time. As he began moving toward the back of the room where his friend was standing, I turned and took a good look at Farley. He was tall, dark, and skinny, and his neck was as long as his legs (okay, not really—it just seemed

that way). He was younger than Willy—in his thirties I
guessed—wearing a pink short-sleeved shirt, a pair of gray
slacks, and an enormous snaggletoothed smile. He was as
glad to see Willy as Willy was to see him.

Feeling happy for Willy, but very sorry for myself (would
I ever see Dan again?), I turned back around and tried to act
casual, as though I were perfectly comfortable in this weird,
way-out atmosphere. I threw my head back, guzzled my beer
like a man, and then made a quick survey of the booths,
choosing the one where I wanted to sit.

The booth closest to the door seemed the most promising.
It was occupied by five fellows who seemed to be around
Gray's age. I couldn't see the faces of the three whose backs
were turned toward me, but their thick hair and well-built
shoulders sent a clear message of youth and energy. Slumped
in the far corner of the booth was a woman. A girl, really. She
was small and serious, and she looked sadder than a kitten lost
in the rain.

Looking pretty sad myself, I'm sure, and feeling so nervous my knees were knocking, I staggered toward the door
and stationed myself right next to the booth in question. Then
I took a cigarette out of the pack in my pocket and held it to
my lips. "Anybody got a light?" I asked, doing my suavest
Robert Taylor, but probably looking a whole heck of a lot
more like Red Skelton.

"Sure," said the young man facing me from the outer edge
of the booth. He took a Zippo out of his pocket and flicked it
into flame. Then he stood up and lit my cigarette. "Would you
like to join us?" he asked, snapping his Zippo closed and gesturing toward his empty spot on the bench. "Please sit down."

"Thanks," I said, slipping into his seat in a flash. I took a
deep drag on my cigarette, set down my beer, and leveled my
gaze at the scarred wood tabletop, trying to think of a good
way to introduce myself and launch my inquisition. "Uh, hi,"
I finally began. "My name's Phoebe." I slowly raised my eyes
to meet those of the people sitting across the table. "This is
my first time here, and I—"

A cherry bomb exploded in my brain. And my entire nervous system went into shock. No exaggeration. If President
Eisenhower himself had leaned over and kissed me on the
mouth, I couldn't have been more stunned. Because sitting di-

rectly opposite me—with his wavy dark hair falling down over his forehead and his deep brown eyes boring like bullets into mine—was the man I had been thinking and wondering about since late yesterday afternoon, when I first saw him standing, half naked, in the doorway of room 96 at the Mayflower Hotel.

"Aunt Doobie?" I blurted, voice cracking. "Is that you?"

Which was the worst possible thing I could have said, of course. Because now—thanks to my unbelievably careless and stupid (but totally involuntary) outburst—the man was on full alert. He was staring right through my lesbian disguise and recognizing the face of the aggressive, inquisitive woman who had disturbed him during his nap at the Mayflower. And whether his name was John Smith, or Aunt Doobie, or Randy, or Dagwood Bumstead—one thing was perfectly clear: he was *not* pleased to see me again.

Five silent but gut-wrenching seconds passed before the man broke his hostile, dead-on glare. He ripped his eyes away from mine and aimed them at door. Then he sprang to his feet, ducked his chin into the collar of his black linen shirt, and—without another glance in my direction, or a single word to the other people at the table—lunged into the crowd and began shoving his way toward the exit.

Oh my god! What on earth is he doing?! Is he running away?

I whipped my head around just in time to see him bolt through the door to the street. And that's when I *really* lost it—my mind, I mean, and what was left of my cool (which had gone on a one-way trip to the moon). I should have held fast and questioned the other people in the booth, of course, found out if any of them knew Aunt Doobie's real name. And then I should have hurried over to Willy to tell him what was going on and enlist his help. But I was too frantic to do either of those things. Aunt Doobie was on the run! If I didn't act fast, he would make a clean getaway!

So what did I do? You guessed it. I jumped to my feet, scrambled to the door, and took off after him.

I HIT THE SIDEWALK RUNNING—EAST on Barrow toward the heart of the Village—straining my eyes through the night, hoping to catch sight of a dark-haired man in black pants and a black shirt. But after I'd gone about seventy-five yards, I came to a sudden stop. It was so dark on the deserted street ahead, I couldn't see anything at all, much less a man in black clothing.

And what if he hadn't come this way when he fled? What if he'd chosen the quickest, easiest, yet shrewdest escape route—dashing under the steel and cement structure of the elevated West Side Highway and darting smack into the teeming, celebrating, fireworks-happy mob near the river? That was certainly the course I would have taken. Except for the rockets' red glare and the bombs bursting in air, it was pretty darn dark over by the docks. And there's no better camouflage than an excited, chaotic crowd.

I turned on my heels and started running back in the opposite direction, past the Keller Hotel, onward across West Street and under the highway. I was so hot I was melting. Sweat was streaming down my face, stinging my eyes and seeping like salty tears into my gasping mouth. I couldn't breathe. When I reached the edge of the madding crowd, I had to stop running for a second, get my bearings, pull some smoky air into my lungs.

Firecrackers were popping all over the place, and every few seconds another cannon would boom. Or another person would scream. Or another bomb would shriek its loud whistle and explode. I was so jumpy I flinched at every eruption. Swiveling my head from side to side and racing up and down the sidelines of the action, I madly searched the throng for Aunt Doobie. Back and forth I ran, like a dog chasing a stick, looking for the man in the black linen shirt—the man I now believed to be a black-hearted murderer.

But it was hopeless. The scene was too crazy. The noise was too noisy. I was too frenzied to see straight. I had to retreat from the fire and fury and fall back to the rear—to the softer, deeper darkness under the highway, where the steady whiz of traffic overhead was almost soothing.

Maybe if I hide here long enough, I thought, *standing still and straight behind this big support beam, Aunt Doobie will think I'm gone—or that I never chased after him in the first place. Maybe he'll emerge from his own hiding place and head for home, or back to the Mayflower Hotel, or someplace*

*else significant. Then I can follow him, see where he goes, try
to pick up some clues to his identity.*

Good plan, wouldn't you say?

Well, that's what I thought, too, but I couldn't have been
more wrong.

Because the next loud explosion I heard was the bang on
the back of my head, and after that came nothing but silence.

Chapter 22

HAVE YOU EVER COME AWAKE WITH A start in the middle of the night, so addled and confused you don't know who, what, or where you are? Well, that's how I felt that night when my lost consciousness began swooping back into my skull. At first I thought I was a crocodile, lying long and flat against the riverbank, but on my back instead of my belly. Then I thought I was a wounded soldier, bleeding to death in a trench in North Korea, while an unknown enemy warrior was raising his sword to strike again. For a few crazy seconds, I actually believed I was an old, gray-haired woman named Aunt Doobie lying on a slab at the city morgue.

"Wake up, Mrs. Turner," a male voice shouted in my ear. "Can you hear me?"

Turner? Turner who?

"Paige Turner!" the voice shouted again. "Are you conscious? Open your eyes!"

Paige Turner? Who's that? What a ridiculous name!

I tried to sit up, but couldn't make it all the way. My aching head was so dizzy I felt nauseous; I couldn't see anything but stars. Quickly lowering myself back to a prone position, I lay still for a couple of seconds, blindly attempting to make sense of my physical situation, trying to imagine where I was. I was lying on something hard, I knew, and from the rough, gritty feel under my fingers, I was pretty sure it was cement. Horns were honking overhead. I could hear loud booms and blasts in the near distance, and the steamy air smelled like gunsmoke.

Oh, goody. I'm not in the hospital . . .

"Hey, move back, boys! Give her some air. She's starting to come around." The same man was talking, but he obviously wasn't alone. "Mrs. Turner!" he shouted again. "Open your damn eyes!"

They popped open on command. And my sight was now fully restored. But what I saw made me want to black out again. There, looming right above me—lowering his boyish face toward mine and baring his teeth like a vampire preparing to enjoy a midnight snack—was the last man in the world I wanted to see: Detective Sergeant Nick Flannagan.

Egads! I screamed the word out loud in my head but somehow managed to keep it off my tongue. (Yes, my self-control actually *does* work sometimes. Not often, but every once in a while.)

Flannagan must have seen the shock and horror on my face, though, because he quickly pulled away and reared back to a squatting position. "How's tricks, Mrs. Turner?" he asked, smirking, gazing down at me like a gargoyle. "How do you feel? Do you know what day it is?"

"I feel like ca-ca," I said. "And as for the day, I'm assuming it's still Monday, the fourth of July. But that depends on what time it is. Is it past midnight yet? How long was I out?"

"Just a few minutes we think." He looked at his watch. "It's ten forty-five now. What time did you come down here?"

"Down where?" I wasn't being coy. I still wasn't sure where I was.

"Down to the river," he grunted. "West Street and Barrow. Sit up. It'll clear your head. Need a hand?"

"No, I can make it," I said, pushing myself up to my elbows, then all the way to a sitting position. The effort made me dizzy again, but just for a second. And when my head stopped spinning, it actually *was* a lot clearer. Gently touching the painful but thankfully not bloody bump on the back of my noggin, I straightened up and surveyed my surroundings.

Two cop cars were parked close by on West Street. One had a cop in it (I'm guessing he was monitoring the radio calls); the other was empty. Two uniformed police were standing to my left and Flannagan was squatting on my right, just a couple of feet away from the steel highway support beam I'd been hiding behind when I was hit. From where I was sitting, I could see the red-lettered HOTEL sign suspended from the corner of the Keller building.

"You look lousy," Flannagan said. "I'm going to call for an ambulance."

"No!" I screeched. "Please don't! I'm fine. Really I am!" I was lying, of course. My head felt like somebody had hammered a nail into it. But if Flannagan sent for an ambulance, I knew darn well what would happen. They'd take me straight to St. Vincent's hospital—and then, even if nothing was wrong, they'd keep me there overnight for observation. Maybe all day tomorrow, too.

And I really couldn't handle that. I had to go to work in the morning! I had places to go and people to see! (Binky was supposed to take me to the Actors Studio, in case you've forgotten. . . . Okay, so we hadn't made a definite date for that excursion yet, but I was supposed to call him at noon, and we would be going there tomorrow. I was certain of it.)

"You gotta be checked out by a doctor," Flannagan said. "You could have a concussion. Or a hematoma."

Hema-what? "Don't be silly," I said. "I don't have a concussion or a hemathingy. I just had a little too much to drink earlier and I guess I passed out. Must've bumped my head when I fell. But I'm just fine now. There's nothing wrong with me that a few hours of sleep can't fix." I actually wanted to tell Flannagan the truth at that point—try to convince him to launch a citywide search for Aunt Doobie—but I was too wary to open *that* box. Who knew what else would come flying out?

Flannagan rose to full height and glared down at me suspiciously. Very suspiciously. Did he know more about my, er, situation than I thought he did? "Okay, then, get up," he growled, stepping back and crossing his arms over his narrow chest. I've got a few questions to ask you. We'll go sit in the car."

I did *not* want to go sit in the car with him. And I certainly didn't want to answer any of his questions. But I didn't want to stay plopped on the pavement either. So, taking the only path that seemed open to me (besides the hospital, I mean), I reached my hands up to Flannagan, asked for his assistance, and allowed him to pull me to my feet. Then I sucked in a chestful of air, squared my shoulders, surrendered my elbows to the two uniformed officers, and let them guide me—as they would a handcuffed criminal—to the flashing patrol car.

FORTY FIVE MINUTES LATER, I WAS STILL sitting in the back of that car. And Flannagan was still sitting next to me, asking one question after another, grilling me like a hamburger, giving me an even bigger headache than I'd had before. I had told him as much of the truth as I could without getting myself, or Willy, into too much trouble, and now we were going over everything again, for the third or fourth time, and I was on the verge of losing consciousness again.

As headaches and hamburgers go, I felt both raw and over-cooked.

But at least the fireworks had stopped. The waterfront was dark and silent now. The ominous presence of the two police cars had put a damper on the frenzied fun, causing the fire-bugs to pack up all their bombs and rockets and move upriver. The area around the Keller Hotel was dead as a doornail, too. Having been alerted that the cops were in the vicinity, the par-tygoers had—very slowly and systematically—exited the bar in small groups and slunk away in the opposite direction, back toward the heart of the Village. (I know this for a fact because I sat there in the car and watched them go. Willy and Farley left together, by the way, looking quite animated and gay. And by that I mean *happy*.)

"Getting tired yet, Mrs. Turner?" Flannagan prodded. "Had enough?" He was taking pleasure in interrogating me. You could tell by the way his thin lips kept curling up in the corners.

"I've had more than enough," I said, "but apparently *you* haven't. How long do you plan to keep me here?"

"As long as it takes for you to tell me the truth."

"And what makes you think I'm not?"

He let out a nasty chuckle. "And what makes you think I'm a stupid fool?" He loosened his tie (finally) and glared at me across the back seat. "Look, I know your game, Mrs. Turner. I know you're a nosy reporter for *Daring Detective* magazine, not just a secretary as you told me at our first meeting. Did you think I never learned how to read? I've seen your name in the papers on several occasions—in connection with one murder case or another—and it's a damn easy name to remember."

Aaaargh!

"But that doesn't mean I was lying to you," I insisted. "Ask my boss Brandon Pomeroy if you don't believe me. He'll tell you I'm a secretary, and nothing *but* a secretary."

"Then he'd be lying, too."

Score one for the perceptive detective.

"Okay, okay! So I'm a nosy crime writer. I didn't reveal myself before because I was afraid you might tell my boyfriend, Dan Street, about my connection to this case. I'm sure you know him. He's in homicide in the Midtown South precinct, and he's forbidden me to inquire into any more unsolved murder cases—ever! If he thought I was working on a story about the Gray Gordon murder, he'd kill me."

"Oh, yeah?" Flannagan jeered. "At the rate you're going, somebody else is gonna beat him to it."

He had a point. I wouldn't have believed it yesterday—even the Baldy and Blackie incidents hadn't convinced me that I was in serious danger—but the Aunt Doobie incident tonight had made a deep and painful impression. Now I *knew* I was at risk.

"If you know what's good for you," Flannagan went on, "you'll tell me the truth—and I mean the *whole* truth—about what's been going on. You'll tell me everything you've learned about the case so far, and you'll stop meddling in the investigation right now. And here's another tip: You'd better quit dressing like a dyke and hanging out with homosexuals. Willard Sinclair, in particular. He might do to you what he did to Gray Gordon."

"Oh, come off it, Detective Flannagan!" I sputtered. "You don't *really* believe Willy killed Gray! You can't! Willy is a kind, gentle, and very *squeamish* man. He's as dainty and fastidious as your grandmother. He couldn't bring himself to carve up a turkey, much less a human being!"

"Leave my grandmother out of this." Flannagan fired up a Camel and blew the smoke in my direction. "You could be wrong about your homo pal, Mrs. Turner. Ever think of that?

Sinclair is our number one suspect. He's the same blood type as the killer."

"Yes, he told me that, but—"

"But what? The proven facts don't mean anything to you? You've decided the fat little faggot is innocent, and that's the end of it? I thought you were smarter than that, Mrs. Turner. You're just begging for trouble. For all you know, Willard Sinclair was the one who knocked your block off tonight."

By this point I wanted to knock off his. "Don't be ridiculous! Willy didn't even know when I left the bar. I shot out of there in a flash because . . ." *Take it easy, Paige. Slow down. Be cool.* I fully intended to tell Flannagan about Aunt Doobie, but I wanted to choose my words carefully, make sure I didn't reveal more than was good for me. Or Willy.

"Yeah, yeah, yeah," Flannagan scoffed. "I've heard it all before. You left the bar because you had too much to drink and you needed to get some air. But you might as well ditch that pack of lies right now. We know what really happened. We've known it all along." The gloating smile on his face was so annoying I wanted to wipe it off with my fist. (When you think you *look* manly, you kind of *feel* manly, too.)

Luckily for both of us, I took the passive (i.e., feminine) route instead. "I'm sorry, Detective Flannagan," I cajoled. "I haven't been totally honest with you. I'm so scared and confused I don't know what I'm saying. But look, I have an idea. Why don't you tell me what *you* know, and then I'll tell you what *I* know. That way, we can compare notes and work out the truth together." I smiled sweetly at him and fluttered my lashes, hoping I could get him to go first.

To my great astonishment, he did. (Sometimes you really *can* catch more flies with honey.)

"We learned by telephone at approximately ten thirty-five tonight," he began, speaking in a lofty, official tone, "that a woman had been attacked at the corner of West and Barrow. The caller reported seeing a dark-haired man in dark clothing hit the victim on the back of the head—with a brick, or a rock, or a hunk of cement—and then run away on West toward Christopher. About halfway up the block, the assailant jumped into the back seat of a black Lincoln limousine, and the car took off for parts unknown."

Black limousine? Baldy. Dark hair and dark clothing?

Aunt Doobie. Or maybe Blackie. Cripes! It could have been anybody! Does Baldy have a wig?

"We arrived on the scene within minutes," Flannagan went on, "and found you lying on the ground in the dark, unconscious and unprotected. There were no onlookers or eyewitnesses—even the man who called us was gone. You regained consciousness almost immediately, though, claiming to feel fine and showing no signs of serious injury. There was a big rock lying nearby which may or may not have been the assault weapon. We're taking it into the lab for testing."

Flannagan wiped his sweaty face with his handkerchief and opened the top button of his shirt. "That's my story," he said. "Now you tell me yours."

I knew it was time to come clean. So I did (well, clean*er*, anyway). I admitted that I was working on the Gray Gordon story, and that I was trying to find the killer (for a variety of reasons, truth and justice being among them), and that I had withheld that information from the police in order to save myself—and Willy—from further scrutiny and admonishment.

"But now I realize that was the wrong thing to do," I said, in total honesty, "and I'm ready to tell you everything I know." *With just a couple of itty bitty details left out.* I took an L&M out of the pack in my breast pocket, lit it with a match (Flannagan never extended his lighter), and started puffing and talking.

Confessing that Abby and I had begun looking for clues to the killer's identity the same day we discovered the body, I gave Flannagan a full account of our expedition to Stewart's Cafeteria, my brief talk with Blondie and Blackie, our infiltration of the Morosco Theatre, and our chance meeting with Rhonda Blake. Then I told him about the list of phone messages Rhonda had written down for Gray.

I didn't tell him that I had stolen the message pad, of course (if he charged me with evidence tampering, I'd be in trouble too sticky to sidestep), but I did tell him almost everything I could remember about the list, including Aunt Doobie's room number at the Mayflower Hotel, and the four messages from Randy. The only call I didn't mention was the one from Binky. I was afraid if I gave Flannagan Binky's name and number, he (Flannagan) would screw up my possible meeting with him (Binky) tomorrow, and then the names of Gray's friends—or, most importantly, his enemies—at the Actors Studio would be lost to me forever.

When he had finished taking notes about Gray's telephone messages, I told Flannagan about my trip to the Mayflower to see Aunt Doobie, giving him a full description of the man who was registered in room 96 as John Smith. Then, continuing to relate the events in the order in which they occurred, I told him about seeing Rhonda Blake and Baldy at the Vanguard, reporting that Baldy had asked the bartender a bunch of questions about me, then departed with Rhonda in a black limousine.

I didn't describe my crazy, terrified flight home from the Vanguard that night (it was too embarrassing for words), but I did divulge the shock and alarm I'd felt when I saw Blackie lurking in the doorway of the laundromat across the street. And then, after that, I gave Flannagan a full account of my excursion with Willy to the Keller Hotel, where I had spotted Aunt Doobie—or John Smith, or whoever—and chased him out to the street.

"But by the time I got outside," I recounted, "the man had disappeared. I ran over to the waterfront to look for him, but so many screaming people were dashing around and so many fireworks were exploding, I couldn't continue the search. I retreated to a secluded spot under the highway and hid behind a support beam, hoping he would reappear. That's when I got hit."

"And you never saw who did it?" Flannagan probed.

"Nope, but I'd bet my last banana it was Aunt Doobie. He has dark hair and he was wearing dark clothing, just like your caller said. And he was definitely in the vicnity." I flicked my burnt-out cigarette stub through the open car window. "But it could have been Blackie, too, I guess. He wears black and has dark hair, and he may have been following me. Or maybe it was Baldy. He has no hair at all, but he has a black limousine. And he could have a wig . . . Oh, god! I don't know who the hell it was! I only know who it wasn't. And you can take my word on this, Detective Flannagan, it *wasn't* Willy!"

Flannagan chuckled. "I know that," he said. "I made that accusation just to get your reaction. Mr. Sinclair is a raving queer, and it's likely he murdered Gray Gordon, but he didn't attack you. He doesn't come anywhere close to fitting the caller's description. He probably doesn't even know the whole thing happened."

Now it was my turn to get suspicious. Why was Flannagan so darn sure on this particular point? Why had he adopted, without question, an unverified account given to him by an anonymous caller? Smelled kind of fishy to me.

"You can't be certain of that," I declared, sneering and smirking, giving him what I hoped was a taste of his own cocky medicine. "How do you know Willy didn't knock me out and then call the station himself and give you a phony description of a phony attacker?" I crossed my arms over my chest, leaned against the car door, and shot him a look that said, *harrumph!*

Flannagan wasn't chuckling anymore.

Now he was laughing out loud.

"If you really think Mr. Sinclair would do something like that, Mrs. Turner," he said between guffaws, "and if it'll make you feel any better, I'll gladly reconsider my position. As far as I'm concerned, that creepy little queer is capable of anything."

X@#%!!*

Do I have to tell you how utterly imbecilic I felt at that moment? Not only had I planted a warped idea in Flannagan's already warped mind, but I had, in the process, cast aspersions on the very person I was trying to protect! I was the world's worst detective. I was a worthless piece of ca-ca. I was a danger to myself and everyone around me. I should be writing about makeup, macaroni, and mops—not murder.

Still, something was really bothering me about the anonymous caller—or, rather, Flannagan's swift acceptance of his supposedly eyewitness tale. Shouldn't the details have been examined more closely? Shouldn't the informant's story have been verified by at least one other witness before becoming a matter of police record?

My head was hurting more than ever.

"Do you think I could go home now, Detective Flannagan?" I asked. "I've told you everything I know, and I'm really beat. No pun intended."

"Of course, Mrs. Turner," he said, with a mocking smile. (At least he had stopped laughing.) "We're finished here. One of my officers will drive you."

"Thanks," I said. "But before I go can I ask you one big favor?"

"What's that?"

"If you happen to see or talk to Detective Dan Street, would you please not say anything about what happened here tonight, or tell him about my previous participation in this case? That's all over now, and I really don't want him to worry about me." (Translation: stop loving me.)

"Ha!" Flannagan snorted. "For a nosy know-it-all, you sure don't know your boyfriend very well. Street's the smartest, most determined dick in the whole damn department. Nobody can keep a secret from him—least of all you."

Chapter 23

I GOT HOME SHORTLY AFTER MIDNIGHT
and went straight to bed. Abby and Jimmy and Otto weren't
back yet—but even if they'd been there, beckoning me next
door for company, comfort, conversation, and a nightcap, I
would have declined. I didn't want to talk to anybody. Not
even Dan. And to make sure I wouldn't have to, I took my
phone off the hook before lugging myself and the electric fan
upstairs.

I don't remember what happened after that. I know I
must've set the fan on the dresser, plugged it in and turned it
on, and then stripped off my clothes and flopped down on the
bed naked, because that was the way I found things in the
morning. The fan was blowing a hot wind over my bare skin,
and my clothes were lying in a jumble on the bedroom floor.

My head felt like a volleyball full of sand, but it didn't hurt
so much anymore. The bump wasn't as swollen as before, and
I was able to pull myself up to a sitting position on the side of
the bed without feeling the least bit dizzy. When I took a look
at the clock on my bedside table, however, my senses went
into a cyclone spin. It was a quarter to nine! I was so late for
work it was sinful.

Jumping to my feet and tearing into the bathroom, I took a
fast shower, dried myself off, and got dressed in a frenzy—

which will explain how I wound up wearing a shocking pink blouse with a red plaid skirt and a pair of green platformed sandals. My stocking seams were twisted every which way, and I applied my makeup in such haste that my poor face looked like an abstract portrait by Picasso.

After my mad dash to the subway, my two connecting train rides (first uptown, then across), and my hot, sweaty scramble to my office building at 43rd and Third, I was a complete wreck. Flying past the lobby coffee shop where I usually bought my morning muffin, I darted into the first open elevator I came to and took it to the ninth floor.

As I exited the elevator and stumbled down the hall to the *Daring Detective* office, I tried to pull myself together—i.e., straighten my clothes, smooth down my hair, act cool. But it was hopeless. (Well, it's *hard* to act cool when you look like a character in a Looney Tunes cartoon.) In an effort to silence the office entry bell and slip inside unnoticed, I opened the door as slowly and quietly as I possibly could and tried to squeeze through it sideways.

My efforts were so fruitless they were foolish. The entry bell jangled as loudly as it always did, and before I was even halfway through the door, all three of my male coworkers— Mario, Mike, and Lenny—were staring up at me from their desks in the large communal workroom, watching me try to sneak inside.

"Look who's here!" Mario crowed, making sure that his voice was loud enough to be heard by our boss, Harvey Crockett (whose private office door was, as usual, standing wide open). "It's our own little page-turner, Paige Turner! And she's only an hour and forty-five minutes late! Guess we're lucky she showed up at all." Mario Caruso, the art director of the magazine, was a short, dark, thickset (and thickheaded) man in his early thirties who liked to cause trouble. Especially for me.

"Good morning, all," I said, squaring my shoulders, tossing my head, and stepping all the way into the office. I was trying to appear self-possessed, aloof, and indifferent to Mario's taunting remarks, but I felt as cool and composed as the melting mannequins in the big fire scene in the 3-D thriller, *House of Wax*.

"Hey, what's the matter with you?" Mike asked me. "You

look awful." Mike Davidson was *DD*'s tall, wiry assistant editor and head staff writer (I was the tail). Mike was a lousy writer, but—thanks to the sexist policies of our woman-hating editorial director, Brandon Pomery—his bylines outnumbered mine twenty to one. "Who picked out your clothes this morning?" Mike jeered, skimming his palm over the shelf of his sand-colored flattop. "Rin Tin Tin?"

Now, do you think that wisecrack was even the weeniest bit funny? Neither did I. I thought it was as lame and sloppy as the pitifully dull stories Mike cranked out for *Daring Detective*. Mario, on the other hand, must have found Mike's quip to be the funniest darn thing he ever heard in his life, because he was laughing so hard I thought he was going to spit up. His fat, swarthy face turned as pink as my blouse, and his spasms of hilarity were so violent his greasy ducktail was coming unglued.

But my dear friend Lenny Zimmerman, the lowly art assistant whose desk was situated in the farthest depths of the common workroom, wasn't laughing at all. He was peering at me through his crooked, black-rimmed, bottle-thick glasses, with a look of intense concern on his pale, narrow face. He knew that something was wrong—that something bad had happened to me. Ever since the day he'd saved my life (which was over a year ago, when I was working on my very first murder story), Lenny had been able to read me like a book.

And that was what he was doing now—turning my pages, so to speak—trying to judge how much trouble I'd gotten myself into this time.

"Pipe down!" Harvey Crockett barked, sticking his large white-haired head through his open office door. "Get back to work! It's ten fifteen!" He gave me a snarly, disgruntled look. "Especially you, Paige. Gotta make up for lost time."

It wasn't just my lateness that had upset him. It was also the holiday. Crockett was a smart but stodgy ex-newspaperman whose only reason for living was his job. He wasn't proud that he was now the executive editor of *Daring Detective* magazine instead of a reporter for the *Daily News*, but he wasn't ashamed of it, either. The actual product or the nature of his work didn't matter that much to him; it was just the *job*. And right now, coming off an unwelcome three-day weekend, Crockett was suffering from job withdrawal.

Caffeine withdrawal, too. "Make some coffee, Paige," he sputtered, "and make it now. This place needs a jumpstart."

"Yes, Mr. Crockett," I said, dropping my purse down on my desk (which, since I also served as the office receptionist, was the one closest to the entrance). I hurtled across the room, hoisted the heavy Coffeemaster off the table where it was always stationed, and hauled it toward the door. Pitching Lenny what I hoped was a reassuring smile, I scooted out into the hall and headed for the ladies' room to wash out the percolator and fill it with water.

As the only female on the *DD* staff, I always had to make the coffee. (That's women's work, in case you haven't heard.) I normally resented being the coffee slave, but today I was grateful for the chore. The ladies' room was quiet and the water was cool. And when I'd finished cleaning and filling the pot, I had a chance to catch my breath, adjust my makeup, and straighten my stocking seams. I couldn't do anything about the mismatched colors of my crazy outfit, but after realigning the buttons on my blouse, and closing the zipper on my skirt, I looked and felt a little better.

When I returned to the workroom and began spooning coffee into the percolator, Mr. Crockett was satisfied. "Bring me a cup when it's ready," he said, stepping back inside his office.

"Ditto," said Mario, who was watching (or rather, ogling) my every move and making ugly smoochy faces whenever I glanced in his direction.

"Me, too," Mike chimed in, never looking up from the story he was pecking out, with two fingers, on his typewriter.

Lenny didn't ask me for coffee. (He rarely drank the stuff, but when he did, he got up and got it himself.) And he didn't say anything else to me, either. He didn't have to. His urgent, puzzled, anxious gaze was saying it all.

I was sorry to be causing Lenny such worry, but there was nothing I could do to ease his concerns right now. If I went over to talk to him, Mario would start making more nasty—and loud—remarks, and then Mr. Crockett would come bursting out of his office to growl at us again. And that wouldn't do anybody any good. Lifting my shoulders in an apologetic shrug, I winked at Lenny and tossed him another quick smile. Then I turned my back on the boys in the workroom and faced a different pile of problems.

• • •

THERE WAS SO MUCH WORK STACKED UP
on my desk I wanted to run back to the ladies' room and hide
out there till lunchtime. There were letters to open and sort,
newspapers to clip, stories to edit and rewrite, galleys to
proofread, invoices to record, photos to label and file. And it
was already twenty to eleven! And I had to call Binky at noon!
And if *DD*'s second-in-command, Brandon Pomeroy, happened to stroll into the office before I left on my lunch hour,
he would see all the paperwork on my desk, and find out how
late I'd come in this morning, and then he wouldn't let me
leave at all.

Which would throw a big wrench in my plans to visit the
Actors Studio.

However, I wasn't *that* worried about Pomeroy coming in
early. Truth was, he hardly ever made it into the office before
lunch. (When you're a close relative of Oliver Rice Harrington—the powerful and wealthy publishing mogul who owns
the magazine you work for—you can show up whenever you
like. And when you're a lazy, jaded snob who breakfasts on
dry martinis, you like to show up late.) Nevertheless, Pomeroy
had been known to pull surprises out of his hat from time to
time, and I was praying that today would not be one of those
times.

After I served my boss and coworkers their coffee, I took
another survey of my work load. The newspapers were taking
up the most room on my desk, so I chose to tackle them first.
Snatching the *Daily Mirror* off the top of the pile, I began flipping through it as fast as I could, looking for juicy crime stories to clip out for our files (one of my more mindless daily
chores). There was one story about Gray, but it was even
briefer and less informative than the article I'd read on Sunday. A wave of sadness washed over me as I cut the piece out
and put it in the labeled and dated manila folder I had set aside
for Pomeroy. (Reading the new crime clips was the only aspect of his job Pomeroy seemed to relish, and if the folder of
clippings wasn't sitting on his desk when he came in, he'd
have a royal snit fit.)

The other three morning editions also ran short articles
about Gray's murder, merely recapping the barest facts and
reporting that the case was still under investigation. Two other

homicides had occured in the city in the past week (one in Harlem, one in the Bronx), and they were rehashed as well.

As I was cutting out these articles and putting them in the folder, I snuck a quick look at some of the day's top stories: The national economy had shown a strong upsurge during the first six months of 1955, smashing all peacetime records; Senate Majority Leader Lyndon B. Johnson had suffered a moderately severe heart attack while visiting a friend in Virginia; The grand opening of Disneyland Amusement Park in Anaheim, California, was scheduled for July 17th.

But the biggest story of the day, bar none, was the heat. WE'RE HAVIN' A HEAT WAVE! one headline proclaimed. NO RELIEF IN SIGHT! cried another. Actually, the temperature *had* dropped a bit—all the way down to 95.8 degrees!—but the humidity was so high nobody could tell the difference. So the papers were jammed with advertisements for products that promised to keep you cool and dry. I gazed with longing at the full-page ad for Ambassador Window Air Conditioners, knowing I'd never be able to save up the 169 bucks I'd need to buy one. But all was not lost; there was hope for me yet. For just seventy-nine cents I could "Beat the Heat with Mexsana Medicated Powder!" Maybe I'd go get some after work.

When I finished clipping the papers, I opened, sorted, and distributed the mail. Then I fixed all the typos, misspellings, and bad grammar in two of Mike's stories, wrote the captions for three four-page layouts, proofread about a dozen galleys, put the corrected stories, captions, and proofs in a large envelope, and called for a messenger to take them to the typesetter. I labeled all the photos and took them into the file room, but left them in a stack on top of one of the file cabinets, deciding I'd organize and put them away later.

In an effort to clear my desk (or just make it *look* clear in case Pomeroy came in), I hid the batch of unrecorded invoices in my top left-hand drawer. Then, at twelve o'clock on the dot, after glancing over my shoulder and determining that none of my coworkers had me under close observation, I hunched over the top of my desk, stealthily picked up the phone, and dialed Binky.

Chapter 24

"YEAH?" BINKY ANSWERED, AFTER THE
eightieth (okay, probably just the eighth) ring. His voice was
so deep and gravelly, I figured I'd woken him up. "Who's calling?" he growled. "What do you want?"

"It's Phoebe Starr," I said, keeping my voice low and cup-
ping my hand around the mouthpiece (I didn't want Mario or
Mike, or even Lenny, to hear what I was saying). "You told
me to call you at noon. Remember?"

He groaned. "I'd rather forget, but you won't let me." He
sounded more than a little annoyed.

"Sorry," I said, "but I was hoping you could show me
around the Studio today. And my lunch hour is starting right
now. I'll meet you anywhere you say." I knew I was being
too curt and aggressive, but I didn't have any choice. My behavior was being controlled by the clock. And my lack of
privacy.

"Cripes!" Binky croaked. "Where's the friggin' fire? You
just woke me up, little girl. I didn't get home until six this
morning, and the only place I'm going now is back to bed."

"Then can you meet me later, when I get off work?" I
begged, still keeping my voice and word-count low.

He groaned again, even louder than before. "A lot of actresses are pushy, but you're the goddamn pushiest! Don't you ever give up?"

"No. I can't afford to. This means too much to me."

"Oh, all right!" he surrendered, heaving a sigh the strength of a hurricane. "Meet me at the Studio at six thirty. I'm auditioning for Elia Kazan at seven. I'll take you in with me and you can watch."

Elia Kazan? The director of Cat on a Hot Tin Roof? *What the heck is that all about!?*

"Thank you so much, Binky!" I said, projecting as much phony gratitude and excitement as I could without attracting the attention of the guys in the workroom. "I'll see you at—"

There was no reason for me to repeat the time or the place. Binky had already hung up.

And the very second *I* hung up, Pomeroy walked in.

I was shocked to the core—both by my lazy boss's extra-early arrival, and by my good timing (which was an equally rare occurrence). "Good morning, Mr. Pomeroy," I said, adopting my most polite (and, according to Abby, puke-provoking) demeanor. "Did you have a nice holiday?"

"No, I did *not*, Mrs. Turner," he said, standing tall in the front of the workroom, removing his beige linen suit jacket and hanging it on the coat tree. "Thank you so much for reminding me." He took his pipe out of his jacket pocket and breezed past me, nose in the air, to his desk right across the aisle from mine. Pomeroy was just six years older than I, and we had worked side-by-side for over three years, but we still—at Pomeroy's insistence—addressed each other by last names only. He even expected me to call him sir.

"I'm sorry, sir," I said. "I didn't mean to—"

"Stop!" he commanded, stretching his arm out, palm first, in my direction. (He looked like an irate traffic cop.) "I don't want to hear any more about it." Pushing his expensive tortoise-shell-rimmed glasses higher on his handsome face, he sat down at his desk, brushed his fingers over his dark brown hair and mustache, and began filling his Dunhill with fresh tobacco.

I could hear Mario snickering behind me. He was enoy-ing watching me squirm. Pomeroy liked it, too. I could tell by the way his mustache was twitching.

I didn't like it at all, though, so—after smashing imaginary pies in both their faces—I got up and went into the file room to file the photos. About twenty minutes later, when I had finished that job, I went back into the workroom, thinking I would just snag my purse and go down to the lobby coffee shop for lunch. I was so hungry I felt faint. (Well, I hadn't had any breakfast, you know!)

"Where do you think you're going?" Pomeroy asked, as I picked my purse up off my desk and turned toward the door.

"Out to lunch, sir," I said. "It's twelve thirty. I always go out at twelve thirty."

"Not today you don't." He crossed his arms over his chest and turned in his swivel chair to face me. "I've just learned that you came in very late this morning, Mrs. Turner. Almost two hours late." He shot Mario a quick glance, then turned his attention back to me. "So I'm rescinding your lunch hour today. Tomorrow, too. You have to make up the time."

"But, sir, I—"

"No excuses, Mrs. Turner. You're supposed to be in the office by eight thirty. You may have forgotten this condition of your employment, but I can assure you *I* haven't. And if you think—"

Pomeroy's tongue-lashing was interrupted when Harvey Crockett barrelled out of his office and came huffing up to the front of the workroom. "I'm going to the barber," he told me, maneuvering his stubby legs and bulging belly over to the coat rack. He unhooked his cream-colored Panama and anchored it on his large hoary head. "After that I'm going to lunch with a new paper supplier at the Quill. If anybody calls, tell 'em I'll be back at two thirty."

"Yes, Mr. Crockett," I said to his back as he bustled up to the door and left.

Mike and Mario were just a few steps behind. (They always go out to lunch together, and they always leave within two or three minutes of Mr. Crockett's departure.) Grabbing their hats and jackets off the coat tree, they nodded to Pomeroy, leered at me, muttered a joint "see-ya-later," and disappeared through the door. Even after the door had swung all the way shut, I could hear them laughing out in the hall. (It never fails. Whenever I get in trouble with Pomeroy, Mike and Mario get in a giddy good mood.)

As soon as they were gone, Pomeroy went back to bullying me. "You seem to think you can come to work whenever you please, Mrs. Turner," he said, taking up where he'd left off. "But you are greatly mistaken. We expect you to work a full eight-hour day, with just one hour off for lunch, and anything short of that is totally unacceptable. Do you understand me?"

"Yes, Mr. Pomeroy."

"Good. Because I have the power to fire you, you know, and that's exactly what I'll do if you don't obey the rules."

"Yes, Mr. Pomeroy."

"And conduct yourself in a proper manner."

"Yes, Mr. Pomeroy."

"And complete all the work that's assigned to you."

"Yes, Mr. Pomeroy."

(Before you throw up, please let me explain my nauseating obsequiousness: I really, *really* needed to keep my job. The few dime-store mystery novels I'd published hadn't earned me enough to pay my Sears and Roebuck bills, much less my rent. And a single working woman needs clothes as well as a place to live, don't you know.)

Pomeroy rose to his feet and gave me a withering look. Then he picked something up from his desk, and stepped across the aisle to mine.

"Did you know this man?" he asked, putting the stack of news clips about Gray Gordon down in front of me and spreading them out like a fan. "He was murdered, last Saturday, in his apartment down in the Village. You live in the Village, too, so I was wondering if you ever met him."

"No, I didn't," I said. *At least not while he was alive.* I was astonished that Pomeroy was discussing a murder case—especially this murder case—with me. Such conversations were always reserved for Mike, since he was the one who would be getting the story assignments.

"Did you ever hear any talk about him?" Pomeroy went on. "Any gossip or anything?"

"Uh, no," I said, reluctant to answer Pomeroy's questions until I knew why he was asking them. "But I did see an article about him in the Saturday *Times*," I added, feeling the need to offer something. "He was an actor—an understudy—and when the star of his show was overcome by heatstroke, Gray Gordon stepped in to play the lead. He made his Broadway debut in last Friday night's performance of *Cat on a Hot Tin Roof*, and the *Times* theater critic said he was brilliant—that he was going to be a big star."

"I saw that article, too," Pomeroy admitted, "and all the murder reports in the papers the next day. That's why I came in early today; I wanted to see what the new reports would say."

"They don't say much of anything."

"Right," Pomeroy replied. "The police obviously don't want any details about their investigation getting out. They must have asked the papers to lay off the story until the killer is caught."

"Yes, that's probably what happened."

"So there isn't enough information for Mike to write a clip story."

"No, I guess there isn't."

"Which is why I'm assigning the Gray Gordon story to you."

What?! Are my ears working right? Did Pomeroy just say he was giving me the Gray Gordon assignment? He must be sick or something.

"Since you live in the Village," Pomeroy went on— actually speaking to me in a civil tone!—"it'll be easy for you to poke around the area, talk to the locals, listen to rumors, and gather intelligence about the murder. Perhaps you'll even dig up some clues for the police. At the very least, you'll be collecting details and descriptions for your story's background."

"Oh, thank you, Mr. Pomeroy!" I said, jumping to accept the assignment before he could change his mind. "I appreciate your confidence in me, and I'll do the very best I can. In fact, I'll start my investigation this evening, just as soon as I get off work."

"See that you do," he said, brusquely turning away from my desk and marching up to the front of the workroom. He took his linen jacket off the coat rack and put it on. "I'm going out to lunch now, Mrs. Turner. You will stay here in the office and do all the work you should have completed this morning. I expect you to be finished by the time I get back." His civil tone had vanished completely.

"Yes, sir," I said, wearing a frozen smile and holding my breath till he disappeared through the door. Then I spun around to face Lenny, thrust my fist in the air, and shouted, "Yahoo!"

Chapter 25

"I DON'T BELIEVE IT," LENNY SPUT-
tered, scooting up to the front of the workroom and sitting
down in the guest chair near my desk. His cheeks were
flushed and his glasses were crooked. "The creep finally
broke down and gave you a *real* story—not just a lousy clip
job!" He leaned closer and slapped his hand down on the
desktop. "I never thought I'd live to see the day! What do you
think happened to him? He must've had a three-martini
morning."

"I don't think so, Lenny," I said, still elated about the unexpected assignment, but beginning to question Pomeroy's
motives. "He seemed perfectly sober, if you want to know the
truth. And he came to work so early! And he said himself that
it was all because of this particular murder story." As surprised as I was that my misogynistic boss had given *me* an important (i.e., lurid and sensational) homicide to cover, I was
even more shocked that it was the Gray Gordon homicide.
Did Pomeroy have some knowledge of my personal interest in
the case, or was the whole thing just a crazy coincidence?

"The man must have grown a new brain," Lenny said with
a sniff. "But it sure took him long enough. I mean, how many
exclusive, exciting, and *true* behind-the-scenes murder stories
does a person have to write before Pomeroy gets the message?

If it hadn't been for Mr. Crockett, your three big inside stories never would have been printed in *Daring Detective*. And they certainly wouldn't have been featured on the cover! And then those three editions would have had the same lousy forty-two-percent sales all the other *DD* issues seem to have, instead of selling seventy-four to seventy-eight percent of a much larger print run. God, Paige! Pomeroy should be shot for keeping you down the way he does. The way he treats you is a crime."

See why I love Lenny Zimmerman so much?

"He probably treats all women the same way," I mused. "I bet he hates his mother."

Lenny's eyes widened in disbelief. His own parents were so wise and wonderful, he couldn't imagine hating either one of them. "Speaking of mothers," he said, mouth stretching into a wholesome grin, "mine made a big batch of potato pancakes yesterday. And she put about six of 'em in my lunch today, along with some homemade applesauce and my usual salami sandwich. Are you hungry?"

"Do babies burp?"

Lenny laughed and stood up. "Stay right where you are," he said, heading for his drawing table in the back of the room. "I'll get my lunchbox." Two seconds later he was back sitting in the guest chair across from me, opening his big black lunchpail (the one I bought him for Christmas last year), and taking out two waxed paper-wrapped packages, which he placed on the desk between us. Then out came a Mason jar full of applesauce.

"So what's your hot new story all about?" Lenny asked, unwrapping the salami sandwich and splitting it in two. "Who got killed?"

"A young actor by the name of Gray Gordon," I told him. "He was stabbed to death in his Greenwich Village apartment, just a couple of blocks over from me. That's why Pomeroy gave me the assignment. He figures I have a better sense of the territory than Mike does, that I'll be able to dig up more information." I took a huge bite of my half-a-sandwich and chomped it eagerly.

"You'd do a better job investigating and writing *any* story," Lenny declared, opening the package of potato pancakes and giving three of them to me. "Mike Davidson has no sense. He should be forced to wear a dunce cap twenty-four hours a day."

I giggled. "And what about Mario? What should his sentence be?"

"That's easy," Lenny snorted. "Mario Caruso should stand nose-to-the-wall for eternity, while legions of *un*blindfolded children pin tails on his donkey."

We chuckled together for a few moments, enjoying the goofy images that Lenny had just invoked. Then we put a lid on our laughter and got down to some serious eating. The crispy, golden, onion-flecked pancakes were out of this world and, between bites, Lenny and I took turns spooning the fragrant applesauce straight from the jar into our greedy mouths. All the food was devoured in nine minutes flat.

"So what's with the clashing duds?" Lenny asked, swiping his finger through a glob of stray mustard and licking it clean. "I never saw you look quite so, uh, colorful. Did you get dressed in the dark?"

"No, just in a hurry. I forgot to set my alarm and I woke up really late."

"Oh, c'mon, Paige! That's not the whole story and you know it. I took a good look at you when you came in this morning, and you had a lot more than punctuality on your mind. You looked like you were running for your life—not just to get to work on time."

(See? I *told* you Lenny had me pegged.)

"And later on I saw you whispering on the phone to somebody, trying to hide what you were doing. You're up to something," he went on. "Something dangerous. And I'll give you five seconds to tell me what it is."

I spent the allotted time deciding whether or not to tell Lenny the truth. I didn't want him to worry about me or feel like he had to watch over me (having saved my life once, he might feel honor-bound to attempt it again), but I didn't want to deprive myself of his protective camaraderie, either (it feels good to have somebody know your troubles and be on your side).

When my five seconds were up, I leaned back in my chair, lit a cigarette, and spilled the beans. All of them.

•   •   •

LENNY STARTED YELLING AT ME THE
very second I finished the tale of my gruesome "holiday"
weekend. "God damn it, Paige! Have you lost your goddamn
mind? This is really critical! How did you ever let yourself get
involved in such a deadly mess?" (So much for protective camaraderie.)

"I didn't *let* myself get involved!" I shrieked. "I was
forcibly involved by fate. And by Abby—although it wasn't
her fault, either. Do you think we *chose* to discover the body?
Do you think we *allowed* ourselves the pleasure of finding
poor Gray slashed to bloody shreds on his living room
floor?"

"Look, I didn't mean it like that. What I meant was—"

"Oh, hush! I know what you meant! You were saying that
I shouldn't have started my own investigation, that it was up
to the police to find the killer, not me!" I struck a match and
fired up another L&M. "But what the hell was I supposed to
do? Just sit back and let Detective Flannagan pin the murder
on Willy Sinclair, even though I know he didn't do it?" I took
a drag on my cigarette, then spewed the fumes out in an angry
swoosh.

"What makes you so sure it wasn't Willy?" Lenny probed,
squinting at me through his uncommonly thick lenses. "All
the evidence points to him, but for some reason you're ignoring it. You know what I think? I think—"

"Please keep your thoughts to yourself," I broke in, speaking in a much nastier tone than intended. "I can't handle any
more opposition right now. Dan's furious at me, Flannagan's
up in arms, and now you. . . . But there's no turning back. I'm
working on *assignment* now, you know. If I don't continue
with my investigation, and produce an accurate, detailed,
well-researched account of the murder, I could lose my job. Is
that what you want?"

Lenny was hurt by my hotheaded response. And I felt so
bad about the way I'd just spoken to him I wanted to apologize on the spot, beg him to forgive me on bended knee. I
would have done it, too, if Mike and Mario hadn't picked that
very moment to come strutting back into the office, posturing
and crowing like two demented roosters.

"Hey, Mike, would you look at this?" Mario said, gesturing toward Lenny and me with a malignant smile on his

sweaty face. "The lovebirds had a little picnic together. Isn't that sweet?" (Mario was jealous of my close friendship with Lenny, so he made fun of it at every opportunity.)

"Yeah," Mike said. "Real sweet."

"Too bad we busted up their cozy little heart-to-heart," Mario needled.

"Yeah," Mike said. "Too bad."

"But now that we're here, and the lunch hour is officially over," Mario went on, "don't you think they ought to stop slobbering all over each other and get back to work?"

"Yeah," Mike said. "Sure do."

"Because if they don't," Mario added, "Mr. Pomeroy will probably find out about their wicked waste of time, and make them work late tonight. And I really would hate to see that happen, wouldn't you?"

"Yep," Mike said. "Sure would." But even he was getting bored with Mario's stupid little game. Looping his hat and jacket on the coat rack, Mike strode down the aisle past my desk and sat down at his own. He rolled a piece of paper into his typewriter and started pecking out another sure-to-be-shoddy clip story.

Without his accomplice at his side, Mario lost some of his spiteful steam. Hanging up his own hat and jacket, he turned to Lenny and inquired, "Did you finish the cover paste-up yet?"

"No, I'm waiting for some repros from the typesetter," Lenny replied. "They should be delivered this afternoon."

"What about the 'Gun-Happy Harlot from Harlem' story? Did you finish that layout?"

"Uh, no . . . it's not due until next week."

"I don't care when it's due!" Mario ranted. "Go back to your desk and get to work on it right now!"

Lenny's face turned beet red, but he didn't say anything to Mario. He didn't dare. Mario was his immediate boss and could have him fired at any time. Without a groan, or even a sigh, of protest, Lenny rose to his feet, plunked the empty Mason jar in his metal lunchpail, and then carried the rattling pail—along with his rattled pride—back to his place at the rear of the workroom.

Deliberately avoiding eye contact with Mario, I crumpled up the greasy sheets of waxed paper and tossed them in my wastebasket. Then I took the stack of unrecorded invoices out of my drawer and began studying the one on top as if it were a new edition of the Kinsey Report. I was so mad at Mario, I was afraid of myself. If Mario said one word to me—or one more word to Lenny—I might tell him where to get off. Or sock him in the nose. Or bonk him on the bean with Pomeroy's marble ashtray. And then I'd either be fired for insubordination, or arrested and charged with assault, or taken into custody and booked for murder.

So Mario and I were both saved by the office entry bell when Mr. Crockett came back from lunch early. "It's hot as hell out there," he said, just in case we hadn't noticed (or read the morning headlines). He hooked his light blue seersucker jacket on one branch of the coat tree and perched his Panama on another. "Bring me some coffee, Paige," he grunted, pushing his wide body down the narrow center aisle of the workroom, thereby forcing Mario, who had been standing in the middle of the aisle, to hustle back to his desk. (Lenny and I shared a secret smile over that one.)

After taking Mr. Crockett his coffee (and ignoring Mario's lewd winks and gestures along the way), I went back to my desk and began studying the invoices for real, putting them in chronological order, tallying the amounts, checking them against my pre-publication records, entering them in the ledger. This tedious job, plus a complete retyping of one of Mike's more heavily corrected stories, kept me busy for the rest of the afternoon. Pomeroy came back about three, but he merely sat down in his cushy swivel chair, turned his face toward the wall, stretched his long legs out in front of him, and fell into an alcoholic snooze. (His morning martini fast had obviously been reversed.)

At the stroke of five, I walked into Mr. Crockett's office and closed the door behind me. "Mr. Pomeroy has given me a very important story assignment," I told him, "which is going to require a lot of after-hours legwork. May I have your permission to leave early tonight? I have to meet an informant all the way across town at six."

(Okay, so I lied about the time. But just by thirty measely minutes! And a harried, hungry, hard-working girl like myself is entitled to a measely thirty-minute dinner break, wouldn't you say?)

Mr. Crockett barely looked up from his copy of the *Saturday Evening Post*. "Okay," he said, switching his soggy cigar stub from one corner of his mouth to the other. "Go on. Scoot."

Chapter 26

I LEARNED FROM THE PHONE BOOK
that the Actors Studio was located at 432 West 44th Street, between Ninth and Tenth, so I took the 42nd Street shuttle to
Times Square. Then I pushed my way through the dizzying
rush-hour crowd to the nearest exit. (I don't have to tell you
how hot it was, because you know that already, right? I mean,
descriptive detail is good up to a point, after which it can turn
rancid. Especially in the heat.)

I had a hot dog with mustard and relish at Nedick's, and a
frosty tall one at a nearby A&W Root Beer stand. And then—
despite the amused gawks my gaudy multicolored outfit kept
attracting—I proudly proceeded to 44th Street, turned left,
and began the two-and-a-half-block trek westward. I was
walking on air. I was working on an important story assignment! So what if I looked like a parrot? A legitimate professional journalist on assignment could wear anything she darn
well pleased.

The theater district was crowded as always. A lot of excited people were standing under the maroon awning and
green neon sign of Sardi's restaurant, trying to peer through
the windows. I figured some famous Broadway star had just
swept inside for a pre-show snack or highball. Passing by the
Majestic Theatre, where *Fanny* was playing, and the St.

James, where *The Pajama Game* was in its second year, I had to push my way through long, disorderly lines of last-minute ticket buyers. After I crossed over Eighth Avenue, though, and headed for Ninth, the street became a whole lot quieter.

And creepier. . . .

All of a sudden I was walking on eggs instead of air. *What if somebody's following me?* I whimpered to myself. *What if Aunt Doobie's on my trail, carrying another hunk of concrete under his well-muscled arm? What if Blackie's crouching like a panther in the shadows, waiting to jump out and claw me to pieces? Maybe Baldy's pulling up behind me in his limousine right now, scheming to snatch me off the street and whisk me down to the docks for a final (i.e., fatal) beating.*

Okay, okay! So my fantasies were probably working overtime. (At least I hoped they were!) It hadn't gotten dark yet, and as many times as I whipped my head around, searching for suspicious characters, I didn't spot a single one. I still felt very nervous, though, and I crossed Ninth Avenue with a sense of dread in my racing heart.

Halfway down the block I reached it—the small, low, red-brick building that housed the Actors Studio. It looked like an old church or theater or some kind of meeting hall. A flight of about ten stone steps led up to the wide, white double-door entrance, but the entire face of the property, including the entryway and the tiny, heavily shrubbed front yard, was closed off by a wrought iron fence. The gate was securely locked.

How's anybody supposed to get in? I wondered, standing anxiously by the iron barricade, looking up and down the nearly deserted street for Binky (or, rather, any young man I thought might be Binky). I couldn't go inside without him. Where *was* he? He was coming, wasn't he? What if he didn't show up? I looked at my watch. It was 6:32. He was late! (Okay, so he wasn't really *that* late. But when you're convinced you're being stalked by a homicidal maniac, two minutes can seem like two months.)

There was a loud creaking noise behind me. I jerked around to see who was there or what was happening, but detected no movement at all. Then, from out of nowhere, a male voice called out, "Hey, Phoebe? Over here!"

Straining my eyes toward the source of the voice, I finally

saw him. Well, his head, anyway. It was a fairly large head
with lots of curly light brown hair, and it was sticking out
from a street-level door on the far side of the building.

"Binky?" I called back. "Is that you?"

"Yeah." He stepped all the way through the creaky door
and walked across a small cement courtyard to the edge of the
fence. "Come down here," he said, gesturing for me to come
closer. "This is the best way in."

Baring my teeth in a huge Bucky Beaver smile, I walked
down to where Binky was standing. "Hi!" I said, extending
my hand over the fence for a shake. "It's nice to meet you, finally. I really appreciate what you're doing for me." He was a
tall, lean, good-looking guy. Not heart-stoppingly gorgeous,
like Gray, but quite attractive in a tense, Van Heflin kind of
way.

There was another gate at this end of the fence and Binky
opened it for me. "So you really *are* an actress," he said,
smirking, eyeing my colorful clothes. "I had my doubts before, but now I see from your way-out wardrobe you're just
like all the other actresses I know. You want to be the center
of attention."

"Looks can be deceiving," I said, just to keep him guessing. (Sometimes, when you're trying to solve a mystery, it
helps to be mysterious yourself.) I stepped through the gate
and walked into the courtyard. "For instance," I added, bla-
tantly scrutinizing the way *he* was dressed, "one glance at
your tightly buttoned collar and long-sleeved shirt tells me
you're either priggish or feeling chilly. But neither of those
hasty conclusions can be true, now, can they? A bartender at
the Latin Quarter couldn't possibly be a prig, and *nobody*
could be feeling chilly in this unbearable heat."

He gave me a chilly smile. "I'm sure you didn't come here
to discuss my clothes, my job, or the weather. And the auditions will be starting soon. Let's go inside." He led the way to
the side door and opened it wide.

"Thanks, Binky," I said, as he ushered me into the building.

"Don't call me that!" he snapped. "Especially when we get
upstairs." He followed me into the dim hallway, then paused
at the bottom of the steps. "Just call me Barnabas, please," he
said, re-collecting himself. "The Studio bigwigs know me by
my real name—Barnabas Kapinsky—and I want to keep it

that way. Binky's too rinky-dink. It's fit for a performing poodle, not a serious actor."

It was time for *me* to do some serious acting. "You're so right, Barnabas," I simmered, doing my best Susan Hayward (she really knows how to emote). "An important director like Elia Kazan would surely laugh at a name like Binky. And isn't that who you're auditioning for this evening? Elia Kazan?"

"Yeah," he said, eyes darting from my face, to the floor, to the well-lit landing at the top of the stairs. "Mr. Kazan's one of the founders of the Actors Studio, and whenever he needs a new face for one of his movies or plays, he looks here first. If he likes my work tonight, my career will be made in the shade."

"Gosh!" I cried, flapping my lashes like a starstruck fool (I felt my role called for a little more pep and hooey). "Aren't you nervous? How can you be so cool? I would be having a heart attack!"

"Yeah, I'm nervous," he said. "But I've been practicing my audition scene for so long, I know it like the back of my hand. I'm going to be a smash tonight. I can feel it."

"I'm so excited!" I fluttered. "Thanks for letting me come!"

"No problem. I work best in front of a big audience—the bigger the better. And the head honchos like to have extra spectators on audition nights so they can get their reaction to the performances. Come on," he said, turning and leading the way up the stairs. "Everybody's here already. You better get yourself a seat."

BEYOND THE UPSTAIRS ENTRANCE HALL, with its many framed photos of Studio luminaries and workshops-in-progress, was a small theater. The six-or-so rows of wooden seats were arranged in elevated tiers, in a wide semicircle around the stage, which was really no stage at all, just the bare wood boards of the floor. Other than the small table and chair set smack in the center of the floor (or stage, or whatever), there was no scenery. An odd clutter of ladders, brooms, stools, folding chairs, and other pieces of battered equipment served as the only backdrop.

"I've got to go in the back and get ready," Binky told me.

"You can sit wherever you like, except for those two empty seats in the front, and the two empty seats in the middle of the fourth row. All the others are up for grabs, and you better grab one before they're gone."

He was right. Most of the chairs were already taken, by a chatty, eclectic assortment of men and women, in many different age brackets, in many various styles of dress, primarily business and casual, but also kooky and bohemian. (I seemed to fit in all four categories at once.) I spotted an empty seat in the middle of the next-to-the-last row and quickly worked my way up the tiers, and past a long line of knobby knees, to claim it.

The second I sat down, I started studying the people in the audience, paying special attention to those who were 1) around Gray's age, and 2) dressed like acting students—i.e., blue jeans, T-shirts, and loafers for the guys; tight skirts, blouses, and ballet flats for the gals. I hoped to zero in on a couple of Gray's closest peers and try to talk to them when the auditions were over. Spying a handsome young man with a dirty blond ducktail in the second row, and wondering if his name was Randy, I craned my neck forward for a better look.

Lord have mercy! I screeched to myself (in the same tone both my Georgia-born grandmother and Willy Sinclair would use). *It's James Dean! I'm sitting five seats and three rows away from James Dean! If Abby ever finds out about this, she'll kill me!*

To say that I was shocked would be like saying Salvadore Dali was a little bit strange. If I had thought for even a second that Abby's fave new screen boy would be here, you can bet your sweet tushy I'd have brought her with me! Abby would have had the famous film idol wrapped around her little finger by now, and if it turned out James Dean had been a friend of Gray Gordon's . . . who knows what stories (or clues) he might have revealed to us (I mean, her).

But as shocked as I was by the sight of James Dean, that was nothing compared to the stroke I suffered when another well-known (to me) man suddenly pushed his way into the audience and sat down in one of the two reserved seats right in front of me. When I caught my first glimpse of him, I almost passed out. My temperature shot through the roof, my heart went into convulsions, and I broke out in such a serious sweat my bangs went from damp to dripping.

It was Baldy!

My first frantic impulse was to slip down to the floor and crawl under my seat. But slipping and crawling were out of the question. There wasn't enough room. And all the closely packed chairs on either side of me were full, making a fast, inconspicuous exit from the row impossible. I was stuck. All I could do was sit there like a stump, holding my breath and hiding my face with my hand, praying to every deity I ever heard of that Baldy wouldn't turn around and see me.

For the time being, my prayers were answered. Baldy leaned his large torso forward, propped his elbows on his knees, and—without a single backward glance—aimed his eyes at the stage. And he continued to sit that way, leaning and staring forward in a seeming trance, until another man entered the crowded fourth row, squeezed his way through the gauntlet of knees, feet, and legs, and sat down next to him.

There was nothing shocking about this well-known man's arrival. He was the director Elia Kazan, and everybody in the audience, including myself, had been expecting him to appear. I *was* surprised, however, by the audience's cheerful and friendly reaction to his unannounced entrance. Everybody was looking at him and smiling. James Dean stood up and saluted. Many people were waving and applauding, and those sitting close enough stretched out their arms to shake his hand. The well-dressed man to my left leaned over and gave him a sporting slap on the back.

Was I the only one in the room who felt uncomfortable being in Kazan's presence? Was I the only one who remembered that just three short years ago, in 1952, Kazan had gone before Senator Joe McCarthy and the House Un-American Activities Committee, and identified eight of his old theater friends as former members of the Communist Party? So what if the man was a brilliant Broadway director? So what if his movies were huge Hollywood hits? Did that make it okay for him to be a snitch?

I was spinning these and many other questions around in my brain when a medium-tall middle-aged man wearing a suit and a tie and a pair of large horn-rimmed glasses stood up from one of the reserved seats in the center of the front row and turned to address the crowd.

"Good evening, ladies and gentleman," he said. "My name is Lee Strasberg, and I welcome you to the Actors Studio. One of our founders, Mr. Elia Kazan, is with us tonight, and three of our most talented young actors will be auditioning for the lead understudy role in his current Broadway success, *Cat on a Hot Tin Roof*. And now it's time to get started. We hope you will enjoy the auditions and continue your support of the Actors Studio."

There was a brief round of applause, and Strasberg returned to his seat.

So that's it, I said to myself. *Kazan is looking for an actor to fill Gray's shoes, and Binky is hoping his own feet will fit.*

Now even more questions were spinning in my dizzy skull. How long, I wondered, had Binky been preparing for this Cinderella audition? Had he begun rehearsing after or before Gray was murdered? How much had he coveted Gray's understudy role? Enough to kill for it? *And what about Baldy?* I reminded myself, staring straight at the back of the man's big hairless head. What did *he* have to do with the whole production?

Going crazy from the storm of questions and my inability to answer any of them, I was relieved when Binky suddenly emerged from behind the stage, then walked out into the middle of the floor and introduced himself.

"Good evening," he said. "My name is Barnabas Kapinsky and I've been a member of the Actors Studio for four years. For my audition tonight I will be playing the role of Brick in a scene from *Cat on a Hot Tin Roof*. It's the pivotal scene between Brick and Big Daddy, which comes at the end of Act Two. Mr. Strasberg will be reading the part of Big Daddy."

Binky nodded to Strasberg and then to Kazan (or was it Baldy?). Then—raking his fingers through his curly beige hair and loosening the collar of his tightly buttoned shirt—he took a step toward the audience, cleared his throat, and began his well-practiced performance.

Chapter 27

BY THE TIME THE AUDITIONS ENDED I was practically jumping out of my skin. It isn't easy to sit squished in a hard wooden seat for an hour and a half, watching the same long scene from the same play three times in a row, and having a major panic attack every time the bald guy sitting in front of you turns his head. Binky's performance was really good—so I didn't mind sitting through that so much—but watching the tiresome auditions of the other two actors (and I use the term loosely) was like waiting for a bus that never comes.

So when the last guy finally finished his presentation, and Strasberg stood up and thanked everybody for coming, I started looking for a quick escape route. I didn't want to talk to Gray's peers anymore, not even James Dean. And I didn't have the slightest desire to hook up with Binky again. All I wanted to do was get up and get out of there before Baldy saw me.

But being wedged in the very middle of the next-to-the-last row the way I was—well, I'm sure you get the picture. I couldn't go my way until all the chatty, slow-moving people next to (i.e., ahead of) me had gone theirs. And the same was true for Baldy and Kazan. All three of us had to sit tight and wait for our rows to clear. Which, believe it or not, turned out to be a good thing (for me), because it allowed me to monitor (okay, eavesdrop on) the following script (I mean, dialogue):

KAZAN:

The Kapinsky kid was good, don't you think? I remember him from the last understudy audition. He gave a decent performance then, too. He was my second choice. He wasn't as polished as Gray Gordon—and not nearly as good looking, of course—but he had a lot of energy and drive.

BALDY:

Yeah, he's okay, I guess. A hell of a lot better than those other two goons. Has he had any experience?

KAZAN:

He's been on TV a couple of times. Had a small role in a *Pepsi-Cola Playhouse* production, and he played a burn victim on *Medic*. They say he did a good job on that one— even though he was wrapped up like a mummy in bandages through the whole show. You never saw his face.

BALDY:

So are you going to hire him, or run some cattle call ads in the papers?

KAZAN:

We need somebody right away. I think we should sign up Kapinsky and save ourselves the time and torture of a cattle call. But what do you think? You're the producer. You have a stake in this, too.

BALDY:

Yeah, but the talent is your territory. I'm just the money man. And my money's on you, pal—so whatever you say goes.

KAZAN:

Okay, I'll tell you what. Go find Kapinsky and tell him to meet us at Sardi's tonight after the show, around eleven thirty. I'll bring Ben and Barbara, and you bring Rhonda. We'll see how everybody gets along. If the other actors like him and want to work with him, he's in.

The fourth row had almost emptied out, so Baldy and Kazan stood up and began making their way toward the end of the passage. I sat still as a statue in my seat, hoping Baldy would just keep shuffling off to Buffalo (i.e., backstage to find Binky) and never look back. In case he *did* turn around, though, and find his eyes drawn to my shocking-pink and red-plaid ensemble, I kept my face turned in the opposite direction, with my wavy, still damp hair draped like a curtain over my profile.

It wasn't that I was insanely terrified, or anything like that. I mean, what could happen to me *here*, in the shelter of the sanctified Actors Studio? And besides, it *could* have been somebody else's big black limousine that Flannagan's anonymous caller had seen down at the river last night. And maybe Baldy had interrogated the Vanguard bartender about me—and given him a secret C-note—just because he thought I was cute.

But I wasn't taking any chances. If Baldy was in any way connected to the murder of Gray Gordon, and if he had any idea that I had become connected to the case, too—well, let's just say I thought it would be a good idea for me to lie low. Real low.

So I stayed in my seat until Baldy and Kazan had both disappeared. Then I quickly exited the little theater and stole into the crowded entrance hall. People were standing around in groups, smoking cigarettes, complaining about the heat, and extolling the virtues of the "Method"—the style of acting endorsed by the Actors Studio. I wriggled my way through the herd, darted down the steps to the street-level side door, and then bolted, like a stallion out of the starting gate, into the steamy night.

Heading back across 44th Street toward Times Square, I was a total wreck. (Yes, I know. I had been a total wreck since this whole thing started! But so what? I'm just a total wreck of a person, and you should know that about me by now. I wish I were less emotional, and a heck of a lot more stable, but I'm not. And that's all there is to say about that.)

It was very dark. As I crossed over Ninth and aimed myself toward Eighth, I felt as though I were staggering, alone, through a murky underground tunnel. There were a few scattered lights in the tunnel—a street lamp up ahead, an illuminated hardware store window over there, a foyer light in the entrance of a tenement building over here—but the overall effect was one of pure and absolute gloom.

Could doom, I wondered, be far behind?

Hardly any people were walking up or down the block, and cruising cars were few and far between. So when the furtive footsteps fell in behind me, I was able to hear them. And when I yanked my head around to see who was there, my response was so sudden and immediate I actually *did* catch a glimpse of a shadowy figure—a slim, dark man dressed all in black, who darted into an unlit doorway before I could see his face. Was it Aunt Doobie? Was it Blackie? I was dying to know the phantom's identity, but too scared to stick around and find out. I tore all the way over to Times Square and hopped the subway home without a backward glance.

WHEN I CHARGED UP THE STAIRS OF MY building and saw that Abby's door was open, I almost sang the Hallelujah Chorus (or some of it, anyway). My best friend was at home! Coltrane was on the hi fi! Cocktails were being served! (Or so I hoped.) I burst into her apartment with a huge sense of relief and a heap of high expectations.

But the scene inside could not have been more *un*expected.

Abby was standing at her easel, wearing her color-streaked white painter's smock, and jabbing at her canvas with a big purple-tipped brush. This, in itself, wasn't so surprising—Abby always wore a smock and listened to Coltrane when she was working on a new illustration—but when I saw who her model was, I was shocked right out of my sandals.

It was Willy! (It seemed Abby had changed her mind about him being the murderer.)

Wearing a scanty homemade toga (Abby must have had an old sheet to spare), and a wreath of ivy (hopefully not the poison variety) on his head, Willy was reclining on a pile of pillows on the floor, and dangling a cluster of grapes (wax, not real) over his open, upturned mouth.

"Hail, Caesar!" I croaked, tossing my purse on the kitchen table and heading straight for the kitchen counter where a big pitcher of rum punch was alluringly displayed. "What's up, Cleopatra?" I called out to Abby, quickly filling a glass with ice cubes and punch. "Let me guess. You're doing a cover for a new magazine titled *Roman Orgy*." I carried my drink into the studio and sat down on Abby's little red loveseat, close to the whirring fan.

"Nope," Abby said, giving me a nasty look, then stepping back from her canvas and studying it through squinted eyes. "It's an illustration for *Coronet*. They're running a three-part serial about the fall of the Roman Empire."

"Oooh! Is *that* what this is all about?!" Willy squealed, feigning outrage. "I thought you asked me to pose in this skimpy little dress just so you could gaze at my gorgeous legs."

I smiled. Willy's short, pale, pudgy appendages looked as if they belonged on a giant baby instead of a grown-up man.

Abby stared at her watch, and then glared at me. "You're way overdue, Sue," she said. "I expected you home three hours ago. When Willy showed up here looking for you, I was so sure you'd be here soon, I convinced him to wait. How come you're so late? What the hell are you wearing? Where the hell have you been?" She was hovering on the borderline between upset and irate. Abby worried about me (and my poor fashion sense) a lot more than she liked to let on.

"It's a long story," I said, not sure I had the energy to tell it. "Where's Jimmy?" (What I meant was, "Where's Otto?," but I didn't have the nerve to put it that way.)

"Never mind where Jimmy is!" Abby sputtered, angrily sticking her brush in a jar full of turpentine and wiping her hands on her smock. "What I want to know is, where the hell were you?"

"Yeah!" Willy chimed in. "That's what I want to know, too!" He pulled himself up and sat crosslegged, like a plump little Roman Buddha, on the floor. "We've been really concerned, you know!"

"So concerned you decided to have a toga party?" I wasn't being snippy (there was no sarcasm in my voice at all, I swear!). I was just poking fun, stalling for time, giving myself a chance to relax (and take a few swigs of rum). I needed to calm down and catch my breath before recounting (i.e., reliving) all my troubles during the last twenty-four hours. And I needed to shore up the strength to face the troubles I felt the next few hours would bring.

"This wasn't a goddamn party!" Abby snapped, yanking her long braid off of one shoulder and plopping it over the other. "We've been *working*. And we only did it to pass the time and take our minds off you!"

"That's right," Willy concurred, snatching the ivy wreath off his head and slapping it down on the floor. Now he was angry, too.

"Oh, all right!" I gave in, returning to my formerly freaked-out state. "I was at the Actors Studio, okay? I went there right after work to watch Binky audition for Gray's understudy role."

"You went without me?" Abby said, pouting. "I told you I wanted to go! Why didn't you call me? I wanted to see James Dean!"

"There wasn't time," I said. "And I had more important things on my mind than taking you to see some pretty boy screen idol."

"Oh, but he's the *prettiest!*" Willy protested. "Mercy! I'd give my right arm to see him myself!"

I rolled my eyes at the ceiling. "Have you both gone soft in the head? Didn't you hear what I said before? I said Binky was auditioning for *Gray Gordon's* understudy role. Shouldn't that little nugget of information have grabbed your attention more than the prospect of seeing James Dean?"

"You mean the *lost* prospect of seeing James Dean," Abby snorted. (Does she have a one-track mind, or what?)

I shook my head in dismay. "Please forgive me," I said, "but I thought we were looking for a *murderer*, not a movie star." To further dramatize my words, I stood up, walked over to the window, pried a tiny peephole between the closed shade and the window frame, and peered down at the shadowy doorways on the dark street below. "When I left the Studio tonight," I added, "a man was following me. He was dressed in black and I never saw his face. I think I gave him the slip, but I can't say for sure. He may have followed me here."

"Oh, my Gawd!" Willy squealed, jumping to his feet. "Is anybody out there? What if it's the killer? Mercy, me! We'd better call the police!"

"Cool it, Willy," I said, returning to my seat on the little red couch and gulping down the rest of my punch. "The coast looks clear. And even if the guy is out there, we don't know if he's the killer. So if we called the police, what would we tell them? And do we really feel like spending the rest of the night with Detective Flannagan?"

"Perish the thought!" Willy said, with a visible shudder.

Abby walked over to the window and looked out. "I don't see anybody, either. Do you think it was Blackie?" She wasn't mad anymore. Now she was as curious and compatible as she should have been in the first place.

"Maybe," I said. "Or it could have been Aunt Doobie. Or even the elusive Randy. I know it wasn't Baldy."

"How do you know that?" she asked.

"Because when I left the Actors Studio he was still inside with Binky."

"Blackie, Baldy, Binky!" Willy shrieked, throwing his hands in the air. "Who the hell are they? A new singing group?"

Abby and I laughed. It really was pretty crazy and confusing.

"You know what I think?" I said. "I think we'd better pour ourselves another rum punch and sit down at the kitchen table for a confab. A lot has happened since I last saw either of you, and I've got some stories to tell."

"I'm all ears," Willy warbled.

Abby grinned and nodded. "Give us the skinny, Minnie."

Chapter 28

AFTER EXPLAINING TO WILLY WHO
Blackie, Baldy, and Binky were, I told Abby about Willy's
and my expedition to the Keller Hotel to try to dig up some
dirt on Aunt Doobie. Then I guzzled some more rum, lit up a
cigarette, and gave them a full report on my face-to-face encounter with Aunt Doobie—and the subsequent encounter of
a big rock with the back of my head. Then—after they'd both
expressed their shock and horror over that little mishap—I
told them about Flannagan's swift arrival and his revelation
that the anonymous caller who witnessed the attack had reported seeing a dark-haired man in dark clothing flee the
scene in a black limousine.

"So it could have been Aunt Doobie who bonked me," I
said, "or maybe it was Blackie. Or Randy, or anybody else in
the world, for that matter. And whoever it was escaped in a
limo which may, or may not, belong to Baldy. Get the picture?"

"Yeah, I get it," Abby said. "It's like a painting by Jackson
Pollock. You don't have a clue what it means."

"Right," I said. "And my trip to the Actors Studio tonight
made the whole scene even more confounding." After reiter-
ating the fact that Binky had auditioned for Gray's understudy
role, I discussed how this opportunistic performance made

Binky a very likely—perhaps the *most* likely—suspect in the murder. Then I told them about Baldy's surprise appearance at the audition, and gave them a word-by-word account of his dialogue with Elia Kazan at the end of the tryouts. I concluded my tale with a recap of my flight from the unknown stalker in black clothing.

"See what I mean?" I sputtered. "The deeper I dig, the crazier and more convoluted the clues become. The only concrete piece of evidence I've managed to uncover is that Baldy is the producer of *Cat on a Hot Tin Roof*." A new thought suddenly occurred to me. "Hey, Ab, do you still have your Playbill from the show?" I was getting excited. "The producer's name will be listed there!"

Abby's eyes lit up. "Of course I still have it! It's right here on the table." She snatched a stack of bills and papers from under the sugar bowl and madly spread them out in front of her. "Here it is!" she gasped, handing the Playbill to me. "You look. I'm too nervous."

I opened the little booklet, turned to the title page with the opening credits, and there they were: "Directed by Elia Kazan" . . . "Produced by Randolph Godfrey Winston." "Eureka!" I shouted, showing the page to Abby and Willy and pointing out the producer's name. The mysterious Randy had finally been found.

"Do you believe that?" I said. "I've been looking for Randy around every corner, and his name was right here on the program, in living black and white, the whole time. I need to have my eyes examined."

"But so what if Baldy's name is Randy?" Willy wanted to know. "What does that have to do with the price of egg creams?"

"It shows that Baldy had a pretty intense relationship with Gray," Abby explained, "apart from the usual producer/understudy connection, I mean. The name Randy appeared on Gray's telephone message list four, count 'em, *four* times in the short period surrounding Gray's death. That's kind of weird, you dig?"

"Yeah, I guess so," Willy said, not totally convinced.

"And what about the fact that he was asking the Vanguard bartender all those questions about me?" I broke in. "Why was he doing that? How much did he know about me already?

Did he know that I was looking into Gray's murder? Had Rhonda told him that I stole Gray's telephone messages? And was it his black limousine that was hovering around the Keller Hotel last night? And if so, why? Was he the one who clobbered me?" A chill ran down my spine in spite of the heat.

"*Oy vey*!" Abby cried. "My head is swimming with all these questions! Everything's so *meshuga*, it's gotten out of hand. And by that I mean *dangerous!* I think we'd better call a halt to this *focockta* investigation before somebody gets seriously hurt. And that means *you*, Paige!"

I was surprised by her sudden willingness to surrender. Abby was usually as tenacious as a pit bull with a meaty bone. "Do you really feel that way?" I asked her. "Because I don't! My feelings are the exact opposite. I think we're really close to catching the killer. I think we're going to break this case in no time!"

"Have you lost your reason?" Abby shrieked. "This is the most complicated, most perilous puzzle you've ever tried to solve. You should have your head examined, not your eyes. There's a very thin line between danger and death, you dig?"

(Okay, so maybe I *had* lost my reason. Considering my recent head-banging—not to mention heart-banging—travails, I might have misplaced it somewhere along the way. It wouldn't be the first time. But I still couldn't bring myself to accept that idea. Call me a cockeyed optimist—or a cockeyed idiot, if you prefer—but I truly believed that the secrets of the Gray Gordon murder would soon be unlocked. And that I would be the one turning the key.)

"So what are you saying?" I croaked. "Are you saying you don't want to go with me to Sardi's tonight? Because I was kind of counting on you and Willy to come and—"

"What?!!" they squealed in unison.

"And help me do a little surveillance," I finished my sentence. "Two of our prime suspects will be there. Binky *and* Baldy. (I couldn't stop calling him that. Even though I now knew his name was Randy, he would always be Baldy to me.) And they'll be sitting at the same table. And Rhonda Blake will be there, too. It's too good a chance to pass up."

"Good for what?" Abby seethed, arching one eyebrow to the apex. "A good chance to be recognized? To be found out? To be marked for murder?"

"Oh, Mercy!" Willy whimpered. "I wouldn't like that!"

"No," I said, taking another sip of rum and eyeing them over the rim of the glass. "I was thinking along different lines. I was thinking it might be a good opportunity for the two of you to see James Dean." (It was a devious trick, but somebody had to do it. I couldn't go to Sardi's alone. They don't admit unaccompanied females.)

"Come off it, Paige!" Abby snapped. "He won't be there, and you know it. You're just dangling a carrot in front of our nose."

"That's right!" Willy dittoed.

"I am not!" I yowled, dangling the carrot even closer. "There's a very good chance he'll be there. Elia Kazan is going to be there, and he directed Dean's latest movie, *East of Eden*, you know! And I read in Dorothy Kilgallen's column that they're very good buddies now. They go out together a *lot*. And you were the one who said Dean is in town, Ab. You said it just the other day. That's the reason you wanted to go to the Actors Studio, remember? So the odds are really, really good that Kazan will invite Dean to join him at Sardi's tonight. I'm not kidding!"

I had ignited a spark in her star-struck eyes. It was obvious. Her lashes were fluttering and her pupils were widening. "I don't know, Paige," she hesitated. "There's a chance he'll be there, I guess, but it's bound to be a small one. There's a much greater chance that the murderer will be there."

"That's what I'm hoping for," I admitted. "And if we're there, too, maybe we'll be able to see or overhear something that will reveal the monster's identity. Wouldn't you like that, Ab? Wouldn't you like to help nail the brutal slasher beast who slaughtered your dear friend Gray?"

She gave me a dirty look. "You're being cruel now, Paige. You're making me think about the horrible way Gray died just to motivate me to want to find his killer."

"Is it working?" I asked her.

"No," she lied, with a wink. "But I *do* want to see James Dean, so you can count me in."

•　　•　　•

WILLY WASN'T SO EASILY PERSUADED.
He wanted to see Gray's murderer caught, but he didn't want
to take part in the catching.

"I'm a coward," he confessed. "I'm a yellow, lily-livered
pansy. I wouldn't be any help to you at all. If one of the suspects just *looked* at me funny, I'd scream and run the other
way." Great beads of sweat had popped out on his forehead
and were beginning to roll down the sides of his cheeks. "And
who gives a fig about seeing James Dean? I'm a very patient
person. I can wait till his next movie comes out."

"Oh, come on, Willy," Abby said, dabbing the sweat off his
face with a cocktail napkin and kissing the tip of his nose.
"We won't have any fun without you." She curled her fingers
thorough his Brylcreamed blond hair, and rested her head on
his bare shoulder (he was still in a skimpy toga, don't forget).

Willy snorted (or was it a sigh?). "I'm a homosexual,
honey. Haven't you heard? Your feminine wiles won't work
on me." The deep pink blush on his face suggested that the
last sentence of his statement was patently untrue.

(Leave it to Abby. She could charm the socks off any male,
straight or gay.)

"We don't need you to be brave, Willy," I urged. "We just
need you to be our escort. Sardi's won't let us in unless we're
accompanied by a man."

"Me? A man?" he jeered. "That's a laugh and a half."

"Hush, Willy," Abby cooed into his ear. "Stop putting
yourself down. You may be a queer, but you're still a real, live,
red-blooded American man. A real *man's* man, you might
say." She let out a soft giggle. "Trust me. A woman knows
these things."

Abby's tactics were taking effect, but too slowly for me. It
was 10:15, and I was hoping to get to Sardi's around 11:15—
before the cast of suspicious characters showed up. "You've
got to go with us, Willy," I insisted. "After all, you're the main
reason we're doing this. If we don't find out who the real
killer is, Flannagan's going to try to pin the murder on you.
And without some hard evidence to the contrary, he may very
well succeed. Your blood type alone could be enough to convict you."

That did it. Willy jumped up from the table, hopped across
the room, and started bounding up the stairs toward Abby's

Vault of Illusions (the little dressing room where she keeps the props and costumes for her paintings). "I can't go to Sardi's in a toga," he yelled down to us. "I'll change back into my street clothes, then run home and put on my good suit."

AS SOON AS WILLY LEFT THE APART-
ment, Abby and I went upstairs to change. We both needed to put on dresses and disguises. Only Rhonda would recognize Abby, but Binky, Baldy, and Rhonda would all be able to finger me.

"Want to be a redhead tonight?" Abby asked. "I just got a new wig. They call it the Rita Hayworth." She held up a white dummy head with long, flowing, auburn tresses for my inspection.

I pinned my own hair back in a bun and tried the wig on. "This is perfect," I said, looking in the mirror. "I don't look like Rita Hayworth, but I don't look like Paige Turner, either. I look a lot like Lassie, but that'll keep me safe from Sardi's celebrity hounds. Dogs can't write. Nobody will ask me for an autograph."

"Ha ha," Abby said, not laughing. "You're just as bad as Willy. Always putting yourself down. You look so fabulous in that wig Kazan's going to put you in his next picture. Here," she said, handing me a black sheath dress on a hanger. "This should fit. Try it with the red belt and red satin pumps."

Thanking my lucky stars, as I often had before, that Abby and I wore the same size (except for our bras), I stepped out of my shocking-pink-and-red-plaid outfit, and stepped into Abby's little black dress. It looked good on me. Especially with the red belt and shoes. But that was the least of my concerns. I was going to Sardi's to snatch a murderer, not a beauty crown.

"Well, hellohhh dahhhling," Abby said, twirling between me and the full-length mirror. "You look lovely tonight. And how about me, sweets? Don't you think I look swell?"

Swell wasn't the word for it. Abby looked, as they say, like a million bucks. She had swirled her hair into a high bouffant and hung long, dangly diamonds (okay, rhinestones) from her ears. She was wearing a low, off-the-shoulder, tight-waisted, full-skirted white dress, white stilettos, silver-rimmed sunglasses (yes, *sun*glasses!), and she was holding a very long, very slender white cigarette holder up to her glossy red lips. The effect was eye-catching, to put it mildly.

"Wow!" I said. "You look stunning. You're going to steal the show. And that's the problem!" I added. "Didn't anybody tell you this is an undercover operation? You're supposed to fade into the background, not shimmer like a star in center stage."

"Phooey to that!" she spat. "You can't be a good snoop if you look like poop."

"Who told you that? Milton Berle?"

"It's common knowledge, silly. The brighter you shine, the harder you are to see."

I didn't have time to argue with her. Willy was ringing the buzzer downstairs. We were off to meet our Cowardly Lion and take the yellow brick subway to the land of Oz.

Chapter 29

WE ARRIVED AT THE RENOWNED RESTAU-
rant at 11:20 and took a table in the darkest reaches of the
plush dining room, away from the lights and the action. Since
the Broadway stars all came to Sardi's to be seen, and the
celebrity-gawkers all came to see them, the tables tucked
against the walls in the back were usually the last to be filled.
(I picked this little tidbit up from Ed Sullivan's column in the
Daily News.) Figuring that the *Hot Tin Roof* clan would be sitting at one of the large reserved tables in the very middle of
the room, I sat down in the chair that offered the best view of
that area.

As I was basking in the glorious air-conditioning and
glancing around at the hundreds of framed and autographed
caricatures covering the bright red walls, a waiter materialized, handed us menus, and asked what we wanted to drink. I
was about to order a Dr Pepper when Willy jumped in and ordered a round of champagne cocktails.

"Jeez, Willy, that'll be really expensive!" I said, as soon as
the waiter walked away. "And I don't have that much money
on me. We should have gotten a pitcher of beer."

Abby laughed. "We're in Sardi's, Paige, not the San
Remo."

"Don't worry about the cost," Willy said. "I'm picking up

the tab tonight. I've been saving up for a Fire Island vacation, but I think finding the murderer is a better investment for my future. You can't frolic on Fire Island when you're in jail."

"Gee, thanks, Willy!" Abby said, patting him on one chubby cheek. She stuck a Pall Mall in the tip of her long cigarette holder and leaned toward him for a light. "You're the best kind of man there is—a *gentleman*." Once lit, she sat back in her chair and put on a big smoking show, waving her thin white holder around in the air like an orchestra conductor's baton.

The restaurant wasn't crowded yet, but it would soon be packed. All the shows were ending. Large groups of people were pouring out of the theaters and surging straight into Sardi's—spreading, like waves on the shore, throughout the vast dining room. I kept my eyes glued to the entrance, watching for Baldy and Binky (and Rhonda, too, though she was not one of my prime suspects). When the waiter set my champagne cocktail down in front of me, I picked it up and took a few sips, never changing the direction of my gaze.

So when Elia Kazan entered the restaurant with his two lead stars in tow (Barbara Bel Geddes and Ben Gazzara, in case you've forgotten), I perked up and took notice. Smiling and chatting continuously, they followed the maitre d' to their table (yep!—one of the ones in the middle) and sat down next to each other, facing the entrance. Baldy and Rhonda came in two minutes later and sat opposite them, facing me. I couldn't hear what anybody was saying, of course (I was seated a good forty feet away), but I could see that all five were engaged in lively conversation.

Binky was fashionably late. He arrived around 11:45 and, holding his head high and his shoulders erect, searched the room till he spotted his party. Then, looking very cool and composed in his pinstriped suit and paisley tie, he slowly made his way to the center of the now crowded dining room and stood next to his empty chair, waiting for Baldy to introduce him to the others. There was a cocky smile on his lean, clean-shaven face.

"That's Binky," I said to Abby and Willy, "also known as Barnabas Kapinsky, the soon-to-be lead understudy in Broadway's hottest drama. What do you think? Does he look like a killer to you?"

Willy shuddered and rolled his eyes. "Oh, yes!" he squeaked. "He really does!"

Abby wasn't so quick to judge. "Gee, I don't know, Flo," she said. "I think he's kind of cute. And if he's as good an actor as you say he is, it'll be hard to determine his true personality. Maybe I should ask him to model for me so I can do an up close and personal study of his character."

"You mean his anatomy," I scoffed, trying not to lose my temper. Couldn't Abby control her libido for a single second? "What about Baldy?" I probed. "Don't you think he looks deadly?"

"He's so big!" Willy sputtered. "And so bald! He terrifies me. He could play the lead in a monster movie."

"You can't judge a book by its cover," Abby teased. "I'll bet he's gay."

"You can be gay and still be monstrous," Willy said, with a sniff.

Abby scowled and blew a perfect smoke ring. "As far as I'm concerned, the only monster at that table is Rhonda Blake." She punctuated her statement by punching her cigarette holder, like an exclamation point, straight up in the air. "By the way, Paige," she added, "you haven't mentioned Cupcake in a while. Are you still looking for her, or have you finally come to agree with me that the mysterious Cupcake is none other than the bitchy Miss Blake?"

"I think Cupcake is a he, not a she," I said.

"What?!" Abby exclaimed. "You're crazy! Cupcake was Gray's *girlfriend*, remember? He stopped seeing me so he could spend all his time with her!"

"Or so you assumed," I said. "But now I've come to a very different conclusion."

"Oh, really!" she huffed. "And what conclusion is that, Pat?"

I drank the rest of my cocktail and set the empty glass down on the table. "I believe Gray was a homosexual," I said, looking her straight in the eye (or, rather, straight in the sunglasses). "I know he slept with you a couple of times, Ab, and I'm sure you both enjoyed the experience enormously, but I'm convinced that Gray loved men a whole lot more than he did women. I believe he broke it off with you so he could commit himself to a special boyfriend, not girlfriend—that Cupcake is, therefore, a man."

Abby tilted her head down, lowered her dark specs, and stared at me over their silver frames. "I don't believe it! It can't be true! Gray was so gorgeous, so masculine, so sexy!"

"All the best fairies are," Willy said, smirking.

"So who do you think Cupcake is?" Abby demanded, snorting smoke out of her nostrils like a cartoon bull. "He must be really fabulous if Gray left *me* for *him*."

I smiled. (If Abby had a sense of humility, she never let it show.) "I don't have a scrap of evidence," I confessed, "but I *do* have a very strong feeling that Cupcake and Aunt Doobie are one and the same."

OUR CONVERSATION CAME TO A SUDDEN halt when the waiter reappeared at our table and asked if we were ready to order dinner.

Dinner? At midnight? Not only was it past my dinnertime, it was past my bedtime, too. I was kind of hungry, though . . .

"Yes, we're ready," Willy said, assuming a very masculine tone, taking complete control of the situation. "We'll each have the filet mignon, medium rare, with roasted potatoes and asparagus hollandaise. And another round of champagne cocktails, please."

Abby and I glanced at each other and grinned.

As the waiter wrote down our order and began collecting our empty glasses, I took another long hard look at the *Hot Tin Roof* table. Everybody was chatting and laughing and eating and drinking—enjoying themselves to the hilt. Baldy and Binky were laughing the hardest. I was dying to find out what they thought was so funny, but how was I supposed to do that? Walk over and stand by their table till they let me in on the joke?

That was when the realization hit me. Rita Hayworth disguise aside, I probably wasn't going to learn a darn thing about the murder tonight! How could I? I wasn't able to hear a word the suspects were saying. And even if I *could* pick up on their discussion, and even if they *did* happen to talk about the murder of Gray Gordon, what difference would that make? They'd just be saying things like, "It's so horrible!"

and "What a shame!" and "Tut tut tut." Not much to be learned from that. The stakeout of Sardi's, I sadly admitted to myself, had been a stupid idea. It seemed all I would be able to do was just sit there and watch the suspects have a good time.

"So what makes you think Aunt Doobie is Cupcake?" Abby asked, as soon as the waiter disappeared.

"Yeah, Paige!" Willy echoed. "You'd better fill us in."

"Oh, it's pretty simple, really," I said, keeping an eye on the suspects while I talked to my sidekicks. "First, there's the use of the word 'Aunt,' which Willy says is a term of endearment between homosexuals, and then there's the fact that Aunt Doobie left a hotel room number in his phone message to Gray. That's a pretty clear indication that he expected Gray to meet him there, wouldn't you say? Add to that the fact that Aunt Doobie was at a party for homosexuals only at the Keller Hotel, and that his virility, youth, and gorgeous good looks were a perfect match for Gray's . . . you see what I mean? All these little clues suggest that Gray and Aunt Doobie were lovers. And since Gray called his lover Cupcake . . . well, you get the connection."

"I do now," Abby said. "And everything you said makes perfect sense. I don't know why I didn't see it before. There's just one problem."

"What's that?" asked Willy.

"Since we don't know who Aunt Doobie is," Abby answered, "we don't know who Cupcake is either."

"Right," I said. "I wanted to go back to the Mayflower Hotel to look for him again, but I couldn't find the time. And he's probably checked out by now. I told Flannagan about him, and gave him his hotel room number, but who knows if the not-so-diligent dick ever did anything about it. I'll call him at the station tomorrow and see what I can find out."

"You should have sent *me* to the Mayflower," Abby whined. "I bet *I* could have dug up some answers!"

"Yes, but to which questions?" I said. "We don't need to know if Aunt Doobie can be seduced by a woman, or how good he is in bed. That information isn't germane to the case."

"Oh, shut up, Paige!" Abby snapped. "I would have found out more than that!" She thrust her now cigaretteless holder, like a sword, in my direction.

"Girls! Girls!" Willy cried, patting us each on our arms to steady us. "Behave yourselves! You're in Sardi's, for heaven's sake. You're supposed to act like ladies."

I was about to apologize to Abby for my rude remark when I saw Rhonda Blake and Barbara Bel Geddes stand up from their table. They said a few words to the men, picked up their purses, and began to walk, arm-in-arm, toward the far corner of the dining room.

"Look!" I yelped. "Rhonda and Barbara are going to the ladies' room together!" I scooted my chair away from the table. "I'm going to follow them in there, see what they have to they say to each other."

"I'll go with you," Abby said, jumping to her feet like a jackrabbit.

"No!" I said, standing to face her. "Rhonda will recognize you—if not from your looks, then definitely from your personality. She'll never even notice me. But here's what you *can* do. While the ladies and I are in the bathroom, you can hop over to their table and work your magic on the men. Not one of them has ever seen you before. I'm guessing you'll be able to direct the scene and find out anything you want to know."

"Good idea," she said, shooting me a devilish look. "Maybe they'll tell me when the hell James Dean is going to show up."

AS SOON AS ABBY BEGAN MAKING HER way toward the other table, I gave Willy a cagey nod and struck off for the ladies' lounge. I was excited and energized. Maybe our Sardi's expedition wouldn't be a total bust after all. Maybe I'd be able to pick up some tiny yet valuable clue that would lead us, if not directly to the murderer, then at least in the right direction.

If I knew Abby, she would come back loaded with information. Way too much information, probably, but some of it could turn out to be useful. If she would just focus her attentions on Baldy and Binky instead of Gazarra and Kazan (which, I realized, was a very big if!), she might gain some important insights (i.e., killer insights). I just hoped she wouldn't make too big a show of herself—give away more information than she took in.

These were the thoughts that were spinning around in my head as I hurried toward the ladies' room. All of my other concerns about the case, including the grave danger it posed to my own personal life and safety, had been shoved to the back burner. I was concentrating on more productive things, primarily the successful execution of my clue-hunting—hopefully fact-finding—excursion to the lavatory.

So when I turned the corner near the bar and caught sight of an amorous couple embracing in the darkened hallway outside the ladies' room, I was so lost in my own thoughts I didn't fully understand what my eyes were seeing. It took several seconds for the unexpected and oh-so-intimate image to take shape in my brain. Even then, the picture was fuzzy and incomplete.

I had no idea who the woman was, but I could see that she was young and beautiful, and that her arms were locked around the neck of a very handsome man. I could tell that her body was pressed so tight against his there wasn't a single molecule of light or air between them. I could see that she was drawing his face closer and closer to hers, and I had no trouble detecting the very moment their mouths came together in a deep, greedy, soul-rocking kiss.

What I *couldn't* so easily perceive or comprehend was the mind-shattering, heart-wrenching fact that the man being kissed—the man so eagerly engaged in enjoying and returning the passionate embrace—was Dan.

Chapter 30

I ALMOST FAINTED. THE SIGHT OF DAN kissing another woman was so shocking and unbearable to me, my consciousness tried to leap out of my skull and take off for parts unknown. But I wouldn't let it go. For some perverse reason, I fought like the devil to hold on—to stay cognizant and on my feet. And once I had balanced myself, I continued to stand there in a zombie daze for several seconds, gaping at the torturous scene before me, absorbing every painful detail like a witless sponge.

The woman was astonishingly beautiful (not as beautiful as Abby, but close to it). With her perfect figure, creamy complexion, and long, wavy red-gold hair, she looked a lot more like Rita Hayworth than I did—a fact that became obvious when she finally removed her lips from Dan's, threw back her head (thus revealing her stunning profile), and released a deep, throaty laugh that sounded so glamorous and seductive I wished I'd been born deaf.

Dan was entranced. I could tell by the way he was studying her every move and expression. His coal-black eyes were crackling with heat, and he was staring at her the way he used to stare at me when something I'd said or done had suddenly put him in the mood.

Heart fracturing into a thousand pieces, and feeling desperate to get out of there before Dan "came to" and caught sight of me, I spun around on Abby's red satin heels and staggered back toward our table in the dining room. Tears were coursing down my cheeks in torrents.

"Oh, mercy!" Willy squealed, the very second he saw me approach. His big blue eyes were popping out of their sockets. "What's the matter? What happened? Did somebody hurt you?" He jumped out of his chair, grabbed hold of my shaking shoulders, and gazed up at me in alarm.

"I . . . I . . . yes," I blubbered. "I'm so hurt . . . I can't b-b-believe . . ." I couldn't finish my sentence. I was sobbing and shivering too hard to speak. People at the nearby tables were starting to stare.

Willy put his arm around me and guided me over to my chair against the wall. "Sit down, Paige," he urged. "Our cocktails have been delivered and our dinner will be here soon. Dry your eyes, have some more champagne, and tell me what happened." He was doing his best to comfort me, but nothing could.

"No, Willy!" I cried. "I've got to get out of here! Right now!" I grabbed my purse off the table and tried to step around him.

But he wouldn't move out of my way. "My God, Paige, what happened to you? I won't let you leave like this. You're too upset! You've got to tell me what's wrong! Abby's still over at Kazan's table. Should I go get her?"

Suddenly reminded that I'd sent Abby to snoop on the suspects, I shot a glance in her direction to see what was happening. It was just as I'd expected. She was seated at the table—in Rhonda's chair between Baldy and Binky—striking a sexy pose, talking a blue streak, and twirling her cigarette holder through the air like a magic wand. Bippity, boppity, boo. All four men were watching her every move and hanging on her every word, completely under her spell.

"No," I said to Willy between blubbers. "Let Abby stay where she is. She might learn something important. But I've got to go!" I wailed. "Please let me out! I don't want Dan to see me here!"

"Dan?" Willy sputtered. "Your boyfriend? Is *he* here?"

"Yes!" I cried, tears starting to gush again. "And he's with a woman. I saw him *kissing* her! Oh, please let me pass, Willy.

If I see them again, I'll die. And if he sees me, I'll kill myself.
I've got to go home this minute!"

"Okay, I'll go with you," he said. "Just let me pay the bill
first."

"No!" I screeched. "I can't wait! And we can't run out and
leave Abby here by herself. You've got to stay with her. You
two should drink your cocktails, enjoy your dinner, and see
what you can find out about the murder. I'm going home now
to cry myself to sleep." I elbowed Willy out of the way and
brushed past him. "Tell Abby I'll talk to her tomorrow."

I was at the Sardi's exit in an instant, and out the door a
split second later. And one breathless moment after that, I was
running like a madwoman for the subway—with my broken
heart in my throat and the Rita Hayworth wig in my hand.

LOOKING BACK, I WISH I'D LEFT THE
wig on my head. Then the dark-haired man in black clothing
might not have recognized me or followed me home. And
then he wouldn't have seen me let myself into my building
and go upstairs to my apartment. And then maybe he wouldn't
have hidden himself in the recessed, pitch-black entrance of
the building across the street and begun watching my apartment like a hawk—or some other deadly predator.

In which case, I never would have sensed his presence behind me on Bleecker, or run to the window and peeked
through the blinds the minute I got upstairs to my apartment.
And I wouldn't have seen him duck into the doorway and stay
there, becoming as much a part of the darkness as the shadows around him. And I certainly wouldn't have crouched on
the floor by my living room window for over an hour, crying
my eyes out over Dan and peering through the blinds (and my
tears) at the street, waiting for the man to step out of the doorway so I could get a glimpse of his face.

*Will it be Blackie's sullen mug or Aunt Doobie's pretty
puss?* I asked myself, dead certain it would be one or the
other, and totally determined—with all the tiny pieces of my
hopelessly shattered heart—to keep watch until I could make
a positive identification.

I might have succeeded, too, if Abby hadn't come home
around twenty past three and started banging on my door with

both fists. "Open up, Paige!" she shouted. "Let me in! I want to talk to you! I know you're crying instead of sleeping, so don't try to pretend anything different!"

I was both upset and relieved. Upset that Abby was interrupting my strict surveillance vigil, and relieved that I wouldn't have to be alone in the building anymore. (If the stalker—i.e., possible *murderer*—had crept across the street and tried to get into my apartment, I would have keeled over and died on the spot!) Groaning under my breath, I jumped up and ran to the door, unlocked it and flung it wide, then hurried back to my station by the window.

"What the hell is going on here?" Abby bellowed, marching into the room like a soldier on patrol. "What are you doing? Why is it so dark? I'm turning on the lights."

"No, don't!" I hissed. "I won't be able to see out, and I don't want him to see in. And keep your voice down! The windows are open. He might be able to hear us."

"Who are you talking about? Blackie? Has he come back again?" She tossed her purse on the kitchen table and scrambled over to join me on the floor by the window. "Where is he? Let me see!" She nudged me aside and stuck her nose through the gap between the blinds and the windowsill. "Oh, there he is!" she shrieked. "I see him! He hopped out of a doorway across the street and he's running down toward Seventh Avenue."

"Oh, no!" I sputtered, madly yanking the blinds away from the open window and leaning out over the ledge. The man was halfway down Bleecker already. All I could see was the back of his black-clad body as he ran past a street lamp.

"Jesus, Abby!" I growled, backing away from the windowsill and out from under the venetians. "I've been squatting here all night, peeping through these stupid blinds forever, never taking my eyes off the creep's hiding place for a second! All I needed was one quick look at his face. Then I would have known, once and for all, if the man was Blackie or Aunt Doobie! So what do you do? You bust in and push me away from the window at the very moment he reveals himself. You screwed up the whole thing!"

"But I didn't mean to!" she cried, getting defensive. "I was just trying to help."

"Oh, yeah? Well, next time you want to help me, please do

me a favor and *don't*." I pushed myself up from the floor, turned on the table lamp, and plopped down on the couch in a huff. "How did you think you were going to help me anyway?"

She made a petulant face. "Well, I know what Blackie looks like, you know! I saw him in Stewart's Cafeteria the same day you did. So I wanted to see if he's the one who's been following you."

"And *did* you?" I asked, dashed hopes rising again. "Did you get a good look at the guy's face?"

"Not really," she said, bowing her head in embarrassment. "You can't see very much through these sunglasses." She took the dark specs off her nose and meekly folded them in her hand.

That was when I started laughing.

It wasn't normal laughter, you should know—not the bubbly, congenial kind brought on by a funny joke or a humorous situation. It was crazy laughter—the fierce, frenetic kind that comes from a place of deep trouble and pain (i.e., more of a howl than a hoot). It was the kind of laughter that, after a brief spell of hysterical cackling, turns into an all-out crying jag.

When I stopped laughing and started sobbing Abby jumped up from the floor and sat next to me on the couch. She threw her arms around me and squeezed hard. "Go ahead, Paige," she cooed, still hugging me tight, "let it all out. Under circumstances like these, crying is the best release. Maybe the only release."

"Willy told you what happened?" I yowled. "Do you know about—"

"Yes," she broke in, "I know all about it." She took a deep breath and squeezed me even harder. "I still don't believe it, though. I'm in shock. I never thought Dan would behave this way."

"M-m-me neither," I blubbered, shoulders shaking so violently I felt they would collapse. "Oh, Abby! I'm so hurt . . . so devastated . . . I'll never get over this!"

"Oh, yes you will," she said, releasing her hold and patting me on the back. "I know it seems like the end of the world, but it isn't. There are worse things than losing a man." Abby meant her assurances to be soothing, but they weren't. How could I take comfort in her words when I knew she didn't believe them herself? "And besides," she added, standing up from the couch and pacing around the living room, petticoats swishing with every step, "how do you know that kiss was real?"

"Because I *saw* it, that's how!" I screeched. "I saw them mashing their lips and bodies together like two halves of a goddamn sandwich. Jesus, Abby! How could you ask me that question and make me relive that horrible scene? Don't you think I've suffered enough?" All of a sudden I wasn't crying anymore. Now I was just ranting.

"Things aren't always as they seem," Abby said, still pacing. "You're the one who taught me that! And how many times have you told me not to jump to hasty conclusions? At least a thousand, I bet!" She stomped over to the kitchen table, snatched a cigarette out of the pack in her purse, stuck it between her lips and lit it. (No holder, thank God. I wasn't in the mood to watch another act in *that* silly show.)

"I wasn't jumping to conclusions," I insisted, wiping my eyes with a tissue and blowing my nose. "I was just facing the facts."

Abby refused to back down. "Maybe you were, and maybe you weren't," she said, scowling. "All I know is, when I saw Dan and that redhead having dinner together, they didn't look the least bit amorous to me. The woman's infatuated with herself, not Dan. She's a raving exhibitionist. She looked flashy, wild, and demanding; Dan just looked bored."

"They had dinner together?" I whimpered, diving into a fresh pool of pain.

"Yes, but he wasn't having a good time."

"Now who's jumping to conclusions?" I said. "I'll give you a hint: It isn't me."

"Oh, hush, Paige! You're always so negative. I had a very good view of their table, and I could see that Dan was miserable. He looked trapped and exhausted. And that's the truth, Ruth."

"Did he see you?"

"No, I don't think so. I thought of going over and saying something to him, but I didn't. I figured you wouldn't want me to."

I heaved a huge sigh of relief and gave her a grateful nod. "You get a gold star for that one, Ab."

"You mean I finally did something right?" Her tone was sarcastic, but her posture was proud. "I was beginning to think you were going to kick me off the case."

I laughed (for real this time). "How could I kick you *off* the case when neither one of us has a right to be on it at all? Except for the negligible fact that I'm now working on a story assignment, this is a totally illegitimate investigation. So it's every girl for herself! Speaking of which, how did you make out at Kazan's table tonight? Did you find out anything interesting?"

"A couple of things," she said, eyes twinkling.

"Like what?" I yelped, tail wagging. (Call me a ghoul, but I felt much better discussing the murder than I did talking about Dan.)

"I discovered that Ben Gazzara is a real dreamboat!" she exclaimed. "He's my kind of man, Fran! He's so yummy and clever you could just *plotz*. I'm not kidding. For Ben, I would convert to Italian. Elia Kazan, on the other hand, is—"

"Abby!" I screeched. "Gazzara and Kazan aren't suspects! They're of no concern to me. And I certainly don't need to know how yummy they are—or aren't, as the case may be. I only want to know about Binky and Baldy. Remember them? They were the *other* two guys at the table—the ones who *are* under suspicion—the ones you were *supposed* to observe. Did you, by some remote chance or accident, happen to discover anything about *them?*!" To say that I was exasperated would be like calling a hurricane breezy.

"Cool it, Paige!" Abby said, crushing her cigarette in the ashtray and shooting me a nasty look. "Why do you have to make such a *tsimmis* out of everything?"

"A what?"

"A *tsimmis*," she said. "It's a stew, a mess—oh, never mind!" She crossed her arms over her chest and stamped her foot on the floor. "The point is I *did* learn some things about Binky and Baldy, and I was getting around to that, but you wouldn't give me a chance. Instead of listening to my story, you had to kick up a big fuss and make me feel like a fool. That wasn't very nice, you dig? And it was a big dumb waste of time, too."

Abby was right. I was a jerk, a shrew, a total *tsimmis*-maker. "I'm sorry, Ab," I said. "I shouldn't have jumped down your throat the way I did. I've had a hard day. Please forgive me."

"Okay!" she chirped, mood changing on a dime. "Now, where was I?" She lowered her gaze to the floor and began pacing around the living room again. "Oh, yeah, now I remember," she said, curling her blood red lips in a sardonic (make that satanic) smile. "I was telling you about Ben and Elia . . ."

Chapter 31

I DIDN'T INTERRUPT HER THIS TIME. I just let her talk until she got it all out of her system. (It was either that or sit through another speech about how impatient and critical I am.) I endured a long dissertation about Gazzara's strong, extra-wide shoulders, and his powerful chest, and his beautiful hands, and his wry sense of humor, and the way his deep, lusty voice made Abby's insides quiver. I was told that Kazan was brilliant and insightful and tender and adorable—and so what if he informed McCarthy's goons that a bunch of his old friends were commies? That didn't make him a stoolie—it just showed he was honest. And you have to be honest to be a good director, you know!

Aaaargh! It wasn't until I had reached the breaking point—the point where I was about to tear my hair out by the roots and run screaming from the room—that Abby finally mentioned Baldy and Binky.

"Both of our suspects are attractive, too," she said. "And guess what! Randy isn't really bald. When you're sitting as close to him as I was, you can see that his head is *shaved*. Do you believe it? I never heard of such a thing in my life! He looks really sexy that way—so *naked*, if you know what I mean—but, still, why would a big, strapping, successful theatrical producer like Randy shave off all his hair?"

"Maybe he has ringworm," I said, hoping to put a damper on Abby's sex fixation and steer the conversation in a more serious direction (i.e., away from hairstyles and on toward homicide).

"No way, Doris Day!" Abby crowed. "Except for a little stubble, the skin on his head was as smooth and soft as a baby's. I ran my fingers over his scalp, so I know what I'm talking about. There wasn't even any evidence of razor burn."

My patience hit the wall with a splat. "Was there any evidence of anything *else*?" I seethed, forcing my words through clenched teeth. "Any evidence, for instance, that Baldy killed Gray Gordon?"

"No," she said, oblivious to my surly tone. "I couldn't tell if Randy has a violent streak or not. I was at their table for just a short while, you know, and he acted sweet as a puppy the whole time. There's one thing I *did* find out, though." She finally stopped her fitful pacing and sat down next to me on the couch. "Randolph Godfrey Winston is a total fruit."

"You mean he's gay?"

"One hundred percent."

"How do you know?"

"It was obvious. Randy didn't respond to me in a manly way at all, you dig? He enjoyed my style and my company, but he never once looked at me as a woman. Not even when I put my hand on his thigh! He studied my clothes and makeup carefully, but he didn't look into my eyes, or at my lips or breasts, the way most men do. Take my word for it, Paige. He's a pansy . . . Hey, I've got a good idea!" she said, light bulb flashing over her head. "We should fix him up with Willy!"

I couldn't believe my ears. "Not if he's a *murderer*, we shouldn't!"

"Oh, yeah, I forgot about that."

See what I was up against? Getting Abby to focus on foul play instead of foreplay was like fighting a forest fire with a squirt gun.

"What about Binky?" I asked. "How did he behave? Did you find out anything about him?"

"Plenty," she said, giving me a frisky grin. "He's got a fabulous build and the most hypnotic hazel eyes I've ever seen. And there's nothing queer in *his* closet. He kept touching my

hand and brushing his leg against mine under the table. If
Jimmy and I weren't tight right now, I would've made a big
play for Binky tonight. He's really hot, Dot!"

I couldn't take it anymore. I jumped up from the couch and
fled into the kitchen. (It was either that or strangle my best
friend.) "I'm going to make a pot of coffee," I told her, struggling to keep my voice and emotions down to a temperate
level. "It's almost five o'clock. I have to go to work soon."

Abby followed me into the kitchen and sat down at the
table, propping her elbows on the yellow Formica and planting her chin in her upturned hands. "Hey, what's your problem, Paige?" she asked. "Why the brush-off? Don't you want
to hear the rest of my story?"

"That depends," I said, filling the coffeepot with water.

"On what?"

I set the pot down on the counter and turned to look her
square in the face. "On whether you have anything to report
about Binky besides his physical attributes and sexual inclinations."

Her cheeks reddened and her nostrils flared. "So *that's* it!"
she snorted. "You've got your uptight tushy in a twist again.
You think I'm too preoccupied with the sex angle."

"Well, aren't you?"

"Yes—but that's the most important part!" she cried. "And
if you weren't such a prig, you'd know I'm right. Whoever
killed Gray was in a vicious rage—so vicious he slashed poor
Gray to shreds. This wasn't one of your average, grab-the-
money-and-run murders, you dig? It was a crime of real *passion*. And where does passion come from, Miss Prissy Pants?
Love, hate, jealousy, or *sex*—that's where!"

Okay, she had a good point. But it certainly wasn't the only
point. I mean, as helpful as it was to know the sexual leanings
of our suspects, it wasn't all we needed to know. Not by a long
shot. And right now I was looking for more practical information. Something useful and definitive. Something we could
roll up our sleeves and work with.

"Look, I know sex is important, Ab," I said, softening my
tone and sitting down across from her at the table. "It's a
major force in life, and sometimes death. It's the primary
cause of most passion crimes. But there are other kinds of
passion, too, you know. People can be fiercely passionate

about their families, or their bank accounts, or their careers—or even their *wardrobes*," I stressed. "Present company excluded, of course."

"Ha ha," she said, with a menacing sneer.

I gave her a friendly wink and went on. "So that's why I was questioning the narrow focus of your investigation, Ab. Especially in relation to Binky. I could be wrong, but it seems to me that something other than sex—namely professional jealousy and a raging desire to advance his own career—might have given Barnabas Kapinsky a strong motive for murder."

Abby cocked her head and arched both eyebrows. "Aha!" she whooped. "I get your drift. You think Binky did it!"

"I didn't say that!" I protested. "I was just saying that *if* Binky *did* kill Gray, it probably didn't have anything to do with sex. It was more likely because he was jealous of Gray and wanted his job."

Abby gave me a sober look. "Well, if that was the case, he got what he wanted."

"Huh?"

"Gray's job," she said. "They gave it to Binky. He starts tomorrow."

"Really?"

"Yes, really!" she said, rolling her eyes. "Why would I lie?"

"But how could he start tomorrow?" I probed. "Doesn't he have to learn the part first and rehearse the role on stage?"

"Sure, but Binky swears that won't take him very long. I heard him talking about it with Elia. He says he knows the whole part backwards and forwards already—that all he needs is a little stage direction."

"Ver-r-ry interesting," I said, wheels turning.

Proud that she'd captured my attention, Abby quickly continued her report. "Elia told Binky he'd have to be at the theater first thing in the morning to rehearse, and that he'd have to stay there for the rest of the day, through both the matinee and the evening performances, to study the play's presentation and be available in case he's needed on stage."

"Gosh, that was fast!" I said. "These Broadway boys don't mess around."

"In this case, they didn't have to. Binky is perfect for the part and very well-prepared."

"Yeah, a little *too* well-prepared, if you ask me."

"What do you mean?"

"I mean Binky must have been preparing to take over this role long before Gray was murdered."

"Ohhhhh . . ." Abby said, as my words sank in. "I see what you're saying. Maybe Binky knew Gray's job was going to become available because he intended to create the opening himself."

"Exactly."

"*Oy vey!*" she shrieked, eyeballs bulging. "Somebody better warn Ben right away!"

"Who? Wha—"

"Ben!" she cried. "Ben Gazzara! If Binky killed Gray just to get the *understudy* role, how far do you think he'll go to land the lead? Ben better get himself a bodyguard immediately. His days are numbered!"

"Simmer down, sis," I said, smiling at Abby's dramatic outburst. "Now *you're* making a *tsimmis*. Let me remind you that we don't have any idea if Binky is guilty or not. In fact, what little knowledge we *do* have points in other directions entirely. The creep who was shadowing me tonight definitely wasn't Binky, and the creep who bashed me on the head last night had to be either Blackie or Aunt Doobie—not Binky.

"We've got more suspects than we can handle," I went on. "We can't run around making any wild, unfounded accusations. And we certainly can't tell Gazzara his life may be in danger. He would call in the cops, and Flannagan would arrest *us* instead of Binky."

"Well, we've got to do something!" Abby blustered. She jumped up from the table and started pacing the floor again.

"I agree with you," I said. "Not because I'm afraid for Gazzara's life—which, at this point, I can assure you I'm *not*—but because I'm determined to discover who ended Gray's life. I'm not kidding, Abby. I'm going to find out who killed Gray Gordon if it's the last thing I do!" (The minute those words escaped my mouth, I wished I'd put them a different way.)

"Any idea how you're going to accomplish this stunt?" Abby asked, suddenly stopping her pacing. She stepped over to the kitchen counter and began spooning coffee into the waiting pot.

"The only way I know how," I said. "By following every lead and digging up all the evidence I can."

"So what's next on the agenda?"

"The first thing I want to do is get inside Binky's apartment," I said. "There are a couple of things I want to look for, and tomorrow—I mean, today—will be the perfect opportunity. Binky won't be home all day, so I'll have plenty of time to pick the lock and comb the place for clues."

"Do you know where Binky lives?"

"Yes, over on Third Avenue between Thirty-second and Thirty-third. I got the address from the phone book. There's only one Barnabas Kapinsky listed, and the phone number matches the one in Gray's message pad."

Abby snapped the lid on the coffee and put the pot on the stove to perk. Then she twirled around, folded her arms across her chest and—speaking in a voice as firm as flint—announced, "I'm going with you."

"Oh, no you're not!" I sputtered. "I can't have you snooping around underfoot, messing up the evidence, making noise and alerting the neighbors!"

"Then I'll go without you," she declared. "I have as much right to case Binky's apartment as you do. You said every girl for herself, remember?"

"Yes, but I didn't mean—"

"I don't care what you meant! I'm going to search Binky's pad and that's final. I've got a good eye and I might spot something you'd miss. So what's it gonna be, Lee? With you or without you—it's all the same to me."

I couldn't let her go alone, but I couldn't stop her, either. "I give up," I groaned. "I'll call you from the office later and tell you when to meet me."

"Good," she said, snatching her purse, sunglasses, and Rita Hayworth wig off the table and heading for the door. "Your coffee will be ready soon. Better drink lots of it or you'll fall asleep at work."

"Don't you want some?" I asked.

"Not a drop, pop!" she said, with a goofy grin. "I'm going home to take a nap."

Chapter 32

AFTER ABBY LEFT, I DRANK TWO CUPS
of coffee, took a shower, got dressed for work, then smoked a
bunch of cigarettes and drank some more coffee. I'd like to
tell you that I went through these motions with a fair measure
of grace and composure, but the truth was I was bawling the
whole time. I couldn't get the picture of Dan kissing that
woman out of my mind. If I'd had a gun, I would have blown
my brains out just for relief. (Okay, okay! Maybe that's a
slight exaggeration—but what do you expect from a writer
named Paige Turner?)

Finally, after an hour or two of sobbing and self-torture, it
was time for me to head to the office. I dried my swollen eyes,
blew my runny red nose, applied a new coat of mascara, and
hit the sidewalk for the subway.

I was in such a muddled frame of mind, I didn't notice the
change right away. In fact, I walked all the way to Sheridan
Square without perceiving any difference at all. But then suddenly, just as I was heading down the steps to the subway station, the realization swept over me like an ocean breeze. My
face wasn't dripping with sweat. My feet weren't sizzling inside my stilettos. My breathing was almost normal. The heat
wave had finally broken!

Exhaling a grateful sigh, I descended the rest of the steps

and ventured into the tiled depths of the subway. It was even cooler underground. I took a seat on the uptown local, which had just pulled into the station, and then, as the screaking train pulled out again, began reading the overhead advertisements, hoping they'd help me keep my mind off Dan. I did not want to start crying again.

In the ad directly across the aisle, a sexy blonde in a slinky black dress was lounging on the "Airliner Reclining Seat" of a new 1955 Rambler, inviting all onlookers inside for a "Deep Coil Ride." Next to her, an ad pushing "Houses for the Atomic Age!" proclaimed the "unique design for these all-concrete blast-resistant homes was based on principles learned at Hiroshima and Nagasaki." And next to that pack of lies danced a pack of Old Gold cigarettes. I say *danced* because the package of smokes was, by some miracle of modern science, prancing around on a pair of shapely feminine (i.e., human) legs. The copy beneath the familiar image said, "No song and dance about medical claims—Old Gold's specialty is to give you a TREAT instead of a TREATMENT!"

Soon tiring of the absurd advertisements, I closed my aching, bloodshot eyes and gave them a rest until we pulled into the Times Square station. Then I hopped off the train and headed for the crosstown shuttle. Turning my head for a second as I was walking toward the gate to the shuttle, I caught a glimpse of a man in dark clothing sneaking along in the rush hour crowd behind me.

Oh, my god! Is this guy going to follow me everywhere? And what's his motive, anyway? Is he just looking for a good place to kill me?

Emboldened by the presence of so many people, and determined to catch the creeper off-guard and get a good look at his face, I pretended that I hadn't noticed him and continued walking ahead for about thirty yards. And then suddenly, without any delay or warning, I jerked to a halt, jumped around in a fast about-face and landed in a menacing combat stance.

"Yeow!!" cried the startled old man right behind me. He was so taken aback by my sudden maneuver that he lurched, stumbled, and dropped his walking stick on the floor.

"Oh, I'm so sorry, sir!" I stammered, hurrying to help him

balance himself, then picking up his cane. "I didn't mean to
frighten you."

"Eh?" he croaked, holding a gnarly hand up to one ear.
"What did you say?"

Oh, dear. Deaf as well as lame. (Can I pick 'em, or what?)

"I said I didn't mean to frighten you!" I shouted.

The old man still didn't hear me. But Blackie, or Aunt
Doobie, or whoever had been tailing me, must have heard me
loud and clear, because when I raised my eyes and looked
around for him, he was gone. *Pffffffft!* Vanished completely.

Just par for the course, I thought, handing the wobbly old
man his cane and tucking my arm under his elbow. He looked
shaken and disoriented. "Can I help you, sir?" I asked, leaning down and screaming directly into his ear. "Where do you
want to go?"

"Er, ah, ub . . . shuttle," he burbled, "eastbound." A thin
line of spit was dribbling down his chin.

I gave him a big smile and slowly guided him toward the
gate, truly glad we were taking the same train. There are times
in a fearful, crazed, heartbroken girl's life when she needs a
little company.

I BOUGHT A CORN MUFFIN IN THE LOBBY
coffee shop, then took the elevator up to nine. As far as I could
tell, nobody had followed me into the building. I still felt a little uneasy, though, so when I exited the elevator and saw that
the long hallway leading to my office was totally deserted, I—
well, let's just say I overreacted (that's a much nicer word
than panicked, don't you think?). I ran (okay, rocketed) down
to the *Daring Detective* door, unlocked it and hopped inside,
then slammed it right behind me and locked it tight again.
None of my coworkers were due to arrive for at least thirty
minutes, and I didn't want any surprise visitors.

But I was *very* surprised when, ten minutes later—after I'd
finished my muffin and begun sorting the mail—somebody
started twisting the knob and throwing their weight against
the door. (At least that's what it sounded like: a large body
thumping repeatedly against a flat wooden blockade.) My first
impulse was to hide under my desk, but I didn't want to behave like a coward (or get a run in my new nylons), so I

jumped to my feet instead. Then I tiptoed over to the door and held my ear as close to the jamb as I dared, listening for clues to the body-bumping knob-twister's identity.

I couldn't tell a thing from the wrenching and thumping sounds, but the reeking wet cigar smell was a dead giveaway.

"Mr. Crockett?" I timidly inquired. "Is that you?"

"Yeah!" he bellowed. "Open up!"

Whew!

I unlocked the door, pulled it wide, and watched my boss propel himself inside and over to the coat tree, smoldering cigar stub clenched between his teeth. Without a single hello or how-do-you-do (or even a query as to why the office door had been locked) he removed his hat and jacket and hooked them on the tree. Then he plucked the chewed-up, nearly burnt-out stogie from the corner of his mouth and squashed it in Pomeroy's ashtray.

"Coffee," he grunted, heading down the aisle of the common workroom toward his private office in the back. "And bring me the morning papers."

"You're in early today, Mr. Crockett," I said to his retreating back. "I haven't made the coffee yet."

As he turned to enter his office he shot me a grumpy look. "So, what are you waiting for? Do it now."

I was so used to Crockett's brusque, disrespectful style, I didn't bother to get upset. I just picked up the heavy Coffeemaster and lugged it into the ladies' room to wash it and fill it with water. Luckily, there were no suspicious, dark-clothed characters lurking in the hallway.

When I returned to the office, sloshing coffeemaker balanced on one hip, Lenny was standing in the reception area just inside the door. He was carrying his art portfolio in one hand, his lunchbox in the other, and he was huffing and puffing like a long-distance runner on his last legs. I wasn't surprised that Lenny was out of breath. When a thin, unathletic fellow is terrified of elevators and has to climb nine flights to get to work, a certain amount of huffing and puffing is to be expected.

"Hiya, Zimmerman," I said, setting the Coffeemaster down on the service table and measuring out the Maxwell House. "How's tricks?"

"Okay," he said, still panting for air. "It's not so ... hot today, thank ... God."

"Yes, the good Lord's smiling on us now," I said. "But it's the least he could do, wouldn't you say? For the past five days he's been laughing his almighty head off." I plugged in the coffeemaker, walked over to my desk, and started arranging the morning newspapers in a tidy pile.

"Hey, speaking of days past," Lenny said, his breathing returning to normal, "where did you disappear to yesterday? You left work in such a hurry, you didn't even say good night."

"I had to go meet somebody, and I couldn't be late. I'm working on an important story assignment, don't ya know." I gave Lenny a conspiratorial wink, hoping that would mollify his curiosity. I didn't feel like discussing the case or telling him what happened at the Actors Studio. And I didn't even want to *think* about what took place at Sardi's.

"Who did you meet?" Lenny persisted. "Did you learn anything new?"

"Nothing significant—unless you want to count the fact that Ben Gazzara makes Abby's insides quiver."

"Who? You mean the actor? What does Abby have to do with—"

"I'll tell you later, Len. Right now I have to take Mr. Crockett the newspapers." I scooped the early editions up in my arms and scurried off to deliver them. Then I exited Crockett's office and scooted back over to the service table to fix him a cup of coffee.

Lenny was still standing in the front of the workroom, anxiously tapping his metal lunchbox against his thigh. "What's going on, Paige?" he demanded. "Why are your eyes so red and puffy? Something happened last night, and I want to know what it was."

"Sorry, Len. Gotta take the boss his java," I said, scurrying away again. While I was in Crockett's office, setting his cup down on his desk, the front door entry bell rang. Glad for the timely interruption, and quickly assuming my required receptionist role, I went out into the workroom to see who had come in. It was Mike and Mario, of course (somehow they always managed to arrive together), and it was probably the first time in my entire *Daring Detective* career that I was pleased to see them.

Surely *they* would keep me from thinking about Dan.

"Gooooood morning, Paige Turner," Mario intoned, big lips curving in a devious smile. "You look very enticing today . . . Isn't that right, Mike?" he asked, giving his partner in crime an exacting look. "Doesn't she look fetching?"

"Uh, yeah, I guess so," Mike said, not sure how Mario wanted him to respond. He removed his hat and jacket and hung them on the rack. "Very enticing," he echoed, just to be on the safe side.

"You can say that again!" Mario went on, hanging up his hat and jacket and walking down the aisle toward his desk, and—since I was standing near his desk—toward me. "You know what I think?" he said, talking to Mike but staring straight at me. "I think she looks like a hot new mystery novel—so juicy and sensational, you want to set her down on your lap, open her up, and turn all her pages."

Mike started laughing, and then Mario joined in. Pretty soon, they were howling like two harebrained hyenas.

"Hey, shut the hell up out there!" Mr. Crockett yelled from his office, never looking up from the newspaper. (From where I was standing I could see that his nose was buried in the *Herald Tribune*.) "Pipe down and get to work!"

Mario sat down at his desk and then Mike made his way to his own. Then Lenny walked back to the rear of the workroom, stashed his portfolio and lunchbox on the floor right next to his desk, and—giving me a stern you-better-tell-me-what-the-hell-is-going-on-soon squint—sat down in his wooden swivel chair and turned toward his drawing board.

Aisle finally clear, I walked back to my desk in the front of the room and sat down with my back to the boys. Then I took a deep breath, picked up my pencil, and—doing my doggone damnedest to read and edit Mike's latest story—started thinking about Dan again.

Chapter 33

MY OFFICE DICTIONARY DEFINED OBSES-
sion as "the domination of one's thoughts or feelings by a persistent idea, image, or desire." I already knew the meaning of
the word, of course, but I looked it up anyway. My obsession
with Dan had reached the sickening stage, and I wanted to see
if the dictionary would offer a useful antidote or cure.

No way, Doris Day. All Random House presented was the
list of symptoms, which—big surprise!—described my state
of mind to a T. Especially the persistent image part. No matter what I tried to focus on that morning—the galleys I had to
proofread, the stories I had to edit, the newspapers I had to
clip—all I could see was the clinch and the kiss (i.e., the
locked-together limbs and lips of my daring detective and his
ravishing redhead).

I was going out of my mind.

I really couldn't stand it anymore.

So when Brandon Pomeroy arrived at the office (early
again, if you can believe that!), I was elated. (Okay, not really
elated, but more like . . . well, happy for the change of scene.)

"Good morning, Mr. Pomeroy," I said, smiling. "Enjoying
the cooler weather?"

"Yes, Mrs. Turner," he stiffly replied. "It's a considerable
relief." He didn't return my smile, but he didn't bite my head

off, either. Could his newfound courtesy, I wondered, have anything to do with my new story assignment?

Pomeroy took his pipe out of his jacket pocket and hung the jacket on the coat tree. As he was walking around his desk to his chair, he spied Crockett's soggy cigar stub in his ashtray and made a horrified face. "That's disgusting!" he hollered at me. (*Jeez!* Did he think *I* was the one who left it there?) "Please take it away this instant! I can't work with a rancid cigar sitting right under my nose."

At least he said please.

I sprang across the aisle and picked up his heavy marble ashtray, which I then carted into the file room and emptied into the large trash can in the corner. (I certainly didn't want to put the stinky stub in *my* wastebasket!) Ordinarily, I would have been fuming (in silence, of course) over Pomeroy's rude and despotic treatment, but today I was grateful for the diversion. It beat the heck out of obsessing over the clinch and the kiss.

Returning to the workroom with the empty ashtray in my hand, I took a look at the clock. It was eleven thirty—an hour before my lunchtime, and a good three hours before the type-setter's messenger was due to come pick up the corrected proofs and stories. *If only I could go search Binky's apartment right now!* I said to myself. *That would save me from having a nervous breakdown over Dan, and I could still get back to the office in time to finish my day's work.* Well, some of it, anyway.

"Can I speak to you for a second, Mr. Pomeroy?" I ventured, replacing the ashtray on his desk and giving him a piercing (okay, pleading) look. "It's about the story assignment you gave me yesterday."

Pomeroy sat up straighter in his chair and granted me his full attention. "Yes, of course, Mrs. Turner," he said, mustache twitching to one side. "How can I help you? What's on your mind?"

I was so shocked by his keen (not to mention cordial) re-action, it took me a few seconds to gather my wits and con-coct a reply.

"I've been investigating the murder of Gray Gordon, just as you directed," I said, leaning over his desk and lowering my voice to a near whisper. "And I've begun to make some real headway. Detective Flannagan of the Sixth Precinct is in charge of the case, and I've learned the identity of his primary suspect. But I think he's focusing on the wrong guy," I added, pausing to let the weight of my statement sink in. "I think somebody else is the murderer, and I'm working around the clock to dig up enough evidence to prove it."

I'd never seen Pomeroy so aroused. He sat up even taller in his chair and began puffing so intently on his pipe you'd have thought it was his last smoke before facing a firing squad. "That's good, Mrs. Turner," he murmured. "Very good indeed. This is an important story, and I expect you to keep your nose to the grindstone until the murder is solved. It would be a real feather in my . . . er, the magazine's cap if you could crack this case before the police do."

Uh oh! I smelled a rat. Why was this particular story so important, and why the strong desire to beat out the police? Pomeroy had never shown such interest in a murder case (or even the magazine!) before. I was dying to ask him a few questions—try to find out who or what had set the fire under his tail—but I was unwilling to change the direction of our dialogue. It seemed more urgent that I find a way to break out of the office and into Binky's apartment.

"I think I'm really close to identifying the killer, sir," I said. "And I got a lead just this morning that could bust the case wide open." (Don't blame me for that last sentence. I was copying Humphrey Bogart.)

"Oh, really?" Pomeroy said, beady eyes turning even beadier. "What kind of a lead?"

"An anonymous one, sir, and I'm not at liberty to discuss it. Not *yet*," I stressed. "It will all come out in due time. All I can tell you at the moment is that it has something to do with the murder weapon, which was never found at the scene. And now it's imperative that I leave the office immediately and go to a certain place to search for it."

Pomeroy glared at me and then looked at his watch. "It's only eleven thirty six," he said, poking his pipe stem between his lips and chewing on the tip. "Your lunch hour doesn't start for fifty-four minutes." (Do you believe that?! Here I was, on the verge of solving a sensational murder and completing an important story assignment, and all Pomeroy could think about was the *time*.)

"If I wait for my lunch hour it'll be too late," I said. "The police might get there before me."

That did it.

"You have my permission to leave, Mrs. Turner," Pomeroy said, blowing a stream of fruity smoke in my direction. "You can make up the time tomorrow."

I EXITED THE ELEVATOR AND WALKED straight across the lobby to the string of open phone booths banked against the wall. Choosing the first available phone I came to, I dropped a nickel in the slot and dialed Abby.

"Rise and shine," I said, as soon as the receiver was picked up. "The time has come for breaking and entering!" (If I sounded excited, it was because I *was*. I was a racehorse breaking out of the gate. I was a feverish bloodhound on the trail of a fresh, hot scent.)

"Huh? What?" It was a male voice and it sounded deeper and dopier than usual.

"Oh, hi, Jimmy," I said. "This is Paige. Let me speak to Abby."

"Can't. She's sleeping."

"Hmmm," I said, stalling, wondering if I should ask him to wake her or just let sleeping dogs lie. I'd done my duty, after all. I'd promised to call Abby, and I had. It wasn't my fault that she was still asleep. (*I*, if you recall, hadn't had any sleep at all!) *And now my time is running out! I convinced myself. What the heck am I supposed to do? Chuck a really important part of my investigation just because my sex-crazed sidekick is catching a few Zs? That would be nuts! Abby can't possibly blame me if I go to Binky's place without her . . .*

I was about to say goodbye, hang up, and head for Binky's when a loud rustling noise came over the receiver, then a series of weird snorting sounds. "Unnphh . . . snick . . . frunkt . . . yello?" Abby honked. "S'that you, Paige? What's up? Are you ready to crash Binky's pad?"

Curses, foiled again.

"Yeah, I'm going there right now," I said. "You want to meet me or stay in bed?" I was, as you may have guessed, kind of hoping she'd opt for the latter.

"I'll be there in twenty minutes," she said. "Don't you dare go in without me."

THE TEMPERATURE HAD DROPPED AT least ten degrees, so I walked the ten blocks down to Third and 33rd in relative comfort (except for my painful high heels, which belonged in a torture chamber, not on the sidewalk). I would have taken the Third Avenue el if it had still been running, but service on the seventy-seven-year-old train line had been shut down about a month ago, and I was left to my own devices (i.e., feet). The elevated track was due to be demolished soon, but for now it was still in existence, looming high over Third Avenue's whizzing automobile traffic, casting its dense, dark shadow for miles.

I arrived at Binky's apartment building shortly before noon and stepped into the vestibule to check the names on the mailboxes. There it was, on the very first box: Barnabas Kapinsky, apartment 1A. I had come to the right place. Thinking I should make sure that Binky wasn't there, I rang the buzzer for 1A. No answer. I waited a few seconds and rang it again. Still no answer. So I rang it a third time . . . and a fourth . . . and a fifth . . . and then, convinced that the coast was clear, stepped back outside to wait for Abby.

Figuring I'd be waiting for quite a while (it's a very long walk from Bleecker Street to the east Thirties, and there's no direct mode of public transportation), I leaned against the wall of Binky's building and surveyed my surroundings. Had Blackie or Aunt Doobie followed me here? I didn't think so. I had checked my back many times on the walk downtown, and I hadn't spied a single stalker in the shadows. And now, although the sidewalks were full of people—workers, shoppers, strollers, lunchgoers—they all looked quite innocent in the bright sunlight and their light-colored summer clothing.

But I kept my eyes peeled just the same.

And that's when I saw it. A long black limousine! It came cruising up Third Avenue like a long black yacht, slowing down to rowboat speed as it approached Binky's building.

Yikes! Is that Baldy's limo? Did it follow me here? Who's inside? Where can I hide? In the vestibule? No! Too Danger-

ous! What if Baldy's bringing Binky home or something like that? I'd really be stuck then!

In a total panic—and for lack of a better alternative—I leapt over to the curb and crouched down on my haunches behind a parked two-tone Mercury (pink and white, in case you're wondering). Then, hoping to get a glimpse of the limo's passengers (and praying with all my might they would be strangers), I duck-walked up to the nose of the Mercury and craned my neck around the headlights, staring through the gap between the parked cars at the traffic going by on the street.

When the long black limo drove into my sight, I felt a surge of relief. At least it hadn't stopped in front of Binky's building. As I gazed up at the slowly passing vehicle, however, and tried to peer through the windows to see who was inside, I felt nothing but defeat. There were thick gray velvet curtains on the windows and they were closed.

"Hey, what the hell are you doing down there? Taking a leak?"

I turned my head and looked up. It was Abby. She was perched on a bicycle.

"Very funny," I said, placing one hand on the hood of the Mercury and pulling myself up to a standing position. "For your information, I was hiding from a black limousine— which may, or may not, have been Baldy's. See?" I said, pointing uptown. "It's on the next block, headed north."

One foot on the sidewalk for balance, Abby raised her head, shaded her eyes with her hand, and gazed in the designated direction. "Yeah, I see it. It's stopped at the light on Thirty-fourth."

"I can't read the license plate, can you?"

"No, it's too far. Should I chase after it?"

"Are you nuts? You'll never catch up. Not unless that bicycle has a motor."

Abby laughed. "No, but it's got everything else. Red frame and red handle grips. Silver fenders. White plastic seat. This beauty is a Schwinn Jaguar Deluxe and it's built for speed, baby!"

"You sound like a commercial."

"Hey, I really like this bike! And it got me here on time, didn't it?"

"Sure did," I said, glancing at my watch. It was only ten after twelve. (Time crawls when you're scared for your life.) "Where did you get the cycle, Ab? From one of Jimmy's friends?"

"No, I borrowed it from Fabrizio, a kid who lives down the block from us. He got it for his birthday. Told me I could use it anytime I want to."

"Nice kid."

"Real nice," she said, dismounting, popping the kickstand and chain—locking the bike to a lamppost. "I owe Fabrizio one." She straightened up and wiped her hands on the sides of her plaid pedal pushers. "Is this Binky's building?" she asked, flipping her braid off her shoulder and nodding toward the five-story tan brick structure behind me.

"Yep!" I said, thrilling to the chase. "Let's get going."

Chapter 34

I RANG BINKY'S BUZZER A FEW MORE
times, just to be on the safe side. He still didn't answer.

"Okay, he's not home," I said to Abby, who was busy reading the other names on the mailboxes. "Let's buzz somebody
on the top floor to let us in." Remembering how Abby had
tricked Willy into letting us enter Gray's building, I figured
we should use the same buzzer tactic again. "Since Binky
lives on the first floor," I said, "we might be able to get inside
his apartment before the person we buzz on the fifth floor ever
gets suspicious or comes downstairs to look for us."

"Good plan," Abby said. "Let's try Mrs. Lettie Forrest in
5C."

"Okay," I said. "I'll do it. Only what should I say when she
answers? Should I pretend to be a messenger of some kind?
Or say I have a telegram? Or maybe I should—"

"Oh, hush! I'll do it!" Abby nudged me aside and pushed
the buzzer for 5C without hesitation. "You always make such
a *tsimmis*!"

"Yes, who's there?" came a tinny female voice over the intercom.

"Is this Mrs. Lettie Forrest?" Abby asked, answering the
woman's question with a question.

"Yes," the woman tentatively replied. "Who's this?"

"I'm from the flower shop down the street, ma'am. I have a delivery for you."

"Flowers? For me?"

"Yes, ma'am. Should I bring them up?"

"Why, yes, of course!" she said, buzzing us in.

That was quick.

We pushed through the humming door and scurried across the tiny foyer to the apartment marked 1A. I gave the doorknob a hefty twist, but it was locked.

"Oh, no!" I whispered. "It's locked!"

Abby propped her hands on her hips and gave me a weary look. "Oh, really?" she croaked. "What a shock! It's so unfair the way people keep locking their doors these days! I don't know what this world is coming to."

"Shhhhh, keep your voice down."

"I didn't bring my purse," she said, ignoring my plea for volume control. "Do you have a nail file or a bobby pin?"

"Yes, but those things don't work! I've tried them in the past so I know. They only work in the movies."

"Hand 'em over," she said, holding out her palm. "Maybe I'll have better luck."

I opened my purse and fished out the items. Then, while Abby was down on her knees wriggling the hairpin in the keyhole and trying to trip the latch with the nail file, I rooted through the rest of the stuff in my clutch bag, looking for something else—*anything* else—that might be useful. "Hey, how about this?" I said, removing an empty plastic photo holder from my new red leather Dale Rogers wallet (silly, I know, but they had a half-off sale in Woolworth's). I held the holder up for her inspection. "I bet this'll do the trick."

Abby rose to full height and propped her hands on her hips again. "A piece of plastic?" she scoffed. "You expect to break open a door with a puny piece of plastic? What's the matter, don't you have anything stronger? A piece of gum, maybe? Or a Kleenex?"

"Oh, c'mon, Abby! I'm not fooling around! I wrote a clip story for the magazine about a cat burglar who used these things to break into people's houses at night. No kidding! He told the police how they worked, and he said they were quiet, easy to carry, and practically infallible. I titled the story

'Plastic-Packing Papa.' Get it? It's a play on 'Pistol-Packing Mama' and it—"

"Hello, flower girl?" Mrs. Lettie Forrest shouted from the top of the nearby stairwell. "Where are you? Are you coming up? Did you get lost?"

We didn't answer her, of course.

"Hello?" she called again. "Is anybody down there?"

We remained as quiet as mice—or cat burglars, if you prefer.

Finally, after a couple more calls and ensuing silences, Lettie gave up. She went back inside her apartment and slammed the door.

I had broken out in a nervous sweat, but Abby was giggling. "Poor Lettie," she said. "When I get home, I'll send her some daisies. But for now, we'd better get to work, you dig?" She stepped away from the door and made a sweeping gesture toward the lock. "It's all yours, babe. Give that wallet thingamabob a whirl. Maybe the plastic is magic!"

And believe it or not, it *was*. I sank into a squat, eased the stiff plastic picture holder between the lock and the doorjamb, gave it a wiggle and a jiggle and—click!—we were in.

BINKY'S APARTMENT WAS SMALL. VERY, very small. The kitchen was the size of a closet and the living room was so cramped Abby and I had to walk in single file to pass through it. Every piece of furniture in the room—the couch, two chairs, a table, and a television set—was set flush against a wall so as not to take up too much space. There was a separate bedroom, but all it could—and, indeed, did—hold was a small chest of drawers and a single bed.

"I don't get it," Abby said. "Binky's a pretty big guy. How can he stand to live in such a tiny place?"

"I don't know, but I'm glad he does. It won't take us long to case the joint." (Humphrey Bogart or James Cagney, take your pick.)

"Where do we start?" Abby asked. "You said you wanted to look for a couple of things. What things?"

"The murder weapon primarily—a butcher knife, or something like that. Also a stash of bloody clothes and a pair of bloody shoes."

"Ick!" Abby said, making a face. "The knife I understand—it could be cleaned up and put back in the drawer like nothing ever happened. But why the clothes? If Binky was the murderer, wouldn't he have gotten rid of anything that had Gray's blood on it?"

"If he was in his right mind," I said, "and if he had the right opportunity. But those are two very big ifs." I thought of my own bloody clothes and sandals, which were still sitting in a bag in the back of my coat closet, needing to be disposed of but totally forgotten until this very moment. "We know from Flannagan that the killer took a shower and changed his clothes before he left Gray's apartment," I went on, "and we know from our own firsthand observation that he didn't leave anything—either the weapon or the gory clothes—at the scene."

"Yeah, so?"

"So what did he do with them?" I questioned. "Maybe he burned them, or buried them, or tossed them in the East River. Or maybe he was so deranged and charged-up and afraid of getting caught that he ran straight home after the killing and hid the whole kit and caboodle in his apartment, figuring he'd get rid of the stuff after the heat blew over." (Bogart, definitely Bogart.)

"Okay, okay! I hear you!" Abby said, shushing me up with her dismissive hand gestures. "That's enough talking. We're wasting time. You take the kitchen, I'll start here in the living room."

"Hey, wait a minute! Why the big rush? You said Binky would be gone all day. There's no reason to hurry. I think we should take it real slow and do a very careful, thorough search of the premises. This is the only chance we're ever going to get, and we can't afford to do a sloppy job. This is really, really important!"

"I dig, I dig!" Abby said (impatiently, as usual). "I'll crawl like a snail, Gail." And to prove it she flipped on the living room light, dropped down to her hands and knees on the brown linoleum floor, then crawled across the room and stuck her head under the couch.

Anxious to get started myself, I darted into the minuscule kitchen, yanked open the drawer (there was only one), and started rummaging through the utensils. I found it almost immediately—a big knife with a broad, sharp blade; the kind used to cut up meat. I could easily imagine the large knife dripping with blood and gore, but the plain fact was—as of this minute, and as far as my unaided eye could see—it was clean as a whistle. Having no idea if this was the weapon that killed Gray Gordon, and no reasonable way to make that determination, I decided to leave the knife where it was for the time being and continue searching for real evidence (i.e., something with real blood on it).

I looked through the overhead cabinets lining the walls of the doorless, windowless kitchen, finding nothing but a couple of pots and pans, a can of beans, a box of Hi Ho crackers, three cans of Libby's fruit cocktail, a box of Wheaties, a jar of Ovaltine, and a motley assortment of dishes and glasses. The cabinet under the sink offered nothing but a blue dishrag and a giant-size bottle of Glim dishwashing liquid. *Probably good for cleaning bloody knives,* I mused. The oven was empty, and—except for a bottle of milk and a half-eaten can of fruit cocktail—the midget refrigerator was, too.

"I found a knife," I said, returning to the living room, "but I don't know if . . . Abby? Where are you?"

"In the bathroom!" she hollered, which was totally unnecessary since the apartment was so small I would have heard a whisper. "I'm checkin' out the clothes hamper."

I walked over to the open door of the bathroom and watched Abby pull a couple of pairs of boxer shorts and a damp bath towel out of a narrow white wicker basket. She was sitting on the edge of the tub, digging around in the hamper like a hobo foraging for food in the trash.

"Is there anything bloody in there?" I asked.

"Not a bloody thing!" she said, sitting upright, brushing a loose lock of hair off her face, then tossing all the stuff on the bathroom floor back into the basket. "This guy is so neat, clean, and organized, all the crap in his medicine cabinet is arranged alphabetically."

"Really?!" I exclaimed. I could feel my eyes popping in surprise.

"No, Paige! No! That was just a figure of speech—an exaggeration used to illustrate a point. You know, for a writer you're not too swift."

"Oh," I said, feeling embarrassed for a split second, but

quickly snapping my attention back to the search. "Did you find anything interesting in the living room, Ab? Anything with blood on it?"

"That's a big fat *no*, Flo!" She rolled her eyes at the ceiling. "There isn't a speck of blood in there, or probably anywhere else in this *focockta* apartment. I knew there wouldn't be. Binky may be a murderer, but he isn't stupid." She stood up from the tub, shoved the hamper back under the sink, and squeezed past me into the living room. "I did find this, though," she said, snatching something that looked like a manuscript up off the table and handing it over for my inspection. "It's the *Cat on a Hot Tin Roof* script, and the pages have been turned and folded and fondled so much they're soft as cotton."

I flipped through the well-worn script, noting several brownish splash stains throughout (Ovaltine, I figured, not blood), and one bright red PROPERTY OF THE ACTORS STUDIO stamp on the back (ink, undoubtedly ink). "The condition of this script shows Binky studied it long and hard," I said, "which supports my theory that he wanted Gray's job, but doesn't prove that he murdered him. For definite proof of that, we have to find something here with blood on it—either Gray's type O, or the killer's type A."

"Then we might as well blow this joint right now," Abby declared. "We're never going to find any evidence of blood in this spick-and-span pad. Binky's way too sharp and clean for that. And I don't think he's the killer, anyway! You know who I think did it? Aunt Doobie, that's who! If he was Gray's boyfriend like you say, then *he* was the one who did Gray in. You, of all people, should know the statistics, Paige. It's almost always the spouse or the lover."

"The key word here is *almost*," I said, with a sniff. "Besides, I've now come to the definite conclusion that Aunt Doobie is innocent."

"What?!" she shrieked. "How did you do that? Did you dig up some new clues you didn't tell me about?"

"No, I just remembered a big clue I'd forgotten about," I admitted, staring sheepishly at the floor, so ashamed of my faulty memory and slow skills of detection I considered looking for a new job. Something in retail, maybe. Or advertising.

Abby threw her hands up in the air. "*Oy!* When the hell are you planning tell me about it? Next Christmas?!"

"Oh, all right, here's the scoop," I said, looking up from the floor but unable to look her in the eye. "Remember when I went to the Mayflower Hotel the day after the murder and knocked on the door of room 96 looking for Aunt Doobie? Well, he came to the door naked, with a towel wrapped around his waist. His neck, chest, shoulders, back, legs, and arms were completely bare, and—as I saw at the time, but didn't recall until today—completely free of any scratches or slashes. He had no wounds of any kind. So he couldn't have been in a big fight with Gray or shed any of his own blood at the scene. Get the picture? Verdict: not guilty."

"Okay, so that acquits Aunt Doobie," Abby said, quickly accepting my conclusion and graciously forgoing the opportunity to scold me for my slack detective work. "But it *doesn't* automatically convict Binky. We've still got Blackie and Baldy to deal with, and—if you ask me, Bea—they're far more likely suspects. I bet they were both down by the river the night of the fireworks. I bet Blackie bonked you on the head and then escaped in Baldy's limousine."

"That's possible," I said, "but even if it's true it may have nothing to do with the murder. I've been thinking about that night a lot, and there's no reason to conclude that the person who hit me on the head is the same person who killed Gray."

"Maybe not, but—"

"And here's another reason I think Binky is the killer," I barreled on, anxious to wrap up my explanations and get on with our search. "Last evening, when I met him at the Actors Studio and sat in on his audition, the heat wave was still going strong. The temperature was 96 degrees, and the Studio wasn't air-conditioned. It was so hot all the other male students were wearing light T-shirts, yet Binky had on a heavy long-sleeved shirt buttoned up tight at the neck and the cuffs. I didn't guess why he was dressed that way then, but now I think I know. I believe he was hiding the cuts and gashes he got while Gray was fighting for his life."

Abby and I stood in silence for a moment while she thought over what I'd said. Then, suddenly, her face turned flame red and her eyes flashed hot in anger. "The bastard," she muttered under her breath, lips curling up over her teeth like a growling dog's. "Let's raid the bedroom, Paige. I'm out for blood now."

Chapter 35

ABBY TACKLED THE CHEST OF DRAWERS
and I took on the bedroom closet. Since it was the only closet
in the tiny apartment, I expected it to be packed tight with lots
of articles besides apparel. But I was wrong. Aside from the
small collection of girlie magazines stacked in one corner of
the shelf overhead, there was nothing inside but articles of
clothing—and very few of those.

Only two hats occupied space on the shelf—a gray felt fedora and a blue and white Brooklyn Dodgers baseball cap—
and the closet floor sported just three pairs of shoes: black
leather oxfords, brown leather loafers, and tan leather cowboy
boots with green stitching on the sides. Spaced along the bar
on hangers were two suits, one jacket, two pairs of slacks, one
pair of dungarees, one coat, and seven or eight shirts. Some of
the shirts had long sleeves, some short, and all but one were
white or solid pastels. The only print had long sleeves and a
maroon background with a pattern of yellow birds and palm
trees.

But no discernible blood. Although I removed each item
from the closet and examined it closely in the light—top to
bottom, front and back, inside and out—there were no incrim-
inating bloodstains to be found. No other kind of stains, either. Even the soles of the shoes were spotless.

"I give up!" I cried, backing away from the closet and plopping down on the edge of the bed. "Barnabas Kapinsky has to be the most immaculate man in Manhattan—except when he's slashing people to pieces, that is. Jesus! How did he do it? How did he cover, or rather, erase his tracks so completely?" I turned to Abby and gave her a pleading look. "Did you find anything in his drawers or under the bed, Ab? Please, please say yes!"

"There's nothing under the bed at all," she said, "not even dust!" She made an angry face, crossed her arms over her chest, and stamped one ballet-slippered foot on the floor. "And there's nothing in the damn dresser but the usual crap—undershirts, shorts, socks, handkerchiefs, a couple of sweaters. I unfolded and refolded every single thing in those drawers, and I didn't find a sign of blood anywhere. Zip, zilch, zero."

My dwindling hope fell to the floor with a thud. And my sorrow rose up to take its place. "I guess that's it, then," I said, in a voice so weak I could barely hear it myself. "We're not going to find any evidence here today. Maybe we never will." My throat tightened up and my heart slowed to a near standstill. "I can't stand it, Abby. I really can't. I'd bet every cent I have that Binky's guilty, but I can't prove it. So Flannagan's going to pin the murder on Willy. I know he will. Just because he's gay." It was all I could do not to start bawling again.

"Not *just* because he's gay," Abby contradicted. "There's also the little matter of his blood type."

"Yes, but that shouldn't even be a factor!" I sputtered. "Willy doesn't have any cuts or bruises or slashes on his body, either. We know that for a fact, remember? Yesterday, when he was modeling for you, he was wearing nothing but a skimpy toga, so we saw lots of bare, unmarked skin. He has a ton of freckles, but not a single scab. They may have found type A blood at the scene, but it definitely wasn't Willy's! Flannagan would know that," I growled, "if he had ever bothered to check Willy's body for wounds."

"Okay, so Flannagan's a lousy detective," Abby said. "and maybe he *is* looking to penalize Willy for being gay. But he's the dick in charge of this case and we've got to go see him right away, Faye. I mean today! The only way we can help

Willy now is by telling Flannagan everything we know about the murder."

"But we don't *know* anything," I said, with a heavy sigh. "All we have are worthless suspicions."

"That's not true," Abby said. "We know a lot of things. We know that Aunt Doobie and Willy don't have any flesh wounds. We know that Binky's replacing Gray in the *Hot Tin Roof* cast, and that he's been wearing long sleeves in sweltering weather. We know that Blackie and Baldy are somehow involved, and that somebody—probably either Blackie or Aunt Doobie—has been following you."

"But we don't even know who Aunt Doobie and Blackie are! And I already told Flannagan about them the night I was assaulted, when he was grilling me in the car. I didn't tell him about Binky, though. At that point there wasn't anything to tell. You know Flannagan will think we're nuts if we go to him with this whole crazy story. Binky, Blackie, Baldy, Aunt Doobie! Jeez, I think the whole thing's crazy myself!"

Abby laughed. "You're right about that, Pat. It's crazy, man, crazy! But it's also the truth," she said, turning serious again, "and it's all we've got, and we have to hand the information over to Flannagan *now*."

"I know we do, Ab," I said, heaving another loud sigh. "I knew it before you said it. It's just that I'm afraid Flannagan won't believe a word we say unless we have some tangible proof. I wanted so much to be able to back up our story with some physical evidence, something that would force Flannagan to stop hounding Willy and start looking—"

"Oh, my god, Abby!" I cried, pulse quickening. "What's the matter with you? You look like you've seen a ghost!"

Mouth agape and eyes bulging, Abby was standing right in front of me, staring straight in my direction. But her gaze wasn't focused on me. It was aimed, instead, at something above and *beyond* me. I whipped my head around to see what she was looking at and found myself peering into the open closet.

"What is it, Abby?" I begged. "What do you see?"

"It *is* a ghost," she whispered. "The ghost of Gray Gordon."

"Oh, come on, Ab!" I twisted back around to face her.

"That's not funny. Stop fooling around. Now's not the time to—"

"Hush, Paige!" she snapped, still staring straight ahead. "I'm not fooling around. I *have* seen a ghost and, you won't believe this, but he just brought us the physical evidence we've been looking for." Abby stepped over to the closet and scraped some hangers to one side of the metal bar. Then she removed the hanger holding the maroon shirt with the yellow birds and palm trees and thrust it forward.

"This was Gray's favorite shirt," she said, looking sad and excited at the same time. "I saw him wear it lots of times. And I can prove it, too! I *painted* him in this shirt when he modeled for an illustration I did for *All Man* magazine. The picture appeared—in full color—in the March 1955 edition."

I thought my heart was going to leap right out of my chest. "Oh, my god, Abby! Is that true? Are you sure it's the same shirt?"

"Of course it's the same one. It's a really weird print in a kooky color combination. How many like this could there be?" She took the shirt off the hanger and handed it to me. As she was putting the hanger back in the closet, she looked down at the floor and gasped, "*Oy vey iz mir!* These belonged to Gray, too." She picked up the cowboy boots and held them out at arm's length. "He really loved these boots. He wore them all the time."

I suddenly felt a little sick to my stomach. "So these must be the clothes Binky changed into after the murder," I said, "after he'd stripped off his own bloody clothes and shoes and taken a shower."

"Right," Abby said, tenderly laying the boots down on the foot of the bed.

Every emotion known to man was churning in my chest. Fury, shock, pride, disgust, despair, relief, elation, horror—I was reeling with the intensity and insanity of it all. "There's no shadow of a doubt now," I said, voice quivering. "Barnabas Kapinsky murdered Gray Gordon."

"And we can damn well prove it!" Abby added, all smiles.

"Should we take the evidence to Flannagan now?" I asked, still in shock that we'd solved the case and unsure what our next move should be.

"You bet your sweet tushy!" Abby crowed. "I can't wait to

see his face. Come on! Let's stash Gray's stuff in the bike basket and I'll pedal straight over to the station. You can ride on the back."

I WAS GATHERING THE SHIRT AND BOOTS together in my arms (and wondering how the heck I was supposed to straddle a bicycle in my extra-tight skirt and ultra-high heels), when I heard Abby gasp again. Thinking she'd found another article of Gray's clothing—a pair of pants, perhaps, or a belt—I turned around to see what had caused her sudden intake of air.

And then *I* was the one who was gasping.

Binky was standing tall in the bedroom doorway with his left forearm clenched like a vise around Abby's neck, and the fingers of his right hand wrapped so tight around the handle of the kitchen butcher knife that his knuckles were white. He was holding the knife up high, within slashing distance of Abby's throat, and the expression on his face was so psychotic it made my blood run cold.

"You fucking, lying, scheming bitch!" he yelled at me. "How did you get into my apartment? I have to kill you now, you know! And your sexy little girlfriend, too!" He jerked his arm even tighter around Abby's neck and stepped backward, cutting off her air supply and dragging her with him into the living room. Abby's eyes popped wide in panic as she struggled in vain to pull his arm away from her windpipe.

"Wait, Binky! Stop!" I cried, dropping Gray's shirt and boots on the floor and hurtling myself through the bedroom door after them. I wanted to kick him in the stomach and knee him in the groin and yank his arm away from Abby's neck, but I didn't dare try. The knife was too close to Abby's throat. One wrong move and—

"Hold it right there!" Binky roared. "If you come any closer I'm going to slice your friend wide open. That's what the slut deserves! Isn't that right, baby?" he said to Abby, turning his head and biting her on the cheek. Hard. "You were a bad, bad girl in Sardi's last night. Rubbing your leg up against mine and pretending to be somebody you're not. I'll have to punish you for that."

Binky's threats were both horrifying and offensive, but they actually served a worthy purpose. They distracted him for a few brief but essential seconds, causing him to loosen his clutch on Abby's neck. Not by much, but enough for her to start breathing again.

"But you should punish me instead of her!" I blustered, hoping to distract Binky further—a whole lot further. "I'm the one who got her into this mess! I talked her into going to Sardi's with me, and I sent her to your table to spy on you."

Binky looked as though he might explode. "You're gonna pay for that, you whore!" he seethed. "I can't believe I trusted you. You said you wanted to be an actress, but all you really wanted to do was wreck *my* career. And I know why! It's because I've got talent! And you can't handle it, can you? You're just like all the other Studio shitheads—James Dean, Paul Newman, Marilyn Monroe, Marlon Brando, Gray Gordon! You're all so fucking selfish and jealous and resentful you just can't stand to see a fellow acting student succeed!"

Every cell in my body was screaming, but I kept my speaking voice down to a soothing purr. "You've got me all wrong, Binky," I said, giving him the sweetest smile my trembling lips could form. "I think you're a wonderful actor who deserves to be a big, big star. I watched you audition for Elia Kazan, remember, and I thought you were fabulous in the *Hot Tin Roof* role. Much better than Ben Gazzara or Gray Gordon ever dreamed of being."

"Yeah, I know," he said, wild eyes gleaming. "If Kazan had half a brain he would've given me the understudy role in the first place! I've got more talent in the wart on my little toe than Gray had in his whole stupid body. The only reason Gray got the job instead of me was because he was so goddamn handsome. Kazan figured his sexy good looks would make him a hit with the broads in the audience—which is pretty goddamn funny since Gray was as queer as a three-dollar bill."

"Really?" I said, putting on a big show of surprise. "I didn't think Gray was gay!" I wasn't trying to squelch any rumors or change any minds, I just wanted to keep Binky talking, no matter what the subject happened to be (as long as it wasn't murder). "In fact, I thought he had a steady girlfriend," I stumbled on. "Somebody he really cared about. He bragged about her a lot, and he always called her Cupcake."

Binky gave me a crooked grin. "Ha! If that pansy had a fucking girlfriend, she must have been a fairy!" Delighted by his own ugly joke, he threw his head back and laughed out loud.

And that was when I made my move.

Shooting Abby a quick wink of warning, I leapt forward and grabbed hold of Binky's right arm with both hands, pulling it and the knife outward (i.e., away from Abby's throat) with all my might. But all my might wasn't enough. I was able to hold onto Binky's arm for no more than two seconds before he shook me off, pushed me away, and—with a single squeeze of his powerful biceps—snapped the knife back into slashing position.

There was only one problem—for Binky, I mean: Abby's throat was no longer in position! Somehow, during the course of the two seconds I'd spent wrestling with Binky's arm, Abby had worked herself free from his other arm and propelled herself—coughing and wheezing—out of slashing range. Hallelujah! God was in his heaven and all was right with the world!

But not for long.

Enraged beyond endurance, Binky jerked the butcher knife up over his head and lunged toward me, swiping the blade downward in a blinding flash. Missed me, slit open the side of the couch. I tried to move away from him, but the apartment was so small there was no place to move *to*. Binky grabbed me by the arm and reined me in, pulling me up hard against his chest in a sadistic lover's embrace. Then, grunting like a pig and glaring down at me with his demon eyes, he yanked the blade of the knife up to a point just under my chin and—

"Stop, or I'll shoot!" bellowed a taut male voice behind me. "Drop the knife on the floor and reach for the ceiling!"

Silence fell on the room like a bomb. Binky stopped grunting. Abby stopped wheezing. I stopped whimpering. Staring, openmouthed, at the person who was standing behind me, Binky released me from his crushing hold, let the knife fall to the floor, and raised his hands in the air without a word (or grunt) of protest.

I spun around on my heels and gazed at the man who had materialized—as if by magic—just in time to save my life. The dark-haired man with the gun in his hand. The tall, lean man dressed head to toe in dark clothing. The sly, sneaky, illusive man whose identity I had been unable to confirm until now. It was Blackie.

Chapter 36

IT WASN'T UNTIL BLACKIE PULLED A pair of handcuffs out of his back pocket and slapped them on Binky's wrists that I began to realize what was going on. Blackie was friend, not foe. Protector, not stalker. Cop, not killer. And any doubts I may have had on this score were quickly eliminated when, just a few seconds later, four uniformed policemen rushed into the small apartment, crowding the narrow living room beyond capacity.

"Step over here, please, Mrs. Turner," Blackie said, maneuvering me toward the bedroom doorway, out of the way of the other cops who, in spite of the strict space limitations, immediately launched into their prescribed police routine. One officer began patting Binky down, one started searching the apartment, one got to work bagging and labeling the knife, and one escorted Abby to the rear corner of the room for safe-keeping. (Abby was feeling just fine, you should know. I could tell by the way she was flirting with her handsome young caretaker.)

"That was a close call," Blackie said, tucking his gun in his belt and scowling at me. "Are you okay? You aren't hurt, are you?"

"No, I'm okay," I said, even though I wasn't. My nerves were jangling, my teeth were rattling, and my knees were shaking out of control. In the interest of appearing cool, however, I chose to withhold that information. "Thanks for saving my life," I said instead.

"Glad to be of service," he replied, still scowling but extending his hand for a shake. "I'm Detective John Dash. NYPD. You may have seen me around. I've been following you for the past four days."

"Yes, I believe I did catch a glimpse of you here and there."

His frown deepened. "Guess I got a little careless."

"I thought you were the killer," I confessed, "looking for a good opportunity to kill me."

"Sorry," he said. "Didn't mean to scare you. I was just doing my job."

"Speaking of jobs," I said, "what happened to your busboy position at Stewart's Cafeteria? Did you quit or get fired?"

He smiled. (At least I think that little upward twitch of his lips was a smile.) "I was on assignment at Stewart's," he explained, "working undercover. I was put there to spy on the Village homos—find out everything I could about the chicken run."

Ugh. I wished I hadn't asked.

"But after you got involved in the Gordon murder," he went on, "they took me off busboy duty and sent me to spy on you."

"Why? Did they actually think *I* was the killer?"

"Can't answer that," he said, scraping his fingers through his wavy hair and giving me a tired look. "And I'm supposed to be asking the questions here, not you. So, whaddaya say you quit grilling me and start telling me what went on here today? Keep it short and sweet. Detective Flannagan will get all the details later."

I gave him a quick rundown of the afternoon's events, then led him into the bedroom where Gray's shirt and boots were scattered on the floor. Blackie—oops, I mean Detective Dash—picked up the boots, wrapped them up in the shirt, and then gave them to one of the other cops to bag. "Okay, that's it," he said, taking the gun out of his belt and sticking it into the slim holster hidden under the leg of his long black pants. "Let's round up the horses and head for the stable."

•   •   •

THERE WERE TWO SQUAD CARS PARKED at the curb. Binky was ushered outside and deposited in one of them, accompanied by the three officers who had attended to him inside. Sullen, silent, and still in handcuffs, he sat with his shoulders hunched and his head hanging low until the car pulled out and sped away, disappearing in the shadows beneath the doomed elevated train track.

Barnabas Kapinsky had taken his final bow. There were no bravos; no standing ovation.

After an argument between Abby and Blackie about Fabrizio's bicycle (she wanted to ride it back to the Village, he wanted her to ride in the car and come back for the bike later), Abby and I were chauffeured to the Sixth Precinct station, with Fabrizio's Schwinn Jaguar Deluxe strapped to the trunk of the car. It was a fast trip and a quiet one. Even Abby didn't feel much like talking.

Once we were taken upstairs to Homicide, however, and seated in the hard wooden chairs across the desk from Flannagan, we both had plenty to say.

"I *told* you Willy Sinclair wasn't the murderer," I said to Flannagan the second Blackie finished briefing him on the afternoon's events. I lit up an L&M and spewed the smoke out in an extra loud whoosh. "If you had listened to me, you could have saved us all a lot of trouble."

"Yeah!" Abby said. "A *whole lot* of trouble. We nearly had our throats slashed, you know!"

Flannagan glared at us and let out a gruff *harrumph*. "You can't blame that on me. If you had kept your snotty little noses out of the case to begin with, none of this ever would have happened."

"Right!" I cried. "And instead of having the *real* murderer in police custody, you'd have poor Willy behind bars—set to go on trial and maybe even receive the *death* sentence—for a murder he didn't commit!" (I don't often break society's strict gender rules and speak so boldly to men in authority—no matter how stupid they happen to be. But in this case, I simply couldn't help myself. I was *mad*.)

Flannagan's boyish, clean-shaven face turned an unusual shade of purple. "How dare you speak to me that way!" he spluttered, banging his fist down on top of the desk. "I'm the homicide detective in charge of this case, and you're just a two-bit pencil-pusher for a smutty crime magazine! You think you know everything about the way I've handled this investigation, and you don't have a clue."

"Oh, really?" I said, with a sniff. "Then perhaps you'd better *tell* me how you've handled it, Detective. A two-bit crime reporter can't afford to be clueless." (Okay, maybe my tone was a tad sarcastic, but not totally. I swear! I was truly curious to hear what Flannagan would have to say for himself—and I wanted to collect all the dirty details for my smutty story.)

But I was losing him and Abby knew it. "Oh, yes, Detective Flannagan, please tell!" she warbled, batting her lashes like crazy, striving to soothe his disgruntled male ego with an ooze of feminine charm.

It worked. Flannagan's face turned from purple to pink. He smirked, loosened his tie, leaned way back in his chair and put his feet up on his desk, filthy shoe soles facing me. "In the first place, Mrs. Turner," he said, "I never even came close to arresting Willard Sinclair for the murder. We didn't have enough proof for that. A matching blood type is strong, persuasive evidence, but it isn't conclusive. So, however low your opinion of the NYPD may be, your precious faggot friend wasn't in danger of going to prison or receiving an unjust death penalty. That's not the way we do things around here."

"Oh, no? Then why were you constantly harassing and abusing Willy—calling him a queer and a pervert and a psychopath, and insisting that he was the one who killed Gray? Is that just the way you get your kicks?" I took one last drag on my cigarette and angrily crushed it in the ashtray.

Flannagan jerked himself up straight and put his feet back on the floor. "You have no right to question my methods, Mrs. Turner," he said, speaking through clenched teeth. "And you're wishing on a goddamn star if you think I'm going to explain my investigative procedures to you."

If at first you don't succeed, try, try again. "But will you at least tell me why you put Black—I mean, Detective Dash on my tail?" I went on. "Did you really believe that *I* was the murderer? I know that the person who discovers the body often turns out to be the killer, but how could you possibly think—"

"I didn't!" Flannagan interrupted, unaware that the hasty placement of his words made his response very funny (to me, at any rate). "I never for one moment thought you were the killer," he grumbled. "I had you followed for different reasons entirely."

"Oh?" I said, curiosity mounting. "And what would those reasons be?"

In spite of his vow not to explain himself, he did.

"I had a hunch you were going to snoop around on your own," he began, obviously eager to reveal and extol his own skills of detection. "I had heard about the other murder cases you meddled in and wrote articles about, and I figured you would try to do the same stupid thing in this case—especially since you and your friend discovered the body.

"So I decided to have you followed," he continued. "I called in Johnny Dash and told him to stick to you like gum, for two simple reasons—one, to see if you might turn up any good clues or actually track down the killer—and two, to protect you if you did. And considering the fact that Dash saved the lives of you and your friend today, I'd say my decision was a damn good one."

He had a point.

A damn good one.

"I see," I mumbled, staring down at the floor, ashamed that I'd been giving Detective Flannagan such a hard time when he'd been doing such a good job (or so it seemed). *If it weren't for Flannagan and Dash*, I humbly admitted to myself, *Abby and I would be on the way to the city morgue right now—or in transit to the Staten Island landfill.* I was trying to find the right words to express my heartfelt apologies and gratitude when Abby jumped in and saved me the trouble.

"Hey, bobba ree bop!" she whooped, catapulting out of her chair and darting over to Johnny Dash, who was standing to one side of the desk, leaning against a wooden file cabinet. "You're my hero!" she cried, flinging her arms around his neck and planting a huge (and I'd be willing to bet open-mouthed) kiss on his unsuspecting lips. Then she hopped over to Flannagan, threw herself down on his lap, pulled his face down close to hers, and repeated the procedure.

Both men were shocked, but pleased. Breathless and blushing. And for several long minutes after Abby danced away and returned to her chair on the other side of the desk, their chests were so puffed up with pride I thought they'd pop.

I hated to put a damper on the friendly fireworks, but I was still curious about the case. "Was Detective Dash following me the night of the Fourth, when I went to the party at the Keller Hotel?" I asked. "The night I got hit on the head?"

"Yes, of course he was," Flannagan answered. "Who do you think called us when you were assaulted? How do you think we got there so fast?"

"So Blackie . . . I mean, Detective Dash was the anonymous caller you told me about?"

"Right."

"That settles it then," I said. "The man who knocked me out was Aunt Doobie."

"The one and only," Flannagan said. "But his real name is Christopher Dubin. He's a thirty-four-year-old lawyer with a wife and two kids. He's also a covert homosexual who was so terrified you would find out who he really is and expose his sordid secret to the world and his wife, that he bashed you on the head with a rock and took off like a bat outta hell."

Christopher Dubin. Married. Two kids. "How did you get all this information?" I sputtered, begging for more. "Did you find him at the Mayflower Hotel? Did he confess to hitting me? Did he admit that he was Gray's lover?"

Blackie, not Flannagan, answered my first question.

"Never went to the Mayflower," he said. "Didn't have to. After Dubin hit you, he took off in a black limo and I memorized the plate number. Then—after I made sure you weren't hurt too bad—I called the station for help and put out a citywide bulletin on the car. As soon as Detective Flannagan and the boys arrived at the scene, I jumped in one of the squad cars, got a location on the limo from the radio, and then tracked the vehicle to its final destination—an East 65th Street brownstone owned by one Randolph Godfrey Winston."

"Baldy," I mumbled.

"Yeah, the guy *is* bald," Blackie said. "Completely. I saw that when he and Dubin got out of the car and went into the building."

"So what happened next?" I asked. "Did you go inside and question them both together?"

"No, he did not!" Flannagan broke in, obviously annoyed that Blackie was claiming so much attention. "Detective Dash stayed outside and kept watch on the building until I got there—which wasn't until after midnight since you took so goddamn long to tell me the truth about the attack and your own little private investigation."

"I'm sorry about that," I said, really meaning it. "I was wrong. I should have told you everything from the very beginning."

"You're goddamn right you should!" Flannagan snapped, tossing me such a gloating, self-righteous sneer I considered retracting my apology.

I didn't do it, though. I was still aching for more details about the case, and I was afraid Flannagan would clam up if I crossed him again. "So you conducted the interrogation yourself, Detective Flannagan?" I probed. "That night in Baldy's brownstone?"

"I sure did," he boasted, sitting back in his chair and lighting up a Camel. Then, snorting two streams of smoke from his nostrils like a dragon, he launched into the longest, most drawn-out, most self-aggrandizing monologue you ever heard in your life. I'm not kidding! He described and explained every single moment of his session with Baldy and Aunt Doobie (i.e., Winston and Dubin), but his focus was on *himself*, not the subjects of his inquiry, and his zeal was reserved for his own "extraordinary" (his word, not mine!) powers of discovery. (*He* determined this, and *he* uncovered that, and then *he* established this, and *he* exposed that, and then *he* . . . well, you get the picture.)

After all was said and done, Flannagan had delivered a lot more details than I'd bargained for. (Don't worry! I won't make you wade through a word-for-word account of his grandiose dissertation. I'll edit out all the pretentious stuff and repackage the rest in a nutshell. Am I a considerate writer, or what?)

What it all boiled down to was this: Christopher Dubin and Gray Gordon had been lovers for five months. They'd conducted their forbidden affair in hotel rooms so that Dubin—a successful theatrical lawyer and respected family man—would never be seen in Gray's company. Because of his fear of being branded a homosexual, Dubin never would have been caught dead at the gay party at the Keller Hotel if: 1) his wife and kids hadn't gone to spend the holiday weekend with her parents in Canada; 2) his beloved gay boyfriend hadn't been brutally murdered; 3) his good friend and gay business associate Randolph Godfrey Winston hadn't persuaded him to meet him at the party for a healing regimen of booze, fireworks, and forgetfulness.

And he never would have bashed me on the head if I hadn't called him Aunt Doobie.

But once that name escaped my lips, Dubin knew that I had recognized him from our first meeting at the Mayflower—when, if you recall, I had also mentioned the name of Gray Gordon. And since the party at the Keller bar was for gays only, Dubin also knew that I now had ample proof that he was a homosexual. As a result, he went nuts and ran out of the bar, looking to get as far away from me as possible, hoping I'd never learn his real name and expose his secret life, which would destroy his public one.

When Dubin realized that I had followed him out of the bar and over toward the river, however, and that I was standing watch under the West Side Highway—right between him and the limo in which his friend Randy had just arrived—his uncontrollable panic took over. He picked up a rock, snuck up behind me, and knocked me cold. Then he fled the scene in the black limousine.

Toodleloo. Bye bye. Over and out.

"What about Baldy?" I asked, when Flannagan finally stopped talking. "Did you find out anything more about him?"

"Besides his real name, you mean?"

Duh. "Yes," I replied, "and besides his profession, too. I already know that he's the producer of *Cat on a Hot Tin Roof*. What I *don't* know is why he was pumping the bartenders at the Village Vanguard for information about me. Did you ask him anything about that?"

"Uh, yeah, I did," Flannagan said, suddenly looking kind of vague, rubbing his pallid, baby-smooth chin with his nicotine-stained fingers. "He said something about seeing you and Miss Moskowitz backstage the night of Gray Gordon's debut, and again the next day, after the matinee. And then, he said, when he saw you *again* at the Vanguard the very next night, he started wondering who you were and why you kept showing up everywhere he went. So he tipped the bartenders and asked them a few questions about you on his way out. That's all there was to it."

"Oh, for heaven's sake!" I exclaimed, utterly amazed (and also a bit amused) that a situation I'd thought so sinister could turn out to be so ordinary.

Abby, on the other hand, didn't even raise an eyebrow. She shrugged her shoulders, gave me an indulgent smile, and said, for the third time that day, "You always make such a *tsimmis*."

Chapter 37

HAVE YOU EVER HAD THE FEELING THAT you were two people instead of one? That one of you was a smart, strong, insightful champion of truth and justice, while the other one was a perfect fool? Well, that was the way I felt that afternoon in Flannagan's office. Like a pair of mismatched twins. Or a monster with two heads. I was brave and decisive one minute, dopey and delusional the next. I was Wonder Woman and Lucy Ricardo combined. I was Brenda Starr with a brain tumor.

"What led you to believe that Barnabas Kapinsky was the murderer?" Flannagan barked, finally getting around to asking for my side of the story. He was glaring at me through squinted eyes, as if I were still under suspicion.

"The long sleeves," I said, "and his buttoned-up collar and cuffs."

"What?!" Flannagan squeezed his eyelids even tighter, peering at me through slits so narrow I was surprised he could see at all. "Long sleeves? Collar and cuffs? I think you'd better explain yourself, Mrs. Turner. And make it fast."

"Well, yesterday was the first time I saw Binky," I began, "and it was so hot that—"

"Binky?" Flannagan croaked. "Who the hell is Binky?"

"Barnabas Kapinsky," I said. "His nickname is Binky."

Flannagan's accusing glare grew even more intense. "You called the murderer by his nickname? I didn't know the two of you were so close."

"No!" I cried. "That's not the way it was! I only called him Binky because—"

It was at that moment—as I was just beginning to explain my theories and actions to Flannagan—that Dan walked into the office. He sauntered down the aisle between the desks and the file cabinets, shook hands with Detectives Flannagan and Dash, gave Abby a smile and me a curt nod, and then positioned himself—arms crossed, legs slightly apart—near the side of my chair.

"Don't let me disturb you," he said, to nobody in particular. "Please go on with what you were doing."

Oh, sure. How could I go on with my explanation when all of my words were stuck in a huge lump in my throat? I couldn't breathe, much less talk. My body temperature and blood pressure were shooting through the roof. My emotions were having seizures in every chamber of my broken heart.

"Yes, go on, Mrs. Turner," Flannagan said, with a smirk. "I believe you were telling us why you called the killer Binky."

I tried to say something clever and enlightening, but the only word that came out was, "Ack!"

"Leave her alone already!" Abby snapped, leaping to my defense like a rabid Jewish mother. "Can't you see she's upset? She hasn't slept in over thirty hours! And she's had a really hard day, you dig? And she caught your murderer for you, didn't she? What else do you want? You should be treating her like a queen—and I *don't* mean a homosexual!"

I smiled. That Abby. You gotta love her.

"I advise you not to speak to me in that manner!" Flannagan seethed. His boyish face was changing colors again. "I'm the head of this department and I—"

"Miss Moskowitz is right," Dan interrupted. His voice was soft, but his tone of authority was coming through loud and clear. "What Mrs. Turner needs right now is a cup of coffee and some peace and quiet, which will improve both her frame of mind and her recollection of events. Therefore, since I have a special interest in this case, I think it best if I show her into a private room and continue taking her statement myself." He leaned down, put his hands on my shoulders, and gently coaxed me to my feet.

Flannagan rose to his feet, too. "But I don't . . . well, I . . . do you really think—"

"Yes, I do," Dan cut in again. He put one arm around my back and began escorting me down the aisle toward the door. "We'll be in the interrogation room across the hall," he said, glancing back over his shoulder. "Please bring us some coffee."

I LOVED BEING ALONE WITH DAN; I HATED being alone with Dan. (I *told* you I was two people.) One of me was so turned on by his intense black gaze, disheveled hair, and determined jawline that I wanted to throw myself in his arms and attach my mouth to his for all eternity (or at least until next week). The other me was still so haunted (okay, incredibly hurt) by the way he'd kissed that redhead in Sardi's last night that I couldn't stand the thought of putting my lips where *hers* had been. Not now. Not ever.

Averting my eyes from Dan's gorgeous face and enticing mouth, I sat back in my chair at the table in the middle of the small interrogation room, crossed my legs, took a sip of my coffee, and hurriedly fired up a cigarette. (I knew if I waited Dan would offer me a light, and I wanted to avoid that painfully intimate gesture.) Staring at me from his chair on the other side of the table, Dan lit up, too.

"Are you ready to tell me the truth?" he asked, in a voice as rich and dark as chocolate. "There's no reason for you to keep any secrets now."

"Why should I bother?" I said, tossing my head back and exhaling a stream of smoke toward the ceiling. "I'm sure you know everything there is to know already. Flannagan has obviously kept you clued in." I was acting as cool as Lauren Bacall, but I was feeling as hot as Scarlett O'Hara during the burning of Atlanta.

"You've got it wrong, Paige," he said. "It's the other way around."

"What do you mean?"

"I mean I'm the one who's been keeping Flannagan in the

know, not vice versa. I've been in charge of this case since the day after Gray Gordon was killed."

"What?!" I shrieked, shocked to the bone. "That's impossible! You were in Maine at the time! And this isn't even your precinct!"

Dan's coal-black gaze stayed fixed on me. "*You* are my precinct," he said, and the way his forceful voice echoed against the walls of the tiny room made my skin dance.

Dan took a swig of his coffee and continued talking. "As soon as I read the reports of the murder in the Maine papers and saw that two young women who lived near the victim had discovered the body, I called Flannagan to find out who they were. And I wasn't the least bit surprised when he named you and Abby. And I knew damn well your involvement wouldn't end there. So the minute I hung up with Flannagan, I called the commissioner and got myself assigned to the case. After that I called Flannagan back, appointed him my second in command, and told him to put his best man on your tail to watch over you and keep you safe. Then, after making arrangements for Katy to stay with my parents for another week, I jumped in the car, and drove all night to get to you."

"But why didn't you *tell* me?!" I cried, trembling with curiosity, gratitude, and outrage.

"Because *you* didn't tell *me*," he said. "When I saw how far you were willing to go—how many lies you were willing to tell so you could keep me in the dark and stay involved in the case—I knew I couldn't trust you to back off and let me handle things my way. And since I couldn't trust you to tell me the truth, I was afraid I would jeopardize the investigation and cause you to put your life in more danger if I told the truth to you. You put me in a real bind, Paige. I was so mad I wanted to kill you myself."

The gross absurdity of our deceitful duet suddenly hit me like a ton of bricks. "Good grief, Dan!" I sputtered. "If I had known that you'd been assigned to the case I would have told you the truth immediately! I swear! The only reason I lied to you was because I knew you'd order me to stop looking for the killer, and I simply couldn't do that as long as Flannagan was in charge. He's a horrible detective, Dan. You've got to believe me! He was trying to pin the murder on Willy Sinclair just because he's gay!"

Dan nodded and took a deep drag on his Lucky. "I realized that myself after working with him for one hour."

Aaaargh! "Then why didn't you come back and tell me what was going on?"

"A little knowledge is a dangerous thing."

"What's that supposed to mean?"

"Like I said before, I thought the truth would hurt you instead of help you."

Uh oh. Dan was beginning to sound as shifty and slippery as somebody else I knew (i.e., *me*). "But how on earth could it possibly hurt me?" I asked, growing more confused by the second.

He gave me a challenging smirk. "You want examples?"

"Uh, yeah, I guess so," I said, wondering what I'd let myself in for.

"How many?"

He was being too cute for comfort. "One will be quite enough," I snapped.

"Okay, how does this one strike you? How do you think you would have reacted to the knowledge that Dash was following you? Would you have been glad that he was watching your every move and working to keep you safe, or would you have dreamed up an elaborate scheme to ditch him so you could conduct your secret investigation in secret?"

"I, er . . . um, I . . ."

"Never mind," Dan said. "You don't have to answer that. I knew exactly what you would do, and that's why I didn't tell you the truth. It was for your own good."

I couldn't think of anything to say, so I busied myself putting out my cigarette and lighting another one.

Dan stood up from his chair and began pacing the floor in front of me, giving me a good look at his powerful physique and devastatingly sexy walk. "This would all be funny if it wasn't so damn serious," he said, raking a wave of unruly brown hair off his forehead with his fingers. "Do you realize how much trouble you've caused? Do you have any idea how close you came to sabotaging the whole case?"

"No way, Doris Day!" I huffed. "In fact it seems to me that the opposite is true. I mean, I *solved* the damn thing, didn't I? Nobody suspected that Barnabas Kapinsky was the murderer but me! Nobody even knew who Binky was!" To say that I was irked would be like calling a heart attack uncomfortable. Would credit ever be given where credit was due (i.e., to *me*)?

Dan stopped dead in his tracks and turned toward me with a look of pure fury on his face. "Yes, and why do you think that was, Paige? Do you think that maybe, just maybe, it was because you *stole* the only piece of evidence that showed a connection between Kapinsky and Gordon? Did it ever occur to you that you were hiding important information from the police—that the list of phone messages Rhonda Blake took down for the victim on or around the night he was killed might be indispensable to the investigation?"

My heart sank to the pit of my stomach and stayed there. "So you knew about that," I mumbled, staring down at the floor in shame.

"You're damn straight, I did! Rhonda told me about it when I questioned her at the theater. She said two extras from the *Bus Stop* cast had come to see Gray, and to get her autograph, and she thought they must have taken the message pad with them when they left because she hadn't been able to find it since. I knew right away she was talking about you and Abby."

I wasn't two people anymore. Now I was just one—the bad one.

"I'm sorry, Dan," I whimpered. "I never would have snatched the list if I had known you'd be taking over the case. Flannagan was in charge at the time, don't forget, and I couldn't be sure that he would ever find the list, or follow up on all the names if he did. So I felt I should take it home and study it carefully, and then turn it over to Flannagan later."

"But you never got around to enacting the last part of your plan," Dan growled.

"No, but I *told* Flannagan about the message pad," I stressed, "and I gave him all the names that were listed. All except one."

"The most important one, it turns out."

"Yes, but I didn't know that at the time! I kept Binky's name and number to myself for only one reason: because I didn't want Flannagan to screw up my visit to the Actors Studio. I thought it was important for me to meet and talk to Gray's fellow acting students—see if any of them were the homicidal type—and Binky was my passport inside."

Dan's face turned from furious to afflicted. "Yeah, and he was almost a passport to the end of your life." He sat back down in his chair and released a deafening sigh. "I don't know what to do with you anymore, Paige. You're impossible! . . . You were right not to trust Flannagan—he's a bigot and a bungler. And I know your motives for getting involved were good. They always are. But you came to within a split second of having your throat slit open!" he cried, throwing his hands in the air. "How am I supposed to live with the knowledge of that? No matter how hard I try to keep you safe, you're always working your way toward another disaster. And nothing I can say or do will make you stop! You're addicted to danger."

"I prefer to think I'm addicted to the truth," I stiffly replied, feeling righteous again.

That did it. Dan's eyes popped wide as golf balls and his jaw dropped to the floor. "The *truth?*" he howled. "That's the funniest joke I ever heard in my life! You wouldn't know the truth if it flew in the window and bit you on the nose."

"I would so!" I whined, sounding incredibly childish, even to myself. "And if you had told me the truth about your involvement in the case, I would have told you the truth about mine!" So *there*.

We sat in silence for a few seconds, each stewing in our own private thoughts.

And then the most extraordinary thing happened.

Suddenly, out of nowhere, when I least expected it—when I was so bewildered and confused I could barely comprehend it—the miracle I had long been dreaming of and aching for occurred. Dan turned his face toward mine, looked straight into my eyes, gave me the most pleasing of all possible smiles, and pronounced the words I had begun to think I would never, ever, ever—in all the miserable, magical days of my crazy, mixed-up life—hear him say:

"I love you, Paige."

"What?!" (It wasn't a very romantic response, but it was all I was capable of at the moment.)

He laughed. "Have you lost your hearing or your interest? I said I love you. I've loved you for a long time. I didn't tell you before because I didn't want anything to change. I was happy with our relationship just the way it was. But now I'm not so sure. Now I'm thinking—"

"You've got a lot of nerve, you know that, Dan?" I was so furious I thought my head would melt. "*Now* you say you love me? Now that you've ripped my heart out of my chest and kicked it around like a bloody football?" (Okay, so maybe that was a bit livid, but it was exactly how I felt.) I jumped out of my chair and began my own round of pacing. "Well, you can cry me a river," I went on, feeling very dramatic, quoting the lyrics of the new Julie London song I now identified with so much. "Cry me a river. I cried a river over you."

"Julie London," Dan said. "I like that song a lot, too. But what does it have to do with us?"

Aaaargh!

"I saw you last night," I said, coming to a sudden standstill and propping my hands on my hips. "In Sardi's. You were wrapped up in the arms and lips of a beautiful redhead. And if you felt even one ounce of love for me at that particular moment, I'll eat Hedda Hopper's new hat!"

Dan didn't move a muscle. He sat still as a stump in his chair, staring up at me with the eyes of a guilty, but thoroughly unrepentant, adolescent. Then he took a long, slow drink of his coffee, set the cup back down on the table, and started laughing.

It wasn't the loud, boisterous, slap-you-on-the-back style of laughter you would hear in a bar or a locker room. It was the deep, personal, private kind . . . the kind that grabs you in the gut and causes intense but near silent paroxysms of glee.

"Well, I'm glad you think it's so funny," I said, stomping one stiletto-heeled shoe on the floor, then starting to pace again. It was either that or start crying another river.

"I'm sorry, Paige," Dan said between spasms, "but if you knew what I was really feeling while I was—as you so eloquently put it—'wrapped up in the arms and lips' of that so-called 'beautiful redhead,' then you'd be laughing, too."

I didn't say a word. If Dan thought I was going to humiliate myself by asking him to explain his stupid feelings, then he had another think coming!

After what seemed like an hour but was probably no more than four seconds, Dan's laughter subsided. He sat up straight, rubbed his face in his hands, and then gave me a dead serious look. "I was disgusted by that woman," he declared. "She's coarse, vulgar, demanding, ostentatious . . . When she was kissing me, the rancid smell and taste of whiskey was so strong I felt sick to my stomach. I went straight into the men's room afterward and rinsed my face and mouth with cold water."

My eyes were downcast, but my heart was soaring. He was telling the truth! I could hear it in his voice. "If she disgusted you so darn much," I said, "why did you ask her out in the first place?"

"I didn't," he said. "I just met her at Sardi's to ask her a few questions about Gray Gordon."

"What?!" I yelped. The man was full of surprises. And I was panting for more. "How was she connected to Gray?" I begged. "How did you find out about her? Why didn't *I* know about her? Did you consider her a suspect? What's her name?" (I'm so cool sometimes, it kills me.)

"Her name is Loretta Cuppano," he said, "but everybody calls her Cupcake."

Oh!

"And, no, she wasn't a suspect," he went on. "I just wanted to talk to her about Gray, see what I could learn about his personal life. According to Rhonda Blake, Loretta and Gray had a brief fling a couple of years ago, when they were both students at the Actors Studio, so I figured she could tell me whether or not he was a homosexual. Confirmed, or otherwise."

"And did she?"

"She said Gray went both ways, but preferred men to women. That's why she broke up with him. She wanted a leading, not supporting, role."

"I take it she's an actress."

"And how!" he said. "She's so showy and pretentious she couldn't possibly be anything else. She's appearing in *The Pajama Game* now."

That figures, I sneered to myself.

"So that's why you met her so late at Sardi's," I said, thinking aloud. "You went there after the show."

"Right."

"Did you know that I was there?"

"Not until later."

"Aren't you going to ask me *why* I was there?"

"Don't have to. I already know."

"What else do you know?"

"Plenty."

"Do you know that I love you, too?"

"Yep."

"Smarty-pants."

Dan smiled, stood up, and walked over to where I was standing. "Are we okay now, Paige?" he said, putting his hands on my shoulders and piercing me to the core with his hot black gaze. "Our truce is signed? The cease-fire is in effect?"

"That's the truth, the whole truth, and nothing but the truth," I vowed.

Then Dan took me in his arms and we sealed our agreement with a long, slow, soul-scorching kiss (openmouthed, in case you're wondering). My knees were weak as water but my heart was going strong, leaping in unbounded delight that Dan and I had finally turned to the same page.

Epilogue

I NEVER FILED CHARGES AGAINST AUNT
Doobie—I mean Christopher Dubin. I knew if I did, the secret
of his homosexuality might come out, and I had no desire to
expose him to the social persecution—or criminal prosecu-
tion—that could result from that sort of disclosure. Yes, he
had assaulted me and knocked me out—but I hadn't really
been hurt all that much. No concussion; no hematoma. And,
anyway, it wasn't as if Dubin had *wanted* to hurt me. He had
just been trying to keep me from finding out his real name. He
had been desperate to protect himself and his family from ha-
tred and oppression. Where's the crime in that?

Willy wanted me to keep his real name a secret, too. Although he isn't totally closeted like Dubin—Willy's distinc-
tive clothes and flamboyantly girlish ways have made him a
gay icon in and around the Village—he still lives in fear that
he'll lose his elderly parents' love, his extended family's respect, and his managerial job at Brentano's bookstore if the
truth about his sexuality comes out. So, when I wrote the story
about Gray's murder for *Daring Detective*, I gave Willy a
phony name. And then, when I started writing *this* masterpiece—i.e., the dime-store paperback novel you're reading
right now—I gave him another one. (Two aliases are better
than one, I always say.)

In my story for *Daring Detective* I avoided the gay issue altogether. After all, it had nothing whatsoever to do with the murder. And I knew all too well what Brandon Pomeroy would do with the information if he got hold of it. He would turn it into the sex scandal of the century. He would plaster the cover of the magazine with lurid headlines like GAY LOVERBOY ACTOR SLASHED TO DEATH IN JEALOUS RAGE!, or QUEER BROADWAY STAR KILLED IN BLOODBATH OF SICK DESIRES!

And the sensational, misleading headlines would just multiply from there. All the newspapers and other crime magazines would pick up the story and run with it (I hated to think how *Confidential* would handle the subject!), and poor Gray Gordon would be remembered as a deranged and depraved pansy pervert instead of a nice, talented young man who'd had a brilliant acting career ahead of him.

And I couldn't, in good conscience, allow that to happen. (Sometimes you have to withhold the truth in order to preserve it.) So I wrote the story straight—never using the words gay or homosexual, and using pseudonyms for the people whose lives would be harmed if another reporter ever learned about the sexual inclinations of Gray Gordon and company. And by omitting all homosexual references, I was able to focus all my nouns and adjectives on the *true* villain of the story—the envious, greedy, vain, brutal, heterosexual murderer, Barnabas (a.k.a. Binky) Kapinsky. He was, after all, the one who *deserved* the bad publicity.

Pomeroy still doesn't know that I soft-pedaled the story. He was so happy to get my exclusive inside scoop for *Daring Detective* that he never pressed me for a sex angle—which was highly unusual since he always demands that every story have a sex angle, whether it's a real one or not. I was surprised by Pomeroy's immediate, no-questions-asked acceptance of my manuscript, until I heard through the grapevine that *DD*'s owner, wealthy publishing baron Oliver Rice Harrington (Pomeroy's second cousin and benefactor), had ordered him to publish more exclusive, first-person stories in *Daring Detective*—or else. Which was the only reason Pomeroy gave me the assignment in the first place, of course. (I should have known it wasn't his own idea.)

I'll be getting a lot more assignments from now on, though, since the issue that featured my Gray Gordon story on the cover was a total sellout. (It seems the next best thing to a sex murder is a show business murder.) Pomeroy's even been giving me more clip stories to write now that my byline has gained some weight. (I write under the abbreviated name of P. Turner, you should know. If I put my full name on my work, I'd be laughed right out of the business.)

Needless to say, Mike and Mario aren't too happy about my new (i.e., higher) status on the staff. Knowing they no longer have the power to get me fired, and finding it harder and harder to make me the brunt of all their stupid jokes, they've been moping around the office like punished children—kids who've been barred from the playground and denied all access to ice cream. It's a welcome change for Lenny and me, and—as you might expect—we've been enjoying their petulant frustration to the hilt.

But my greatest new source of enjoyment is Willy. He's become a very dear friend of mine and Abby's, dropping in on us often, bringing us flowers, fruit, candy, champagne, and the pleasure of his ebullient company. He also brought me a beautiful new set of four crystal champagne glasses, which have—thanks to our mutual fondness for fizz and bubbles—been put to frequent use.

Now that he's no longer a murder suspect, the bold, unfearful side of Willy's personality has emerged, and we're seeing him at his wise, funny, charitable, insightful, and oh-so-lovable best. Abby is downright crazy about him. And Otto has made his deep affection for Willy known by curling up in his lap—instead of mine!—at every opportunity. At first I was jealous, but I've gotten used to it now.

Even Jimmy likes him. The last time we all got together (for pizza, smoked oysters, and champagne) Jimmy insisted on reciting his new poem, and—though I can't be one hundred percent sure, of course—I would swear it's all about Willy:

> When the whistles blow
> And snow falls
> The sun shines still
> As we know.
> Never been rightly teached
> Love's always up front
> Only way to go!

Okay, maybe it isn't about Willy. Who the hell can tell? All I know is that Jimmy laughs a lot when Willy is around, and participates more in the conversation (if you can call it that), and he even lets Willy take Otto out for an occasional walk—which is Jimmy's way of showing that he trusts you.

Dan trusts Willy a lot, too. Though he hasn't spent that much time with him—Dan has to work late most nights, solving one grisly homicide right after another—he's very glad that I have a new friend to keep me company (and out of trouble) when he's working on a new case. I suspect Dan's especially glad that my new friend is a *man* (better protection, don't you know), but one he never has to worry about or be jealous of. He hasn't said as much, but he doesn't have to. I know the way his wary, watchful (and intermittently wicked) mind works.

As for Dan's relationship with *me*—well, that just couldn't be finer. He introduced me to his daughter a little over a month ago, and he's been taking us both out to Schrafft's and to the movies every Sunday since then. And you know what that means, don't you? It means Dan trusts *me* now, too. It means he believes our relationship is really going to *last*.

Katy is really great, by the way—a petite blonde with a keen mind, a fabulous sense of humor, and a wealth of human understanding far beyond her fifteen years. We like each other as much as Dan predicted we would. We even like the same kind of movies. I got a bang out of her favorite, *Seven Brides for Seven Brothers*, and she got a big kick out of mine—*Lady and the Tramp*. (No lie. I've seen it three times.) I look forward to getting to know Katy better, and I know Dan's really happy about that. I can tell by the way he keeps staring at us when we're together, with a goofy, mile-wide grin on his face that puts Red Skelton's cockeyed smile to shame.

But who am I to talk? I've been walking around with a permanent smile on my kisser ever since that day in the police station when Dan first told me that he loved me. I've tried to hide it, but I can't. I've done scowling exercises and eaten about a thousand lemons, but nothing works. No matter how hard I try to force my features into a frown, they pop right back into a beaming smile the instant I relax my cheek muscles. Abby says I look like a dumbstruck fool.

"I can't take it anymore," she said to me this morning over

coffee, holding her hand up to shield her face. "Your freaking teeth are shining in my eyes!"

"I'm sorry, Ab," I said, laughing. "I just can't help it. I'm floating on cloud nine."

She groaned and gazed up at the ceiling. "*Oy gevalt*, Paige! How many times do I have to tell you? Cloud nine is for the birds; it's the *mattress* that counts!"

I laughed again. "Thanks for the advice," I said, "but Dan and I are sticking to the couch for now."

"Still waiting for the stupid wedding band?" she scoffed.

"Well, no, not really . . . but I saw a pretty nice one in Macy's the other day."

Penguin Group (USA) Online

What will you be reading tomorrow?

Tom Clancy, Patricia Cornwell, W.E.B. Griffin,
Nora Roberts, William Gibson, Robin Cook,
Brian Jacques, Catherine Coulter, Stephen King,
Dean Koontz, Ken Follett, Clive Cussler,
Eric Jerome Dickey, John Sandford,
Terry McMillan, Sue Monk Kidd, Amy Tan,
John Berendt...

You'll find them all at
penguin.com

*Read excerpts and newsletters,
find tour schedules and reading group guides,
and enter contests.*

Subscribe to Penguin Group (USA) newsletters
and get an exclusive inside look
at exciting new titles and the authors you love
long before everyone else does.

PENGUIN GROUP (USA)
us.penguingroup.com